CAMPBELL'S KIDS

For Rod Campbell.

Inspiration flows both ways.

PROLOGUE

The wildfire looked exactly like the face of an old man grimacing in the pain of the moment of death, his emblazoned face capped with white hair of steaming sap roiling up from the green backdrop of trees. The features of the face—closed, wincing eyes, eyebrows, nose, mouth, chin, even the wrinkles of his neck—were defined by the silhouettes of imperiled trees. Piloting the plane with his feet and knees, Derek Saunders took a whole series of shots out of the open door of his Cessna with his digital Pentax. He took a look at the last shot and handed the camera to Roy.

"That'll translate well onto the front page," Roy Farquhar yelled above the thrum of the engine. "Hell, every paper in North America will run it!"

Derek peered through the windshield and the passenger window on the starboard side looking for the Alberta Forestry Service helicopter they'd seen monitoring the fire. "Where'd it go," he shouted, "that chopper?"

Roy pointed downward at the blurred circle of the rotor. "Flying low!" he said. "One o'clock."

Derek maneuvered the plane in a half rotation so he could see it for himself. "Three o'clock," said Roy. "Two bombers!" They were bringing in the big guns, no doubt about it. "Hadn't you better turn on your radio?"

"Fuck that! They'll just tell us to get the hell out of the way!"

This was the fourth forest fire in this part of the Clearwater Forest Reserve this week—none of them caused by lightning. The other fires, still smoldering, were under control now, volunteer firefighters battling them on the ground. The fire marshal had found evidence of arson at the site of origin of at least two of the fires, which is what had brought Roy Farquhar out on this mission. For years the West Country, as the foothills of the Rocky Mountains were known, had been one of his beats.

This was an archetypal wildfire, costly for the millions of dollars of pulp wood it was destroying as well as the threat not only to wildlife but also to the oil wells peppered throughout the district. Someone had to pay for this holocaust.

Derek swooped down as close as he could to the billowing smoke without encroaching upon the run of the water bombers coming from the north. "Where are they getting their water?" asked Roy.

"Probably Abraham Lake." Derek craned around to look out the open door again. "What the hell's he doing down there?" He took several shots of the helicopter framed by flames, then handed Roy the camera. Then, taking the controls in both hands, he peeled off to port, away from the flames, before leveling out again. "We can get better shots from a distance, anyway," he shouted.

Roy watched the whirring rotors of the forestry chopper hovering between them and the flames as the first bomber came in, dumping its load ahead of the main blaze, soaking the scorched trees. The second water bomber hit its target dead on, creating a maelstrom: a huge ball of smoke and steam that resembled a nuclear mushroom cloud. Roy took a shot of it through the windshield with Derek's camera before handing it back to the pilot.

There were boundaries: Derek was the photographer on this assignment, not he. He was just the reporter. They worked well together as a team as long as they maintained their well-defined roles. Derek wouldn't even try to put a news story together, and, in his opinion, Roy's photography rarely rose above the level of domestic snapshot.

Below them, the forestry helicopter descended even lower over the trees, making miniature tornadoes of smoke. Roy stabbed the air with his finger. "What the hell's he doing? Fanning the flames?"

Derek pulled the plane around for another series of shots as Roy peered across his lap through the pilot's open door, glad for the broad seatbelts that kept them both from tumbling out. Once again Derek was steering with his knees. He changed lenses, focused, and then handed Roy his camera. "There's a bear down there, just ahead of the flames," he yelled. "Maybe they're trying to chase it off. I'm gonna get in closer."

"Here comes another bomber!" Roy warned Derek. "We're right in its flight path!"

"Shit!" Derek peeled off again, diving toward the greenery of the unburned forest, then leveled out above the trees.

"Why don't you turn on the fucking radio?" asked Roy, his heart beating rapidly from the scare.

"Because all we'd ever hear on it is 'Thou shalt not!'"

The water bomber came in low, heading almost directly for the hovering forestry helicopter. Roy could just make out the black shape huddling in the smoldering trees. Little more than a cub, he thought. Probably a yearling.

At the last minute, the helicopter veered aside. The water bomber let loose its load, scoring a direct hit on the animal and the trees immediately around it. As the large plane gained altitude, free of its load, the helicopter swooped in over the steaming forest as if to take a closer look at the poor beast. It fanned the steam into a vortex as it set down in a tiny clearing.

"Looks like they're gonna try to scoop the bear!" Roy yelled. He glanced at his watch and jotted the time in his lined notepad. *The forestry service puts several million dollars worth of equipment on the line to rescue a terrified bruin? Scandalous!*

"Assholes. Well, we're done here. I'm running low on fuel." Derek reached out and grabbed the handle to close the door. He took one last pass over the helicopter, which had landed within a hundred meters of the wall of flame.

Roy snapped pictures through the starboard window. The rotor was still spinning, blowing aside the smoke and steam to reveal a circle of writhing green weeds. One of the foresters jumped out of the helicopter into the steaming undergrowth, running toward the bear, which bounded away into the trees. *Got that*, thought Roy. The forester glanced up at the Cessna as they passed overhead—and actually gave them the finger! Roy kept snapping away. *Got that, too*, he thought with satisfaction. Then they were homeward bound.

Roy accessed the images he had caught on the digital camera. Snapshots, blurry all, despite the anti-shake technology built into the lens. He chose the tiny image of the forester standing in the steam, seemingly backed against a wall of fire. He zoomed in on the forester, then closer on his arm, then even closer on his blurred hand giving them the finger. He showed it to Derek, who chuckled.

"What about the bear?" he asked.

Roy went back a couple of frames, then zoomed in once again on the blurred black form crouching in the trees, trying to make sense of it. Where was its mouth? Its hind legs? What the hell? The animal was black with a blaze of white. Was that common in black bears?

He zoomed in even more but the image was too blurred to be recognizable beyond its size and color. A juvenile bear at best. He went back out and picked another image of the animal at the edge of the clearing. As Derek glanced at the screen on the back of the SLR with mild curiosity, Roy methodically zoomed in once again.

"Holy God!" he gasped as he stared at the screen, holding it toward Derek so he could see. Derek frowned.

"What is it?"

"That's a cowl," he said, pointing to the center of the screen.

"Cow? Out here? Nah!"

"Not a *cow*," said Roy. "A *cowl*. As in *habit*!"

"Huh?"

"That's no bear down there. It's a bloody *nun*!"

PART ONE: MAGGIE

1

At least I know I'm dead.
Angels. Demons. God. The Devil.
Good. Evil. Nothingness.
Amnesia. Black on black.

Found but not "missing." No ID.

Foresters. Pilots. Firemen. Police.
Nurses. Orderlies. Doctors. Reporters.

Starvation. Chronic malnutrition. Coma.
Subdural hematoma: large encysted blood clot.
No hair. Fresh facial burns. Old burns scars.

Name: Unknown. DOB: Unknown. Gender: female.
Weight: Approx. 30 kilos – 66 lbs. (Query: Progeria?)

X-rays: Hairline at the hairline.

"Old injury. Must've struck the windshield."
A voice of disdain: *"Obviously not wearing a seatbelt."*

I feel a new pressure: finger and thumb above and below my right eye. A ring of bright light blasts me out of the black vastness of the unknown. I flinch, shrinking away from an immense cyclopean eyeball, its gross cilia encircling squiggly capillaries. Then the blinding monster swallows my other eyeball, whole. God growls as He directs the speculum away from my right eye and back again, checking the reflex.

"Sister?" he mutters. "Do you hear me? Are you awake?"

I squint at the unaccustomed brightness of the fluorescent lights in the hospital ward. He scrutinizes my face, reading the unspoken questions riddled there.

"I'm Dr. Lenski." I see a tanned, ruddy complexion under silver-flecked sandy hair. "You're in the Burn Unit at Red Deer General." He exaggerates his enunciation, almost yelling. He must believe that I am deaf. He stares directly into my eyes, waiting for a response.

Burn unit. That explains the sudden overwhelming agony that still scorches my face like a blowtorch. I reach up and grope at the bandages on my face. Gently, he grasps my wrists and pulls my hands away and down. "It'll be itchy for awhile but try not to scratch, okay? We've had a mask designed for you. That should help."

I glance about, searching for context. An unscabbed spot of skin on the back of my hand is bruised greenish-black around the tape where the IV drip enters my body. I trace the tubing past the plastic hospital ID bracelet up to a half-empty plastic bag hanging from a stainless steel stand, then read the tag.

Sister Jane, it says, a name repeated on my plastic hospital bracelet: *Sister Jane Doe*.

The doctor follows my gaze. "That's the moniker the triage unit gave you when you first arrived," the doctor explains. He flips to the bottom sheet on his clipboard. "They had to cut your clothes off you, it appears, to access and treat the burns." He holds the clipboard before him, pen poised. "Do you remember your name? Address? Telephone number? Age? Date of birth?" Query after query. No time to think.

I shake my head slightly in an all-embracing *No*.

Dr. Lenski pats my arm. "It'll take you a while to adjust," he says. "Just tell the nurse, should you remember. Or write it down. I'll give you a pen and paper. We need to know more about you before we can treat you properly, you see. Any allergies, for example? You must have a family, right? Do you belong to a convent?"

I shrug. I remember nothing.

"The police have checked the missing persons files, and there has been speculation by the press as to who you are. But we don't even know how old you are. Thirty? Forty?" He sighs impatiently at my silence, then flips a page on his clipboard, running down a checklist of questions. "Family, then. Are you married? Divorced? Single?" He looks up expectantly. "Surely you remember whether you're married?"

I shrug and shake my head, puzzled. I really don't know.

Yes, surely I would remember being married!

"Widowed, perhaps?"

I shake my head a little more vigorously. It didn't seem likely.

"So, a husband? Children? No? What about siblings? Any brothers or sisters?"

A half-remembered command surfaces like a bubble rising to air:

Find your sister!

Slowly, I nod.

"Ah, now we're getting somewhere. How many?"

Sister, singular. I raise my index finger.

"What's her name?"

I puzzle over this, then shake my head and give up. I didn't actually remember a brother or a sister—only the admonition that I should *find* one.

A nurse comes into the room and hovers at the foot of my bed. "Well, hello, Sister Jane!" she says effusively. "Welcome back! I'm Jennifer, your nurse today."

"What about the other sisters in the convent, the nuns, do you recall *their* names?" asks Dr. Lenski, pointedly ignoring the nurse. "Or the name of your mother superior?"

"She's more likely to remember her real mom and dad. What were *their* names?" says Jennifer.

"Do you mind, Nurse?"

"Well, I'm just saying. I spent a couple of months in a convent and never did find out the name of the mother superior! Or any of the nuns, come to that! You must be famished, Jane! Would you like something to eat? Some soup, perhaps?"

I nod.

"Any particular kind?"

"Campbell's." It was the first word I had uttered.

Dr. Lenski and Jennifer exchange glances, their eyes wide in surprise and delight.

"Oh, aren't we funny!" says the nurse. "Fussy, too. Tomato? Mushroom? Chicken noodle?"

I shrug. The flavor doesn't matter.

"I'll see what they have." She disappears into the hall.

Dr. Lenski writes a note on my file, then sets a few spare sheets of paper and a pen beside my pillow. "I want you to write anything and everything that comes into your head," he says. "Or draw. Whatever you want. Doodle away. Put it all down. *Everything* is important. Got it?"

I nod.

"Very good. Progress!" He squeezes my arm reassuringly, then leaves.

Jennifer comes back a few minutes later with a covered Styrofoam container. She keeps one hand behind her back.

"Since you specified *Campbell's* soup, the kitchen's in a bit of a dither. All they have is homemade. But maybe this will make up for it. The Campbell Kids," she announces, flourishing a bright red-and-white mug. "It's been on the top shelf of the kitchenette in the nurses' station for years! Lord knows whose it was."

The mug sports caricatures of round-faced, rosy-cheeked children. One little girl with blonde, curly hair holds her nose and closes her eyes as she jumps off a vibrating diving board into the silvery-blue water of a lake. She is dressed in a blue bathing suit and wearing a red life preserver around her waist—the same color as her cheeks. Another child with red hair looks on, eyes wide. He wears striped swim trunks and a red muscle shirt sporting a "C." On the other side of the handle, the same red-headed boy sits on a rail fence dressed in a red sweater with a similar "C." He holds out his right hand as a perch for a bluebird, while a girl in a yellow dress with a matching yellow ribbon in her red hair sniffs at a posy of daisies. She gives the boy an adoring sidelong gaze as he sneaks his arm around her waist.

"It's the real McCoy!" says Jennifer. "See? *'M'm! M'm! Good!'* all over it!" She transfers the steaming tomato soup from the Styrofoam container into the mug, then spoon-feeds me as if I were a child. I take a tentative sip from the spoon, savoring its unfamiliar richness, anticipating its heat. "Your habit was burned along the hem and sleeves. The cops took it away to try to trace it."

I open my mouth for another spoonful.

"As the doctor no doubt told you, they've been trying to find out who you are for weeks. When they first changed the bandages, one officer came in here with a three-inch-thick binder of missing persons and went through it trying to compare your features to photographs of missing women. No luck. They even took impressions of your fingerprints, just in case you're in a registry somewhere—no luck. Then a reporter put two and two together, with the help of some Cree and Stoney Indians from the reserves west of Rocky Mountain House. It's been in the papers. Figures your mother was a nun—you were wearing her habit. They took that, but at least they left you your boots!"

Her voice sinks to a conspiratorial whisper.

"Hey, we've contacted your son. If you are who we think you are, you are—" She scoops another spoonful into my mouth. "Sorry, I forgot. I'm not allowed to tell you who they think you are. Stupid, really. Mother of four kids—you can write that down. And the widow of—"

She reads the alarm on my face and halts, realizing she has again stepped out of bounds.

"No, no, this is a good thing. Didn't Dr. Lenski say? It's in the papers—even on TV." She glances at the door, points to the mug, then whispers, "You're Maggie Campbell, the widow of Philip Campbell—Alberta's most famous artist!"

2

I remember trying to follow the creek as it meandered through the mountainous foothills and funneled through a barely passable gorge. As I traversed the valley beyond, I heard a distant rifle shot. It seemed mountains away, and it stirred my blood with first a longing and then a terrible fear. We had always retreated to the most inaccessible parts of the forest when the hunters arrived for the fall kill.

They would not let a girl like me alone, so injured yet so lovely. They would try to take me from her, Tuanahaki told me, as she watched me bathe at the muddy edge of a hot spring, feasting her old eyes on my breasts and pudendum, a blanket draped over my shoulders to ward off the chill and clouds of blackflies. If they knew I was here in the woods, they would search until they found me, and they would scoop me up and take me away from her and her away from me and say that she was mad. They would lock her up in a cage like an animal. It had happened before.

They would never catch Tuanahaki. Not now. But I still feared what those hunters might do to me if I revealed my presence. So instead of pursuing the sound of the rifle, I followed the creek downstream until the sun hid behind the mountains. I gathered dried moss and old man's beard for tinder, and using one of half a dozen books of matches stuffed into the inner pocket of my habit soon started a small fire, on which I placed green spruce twigs to smoke away the flies. I huddled in my blanket, regretting that I had not brought more. Determined to travel light, I had left a whole pile of blankets beside Tuanahaki's grave.

On the second day, I heard half a dozen shots, three in a cluster. Though distant, I could smell the smoke of spent carbon and cordite, which hung in the air like mist, a persistent reminder of their presence. By the third day, the smell of smoke had become even more pronounced. Perhaps the hunters had pitched a tent and started a campfire of their own nearby. I didn't even bother to light a fire that morning, lest I give myself away.

Later that day I reached a forestry trail. Walking was easier along the rutted road, and I trudged along, lost in a haze of speculation and reflection so muddled that I could hardly extract anything meaningful from the images. I hadn't noticed how high I'd climbed along the trail, but now, suddenly, the trees fell away and I was skirting a low mountain, looking over the tops of the trees to where the forest ended at another ridge ten miles away to the south.

I first smelled the acrid odor of burning needles and green wood as I reached the top of the trail where it began to descend again into the forest on the other side of the hill. Then it dawned on me that the light flickering above me on the western slope was a mirroring not of twilight but of fire—of a forest fire not yet seen or felt but tasted and smelled! Curious, I limped along the trail etched into the side of the mountain until the billowing smoke formed a towering column before me, miles wide. From here I could see the full extent of the blaze coming in behind me from the northwest. That black expanse was where I had been walking the day before!

Wafts of smoke mingled with cloud before spiraling up the valley toward me. For a moment I felt surrounded, but then I saw that the stiff evening breeze blew from the southwest, so the fire was no immediate threat. Yet it was obvious that I could not progress beyond that fire. I sat down on the moss on a rock near a spring on the side of the mountain, where I had a ringside seat of the forest ablaze. The crackling of the fire and the showering bursts of spruce sap grew more explosive as the blaze expanded. For the first time in days I felt warm at night. And, stupidly, I fell asleep.

I awoke to the sound of a water bomber roaring by overhead. At least three planes were dumping water on the flames. When they left, I became aware of another roar, that of the fire itself, and the whine of a powerful motor. A distant pump-truck sprayed the forest from the road on the far side of the fire.

The wind had shifted during the night so that now it ate its way south along the western side of the mountain. Only slowly did I become aware of the encroachment of the fire, which now surrounded me on three sides, with sheer mountain behind me and a mere corridor of unburned trees in front leading down to the trail. The mountain farther over where the flames had reached served as a chimney—I would not survive if I did not move, and now! Seizing my blanket, I picked up the skirt of my habit and scrambled the remaining distance down through the trees in a panic. Below, terrified squirrels chattered their way across the firebreak formed by the trail.

I was drawn to the flames as a moth to a campfire. There was simply no place else for me to go. I wished I had the energy to follow a herd of elk, which somehow scrambled up and around the tongues of fire that licked at the base of the mountain half a kilometer away.

A wall of flame roared like a giant blowtorch over the gravel trail. Beyond it I could see an area of level ground bereft of trees, which the fire had already passed over. In order to get to the clearing, I had to put all my instinctual fears on hold and run through the flames. Had to. It was my only chance.

I draped the blanket over my head and grasped the cloth of the habit around my chin, then ran blindly down the trail toward the road. A flaming tornado blasted across it, igniting my blanket.

Abandoning it, I detoured through the last remaining stand of trees toward a clearing a hundred meters away.

I had just started my desperate sprint for the clearing when above me through the flames I heard and then felt the clacking of a helicopter's blades. Tuanahaki and I had always hidden from the forestry helicopters, and now I reflexively cowered away from the familiar racket. I hesitated for only a moment, but it was long enough for the hem of Tuanahaki's habit, already scorched, to catch on fire. The flames spread to a wisp of hair hanging over my forehead, singeing my face. I plunged sideways into the woods and hid my face in weedy undergrowth, shrieking in agony and unspeakable fear as another monstrosity let loose a deluge above me, at once dousing and fanning the flames, converting them to boiling steam blasting my face and hands. Then the chopper was back, stirring a whirlwind of smoke and grit and smoldering needles into the cauldron of soot and green steam that roiled around me. The trees too writhed. I could feel my face becoming a mass of bubbling blisters; in my peripheral vision I could actually see the skin bulging away from the meat of my face.

The helicopter blew the flames back away from me where I huddled in the underbrush. Another water bomber roared in overhead at that instant and let go of its load directly above me, just as the helicopter swooped up and away. The water boiled into smoky steam in an instant and quelled the flames. Almost immediately, the helicopter landed in the sodden trail. Somebody jumped out.

"Hallooo!"

I shivered in terror, holding Tuanahaki's crucifix in my clasped hands. I couldn't get it to work! I couldn't pray. She hadn't taught me how.

"Are you all right? Where are you, Sister?"

Lying beneath a scorched pine tree, hardly breathing, heart about to explode in my aching chest, the images all mixed up in my head. I understood nothing; I was mindless in a sea of panic and fire. Flames surrounded me as I toiled through the newly dampened underbrush toward the helicopter, which still marked time, fanning the flames back to life. Thick smoke rolled in around my feet as the blaze consumed the damp underbrush, tasting the pine and spruce needles with tongues of steam. The damp smoke embraced me, kissed me, choked me. I ran headlong into that cauldron, resigned to die—and stumbled onto the trail not fifty meters from the helicopter.

"There she is!"

The voice sounded like a distant echo beneath the clatter of the rotor. I no longer cared what happened, abrogated my rights to the helicopter men. My face was a giant blister, my hands red, raw beestings of hurt.

"How the hell did you get around there?" panted the forester as he ran up to me. The boiling smoke billowed around me, and I coughed it away, barely able to breathe. It stung my burned and blistered skin, stung my eyes. I could no longer see.

Tuanahaki's crucifix dangled at the end of the useless rosary. I could not speak but stood up, shakily.

"You'll be all right now, Sister." It was a friendly voice, compassionate and strangely masculine. "Here, I'll carry you, okay? What's your name?" He scooped me up. "My God! You hardly weigh a thing!"

The pilot yelled a warning from the helicopter. "Hurry, damn it! The fire's beginning to build!"

The forester spat soot. He pulled his jacket up over his head as fresh flames burst around us. He ran with me to the helicopter and tossed me into the metal monster before climbing in after me. Almost immediately the clacking vibration intensified with the roar of the motor.

What unending agony!

Hysteria, that's what it was. Hysteria. When all sense of time has been lost and the present is one long wail.

3

Jennifer brought in a package of a dozen Bic pens—six blue, three black, two red, one green. I doodled at first, but soon my doodles took on the form of pictures, then letters, then simple words, and within hours my handwriting began to come back, wobblily. Yet if my writing was wobbly, my fractured mind was wobblier still. It kept wandering as I doodled and sketched my way through page after page, starting with crude copies of the Campbell Kids diving or sitting on a fence, then detailed images of flowers and trees (green ink), the forest ablaze (red ink), smoke billowing (black ink)—water bombers and helicopters (black on a backdrop of blue), and crude cartoon caricatures of nun after nun after nun.

There were no simple answers or excuses. It was all a riddle, the remembered and half-remembered details, the bits of fact and bits of fiction disordered and reorganized in time. I had no answers. Not at this juncture. Maybe never. I had only barely learned to recognize that I had a past. How could I catch up with what I had missed when I didn't know until now that I missed anything at all?

After a week, they moved me from the Burn Unit to Head Injury and from there to the psych ward, the only place, they said, where they had a spare bed. Although the staff psychiatrist interviewed me upon "intake," he and the nurses were more businesslike than Jennifer and Dr. Lenski. My only visitor was an RCMP corporal who sought to obtain my "Jane Doe" signature on waivers for actions already taken, including permission to take an impression of my fingerprints and samples of my blood.

"Did they find a match?" I asked eagerly.

He looked at me curiously, almost with suspicion.

"My fingerprints, I mean?"

The officer caught his own nod and converted it into a shake so that his head did a half-rotation in each direction, down, up, and side to side. "Not yet," he said as he handed me the pen.

Once I had signed the waivers, he plied me with questions that I simply couldn't answer—name, address, closest living relative, how I came to be in the forest where I was rescued, where I was going, where I had come from, and my activities immediately prior to the forest fire. Then he pointed a tiny digital camera at me.

"Do you mind if I take your photograph?"

I was conscious of my burns and wrinkled skin. "No," I said, putting up my hand. "I mean, yes!" *I do mind!*

The camera clicked anyway.

"Don't you *want* to help us find out who you are?"

"I thought you *had* found out! Aren't I—Mrs. Campbell?"

"You tell me. *Are* you?"

"Honestly? I don't know."

He pointed to my wrist band. "Well, until you do, in our books you're still 'Sister Jane Doe.' Not that we're convinced that you are a legitimate nun. More of a costume, right? But we had to ask ourselves, 'Why was she wearing that habit?' Hand-stitched, homemade from a pattern used exclusively by the Convent of the Blessed Virgin in Calgary, where the wearing of habits was discontinued fifty years ago. The mother superior told us that whoever made that habit would have to be in her seventies, if she's still alive. So it's not yours, right? At least, not yours to wear. It's a hand-me-down?"

I nodded slowly.

"So let me guess, it's your mother's?"

Tuanahaki's!

"Then yes, it does look as if you might be Margaret Campbell."

4

The next day a reporter arrived, somehow evading nurses, doctors, and security cameras to get to my room where I was resting on my bed, eyes closed.

"You faking?" he asked from the door.

I opened my eyes wide, shocked, and shook my head. He had chestnut brown hair with a squarish face and eyebrows a bit too bushy for his slightly sunken eyes. He cradled a blue three-ring binder under his arm.

He grinned. "The amnesia, I mean. There was a case in Montreal where the guy conned his doctor and the police for years!"

"Who are you?" I croaked.

"Roy Farquhar, *Red Deer Record*." He glanced behind him before pushing the door to, leaving it open just a crack. "Actually, I'm not allowed in here. 'Permission denied.' But let's just say that I believe in freedom of the press." He straddled a chair as I struggled to sit up in bed.

"I could have you arrested," I said.

"Occupational hazard. Speaking of which, have you been charged yet?"

"What?"

"The police. They're considering charging you."

I pondered this. "With what?"

"Arson. They found a book of matches with your fingerprints on the cover near the spot where the forest fire began. Word is the book of matches was identical to others found in your clothes. So first question—assuming my source is correct, which it always is—how did they know they're your fingerprints? Did you give them permission to take impressions?"

I shook my head. "But they had me sign a—"

"Waiver? Yeah, figures. You should call Legal Aid and get a lawyer. In the meantime, don't say anything to anybody, especially the police. And sure as hell don't sign anything else! Sounds like they conducted an illegal search of your clothes as well. Don't worry; they won't be able to use any of that at your trial."

"Trial! But I didn't do anything!"

"Did they tell you you have the right to remain silent and to have a lawyer? And that anything you do say may be used against you?"

"No."

"Good. Anything you've said to the cops up to this point can't be used against you—including the waiver. Just don't talk to anybody else. I mean, do not talk to *anybody*—doctors, nurses, lawyers—"

"You?"

He laughed. "*Especially* me! About your recent past, that is. But what you can tell me about is your distant past—that's what I'm most interested in. See, I've been writing about your family—especially your husband—for years. I met him at gallery openings a couple of times. And I kinda got in on the ground floor, investing in his art. Or at least, my parents did—my mother was pretty savvy in that department. So when word got out that Phil Campbell had shot himself—"

"*What?*" The news of my husband's demise was almost as shocking as the news of his existence.

He handed me the three-ring binder. "It's all in here," he said. "Photocopies of news stories about your family I wrote years ago."

I hesitated to open it. "How can you be so sure it's *my* family?"

"How many women can claim that their mother is a nun? That was the clincher—for both me and the police. Your married name is Margaret Campbell, nickname Maggie. Your maiden name was LaPierre. Ring a bell?"

A whole cacophony.

"You, Maggie, are rich! The widow of a well-known artist."

Canada's most famous.

"Your husband painted several portraits of you—I mean they're recognizably *you*—mostly nudes, sometimes with stylized mountain landscapes in the background."

"*Nude* portraits?"

"Hey, he was your husband—you were his wife! You were still young—"

That grated. "I am still young," I said. "How old do you think I am?"

"I dunno—pushing forty."

"But I was a girl—I was a girl!"

"Of course. And now you're a woman."

"But I don't remember being a woman; I don't even remember being married, let alone having four children!" That part of my life was a complete blank.

"So you remember them! Tom will be impressed. I have a call in to him, but he doesn't return his calls. It's hard for him to call long distance from in a federal pen. He's probably the *only* person who can positively identify you. Last person to see you alive—when you took off with Dick Thompson, remember that? Your plane crashed not long after takeoff from Camas Lake."

This was all news to me.

"You must've been thrown clear of the plane and wandered away from the site of the crash. How you survived in the woods all this time I can't imagine! It's all there in the binder."

Strangely, I could visualize the instrument panel of a small plane. But I didn't remember crashing.

"I have *how* many sons?"

"You had three sons and a daughter. Tom was the eldest."

Had. Was.

Farquhar glanced at the door, which he had left slightly ajar, and pressed his finger to his lips. I heard voices in the hall. "It's all in the book," he whispered.

The door opened, and Dr. Lenski stood there, fuming, flanked by an RCMP officer and an orderly.

"I couldn't have made myself any clearer that you are not welcome here!" said the doctor to the reporter. "I've a good mind to press charges!"

"It's a free country," countered Farquhar. "She can speak to whomever she wants!"

"No. This is a secure psychiatric ward. My patients are compromised. Sister Jane doesn't even know who she is!"

"Only because you've kept the obvious from her! Why is that, 'Doctor'?"

"We have not yet done a full assessment. We still don't know who she is, or where she came from, or even when and where she was born—despite your speculation. Orderly, escort him off the property!"

The burly orderly gripped Roy's arm. Roy shrugged him off.

"I wouldn't advise you to resist, Roy," said the officer.

"Don't talk to them, Maggie!" Farquhar said as he left the room. "They've already wrongfully convicted at least one person for arson—your *son*!" Then from down the hall: "Demand to see a lawyer!"

I stared at the policeman in alarm. His smile only increased my fear, especially when he pulled a small digital recorder from his pocket and pressed a button. A red light shone. "Yes, you do have the right to a lawyer—and the right to remain silent," he said gently, "but first I'd like you to hear our concern. Do you mind if I record this?"

I nodded.

"Do you mind answering verbally? I can't record a shake of the head."

"I don't even know who I am," I said, parroting Dr. Lenski and looking to him for support, "although I think I might be Maggie Campbell."

"Thank you for that," he said, making an entry in his notebook. "I'm Corporal Roberts. But this matter has little to do with your speculated identity. It has more to do with you as 'Sister Jane.' It now appears that you, whoever you are, were trapped in a forest fire of your own making—a wildfire that caused several million dollars' worth of damage to prime pulp woods."

I shook my head in denial.

"There is no doubt! You had several books of matches in the inner pocket of your habit when you first arrived in Emergency. Two identical books of matches, one of them empty, were found near a campfire from which the fire spread into the forest. Consider the cost to the public purse, not just in burned timber, but the fire crews, the water bombers, the helicopter—"

"Your hospital bills," added Dr. Lenski.

"That's why the Crown is contemplating laying formal charges against you as Sister Jane Doe, also known as—" He wrote in his notebook. "Margaret Campbell. There."

I was in shock. "I—I don't remember," I said, fighting back tears.

"And that is why I recommend that you consent to a period of psychiatric observation," said Lenski hurriedly.

"The Crown will request a thirty-day psychiatric examination from the court," said Roberts. "Amounts to the same thing. Or a third option we discussed—Dr. Lenski and I can sign an order of committal. In which case we might not pursue criminal charges."

Dr. Lenski handed one of the forms to me. It was filled out in the name of Sister Jane Doe. "So which is it? Consent? Or certificate of committal?"

"Committal? Committal for what, 'Doctor'?" I challenged, mimicking Roy Farquhar. I hadn't intended to sound so vitriolic.

Dr. Lenski flinched and his eyes narrowed. "Jane, I'm trying to avoid losing you in the system, here—and that's exactly what will happen if the police pursue these charges and the courts get involved in your case. You don't seem to realize what big trouble you're in!"

I recalled what Farquhar had told me about illegal search and seizure. "They don't have any evidence," I said.

"I wouldn't put any eggs in *that* basket!" said Roberts.

"Jane, I'm on your side, here! Your consenting to psychiatric observation and assessment is a way out of your current dilemma. It will all be the same anyway, don't you see? Whether by committal or court order. Don't make it more difficult for yourself than it has to be!"

"So if I consent, I won't be charged with anything?"

"Depending on the results," said the corporal.

Lenski looked at the policeman with raised, expectant eyebrows. "It is my understanding that if she consents, she will *not* be charged with anything, correct?" said the neuropsychologist pointedly. "Look, she's been through hell. It's clear she is suffering from amnesia and post-traumatic shock. Besides, how can you lay charges when you don't even know her name?"

Roberts shrugged. Sighed as if making a huge concession. Nodded his reluctant agreement.

Dr. Lenski handed me one of my pens. Blue. And not knowing what else to do, I signed the consent form, copying word for word from my hospital bracelet: *Sister Jane Doe*.

5

The blue binder contained copies of articles from Farquhar's byline clipping file and several glossy eight-by-ten photographs. The first was an aerial photograph of black patches on brown grass. As I examined the image more closely I made out the smoking ruins of two substantial buildings and smaller outbuildings, surrounded by blackened lawns brown at the edges, and at the perimeter untouched by fire, evergreens and aspens. Two yellow pontoon planes marked POLICE floated beside a wooden dock at the extreme top right corner of the photograph.

A worn dirt path led from the jetty through a small hay field to the charred remains of the first building. The barn, recognizable by a rust-stained corrugated steel roof, had collapsed inward on itself. The grass behind the barn had burned halfway up the bluff to the upper house. Judging from the shadows, one windowed wall of that house remained standing, and the floor looked relatively intact.

A trail joined the two cabins, running up the bluff at an angle. Otherwise, there was no clear connection between the two blackened areas.

The next photo, taken from the ground, displayed the image of a charred staircase in the center of the lower house. For some reason that staircase triggered in me an apprehension that made my heart beat faster. I gasped and my lips went dry.

Someone died there! Was it my husband? My sister? My kids?

I stared at the photograph again, working out the details: an old woodstove here, a haze of black rubble surrounding a tub of water there. But inevitably my eyes were drawn back to the staircase, and I shuddered, feeling decidedly clairvoyant. I took in other details I hadn't seen before: the old woodstove was connected to the soot-black chimney by an L-shaped stovepipe. The tub of water nearby looked like a small copper sheep dip. Why had the water not evaporated in the fire? Why had the copper not melted when everything around it had burned to cinders? A tub of similar shape in the foreground beside the stairs had melted to practically nothing.

I flipped over the top photograph. On the back was a purple stamp mark with *Order from* printed clearly across the top, then the scrawled name *Derek Saunders, Red Deer Record.* I made a mental note of the name.

I flipped to the first newspaper clipping, where the same photograph was reproduced in blurred form. More startling than the photograph was the headline.

ARSON SUSPECTED

TWO CABIN FIRES CLAIM EIGHT LIVES

My insides turned upside down. I flipped to another page, and another, and another, each with more clippings and pictures, and more, and more. The room, the scrapbook, all things tangible, whirled around me faster and faster until I fell back into my pillow.

Farquhar had given me an identity complete with family with one hand, and had taken it away again with the other. All that day and the next that first headline would keep flashing in my brain:

ARSON SUSPECTED

TWO CABIN FIRES CLAIM EIGHT LIVES

I ate no supper, no breakfast, no lunch, just lay there, fearful, contemplating the implications, afraid to read the text of that news story or any other. I lay there imagining burned bodies scattered throughout the ruins. I had been right to feel a shudder of horror at that central staircase. Not just one but several people had died there, my own children among them. The victims of arson.

Eight people. Two fires. And the perpetrator was my own son, Tom!

At last I screwed up the courage to open the scrapbook again. Two fires, probably set hours apart. Three bodies extracted from the ruins of the upper cabin: an infant girl of three and two adults, one male, one female. Worse: "*Police say five children perished in a second fire in another house on the same foothills farm, four of them burned beyond recognition. Names of the dead, two girls and three boys, have not yet been released.*"

A second illustrated news story was more definitive:

Reclusive artist among dead

TWO FAMILIES LOST IN WEST COUNTRY BLAZES

by Roy Farquhar

Record Staff Reporter

NORDEGG—Well-known local artist Philip Campbell, 37, has been identified as one of eight victims of two cabin fires police believe were deliberately set. Six of the dead were children.

Three of Campbell's four children, Roger, 12, William, 9, and Colleen, 3, died in the double blaze. Also killed were Campbell's sister-in-law, Alice Thompson, 35, of Edmonton, and three of her four children, Emily, 16, Willis, 14, and Sandra, 11.

Two teens who survived the double blaze are being detained for questioning. Under the provisions of the Youth Criminal Justice Act, they cannot be named. Police said one of them was hospitalized with unspecified injuries.

Police are treating the fire deaths as suspicious. Fire marshal Peter Armstrong said an accelerant had been used to start the blaze at the lower cabin. "Naturally we are concerned whether both fires were deliberately set."

I examined the accompanying photographs more closely. One, a promotional shot of the red-haired artist as a young man, was simply credited "File photo." The caption read,

Artist Philip Campbell among fire dead

Three of his four children lost their lives in arson blaze

The other photograph of a man, woman, three girls, and a boy was credited "*CP* wirephoto—courtesy Elizabeth Thompson":

The Thompson family in happier times

From left, Emily, Sandra, Richard, Alice, Willis, and Margo

Rather than looking at the camera, Margo, a skinny, prepubescent blonde, seemed to be sharing a joke across the tableau with her plump older sister. They were both laughing. Sandra, who couldn't have been any more than seven when the picture was taken, stared somberly straight ahead. Willis glared at the camera, his ears sticking out on either side, his sneer revealing teeth too big for his head. The father, Richard, of dark complexion, had a smile on his face as he looked at Emily, while Alice—who looked very much like me—stared intently at the top of Willis's head as if examining it for lice.

The next news story, illustrated with black-and-white blowups of Emily, Sandra, and Willis drawn from the same family portrait, served only to confuse matters:

Arson suspect's leg amputated

Sandra, 11, bound, gagged, burned

I read with shackled horror how Sandra, the first victim to be recovered from the lower house, had been found tied securely to a chair in a locked broom closet under the same charred staircase that had given me goose bumps. "The tissue of her lungs appeared bright red with traces of black soot," the provincial pathologist was quoted as saying, adding that she had died not from her burns or smoke inhalation but from asphyxiation, specifically "oxygen deprivation." Dr Sutcliffe said other ashes recovered from the house had been identified as those of Sandra's sister

Emily Thompson, 16, of Edmonton; their brother, Willis, 14; and two of their cousins, William and Roger Campbell, 9 and 12, of Nordegg.

"Fire marshal Peter Armstrong said traces of marked agricultural fuel had been found all around the building, including the front of the house. A large elevated gasoline tank fifty meters to the rear of the house had ruptured, fueling the blaze, he added."

A week later, this article had appeared, illustrated by the same promotional photo of my husband:

TOT FOUND NO COMFORT IN DEAD DAD

MURDER-SUICIDE?

by Roy Farquhar
Record Staff Reporter

CALGARY—Reclusive artist Philip Campbell and his sister-in-law Alice Thompson died from shotgun wounds to the head days before their bodies were incinerated in a house fire southwest of Nordegg, says medical examiner Dr James Sutcliffe in his preliminary report on the deaths.

The single shot to Campbell's head created a wound consistent with self-inflicted injury, he said, confirming earlier, more speculative reports. Dozens of lead shotgun pellets had penetrated the skulls of both victims.

Dr Sutcliffe said blowfly larvae helped him determine that the deaths had predated the fire by several days.

Police say the partially burned body of Colleen Campbell, 3, was found huddled with those of the two adults.

Dr Sutcliffe said Colleen had heavy soot deposits in her lungs, indicating heavy smoke inhalation, the likely cause of her death.

RCMP Cpl Michael Roberts said firemen had found a suicide note, apparently signed by the artist, saying he was "so, so sorry.... Please, please forgive me." He added that a charred shotgun had been recovered from the ruins of a second house-fire on the property, in which five other children had died.

And a month after that:

11 counts in arson deaths

TEENS CHARGED WITH MURDER

by Roy Farquhar
Record Staff Reporter

ROCKY MOUNTAIN HOUSE—A girl of 13 and youth of 17 have been charged with a total 11 counts of first-degree murder in connection with a double arson that nearly wiped out two families southwest of Nordegg.

Police allege the teens conspired to set fire to the house last August. The boy's gangrenous leg was amputated in emergency surgery the day after the fires, and he has been hospitalized ever since. The girl has been in the custody of her grandmother.

Duty counsel Sharon Meyers reserved plea on behalf of the teens. Under the Youth Criminal Justice Act they cannot be named.

Crown counsel Betty Douglas said the duo were charged with the arson deaths of William and Roger Campbell and Sandra, Willis, and Emily Thompson, who ranged in age from 9 to 16.

This story and several to follow were illustrated by the same recycled file photos: Philip Campbell's promo shot and individual pictures of Alice, Emily, Willis, and Sandra blown up from the family portrait. There were no photographs of my children.

The last item in the scrapbook was a short obituary:

THOMPSON

Elizabeth Thompson, 72, of Edmonton, a retired schoolteacher, died Monday after a long illness. She had suffered a stroke a few days after learning that granddaughters Emily and Sandra Thompson and grandson Willis Thompson had died in a Nordegg house fire last summer. She was predeceased by her husband, George, a realtor, and by her son Richard, an art promoter who died in a plane crash three years ago. She is fondly remembered by granddaughter Margo Thompson, 14, of Edmonton, her sole surviving relative.

I gazed again at the top photo, the one where the staircase stubbornly refused to collapse into the rest of the rubble of my home. Up there somewhere, my two young sons had burned to death in a fire set by their cousin and their own brother, my only other son. Roger and Billy, like Colleen before them, had suffered hell itself.

But so had I. That night, in nightmare, I saw the inside of the plane as we dropped down, down, down toward the dense lodgepole pines surrounding a tiny beaver pond fed by an alpine rill. Flames engulfed my mind along with the echo of my screams. But the image of impending disaster was overshadowed by the even starker image of the charred staircase. The screams were the agonized shrieks of my two younger sons, Billy and Roger, my nieces, Sandra and Emily, and my nephew—what was his name again? As I visualized the photograph, I could hear us *all* screaming.

I choked on my grief: *I was there, yet did nothing to save them?*

What had those articles said? Sandra, locked in a closet, had been tied to a chair and gagged. Neither she nor the chair had burned, because the cupboard had been starved of oxygen. She had suffocated. *So how had she been able to scream?*

It was a deceit, I rationalized, some trick of the imagination. I had not really heard anybody scream, not Billy, not Roger, not my nieces or nephew. I had simply inserted myself into the picture, could put myself in any picture: in the plane, on the stairs, under the stairs, beside the stairs!

I closed my eyes against swimming dizziness as, down the hospital hallway, someone pulled the plug on a whistling kettle.

I recalled the newspaper accounts of a ruptured gasoline tank. I visualized an elevated tank being struck by lightning, twin forks striking both buildings, a blitzkrieg of fire and water and smoke roiling in a tornado of dusty air. *Boom!* In the dream, I touched my burned face with my fingertips, felt for an instant the searing pain that obliterated everything around it.

"*Explosion*," I whispered, fixing on a memory more tangible than the others. Memory of the pungent odor came back with the roiling wall of flame, sickening and thick and choking, along with the rank odor of my own burning flesh and hair. *Gasoline,* I realized in horror. *Purple gas. Pails of it!*

Pails and pails. I visualized myself carrying two pails from a yoke, like a milkmaid. The pails themselves were purple, as was their contents. On the side of each pail, scrawled in purple capital letters, were the words *PURPLE GAS.* It looked potable, like grape juice.

The gasoline ignited behind me and in front of me and all around. I scrunched my eyes shut, warded it off with my arms. I was on fire! Then another explosion, even larger. I was flying through the air. I couldn't move. My face! My face! My face and hands!

A uniformed forester emerged from behind a veil of smoke. I dismissed the image with an irritated shake of my head as I refocused on the fractured memory beneath. How could I be so mixed up?

One of the boys screamed, "*We're on fire!*" Roger opened the back door, saw me, and slammed it again.

Why is he so afraid? I'm his mother*!*

Then another, higher scream above the roar: "*They got bombs! BIG bombs!*" Someone smashed out the attic window. A gun fired from inside the house, from upstairs in the attic, above the roar of the fire.

I saw the barrel of the gun. Two barrels. The shotgun! It couldn't have been Billy; he was too small. It couldn't have been Roger; he was at the back door. It was—*Willis*! He was standing in the attic window shooting at anything that moved when the fire broke through.

You see? It wasn't my kids! It was Alice's! Tom wasn't even there!

Yet he and Margo had both admitted to setting the fire.

They killed my little boys!

It was all there in the newspaper articles, of course. A ruptured gasoline tank had fueled the flames, no doubt causing a tremendous explosion. Marked agricultural gas had been used as an accelerant. The unidentified teenage girl—obviously Margo—had admitted to setting fire to the gas-soaked building. In one of the articles, the Crown alleged that she had used a broken piece of shiplap obtained from the smoldering remnants of the upper house, a piece that matched the splint on Tom's broken leg.

The fingerprints of both accused had been found on the extinguished torch—hard evidence that Tom and Margo would not have been able to refute had their cases gone to trial. The fingerprints had precipitated the guilty pleas, according to the news clippings. The girl's fingerprints had also been found on the outside of a galvanized steel bucket containing a residue of purple gas.

I had inserted myself into the scenario in the dream, visualized what had happened, but could not make out the perpetrators. Instead, I myself was condemned.

6

Despite Dr. Lenski's implied assurances to the contrary, I became lost in the system. Once I was locked away on the forensic ward of Alberta Hospital at Ponoka, he seemed to forget all about me. I was quickly deprived of any means to record my thoughts, dreams, or emerging memories because I was considered a chronic arsonist, a pyromaniac.

One night shortly after my arrival on the ward, I woke up having to go to the bathroom. I was hungry, so I walked in my hospital mules down the hall to the kitchenette, which we patients were allowed to use for late-night snacks. I tried to make myself some toast, as I had seen other patients do, and while I was waiting ran some water into the sink to wash a dozen dirty mugs that had accumulated. The toaster started smoking and simply wouldn't turn off. I pushed and poked and twisted every button, to no avail. The unit was growing hotter, and my prodding pushed it under the paper towel rack. To my horror, the toasted bread burst into flames and ignited the hanging paper towel. The smoke triggered a smoke detector, a horrible screech right above my head that made me reflexively clap my hands to my ears. Someone pulled the fire alarm—a serious business in a hospital.

I was still in the kitchenette when several nurses and orderlies arrived in a panic. An orderly blasted the toaster with a fire extinguisher, which knocked the toaster off the counter into the sink, causing it to short out, blowing a fuse.

By then, several patients had gathered around.

"I seen her! I seen her! I seen her diddlin' the controls," said one woman. Which of course was true.

"Pyro!" said another patient. "I'm movin' out!"

The psychiatric staff used my "history" to justify locking me in a padded cell for the night. The next morning, I received a visit from Dr. Romano, the staff psychiatrist.

"This habit of playing with fire has got to stop," said Dr. Romano. "Last night you put the whole ward—the whole hospital—at risk by turning the toaster on high and watching the toast burn, pushing it down again and again until it ignited. Three people say they saw you fiddling with the controls."

I shook my head vigorously. "It wouldn't turn off," I said.

"You could have pulled the plug."

I hadn't even thought of that.

They let me out only after I agreed to some house rules of my very own. The kitchenette was off-limits. I was allowed pens, but what good were they when I was issued paper one sheet at a time and could use it only under supervision, lest I set fire to it? They confiscated Farquhar's clipping file and photographs, and I wasn't allowed access to current newspapers either. Under supervision, I could visit the library and read whatever I wanted except for medical books that might encourage self-diagnosis, but I could not check anything out of the library to take to my room to read. Not that there was much of a selection: mostly trashy novels and Harlequin Romances.

I did not have access to a telephone.

Because I was there by consent rather than by court order, no psychiatrist other than Dr. Romano saw me from the time of the kitchen fire until my thirty days were up. Only when I demanded to be released did an anonymous staff psychiatrist deign to interview me to see how I had "come along." Realizing that I had indeed been lost in the system, he made up for lost time, simply reiterating the observations and notes (with applicable dates) of orderlies and psychiatric nurses with whom I had interacted—including Dr. Romano's and the nurses' stilted accounts of the toaster incident. On the basis of my simple request that I be released—the only thing we ever talked about—the new psychiatrist concluded that besides my "obvious" chronic pyromania, I exhibited compulsiveness, hostility, bipolarity, heightened aggression, delusion, paranoia, and frequent hallucinations, all symptoms, he noted, of advanced chronic paranoid schizophrenia. He also diagnosed "possible multiple personality disorder and/or schizoaffective disorder," for which he prescribed a regimen of drugs that literally left me reeling. Pegging me as a gas-sniffer, he put me in a substance abuse program, listing agricultural gas rather than drugs or alcohol as my preferred substance of addiction, and explaining that this was in his opinion a contributing factor to my chronic progeroid syndrome and repeated psychotic breaks.

I was permitted to walk in the confined yard of the women's forensic ward, so I wrapped myself up in cocoons of insulating clothing and wandered about in mind and body. Usually, I walked alone. Nobody encouraged me to fit together the tiny clumps of my personal jigsaw—they gave no credence to the bits and pieces I had fitted together already, with Farquhar's help. They all believed that I was insane.

And at one level, I did too. I began to doubt even the memory of Tuanahaki. After all, had she not sent me on a fool's errand: to look for my sister? Yet even as I doubted, I saw her more clearly than ever, and nowhere more clearly than on her deathbed.

"You have been a good friend, *Nitanis*," she murmured. "An old woman needs a friend. Where I am going, I shall have many friends. It is your turn now to seek a friend on the earth. Find your sister. Maybe she can help you find yourself."

She smiled slightly, nodded, slowly closed her eyes, and slept, her head propped against her worn pillow, the fur-bare pelt of a beaver. I adjusted the patterned blanket that sheltered her from the chill air, and then out of a lasting affection for her, placed my hand gently in hers. It twitched slightly, and then her fingers gripped mine with gentle pressure. Her brown skin, up to that time hot from fever, felt leathery and cold. Her long nails, lighter in color than her skin, were each rimmed with a crescent of black from grubbing in the soil for roots and herbs.

For almost the whole day I sat there, brushing away blackflies and mosquitoes from her face, slapping at any that ventured near my own, and I chanted mournful chants and whipped my bare back with a bough of spruce as she had taught me. Her fever had gone, but so had her will to live. I left the door to her death lodge open, so that when she died her spirit could easily depart for the other world, or stay, as it chose.

At length numbness invaded my knees and ankles and spread into my thighs as unbearable pain, so I extracted my hand from hers to stretch and reposition my body. The sun was already setting by then, judging from the ochre-tinted clouds; I could not see the sun. Both of us had been chilled in the storm three days before. Tuanahaki had refused the saskatoon berries I'd salvaged from the frost. We had finished the last can of soup, so long a staple. She had just lain there for three days sipping tea occasionally, sweating more than she sipped. Even the roots of dogwood and columbine, the bark of diamond willow, and the leached seeds of cones from the fallen pine she had refused, although she'd assured me that they were good for fever.

"My time is near," she kept saying, almost with relief. "My time is near, so near." And then, "It is time. Time for me to go. Time for you to go find your sister!"

That was her last word: "Sister." No wonder I had remembered it first!

I clung to her hands fiercely for perhaps an hour after that, before her fingers became noticeably colder than mine, and it was over.

I smeared my face with a layer of aspen ash, which turns as white as guano when it dries. My grey-streaked bronze hair had matted into dreads, which I cut off with large scissors designed for cutting canvas. I stripped off all my clothes and smeared the rest of my body with what was left of her mud. And I wailed the ghost dance songs she had taught me, pounding my fists together, one above the other before my chest as I knelt over her, my body lurching and trembling with the grief of her passing:

> *O you who pities us the Holy One we pray to*
> *Help me in what I do tonight!*
> *Help me in this my dance of death!*
> *Help me in my song!*
> *May Tuanahaki find happiness!*
> *O pity her!*
> *Pity her body!*
> *Help her spirit journey to your kingdom!*

She still wore her nun's habit, ragged from years of wear, over the rest of her clothes. As winter approached, we both dressed layered against the cold—I wore what was available, mostly men's clothes, undershorts modified by tying a knot in the waistband, rolled-up slacks, and rolled down socks, and my red-and-white floral dress over top. As well as her black cotton habit, she wore a cowl, wimple and veil, stockings, jeans, and an extra skirt. A three-inch wooden cross hung from a rosary at her waist, and she wore a smaller, bent crucifix around her neck.

Removing everything except the small crucifix, I washed her naked, wrinkled body, then carefully unrolled her deerskin medicine bundle to make a mat. I breathed the fragrant incense of sagebrush and spruce and sprinkled it over her, then painted her face with white ash, encircling her eyes, mouth, and nose with burnt ochre. I ochred her wrinkled nipples, too, and darkened her hair and pudendum with spent embers so that in death she looked younger than she had in life. I kissed her on each ochred patch. Taking off my own clothes, I stretched out on top of her, our nakedness combining, both of us skin and bone, willing my life force into her body, her insights into my mine, connecting forehead to forehead, nose to nose, lip to lip, breast to breast, belly to belly, thigh to thigh, each of us a reflection of the other. I fell asleep on top of her, a transference of impressions and affections, not knowing which world was the more real.

I awoke, goose bumps from head to toe. It was already dark. I reached for the first clothing that came to hand: Tuanahaki's habit. Her smoky body scents were strangely comforting.

As my final gift to her spirit, that it might travel if it chose in dignity, I gave her the only garment I could remember owning from a previous life: my red-and-white floral dress. Then I wrapped up her medicine bundle as closely as possible to the way it had been and used it as a pillow. Dressed in her habit, I huddled in its folds, using it as a sheet among wool blankets. Oh, how I willed the sun to return!

Tuanahaki's passing seemed at first a great desertion. But she had taught me that death was an integral part of the grand cycle of life. She had spent more than half her life in these woods in the shadow of the Rocky Mountains, hunting, fishing, gathering berries and nuts, huddling in vacant cabins long forgotten by foresters, trappers, and prospectors, watching, waiting. Her life in the woods was a kind of penance, she said, for her sins and the sins of the fathers. She had taken an oath of solitude, cloistered in the woods, avoiding all human contact except for mine. Yet it was not the ways of her abandoned convent that she had taught me as her initiate. It was the shamanic ways learned as a child from her father and brothers, who formed the core of an isolated band of Cree trappers and guides. For a few years, Tuanahaki's band had competed for survival with the Stoney and Cree reserves farther north and east.

I buried her where she lay in her death lodge, dragging large rocks from the creek in a hundred trips through the underbrush until I was satisfied that no crow or raven could beak its way to her body, no coyote could enter and paw aside the stone. Then I sprinkled the stone with musky sagebrush and spruce needles, crushed until they gave up their scent to purify the air and earth.

When I had finished, her grave looked like a lair within a larger lair—not even the flies had found her.

> *May this my dance lead me the right way home!*
> *Pity my body!*
> *Help me.*
> *May I grow as old as Tuanahaki before I die!*

I left my *nimama* then, her death lodge wide open to the elements so that she might seek egress as her spirit willed or that others of her kind might join her in her lodge and make it into a holy place.

I did not know what month it was, although the days were growing noticeably shorter and the nights colder. Although it had not snowed, night frost remained most of the day in the shadows of the trees and on open grass and weeds until noon.

Except for seasonal shifts, time had never seemed to matter all the while I had been with Tuanahaki. I could not even count the years I'd been in the bush by the number of winters, for they had telescoped, so that the time I had spent with her seemed at once one month and many months, one year and many years. There seemed to be the present year, from spring to fall, from the great thaw and return of the birds to their recent departure; but all the rest, the long winter and winters before, seemed one long, painful season, for we had suffered, and every day seemed long from the ache of cold and hunger. I only know that several years passed from my first joining Tuanahaki in her wandering to my leaving her in her death lodge in the foothills of the Rocky Mountains, the rocks of her grave and my dress her only memorial.

If there is anything else but this and my memories of her, she will let me know.

7

On the forensic ward, the staff refused to call me "Maggie" or Margaret Campbell, saying that they were under strict instructions not to reinforce a fiction. Instead, they persisted in calling me Sister Jane. "And that *isn't* a fiction?" I protested. When I refused to answer to "Sister Jane" or "Miss Doe" and insisted that the other patients call me Maggie, the nurses shook their heads and clucked compassionately that I was still delusional.

Any reference to Tuanahaki was taboo. She was my "imaginary friend." They simply did not believe that a nun would skulk about in the woods year after year in her habit, complete with cowl and wimple. They did not believe me when I said that Tuanahaki could merge with the trees like a shadow. Yet that was her magic: She could emerge in the perceptions of others almost at will, then disappear again. When I told them I had seen her shapeshift into a red-tailed hawk, a coyote, a timber wolf, a deer, an owl, a polyphemus moth, they shook their heads and took my temperature.

There is a darkness in my past that Tuanahaki helped me lose; I do not quite know how. Say that at a time when the only reasonable course seemed to be to hurl myself off a cliff, she showed me a glimmer of light. I could not then remember why I was all alone, did not know where I was, just knew that I was exhausted, terrified of the Thing, the darkness in which there seemed to be nothing because it was too horrible for the human mind to conceive of it and live! I had been running, crashing through the woods, mindless and lost, not caring about anything but getting away from the horror that attacked me swinging from trees on either side—scratching, whipping me at every turn. Stumbling over a felled tree, I crashed headlong into the undergrowth and lay there not crying but heaving, heaving and moaning, aware of the noise I was making as if from a distance, trying to stop but unable to control myself.

Tuanahaki brought me back, soundlessly, gently. Her black cloth habit and white wimple seemed ludicrously out of place among the trees. But what appalled me most about her was her face. It was caked with whitish mud—*totally* caked except around the eyes, nostrils, and mouth.

I felt her presence before I saw her, then in another dimension felt the cold compress on my forehead, dabbing my scratches. She lit a tiny fire a few yards away from where I lay and dangled a little skin pot above it from a bent sapling. I jumped when I first saw her face, and my first impulse was to run again, to hide, or to strike out at her to make her go away. Sensing my alarm, the old woman moved away to the fire and added another handful of wet twigs and stirred them so that the fire sizzled and popped and the mud face flickered. Then she came back and tugged at my elbow, lifting on it until I gained my feet. Neither of us spoke. We still just experienced each other's presence, and that seemed to be enough, for the moment.

The truth is, I was overawed by her presence. I could do only as she bade me, nothing more or less. She gestured that I should sit opposite her, facing the fire. I felt cold shadows as if icicles were pressed between my shoulder blades; she, rather than her fire, seemed to be the source of warmth.

It seemed hours before either of us moved, and then she leaned forward to stir the fire again and add some more twigs, and she poured something from the skin pot into a little leather cup. She offered the hot liquid and I took it and sniffed it and then sipped. It was insipid, probably just hot water with a few roots added, but it warmed and cheered me, and I grew less afraid. And as she looked on, I forced a smile.

She seemed to sense that it was insincere and did not return it—seemed in fact to shut me out as if there were no room any longer for postures, and suddenly I could contain myself no longer: I wept desperate tears for what had been, for what had happened, though I knew not what—for the horror and fright of it all. If anything at all was betrayed from behind her mud mask, it was the expression in her eyes that bespoke simple, limpid compassion, welling as they were with tears of her own. And then she started talking in a tone so soft that I could do nothing but listen to her drone, accented yet eloquent.

"They say we are spirits of the damned," she intoned, "not to be spoken or thought of, not to be believed in. But we are not spirits of the damned. We are spirits of the blessed, as all spirits of the hurt are spirits of the blessed. We have been hurt. We have been used and tossed aside." She reached across the fire as if it did not exist and gripped my wrist. "I have been watching," she whispered hoarsely in an agitated voice. "I have seen much, as you have seen much, that is not good."

She paused to sip some of her herbal tea, and then read my expression of surprise.

"My father, Piyesiw—Thunder Maker—had a Cree mother, a Blackfoot father. Rather than live like a caged muskrat on the reserve near Fort Macleod, he became a squatter in these foothills, land taken over by the white men to whom it never belonged. At first, nobody challenged him in his trapping. Pelts in the forest were plentiful and most Cree and Stoneys stayed on their reservations to the east. In fact, white poachers were his only threat.

"My father sent me away to the mission school at Rocky Mountain House to learn English, but he did not foresee that I would go on to a convent in Calgary and become a Sister of the Blessed Virgin. This black habit that I wear became my uniform.

"Soon, my education ended, for the mission schools were universally regarded with suspicion, though I could claim no abuse. The Church disbanded the schools, and I returned to my father's camp. But because I had given a vow of chastity and could not marry, Piyesiw was ashamed of me, and the others, men and women alike, regarded me with scorn."

She stopped, at that, and poked absently at the smoldering ashes of her fire. Then she unrolled a long piece of canvas that may once have been a tent, from which she took and unrolled two blankets and her old beaver pelt—the same one her head was lying on when I buried her. And we lay on the canvas and covered ourselves with blankets to make ourselves comfortable and warm, curled up together. At first I found her pungent scent distracting: a combination of smoke and pine and perspiration with a hint of urine. But soon it became a reassuring balm. And I slept. We slept.

It seems, upon reflection, such a dream! Even now the knowledge Tuanahaki conveyed in that hushed conversation on the top of the treed bluff overlooking the studio cabin seems sacred, a secret that the vulgar world outside should never share.

Did I really hear her that well?

Have I embellished her English?

How did I first come to live with her in the bush and learn her lore? How did I get to the woods? Desperately I sought an answer, but my fractured mind balked at the very challenge. It seemed that I would have to find the answers somewhere else. For my soul had willed me to forget.

I regretted that I'd ever tried to come back to "civilization." Would it not have been better to have died with Tuanahaki, curling up beside her, letting hypothermia lull me into the spirit realm? She'd told me about her own experience with Ponoka, which the Blackfoot call "The Place of Lost Souls." The Cree name, by contrast, means "The First Bridge," referring not to the first step back to sanity but to early post-contact history—the first bridge across the Battle River.

I suppose in one sense it was fitting that I should be put there, for who needed a bridge between the two worlds I had encountered more than I?

And what soul was more lost?

8

Just before Christmas, following a snowstorm, the weather turned bitterly cold. The red-nosed staff joked on their arrival—insensitively, given the plight of us patients—that nobody in their right mind would go outside in *that* weather. The windows had iced up inside and out. As Christmas approached, most other patients seemed to receive guests, some on a daily basis. But I remained alone.

By then, I had completed the "rehab" program and received a certificate to prove it:

ALBERTA HOSPITAL PONOKA

This is to certify that

(John/Jane Doe)

has successfully completed the

Drug and Alcohol Rehabilitation

program

(signature)

(name and office)

The unsigned certificate, a form to be downloaded from a computer, had been printed off unrevised, complete with instructions. My only Christmas gift was a sad, sick joke.

That was when I decided to escape. While the other patients were preoccupied with pre-Christmas activities, I laced on my boots, then folded up my "certificate of rehabilitation" together with the copy of Dr. Lenski's consent form and shoved them in my pocket. I poured a little hot coffee into my treasured Campbell's soup mug—my only possession—and quickly dismantled a large armful of Christmas decorations that had been put up in the television room the night before. When a bevy of guests was ushered through into the forensic ward, I managed to catch the door before it whooshed shut and, disguised by the pile of decorations, made my way to the less secured hallway, which curved around the building from the forensic ward to a central intersection of halls, complete with small shops. Once in this common area, I kept walking, turning right toward the cafeteria, then left, then eventually left again into the wing used by Grant McEwan College for the psychiatric nursing program.

The place was virtually empty, and I sought refuge in the college library. One of the desks had a telephone. Still clutching my soup mug, I telephoned the *Record* office in Red Deer collect, person-to-person, asking for Roy Farquhar. My breath came in little pants as the seconds ticked by. Then a brusque voice, full of impatience and hauteur, virtually barked into the receiver.

"Farquhar here!"

"You have a collect call from Jane Doe," said the operator. "Will you accept the charges?"

"Is this a joke?"

"I don't think so, sir."

"Where's the call originating?"

"Ponoka. Alberta Hospital."

"Ponoka!" Silence. Then: "Whoa. Alberta Hospital, Ponoka?"

"Yes, sir. Will you accept the call?"

"Tell him it's *Sister* Jane," I said to the operator. "Maggie Campbell."

"It's *Sister* Jane Campbell," said the operator. "Maggie."

"Maggie? Sure, I'll accept the call!" The operator disconnected herself with a click. "You're back at Ponoka?" he asked.

"I've never left."

"What? Corporal Roberts said they'd released you!"

"Yeah, to the custody of the hospital. They transferred me to the forensic ward two months ago. After you left that last time, I consented to a thirty-day psychiatric examination. That was up a month ago, so I want out of here!"

"No doubt!"

"Hey, I want—I need to talk to you. I mean privately, face-to-face. Because they still haven't resolved who I am. You seem so sure that I'm Maggie Campbell, and it resonated, especially when I went over your clipping file. But they confiscated it when I was transferred to Forensic. I've been able to visualize faces to go with the names ever since—Phil and Richard and Colleen and Billy and Roger—even Tom."

"I don't get it. Why are they still holding you there?"

"It's winter, and bitterly cold out. Policy requires them to keep me here until someone volunteers to put me up—to 'house' me. But nobody wants to house an accused arsonist! So I don't have anywhere to go. Which is why I need to talk to you."

"Okay," he said. "Let's see, it'll take me—" He paused. "Let's say an hour. Where can we meet?"

I knew the people on my ward would be looking for me shortly, certainly if I didn't show up for lunch. Nor could I stay undetected in the college library for long, especially once they sounded the alarm.

"What times are visiting hours?" he was saying.

"Better not come in as a visitor. They monitor visits." I looked searchingly around me and saw the washrooms. "Meet me in the Grant McEwan Centre. That's the first building to the left of the main entrance. Come in through the college entrance. I'll be in the men's washroom."

"The *men's*?"

"They won't think of looking for me there."

"Hey, you won't get into trouble over this?"

"I hope not."

"I'll grab the file, see what I can find. See you in an hour!"

I went into the men's washroom and sat there. And sat and sat and sat. It did not occur to me at the time that attempting to escape from a forensic facility was highly illegal, possibly dangerous. I was conscious rather of the impropriety and absurdity of sitting in a men's public washroom. Although at first no one came in to use the facilities while I was ensconced on the john, a nagging voice warned me over and over that this was naughty, this was immoral, this was sinful, this was taboo. To supplant these thoughts with the imagery of innocence, I stared fixedly at my mug, specifically at the image of the little ruddy-cheeked Campbell Kid holding her nose as she dove into the water, the boy in the red shirt smiling in the background. As so often happened these days, a whole series of associations jangled in my head as I dozed off, then surfaced, dove in, then surfaced yet again.

I jarred awake. Someone was humming "Rudolph the Red-Nosed Reindeer" to himself as he used the urinal, oblivious to my presence. He cleared his throat. Spat. His feet were inches away from my cubicle. I could see the fine mist of his urine bouncing back onto his shoes. Oblivious to that, too, he shifted his weight, farted, zipped up, and went to the sink to wash his hands. I heard a towel rack spin, then the door whooshed open and wheezed shut behind him.

Gradually, my heartbeat slowed. But then: "*What are you doing in the men's toilet?*" The strident voice of a woman. Was it a teacher? A nurse? A psychiatrist? Tuanahaki? No, this woman was too fanatical, too judgmental to be Tuanahaki. Another nun, perhaps? My mother superior? Or was it merely my conscience?

"*Embarking on another little tryst?*"

I had the overwhelming urge to pee, and did so. But the voice still sounded in my mind.

"*I want to talk to you about you and—you-know-who!*"

"I have no idea what you are talking about," I muttered aloud.

"*You were down at the hot springs, swimming stark naked!*"

I visualized a young man's tanned, nude body as he pulled himself dripping out of the water onto the moss-covered rock. For a second as he paused to pick up a towel, he looked exactly like Myron's "Discus Thrower." Who could not adore the athletic form of such an archetype!

The woman in my mind perched primly on the edge of the sofa, the epitome of self-righteous indignation.

"*You were sitting on the fence, kissing and holding hands.*"

"So?"

"*—and you let him touch your breast.*"

"Maggie?"

I came back from my reverie with a start, still staring at my mug.

"Uh, yeah. Mr. Farquhar?"

"Yeah. Hi!"

"Just a minute." I stood up off the toilet and automatically it flushed! Embarrassed, I emerged from the cubicle.

He examined my face. With three square meals a day and little exercise, I had filled out a lot since he had seen me last. "You look— well," he said tentatively. Conscious of the cavernous echoes from the tile floor and porcelain urinals, he added, "We can't very well talk here. Is there some place more private we can go?"

"How about your car?"

"Whoa!"

"Anywhere else, we'll be noticed."

He shrugged, then held the door to usher me out of the washroom. We passed the library into the lobby and its convenient closet. I swiped someone's coat off a hanger, then walked beside Roy down the concrete steps outside toward his car, the fake fur collar turned up to hide my face, clinging tightly to his arm to keep my balance.

He had parked in a designated visitor parking area across from the front entrance of the college. He opened the passenger door for me and then went around to the driver's side and climbed in. He glanced at me nervously, again taking in my residual facial scars, my pallor. "So—where do we go from here?"

"Your place," I said.

He laughed. "I can't do that!"

"Why not?"

"It's just like—busting someone out of jail!"

"No. This is a hospital, not a jail. I consented to be detained. I can withdraw my consent at any time after thirty days, and it's been more than *sixty*. The only reason I'm in here is because I have no other place to go."

"But you'll have to check out and everything."

"I *have* checked out everything, and there's no other way."

"Officially *discharged*, I mean. I don't know if I want to get implicated in what could amount to a prison bust!"

"You already *are* implicated. You said you needed help with your biography on my husband."

"Right. But you didn't seem to remember him too clearly."

"I'm remembering more and more. Yes, it's spotty, but I do remember posing for him. And flying with Richard. And how Tuanahaki and I survived all those years—especially in the winter. We ate berries in spring, fish in summer, snared rabbits in winter—and ate tin after tin after tin of Campbell's soup. That was the mainstay of our diet."

"Where'd you get that?"

"Tuanahaki had stocked up, somehow. We eventually ran out," I added with a sigh. The beginning of the end.

"What do you remember about Tom and Margo?"

"Nothing," I admitted. "Why?"

"He still won't talk to me. When I first floated my theory, I tried to arrange through Corporal Roberts for you to visit Tom, perhaps vice-versa, so he could ID you, but he refused to cooperate. Claimed that you abused him as a child. That was one of the arguments his lawyer used to oppose elevation to adult court for trial, and later at his sentencing—"

"That I *abused* him?"

He nodded. "Sexually. When he was thirteen—you were going through a crisis in your marriage. He said you weren't getting any from your husband so you turned to him instead. Taught him everything he knows. He regarded it as consensual."

I visualized a naked body gleaming in the sun. "It *was*," I said.

Roy looked at me sideways. "Of course, the courts wouldn't look at it that way. Age of consent. Incest. Margo told me Tom's still furious you 'dumped' him and took up with *her* dad—Dick Thompson. As is Margo—she's very protective of her late father's reputation! Long story short, neither one of them is willing to make contact with you, or even to visit."

"'Dumped' him? How can I have 'dumped' him? He was my *son*!" I was shivering. "Do you mind heating up the car? I'm freezing." He started the motor and we sat there until it warmed. "How about we go for a coffee?" I suggested. "I hear there's a great Tim Horton's in Ponoka."

"You know I can't take you off the grounds."

I folded my arms and stared straight in front of me at the winter wonderland beyond the windshield.

"If what you say checks out, we can get you out of here in no time—legally and above-board."

"Technically, I am free to walk out of here whenever I want to. Otherwise they'd keep me locked up, don't you think?"

Farquhar was weighing everything I said very carefully. "I thought you *were* still locked up. Aren't you still on the forensic ward?"

I nodded reluctantly.

"What's to stop you from applying for a release?"

"That would take *months* to process. You don't understand. I've got to get out of here *now*! They're in denial that I'm in here by consent. They've already dismissed the consent form as if it's a bookkeeping error—they'd confiscate my copy of it, if they knew I had it, pretend it never existed. They'll *never* release me until I have someplace to go—but I don't know anyone out there, except you." I carefully unfolded the copy of the consent form Dr. Lenski had made for me two months before and showed it to Farquhar. "See? I consented for thirty days, two months ago. So if I leave here, they cannot demand my return. Believe me, if I had someplace to go, there's absolutely nothing to keep me from walking out of here!"

"*Habeas corpus*," said Farquhar thoughtfully as he scanned the document. "Hmm. You signed it 'Sister Jane'?"

"It was witnessed by Dr. Lenski." I pointed to his scrawl.

"Pompous ass! Listen, we're off to a good start today. I'll come back as soon as possible to record your account of what happened, how you escaped from the plane crash."

"I don't remember that yet. Not clearly, at least."

"Why am I not surprised?"

"That's the main reason they keep me here on drugs—so that I *won't* remember. They think my memories are too traumatic for me to handle. But how can anyone know *that* when they don't even know what memories are there? How does keeping me here medicated out of my mind help me discover who I am and what happened to me?"

I slapped the consent sheet into his hand in frustration. Would nobody see sense?

Farquhar scanned first the document and then my face, taking in my scars, my wrinkles, my pleading eyes. I think he must have seen the mingled hope and despair I held there, saw too a challenge. He didn't say anything more. He put his Volvo into reverse, backed out of the parking stall, and drove slowly through the hospital grounds toward the main exit. I slumped down in my seat as we passed the administration wing. He turned right and we drove north for a couple of miles before taking two lefts onto Highway 2A. I felt a wave of exhilaration as the car picked up speed outside the city limits.

Roy's hand rested lightly on the round gearshift between the bucket seats. Gingerly, I put my hand on his, then gently patted it and flashed him a grateful smile.

9

Roy Farquhar's "home" was a cozy but untidy furnished apartment on Red Deer's busy 55th Street. The walls were covered in art—mostly original paintings, several of them by my husband. Of course, I'd seen Phil's signature before—it looked like a copyright sign preceded by a P and followed by a lower case L: *P©l*.

"What would you like to drink?" asked Roy as soon as we got settled.

"I dunno. Surprise me." Which he did again and again, with tequila, I think it was—the bottle had a bug in the bottom of it—and soon my mouth was moving faster than my mind. Still, I didn't like the light-headedness that soon overtook me so that I could hardly stand. "You're geddin' me drunk," I accused him as I held out my empty glass for more. But by the time he filled it, I had fallen asleep. I was vaguely aware of coming to for an instant as he lifted me from the arm chair and set me down on the sofa, positioning a soft pillow behind my head and covering me with a blanket.

"Sorry," I managed to murmur. My head was pounding and I wanted to throw up.

"It's all right," he said. "We can talk some more tomorrow."

I awoke at about four that night with a terrible headache and an intense thirst. I turned on a lamp in the living room and staggered to the kitchen. From the bedroom I could hear Roy's gentle snoring, hardly identifiable as human. I poured myself a glass of water from the tap, but it tasted rank, so I opened the fridge and poured myself some milk. Then I returned to the living room and sat on the sofa for several minutes, closing my eyes against the spinning, swimming giddiness that engulfed me. *Withdrawal*, I thought. I had left my meds at the hospital. All of them. Had not given them a second thought until now. I must have sat there for half an hour, vaguely conscious of passing time only because the odd truck rumbled by outside, rattling the windows, each one seeming to take forever to pass.

By the light of the lamp, I became aware of a large painting hanging on the interior wall of the living room, a landscape of dark woods in the foreground and rugged mountains in the background that seemed familiar, as did Phil's telltale signature. On the adjoining wall over the sofa where I had been lying were two smaller Campbell paintings – another landscape and a vaguely familiar portrait of a middle-aged woman.

I turned my attention to the file that Farquhar had brought in with him from the car and realized immediately that he was a journalist who did his homework. There were several clippings about fires in the West Country, including an article about the forest fire for which I was deemed responsible. Deeper down were notes torn from a spiral notebook, then entries of a diary from years before.

Oct 21

Found nr Lower Cabin site:

1. *Charred air rifle*
2. *Sprung wolf traps (2)*
3. *Partial skeleton (prob. canine: dog? small wolf? coyote?)*
4. *Dead cow (?), burnt, putrefied, partially buried (in barn)*

Campbell's Kids

Found in ruins of Lower Cabin:

1. *Cast iron wood stove, well preserved, connected to chimney*
2. *Copper sheep-dip tub, floor burned through, collapsed*
3. *Metal coil mattress springs (5 sets)*
4. *Metal "guts" of easy chair*
5. *Broken dishes, glassware, etc. (lots!)*
6. *Bent and melted cutlery*
7. *Charred saucepans, cookware*
8. *Cast iron manual water pump, not working (seized up)*
9. *Floor completely collapsed except around stairs, stove*

Found in ruins of Upper Cabin:
In kitchen:

a. *Cast iron wood stove, well preserved*
b. *Broken dishes, glassware, cutlery, etc.*
c. *Charred saucepans, cookware*

In living room:

a. *Floral sofa, charred but more or less intact*
b. *Partial sculpted rug, charred. Floor intact*
c. *2 armchairs, barely recognizable*

In front bedroom:

a. *Set of bunkbeds, intact. Smoke damage*
b. *Single bed*
c. *Chest of drawers (emptied by police?)*

Master bedroom inaccessible (still police crime scene!)

a. *Appears to have double bed*
b. *Floor intact (trap door?)*

At rill Nr Upper Cabin Site:

1. *Washboard*
2. *1 pr. boys' Jockey undershorts*
3. *1 pr. women's panties*

Oct 22

Heavy frost. Got to get out of here before winter sets in! Followed well-worn trail 1 km east to rail fence. Ashes of campfire containing

1. *broken end of bow, including nylon string*
2. *partially melted suction cup (kid's arrow?)*
3. *loose coils of baling wire*

Hiked to jeep seen from air. Reached it 5:20 p.m. Deeply imbedded in muskeg, no tracks leading to it. License number current; keys still in it; battery dead.

Here a note had been inserted: *MVB check: reg. owner Philip Campbell.*

So absorbed was I in trying to decipher Roy's handwriting that I did not notice him standing in the doorway observing me. As soon as I saw him standing there, I shut the file, feeling guilty.

"Oh, I don't mind if you read it."

"I thought there might be something about the plane crash."

"There is, if you dig deep enough. It's in reverse chronological order, so it's probably near the bottom of the pile."

I gazed around the room. "Where'd you get all these paintings?"

"My mother. That's how I first became interested in your husband. Naturally, I followed his career, even interviewed him once, years ago, in connection with a show he mounted here in Red Deer. Then he had a big opening in Edmonton. Then Toronto, Ottawa, Montreal, New York, London. Just took off. The wildness of the Rocky Mountains and the Kootenay Plains that he captured in his larger canvases has a voice of its own, popular in urban settings." He added, "Now, my mother's collection of his art is worth a bundle!"

"How many does she have?"

"Hundreds of his earlier paintings. And dozens of sketches. They quadrupled in value the day he died. Funny, how that works. But you must know that already. You lived with him during his most prolific period. His muse. You remember modeling for him? You must've watched him paint!"

Struggling to resurrect a memory, I had a sudden image of an artist with reddish hair craning around the canvas as he painted my portrait. There was something predatory about the way his eyes seemed to caress my flesh. I wore nothing but my goose bumps.

Then, and now. I shuddered and backed out of the memory, trying to pack it away.

"I'm obsessed with him, to tell you the truth," Roy was saying. "Famous artist struck down in the prime of life by something so dark as a murder-suicide."

An image of this horror flashed in my mind in silhouette. "Yes, I read that in your article."

"According to Margo, Phil shot her mother – your sister Alice – with a shotgun, then turned the gun on himself. Murder-suicide. The girls guarded the crime scene like a shrine. Wouldn't give the boys access, not even to the food which was stored there. When Colleen tried to sneak some food out to Tom, Emily locked her in the master bedroom with her dead dad as a punishment. Tom admits that he organized a raid by the boys to try to rescue Colleen and free up some food. He couldn't participate in the raid himself because he had a broken leg – but there was never any doubt that he was the brains behind it. In the course of the raid, Willis set fire to the place, 'Accidentally on purpose,' Margo said. Colleen was trapped inside the cabin and died in the blaze."

An image of a little girl flashed through my mind, a face behind wooden bars surrounded by roiling steam. I felt physically ill.

"*Colleen!*"

"Yes," said Roy. "Do you remember her?"

"And—Margo?"

"Your niece. She was there. She claimed she tried to fight the fire, but the boys prevented her."

"The boys," I said. "Tom?"

"No, not Tom. Your other sons, Roger and Billy—and your nephew, Willis. He was the leader."

I shook my head free of cobwebs. It was all so confusing.

"Alice had taken her family to Camas Lake from Edmonton for the summer holidays," Roy explained. "The two families were vacationing together when things went sideways. Phil and Alice did not get along. Not surprisingly! As you may recall, your sister was a Jehovah's Witness, too much of a fundamentalist to be comfortable with Phil's lifestyle. Your husband spent most of his time in his studio, obsessed with his work. Margo claims he left his kids to their own devices, leaving Tom in charge, for days at a time while he went off to paint. So there was quite a bit of tension after Alice arrived with her family. In your absence, she was expected to be a surrogate mom. And Phil could not tolerate Alice or the girls intruding on his privacy. Margo claims that once when she approached his studio the back way, he took a shot at her. Must've been a shotgun, because it denuded the sapling she was hanging on to. Scared her to death!"

"And then he shot Alice," I said, still trying to wrestle with that stark dimension of reality. "Why?"

Roy looked at me as if to say, *You just don't get it, do you?*

"Margo thinks they were having an affair."

I flinched. "My sister? With my husband?"

"I'm sorry. But it's not surprising, really. You went missing two years earlier in the plane crash that killed her husband."

I had a half-formed memory of the cockpit of a plane, the stall, then the fall side to side, a falling leaf swooping back and forth, engines cut, prop fanning—

"The inquest into the murder-suicide was overshadowed by the horror of later events," Farquhar was saying. I tried to track.

"The fire?"

"Fires, plural. The kids became embroiled in some kind of feud. The boys were out of control—"

"Colleen—"

"Yes. Your nephew set fire to the house."

"Colleen was trapped inside!"

"Yes. Margo said it spread from the kitchen. The pathologist said Colleen was overcome by the smoke. Firemen found her clinging to her father's dead body—"

Tears welled in my eyes at the thought of my little girl suffering so.

"And the other fire?" I whispered.

"*Your* house—the main Campbell residence."

"In which Roger and Billy died," I whispered, remembering the news stories. "And Emily, Sandra, and Willis."

Farquhar nodded grimly. "Wiped out half the family. That was the one set by Margo."

My throat had clamped shut so tight that I was strangling. "That monster Margo killed my kids!" The enormity of her crime was beginning to sink in. "Billy and Roger and Colleen all burned to death?" I was nearing hysteria. "Oh my Jesus God Christ!"

"She admitted to setting the fire," said Farquhar. "But the court was not convinced she acted alone. She had no motive. The judge said there had to be a controlling mind. That's why your son Tom was convicted of five counts of manslaughter and criminal negligence causing death."

10

That was why he had decided to write my husband's biography, Roy Farquhar explained. "I already had a good grasp on his art, because my mother has an art gallery in Ottawa that features his work. Has for years! And I used to prepare the catalogues for the printer. That's why I asked to be assigned to the story.

"Phil had a flair for taking a picture postcard of almost anywhere and painting it on canvas to make it look like home. So he was popular with politicians. My mother gave Richard orders from politicians and their wives to paint favorite scenes from their ridings on large canvases that would decorate their offices. The cost of the painting was covered by a special budget through Alberta Culture. Later, in Ottawa, she set up her Parliamentary Art Gallery and performed the same service for federal politicians. Of course, one politician gets one, every politician has to get one, so it became a non-partisan service: You supply a postcard and get back a massive original oil painting of the classic scene, stylized to reflect the true talent of the artist. That's how Philip Campbell came to be a household name.

"When my dad became Minister of Foreign Affairs, my mother found a whole new market in consulates and embassies.

Same idea: favorite postcard becomes abstracted to oil painting with a Canadian flair, bearing the signature of Philip Campbell. Phil painted to order, and every month Richard flew in to Camas Lake to collect the finished paintings. He flew them back to my mother's gallery in Edmonton, and later after we moved to Ottawa he shipped them there. Phil became one of the most prolific artists in Canada—today he's represented internationally everywhere from MOMA to the Tate.

"So naturally, as a fledgling journalist, I was interested in his art. Especially when Richard's plane went down—and you went missing. That was a shocker!

"My mother blanched when she heard the news from Richard's mother. She hung up the phone, turned to my dad, and said, 'They've killed the goose that laid the golden egg!'"

"'They've'?" I asked.

Roy laughed. "That's exactly what I asked my mother. 'Figure of speech,' she said. The golden goose was obviously Richard Thompson. But who was 'they'?"

He paused, reflectively.

"Well?" I asked.

"I never did find out. But my mother went to his funeral. Took over, in fact. Richard's mother and mine had been best friends, but Elizabeth couldn't handle the strain of a funeral. Must've been heart-wrenching to see all her grandkids lined up at the closed casket saying their goodbyes to his photograph. He was burned beyond recognition.

"My mother had to prevail upon Phil to attend the funeral. My father arranged his transportation to Edmonton. The police suspected foul play, because the traces of gasoline left from the wreck were marked gas—agricultural gas. A lot of high test gas—it checked out as aviation fuel—had been dumped into Camas Lake, polluting it with a sheen that lasted until the lake froze over. Killed everything in it."

"So the tank was drained?"

"Both tanks. And replaced with purple gas. The same gas that was later used to fuel the fire at the Campbell house. There was a ready supply."

He flipped to the back of the file.

"Richard had filled up with aviation fuel before leaving Edmonton. Had plenty of fuel to get there and back." He found what he was looking for. "But see here? 'The coroner found that a cheap, low-octane agricultural fuel had been used in the vintage plane and that this had fouled the spark plugs and flooded the engine, causing a stall.'" He flipped a page. "Then over here, Phil is quoted as saying he had brought in a thousand gallons of agricultural gas to the farm ten years before, when he was farming. Richard must've used that to top up his tanks. He probably didn't realize just how stale that gasoline was!

"Suffice to say, your husband—my mother's hero—suddenly became a person of interest in a murder case. The press turned up at the funeral in force—including me! And who should be there at the door turning us away but my good old Ma!"

"Protecting her interests?" I said.

"Like Mother Goose!

"In one of the interviews I had with Tom, he told me Richard had spent the night before the crash at Camas Lake—he'd flown there from Edmonton the day before. Tom said you and Richard flew out together first thing the following morning, or tried to. Of course, the coroner's report—a copy's in there somewhere—was limited to Richard's death. Doesn't mention you at all. After all, his was the only body they found. The coroner concentrated on the cause of the crash, which he chalked up to equipment malfunction owing to the wrong kind of gasoline. Fouled plugs but no foul play."

"Who reported the crash?"

"Nobody. Richard should have radioed in the night before to change his itinerary but didn't. His old plane was not equipped for night flying; the instrument panel was smashed in the crash.

It did have a transponder, but it was disconnected. An automatic search began when he failed to follow his flight plan. He was supposed to have flown alone from Edmonton to Camas Lake in the morning, returning in the evening before sunset, there and back in one day.

"Once Search and Rescue found the plane wreck, they brought in a helicopter and later the coroner and investigators from the Transportation Safety Board. They took out Richard's body and later removed some of the wreckage, including the engine, for analysis. Dusted the doors and dash for fingerprints—whatever hadn't been burned. That's as far as it went. Alice initially filed a request for an inquest but later withdrew it after the coroner's report came out."

"So my sister abandoned me, too!" I said, half to myself.

"I don't think there's any doubt she knew you were aboard. But—she had lost her husband. It's understandable that she may have been in denial that you were with him.

"According to the report, the passenger door was open, consistent with someone kicking it out—or trying to—but also consistent with it buckling under the force of the crash. Richard's seat belt was undone and he was found sitting on the port seat, lying back against the port door. The investigators lifted several latent fingerprints from the outer handle of the passenger door, at least one of them repeated on the inner handle. A search for you was mounted, fanning out from the wreckage—but it was called off after a week. You were officially listed as a missing person, joining hundreds of other women on the list. Been on it ever since."

11

Roy pointed dismissively to a large colorful book on the low coffee table in front of the sofa I sat on.

"I've already published a coffee table book of your husband's art," he said, "thanks largely to my mother. The gallery published it. It doubled as a fancy catalogue—but it looks impressive on the portfolio. At least to publishers who are looking for published writers."

I began to flip through the glossy images that emerged from each page like butterflies in full wing. He laughed at my obvious fascination with one painting of a nude, quite different from Phil's usual landscapes.

"Some of them might trigger your memory," Roy suggested.

"Did you go to many of his shows?" I asked.

He nodded. "Besides the first ones in Alberta? Several, mostly in Ottawa."

"But as his wife, surely I would have been there? Surely you would have met me?"

He shook his head. "Each time he came with Richard, who helped organize them."

I continued to flip through the book of Philip's paintings, starting at the back and working forward systematically, a page at a time. A few of the scenes looked vaguely familiar.

"So I wasn't a very supportive wife?"

"It must've been difficult living with someone that creative, so driven. He believed, as do I, that every successful artist must be obsessed with his art, almost to the exclusion of all else. I thought I understood him, because when I get going, get past the writer's block, I'm almost as obsessed as he, although writing's a very different medium from painting.

"Back then, I believed that the only way I could come to understand Phil's death was by placing myself in that setting, mulling over what had happened at Camas Lake and what I knew of the facts, trying to get a feel for the place.

"I don't mind telling you, I was spooked! I didn't know I was superstitious until I was alone in the woods where every cracked twig became a new threat. Death seemed to stalk that valley as if it were a person. Death in the two cottages. Death in the barn, death down by the creek—that's where I found the remains of a horse, chewed apart by wolves. The deaths seemed to have come in waves.

"After a week I had had enough. I didn't think anyone could survive in the bush longer than seven days, let alone—God, it's seven *years*!"

It took me a moment to realize he was alluding to me. "You get used to it, I guess." *Tuanahaki made all the difference*. "There must be portraits of me in here?"

"I believe so. Of course, you would've looked—"

"Younger," I finished for him.

"—more robust."

I stopped at one of the portraits. The model was not named, but the figure had light auburn hair, stern features, and a pale face that might once have been freckled. In the next portrait, she was more relaxed, laughing. Then my heart skipped a beat, for the next image—there could be no doubt—was an uncharitable representation of . . .

"*Tuanahaki!*" I gasped. "This is Tuanahaki! She used to wear a mudpack like that. See the habit? That's the very gown

I wore when they found me and brought me to the hospital, the one with the matches in it!"

I turned the book so Roy could see for himself.

"The painting's called *Nisokos*," said Roy doubtfully.

"'Tuanahaki' was my special name for her. It was the first thing she said to me: It means 'There's always room for one more.' I thought she was telling me her name. But that's her, I swear!" I closed the book, afraid to delve any deeper.

"So it all fits!" said Roy.

12

The following morning, I awoke to the shriek of a hawk protecting its nest. Farquhar, face white with shaving cream, came into the living room and fumbled around, trying to get the telephone receiver to his ear before the other party hung up.

"Hello?"

"Farquhar?" I could hear the voice of the other man clearly. "Where are you, for crying out loud?"

"At home. What number did you think you dialed?"

"You know what time it is?"

"Yeah, I'm sorry. I slept in."

"Did you get anything yesterday? You took off in such an all-fired roar."

"Nope. False lead. Could have been a beaut, though."

"Nothing?"

"Nope."

"Well what the hell are we going to do with the City Page? It's the holiday edition, and we've only got an hour to deadline! Get your ass down here right now, God damn it!"

I heard the other party hang up. Farquhar put the receiver back in its cradle. Then he picked it up again and slammed it down. His eyes blazed and he looked for a moment rabid, with the dried suds around his mouth and chin.

"Son of a bitch," he said. "They think they *own* me!"

I opened my mouth to say something, then realized I had nothing to say, so I shut it again.

"Why don't they run a morning paper like everybody else?" He slumped down into the armchair nearest the phone, and then wiped the dry bubbles from his face with his sleeve.

"Can't you interview me?" I asked.

"Don't *you* start!"

"Just trying to help."

He looked at me and blinked. "Sorry," he said. "No, they want a news story for the second front. Your story's more than a news story. Yours is a feature, a human interest story." He returned to the bathroom to resume shaving.

The telephone rang again.

"Fuck! Would you get that, please, Maggie?"

I picked up the receiver. "Hello?"

"Hi, is Roy there?" The voice was very faint.

"He's busy at the moment," I shouted.

"It's Jim Harris. Tell him to get unbusy!"

I cupped my hand over the receiver. "Roy, Jim Harris says to make yourself unbusy."

"Tell him to screw right off."

"But—I don't even know him."

Roy let out a guffaw. "Tell him I'll be there in a minute."

I put the receiver back to my ear and only then realized that I had had my hand cupped over the wrong end. "He'll be here in a minute," I said.

Roy came out dressed in a sports shirt and old jeans, as if the last place he planned to go was to work.

"Yeah, Farquhar," he said, holding the receiver away from his ear.

"What do you mean by telling me to screw off?" the tirade began. This time, Roy did not even engage. "I want a story by nine, or you're fired!"

"Fuck off, Harris! You don't have the authority to fire me. I outrank you on the seniority roster, you little pissant! Just because you opted to become assistant city editor and I decided to stay on as a *real* journalist—"

"I just can't work with you!"

"Then quit."

"*You* quit."

"Oh, okay, all right. *I quit!* Satisfied?"

"That's all right, Farquhar," said the voice, "because now you're *really* fired!"

"Whatever."

Harris hung up again. Roy gently replaced the receiver and sat down beside me on the arm of the sofa. He began counting as if he were a referee standing over a decked fighter at a boxing match.

By the time he got to seven, the telephone rang again. Roy picked it up, holding it tilted so I could hear.

"Hello?"

"Roy?"

Syrupy voice. "Oh, hi, Jim! I've been expecting your call!"

"Ah, come on, Roy. Look, I'm sorry. God damn it, we can't operate without you, not today. Everybody's off on holiday. We just don't have enough bodies to go 'round."

"That's *journalists*, Jim. Not bodies. *Journalists.* Can you get your mind around that?"

"Why don't you come in and let's discuss it."

"No thanks, Jim."

"Come on, don't be a prick about this, Roy."

"I've just had it up to the teeth with the whole damn operation."

"Look, I was mad. You walked out on us yesterday afternoon, and you skipped an assignment last night."

"I did?"

"Up at the college. That student play?"

"Jesus, Jim!"

"Well, you were down for it, and it was a good photo op, something Christmassy, and then you took off on this hot little story and you didn't get back. We need you, man. Even Milly's away for Christmas. I don't have anybody I can rely on."

"Okay, just for today. And—yeah, I'll take that raise."

"What?"

It was Roy's turn to hang up. He rose from his chair, stretched, and grinned at me.

"What are you doing tonight?" he asked.

"I hadn't really thought about it." And then, with a sudden pang, "You want me to leave?"

"No, silly. We can have dinner at the Lodge, the most popular restaurant in Red Deer."

"That would be very nice. But I have nothing to wear."

"We can fix that. By the way, I have a tape of Tom and Margo I recorded before Tom got busted for breach of parole last year. You are mentioned in a couple of the tapes, if you want to have a listen. Catch ya later!"

He left then, and I went to the window to watch him jaywalk across the four lanes of 55th Street and then cross the park on the other side—a shortcut to his office.

I looked more closely at Roy's tribute to my husband's art, which included a photograph of the artist as a young man—not exactly a portrait, although there was a self-portrait in there as well, very Van Gogh, when I think about it. Both looked very familiar. There were several studies of a young woman—in some, more than one—swimming or sunbathing, surrounded by surrealistic flowers, irises and water lilies. And a young man, obviously naked. Was that Tom? Or was it a self-portrait?

13

Inevitably, I turned to the DVD and CD tower. On the top shelf, tiny cassette tapes were filed separately but chronologically beside a miniature tape recorder. He'd said he'd interviewed Tom and Margo within the last year. Several of the tapes were labeled with Margo's name but only one with Tom's.

It took me half an hour to figure out how to work the tape recorder. I zipped through the cassette a little at a time, fast-forward, then rewind, listening to this sentence and that until I heard Tom describing his father and his habits. It was all a revelation to me.

My dad used to go off for weeks at a time, painting trips, workshops, openings—what artists do, I dunno where all he went—Edmonton with Richard, for sure, quite often, but when he come back he'd talk about New York, London, Montreal—Christ! Sometimes he would be gone a month. Other times he would be up at his studio for a week, two weeks at a stretch, paintin', leavin' Mom and us boys to fend for ourselves.

The upstairs was just a fixed-up attic, where us boys slept. Downstairs, there's the master bedroom at the end of the hall. The livin' room's the smallest room in the house—doubles as an office. Mostly we lived in the kitchen. No privacy at all. If we wanted a hot bath, we'd have to fill up that copper tub—the one in your picture—hot water from the boiler on the side of the woodstove, then add cold water from the hand pump. Kinda rusticky. The only way to bathe was in front of everybody else. Not such a big deal while we were boys—Mom 'n' Dad would bathe there like the rest of us, and it got so we didn't take much notice, we'd seen each other naked so often.

But when I reached puberty, I wanted more privacy. Seemed like everybody in the family was countin' pubic hairs. My ol' man hadn't told me jack shit about sex an' that, although I had a fair idea how things worked from watchin' animals. I began to grow in all directions at once, and of course at thirteen my voice changed, and besides the pubic hair I got pimples an' grew a bit of a beard. And I become—sensitive. My thing, I mean. Got so I had a rod on every ten minutes, day or night: every time I went to bed, every time I took a walk, every time I took a bath. That was particularly bad, 'cause it wasn't private. Got so shy I wouldn't take a bath for weeks. Whenever I went for a walk it would rub against my pants and there I'd get another stiffy. Every night I'd play with it. And naturally I started jackin' off—I'm talkin' serious masturbation here!

Trouble was, my bed was a rickety cot, and every night the bed would be jumpin' all over the attic. Kept my mom downstairs awake more 'n once, I guess. Anyways, this one time she comes up the stairs right into our bedroom to see what's goin' on. I hear her on the stairs, so I'm lyin' there stock still, holdin' my breath in one hand and my dick in the other.

My curtain was open—I'd been lookin' at a Sears Wish List by the light of the moon. Pictures of panties did it for me back then, I guess. Mom comes over and sits down on my bed and asks me what I was doin'.

"Nothin'," I say.

She smiles, knowin' she's caught me in a lie. She pulls back the covers and looks longingly at the cock in my hand, "Nothin', huh?"

I get all defensive. "What do you expect me to do around here," I say, "shag a sheep?"

"Shhh! Rog and Billy are sleepin'!" Which they were, at the other end of the attic. Then she says in a mockin' voice, "Is that what you think about when you're doin' that? Shaggin' sheep?" She sees her Wish List on the floor beside my bed where I'd dropped it when I'd heard her on the stairs. When she bends over to pick it up, her housecoat falls open so that her boobs dangle, hangin' there a few inches from my face. She doesn't have a stitch on underneath. She stands up to look at the catalogue, her breasts and round belly and her furry snatch all lit by a shaft of moonlight. She glances down at me, then snaps the book shut and says, "I always wondered where this went." Her breath comes short, and she whispers in a trembly voice, "If you really want it, you can always come downstairs an' get it!"

I lay awake for about an hour, my heart poundin' like crazy, knowin' she was lyin' wide awake too jus' waiting for me to go downstairs to her room. Or maybe not. Maybe she was jus' testin' me. Or maybe I had misunderstood her meaning. I couldn't be sure. An' I begin to think of her, y'know, like not in a good way. Her breasts and belly and pussy bathed by the moon. I mean, it was nothin' new—I'd seen her naked often enough. But I'd never noticed her, I'd never once thought of her that way before.

I couldn't get out of my mind what she'd said about goin' down to get the Wish List. So I get up, put on a shirt, an' sneak downstairs to the master bedroom. The door's open. There's a candle burnin' low on her dresser, reflected in the mirror. The catalogue's beside it. I glance at her in the double bed, then realize she's still awake, lookin' at the door, watchin' me. Waiting. I can feel my heart beating in my ears. My cock shrivels up to nothing, I'm so scared.

I didn't say a word. Nor did she. She beckons me in with fluttery fingers. As I come near the bed, she lifts up the blanket an' holds out her arm. I sit down sideways on the bed beside her, half expectin' a lecture. She pulls down the sheets so I can see her breasts, her pussy. She's stark naked. My mouth goes dry. I can feel my cock coming alive.

She holds her right breast in her hand, offering it to me, the nipple hard and dark. "See how you make them stand on end?" she whispers. "They want to be sucked. They need to be sucked!" God, that just turns me to jelly inside.

She pulls me down beside her and practically feeds me her right breast. It felt weird to have the nipple in my mouth—but comfortable. She holds my head to her breast as I suck, an' murmurs, "Harder, harder!" Her hand goes down to feel my rock-solid cock an' she holds it and gives a sort of gasp. I feel about ready to explode. I mean, I'd been jackin' off when she first interrupted me, but I hadn't come.

My balls feel like they've been crammed into shoes two sizes too small. She takes her nipple out of my mouth, kisses me, then quickly takes me in her mouth. Oh, God! Jus' long enough to make me wet or I would've come in her mouth for sure. An' before I know it she's pulled me over beside her on the bed and she kind of straddles me, an' I was like all the way up inside her like instantly without doin' a damn thing, an' I jus' couldn't believe it, it was so soft and wet and warm and wonderful. An' she was like writhing on top of me an' screaming scary shit and bang! Just like that, I come inside her. And she screams and keeps working on my dick, moving her hips in circles and up and down. She squeals as she squeezes down against my pubic bone real tight, holding her clit against the base of my cock until she comes with a groan. I can feel her suckin' my dick up inside her with each spasm of her orgasm.

We both lie there pantin', trying to catch our breaths. But neither one of us can keep our hips still; hers are still swirling and mine are thrusting like aftershocks following a quake.

I'm not fully hard anymore but somehow I'm still inside her, and she's squeezing me with her cunt, sucking me in and pushing me out again, in, out, in, out. She giggles like a little girl as I gradually get harder and kisses me and hugs me and rolls me over so I'm on top, an' then she says, "Boy, have you got a thing or two to learn!" An' she kisses me all over my face, no French stuff, though, just surface kisses, and she laughs an' laughs. And I laugh too, but more nervously, because I'm still scared shitless about what we jus' did. You have no idea how fucked up that is—to have sex your own mother!

That first time, I guess it was late and we were both very nervous and kinda tired, we just did it the once an' she shooed me off upstairs, and I slept the rest of the night in my own bed. Sort of. But after that I knew what to expect whenever she invited me down, and over the next two or three months—well, it's safe to say she taught me practically everything I know!

I gasped for air. Had I really done that? To my own son? How could I? Surely some fail-safe mechanism should have kicked in to prevent it? Was this why my brain refused to let my mind remember?

I knelt in front of the tape recorder, waiting for the shock and nausea to pass as the tape continued to feed silently from one side of the cassette to the other. That was *me* Tom was talking about! And Roy had been privy to this! Having heard, perhaps even recorded, this tape of Tom, Roy must have had a notion from the outset—perhaps a sick hope—that I was some kind of nympho, that I was "easy" and available. I blushed in humiliation and willed myself to be someone else, *anyone* else, but Maggie Campbell. The woman Tom had described, so bereft of conscience and morality, could not possibly be me!

14

Roy returned to the apartment at four that afternoon tired but buoyant, a plastic bag swinging from his hand.

"Merry Christmas," he said, producing a colorfully wrapped present.

"Thanks!" I said, beginning to open the package. "Sorry I don't have anything for you."

"I picked you out some clothes, just jeans and a top. I had to guess at your size, figured eight was about average. But they said I can take them back if they don't fit. Just don't take off the labels."

I took the package from him and opened it, taking the red blouse out first. It was on the large side, but close enough. Then I held the jeans up against me. Way too big.

"The clerk said that kind shrinks when you wash them."

"I'll have to roll up the legs a little, and I can pin the back."

It felt good to climb into new clothes, even if they didn't fit. Still, Roy winced when I came out of the bathroom to model them.

"Let's go back and exchange them right away," he said.

"Won't they get a little suspicious if I walk in there with nothing on but the clothes I'm exchanging?"

"That kind of detail goes right by them at this time of year. Everyone returns stuff."

We went back to the store, taking the car so that if there was nothing suitable downtown we could go to one of the malls. Roy hadn't bought me a belt and his own were way too long, so I had to keep my pants hitched up in front with my left hand as we walked down the sidewalk to the store.

Every garment on the racks seemed to me to be the very thing. I would have bought them all, had I the money. The clerks lost all patience, especially since I was "trading in" the clothes I had originally been wearing. I tried on dress after dress, catching up on five years of fashions in a single afternoon.

With each new change of outfit I thrilled at the sight of my body. Although my face was a mass of wrinkles—it still is—I became aware for the first time of my shapely figure. From the shoulders up I looked plain enough, but from the breasts down, I was all woman. I flirted with Roy as I modeled each dress, pretending to walk the catwalk.

At last I decided on one of the cheapest outfits in the store, a purple suit on sale (and no doubt already out of fashion), which accentuated my bust and butt while showing off my legs. I brushed my hair in the changing room and wore the suit out of the store.

Ten minutes later, we arrived at the restaurant. We sat on an indoor patio overlooking tropical plants and a huge pool. Roy chose a wine and then we went to the salad bar—a feast in itself. The Christmas buffet, complete with turkey, ham, and chateaubriand, awaited along with English trifle, Black Forest cake, plum pudding—all the fixings of a Christmas dinner that I could never recall having experienced in my life. Armed with salads, we returned to the table to talk.

"So, have you remembered anything?" he asked point-blank.

"A little." Dr. Lenski had told me I might remember the latest things first, then earlier events, then gradually I'd zero in on the event that caused the trauma. "My memory casts back and forth in time, occasionally sets down. If I'm lucky there's a strike—little bursts of detail that don't seem to make sense, but I'm able to put more and more pieces together. Eventually, I hope, I'll have a complete picture of my past."

"How far back have you remembered?"

"I really don't know. So far it's been about the recent past—the forest fire and Tuanahaki."

He sat down in the armchair and flipped through a notepad, reviewing his notes. "What was that name again?"

"Tuanahaki. She's the one who helped me survive in the woods."

He made a cryptic note in his pad: *Dyawannahanky?*

"I listened to the tape of your interview with Tom," I said, "the one in which he describes how I seduced him."

"Ah. Wow." He looked at me, trying to read my mind. "Ouch! No, that wasn't my interview. His lawyer recorded that statement prior to the sentencing. She figured it would help if the court knew he'd been abandoned by his father, only to be sexually abused by his mother. But she didn't use it, because it was so explicit and might have reflected badly on him. She gave it to him with the rest of his file when he was contemplating an appeal. He didn't want his file in the prison, so gave it to Margo for safe-keeping. She found the tape in the file box but didn't have a tape recorder, so I took one up there and we listened to it together. She was some upset! In trying to comfort her, I forgot all about the tape still being in the machine, so it ended up here. Was he telling the truth, do you think?"

His blunt question caught me by surprise. But I recognized an opening: *No! It's a lie!*

"I don't remember doing that at all, any of it! The very *thought* of it—of doing that to—with my own son—" I shuddered. "Ugh! He's lying. He's got to be. It's so unlike—what I feel *capable* of doing. I can't even visualize it as a possibility!"

"We're talking eight, nine years ago. You were younger then—"

"No! The answer's *no*. A thirty-something-year-old seducing my thirteen-year-old son? That's just *wrong*! I am his *mother*."

Then: "What must he think of me? I mean, for him to say that I did *that*!" I looked at him. "What do *you* think of me?"

"Hey, it isn't my place to judge."

"How can you *not* judge, having heard that? No wonder I have amnesia! It makes me not want to be me! Maybe that's part of my craziness. I can't even remember having been married, let alone being a mother—what, four times over? I don't remember any of that! It's as if my entire adult life has disappeared. And judging from what Tom said, it's for the better."

"But if it was all a lie—"

"Am I really the incestuous whore Tom describes me as being?"

"That's a little harsh."

"No. I'm not that person. It wasn't me. I'm not his mother." Then, lamely: "I want to be someone else."

"You are who you are. Are you saying you don't remember Tom?"

Actually, I did. More and more. I closed my eyes, trying to visualize the young man I had come to think of as him—a dark-haired teenage boy perched on the top of a rail fence. Where did he figure in the scheme of things? In my mind's eye, he wore a wine-colored plaid shirt, faded blue jeans, worn-out Nike running shoes. His green canvas-covered cedar canoe rested against the top railing, one end pointing to the ground, the other to the sky. Was it by prearrangement that I rode up the trail toward him on—Angel, that was the horse's name!—my dog—Ragtime!—following along behind? I was dressed simply in pink cotton shorts, a yellow tank-top, and sandals. I smiled at him. He was chewing on a straw but spat it out as I approached. He looked at me critically with a roving eye.

"Saddle's loose," he said.

My saddle had shifted to one side on the horse's back. "Oh, so it is," I said. I tried to straighten it with my thighs. "Will you make it tight for me?"

He swung down off the top railing to open the gate. "Only if ya promise to return the favor." He laughed heartily at his own joke, then even harder at my obvious flustered embarrassment. "Get off of it," he said. "The blanket's fucked."

I lifted my leg away from the saddle and looked down. "Rucked," I said starchily. "The blanket's *rucked.* Can you fix it?"

"Sure. Ride on through." He was still chuckling to himself: *Got you good!*

Was that boy really Tom, or was it Phil at an earlier age—no, Phil had *reddish* hair, judging from his self-portrait—or was it someone else altogether, some fantasy figure conjured by a photograph, a painting, or an innocent caricature of a Campbell Kid sitting on a fence? The figure in my memory straddled all these realities. When had that happened, if it had at all? Where?

As the horse walked by him through the gateway, Tom's fingertips alighted on my knee and rode along the top of my thigh. Only when his finger caught the cuff of my shorts did I reflexively slap his hand away.

"Bad, bad boy!" I scolded, hiding my embarrassed grin.

"Sorry," he said, one eye looking at my face, the other fixated on my leg. He held the bridle as I swung down off the horse, but the saddle shifted and my left sandal slipped through the stirrup. I lost my balance, but he caught me, one hand around my left shoulder, the other supporting my right butt cheek. *Touchdown!*

Oh my God, he's hot!

He took the pressure off my ankle as I disentangled my foot, first from my sandal and then from the stirrup. "Dangerous to ride with sandals on," he panted in my ear as he set me gently on the ground.

"And shorts," I added, pushing his hand gently but firmly away from my leg for the second time. This could get tiresome.

I was blushing not from anger but from arousal, and he knew it. He shut the gate, then approached the horse and released the cinch on the saddle. He flattened and smoothed the saddle blanket, and the horse jerked its head upward as he cinched the saddle. Then he walked along the fence to the canoe, which he slid easily over the top rail toward him.

To complicate things, our dogs carried on as if they were the last pair of their species on earth. Ragtime, a Springer spaniel, braced his hind legs as he plunged into Baloney, only to lose his footing as she stepped forward then back, trying to brace her hind end to accommodate him. Ragtime chuffed away like a steam engine as, tied together, they worked their way off the trail into the privacy of the woods.

"Jeez, I di'n't even notice she was in heat!" Tom said. He feasted his eyes on my nipples, which unbidden pressed out of the fabric of my tank top. "It's sometimes hard to tell."

"I wonder what their pup will be," I mused aloud, my mind in neutral.

"Pup? *Pup!* The way they're carryin' on, she'll have a dozen at least!"

"Yeah? Well, I bet—no more than six!" I said, recovering.

We shook on it. But what a shake! It went right through me like an electric shock from arm to breasts to belly to groin. His eyes twinkled above a smile that blew me right out of the pasture. My nipples sang.

He cinched up Angel's saddle even tighter for me and helped me remount, then rested his hand for a third time on my leg. He looked up at me, his chin on my bare knee.

"You're right," he said, running his forefinger up and down the inside of my calf. "You shouldn't ride a horse wearin' shorts. It's real hard on the insides of the knees." He turned out my leg and kissed me there to show me. His gaze took in the inside of my thigh as I tried reflexively to close my legs, pressing inward against the saddle. "'Specially pink shorts," he murmured, "with matching panties."

I pinched my legs together even tighter, and Angel took this as a command. But Tom still had hold of the left rein. I slapped his hand with the end of the reins and pushed him away. The horse danced a reel around him. It was all I could do to keep aloft. "Third strike, and you're out!" I said, wrestling to regain control. "Enough is enough!"

15

Tom laughed and returned to the fence, where he picked up the bow of the canoe and half crawled beneath it. Straining, he balanced the canoe across his shoulders, gripping the sides tightly in front so that his knuckles looked like white and pink petals against the green paint. He jogged awkwardly across the rocky pasture under the canoe on hyper-extended legs. Angel and I trotted behind. Occasionally, the canoe tipped forward and I could see his muscular butt cheeks, tight against his jeans.

By the time we reached the woods, he had developed quite a sweat. I dismounted as he rested for a second then, holding Angel's reins in one hand, I helped him carry the canoe down through the last stretch of the portage over mossy limestone rocks to the creek, a hundred yards or so down a steep bank. He went first, examining and testing each exposed root on the way down. My sandals slipped and squelched through a squishy bed of needles sodden with water trapped in pockets of rock.

When we reached the creek, he thrust the bow of the canoe into the water. It bobbed as he pushed it farther into the current. He tied the stern line to a sturdy dogwood bush and wiped his forehead, passing a frayed sleeve across it, then tethered Angel to the adjacent bush. He slipped off his shirt and flapped it under his arms, swatting away the mosquitoes and cooling himself.

The sun glistened on his moist, tanned skin, revealing ugly grooves on each shoulder blade.

"You've got marks," I said, impulsively feeling with my fingertips the long, narrow dent across his shoulders left by the paddles lashed to the crossbar of the canoe. His skin was slippery with sweat. "The wood cut into you."

"Nothing," he said, shrugging me off. He unbuckled the belt of his jeans and zipped down his fly. "I'm all sweaty. Up for a swim?"

He wore no underpants. My heart thumped in my chest as, naked, he disappeared down a hidden trail behind some willow shrubs.

"Last one in's a toothless beaver!" he called with a laugh. Then some distance away there was a tremendous splash that was for me an invitation and a challenge.

When I dove into the hot spring pool, I was as nude as he. "It's *freezing*!" I cried with a surprised squeal as I dog-paddled in a circle.

"The crick keeps it cool. The hot spot's over there." He nodded to the center as he swam to the edge of the pond. "Want a flower?" He snapped off a large white water lily with prominent yellow stamens and anther. "This is about the biggest."

I swam closer and allowed him to thread it through my hair. Then he disappeared beneath the surface. I too dove, and we swam toward each other under water. I stuck out my tongue, while he thumbed his nose in reply as we surfaced together.

My water lily was floating near the rock, bobbing in the waves we had made.

"Beat you to it!" he challenged, and once again we plunged and swam. He wheeled, holding the water lily between his teeth, panting on each side of the stem.

"Now it's your turn to wear it," I said, taking it from his mouth and sticking it in his hair. I continued dog-paddling around the pool. "Now, where's that hot spring?"

"Follow me!"

He dove out of sight, once again leaving the water lily bobbing on the surface. I too dove down, feeling the freshness of the cool water—what a switch from household chores! We swam down, eyes open, side by side, holding our breath, until I felt a warm current of water rising past me, dissipating into the larger pond. It was like a stream from a hot water tap, which I followed up to the surface. I took a deep breath and dove again.

Incredibly, he was still down there. He pointed to a flat rock about fifteen feet down, from beneath which the hot water was swirling, twisting the weeds slightly. He signaled for me to wait as he went up for air, but I followed him up, squinting in curiosity at the fullness of his male anatomy. His testicles dangled, seeming to float independently in the water as he kicked his legs. Had he examined me this intimately when I had surfaced? Is that why he'd stayed down so long? Funny that at the time I hadn't cared!

I found the tiny circle where the water was noticeably warmer. Still, I abandoned it for the rock island. I pulled myself out onto it and lay there, content to bask away the afternoon in the sun as he skirted the pond picking a bouquet of wild irises, which he handed to me when he hauled himself out of the water beside me. He gave me the bouquet, all but one flower, which he sniffed, then threw it like a dart into the water. "See if you can beat that!"

I selected an iris, sat up, aimed it, and released it in the general direction of his missile, self-consciously aware that every arm movement made my breasts jiggle. The flower veered suddenly and flopped back into the water several feet short.

He crouched behind me. "You need a lesson throwin' overhand," he murmured in my ear. "Here." He took an iris from the bouquet, put it in my right hand, then held my arm in the air. "Swing it like this. Keep your wrist free. No, no, loosen it up. My dad taught me this. Now, pivot at the elbow, not the shoulder. That's it. Free it up, now, free it up!" With his right hand he swung my arm back and forth as if he were casting for trout, until my arm flowed smoothly. "Now, hold your body firm!" His left arm encircled my waist. "That's it. Now *throw*!" He snapped my arm forward.

Somehow my right breast had ended up cupped in his left hand. He nuzzled the right side of my neck. "You're s'posed to let go of the damn flower!" he mumbled into my shoulder.

I reached up with my throwing arm and grabbed his hair. "Like this?" I said. And I flipped him right over my shoulder. Unfortunately he landed half on the rock, half in the water, grazing his hip. He scrambled higher up onto the rock, still laughing but nursing his leg. His eyes were crossed, as if he had been hit on the head. "Just a reminder who's in control," I said.

A pair of horseflies circled buzzing around us, and the mosquitoes descended, first singly then in a swarm. We jumped back into the water. He dove deep, and when he came up I splashed water in his face, and then dove down and swam under water. He was breast-stroking in a circle, waiting for me to surface. I came up underneath him and grabbed him by the waist. Surfacing, I tickled him until he writhed in the water, giggling in high excitement, mocking retreat.

He rolled over then, and I realized that my tickling had aroused him in ways I had not intended. His penis was huge! He wheeled around, mischief written on his face. I struck out for the bank, but it was too late. He plunged after me and grabbed an ankle, pulling me down, avoiding somehow my free, kicking foot. I felt his naked body rub against me, felt his hand on my breast again, the left one this time—felt his legs holding me in a scissor-lock as he ran his hands over the front of my kicking thighs, then my crotch. He kissed me on the neck, on the cheek. I wriggled free, and he surfaced beside me, laughing.

With white rage, I mustered all my force in a slap to his face that resounded like a beaver tail slapping water. Then I swam for shore.

16

I slept on Roy's sofa again that night, or rather lay there in waking dream. When I did finally fall asleep, later that night I woke panting with a panic that left me without breath. My mouth and throat felt dry as talcum, and I drank the remainder of the glass of milk that I had poured for myself when I first snuggled down on the sofa. I trembled for a few minutes, hugging myself, holding myself in. I had relived with shackled horror the nightmare of nearly drowning. I had vomited water and coughed as if I would never stop.

The pool. I had almost drowned in that pool!

Someone hugged me and stroked my hair, whispering to me in the same indecipherable mantra over and over in androgynous chorus far, far off beyond comprehension or caring. My husband? My lover? Adonis? Jesus Christ? My savior, certainly. The pond itself seemed a mystic tunnel to the beyond.

Tom?

Someone—a man—carried me, wading with great effort across the creek and up the hillside to his studio.

No, it wasn't Tom. Not this time. It was Phil! Definitely Phil!

He lay me down on his cot. I remember vague sounds of clanging and banging as he stoked his old potbelly stove with kindling from a woodpile outside the door. By the time the stove roared, spewing heat, I was shivering with the chill of wet fabric against my flesh. My teeth chattered. Yet I could not summon the will or even the energy to cover myself. I just lay there until my involuntary shuddering shook the cot.

Phil noticed me shivering. Only then did he remove my drenched clothes. His fingers trembled and his breath came short as he dried me off with a towel warmed by the stove, stroking my breasts and belly and each leg and arm gently with the towel. He touched my swollen forehead with his fingertips, then bent over me and bussed my hairline as if to kiss it better. He covered me with a blanket, then fished under the bed and brought out a bottle of some kind, from which he drank deeply. Then he removed his own wet clothes.

Naked, he turned to the stove to pour some coffee, then set a canvas in place on a paint-riddled easel as, exhausted, I fell asleep again.

I woke to feel the stove going full blast, the cabin uncomfortably hot. I lay on my back on the cot, still nude. Phil breathed rapidly as he sketched me with manic strokes, then placed the wet canvas against the wall behind the stove and set another onto the easel.

The sun was well up by the time he finished his second sketch. He leaned back to view it from a new perspective, and then poured himself a coffee.

I tried to take in the details of his studio. Paintings hung on every wall, along with an assortment of photographs, several of young women. One of a couple of boys, each carrying a gun and a dead rabbit, over which was scrawled, *Phil and Richard. Best of pals.* A large framed portrait dominated the wall between the windows directly across from the cot on which I lay, a painting of a young but attractive woman with red hair and a fierce aspect. The portrait mirrored a large photograph on the bookshelf, a framed sepia print of the same woman, with the identical pose and many of the same features as the painted portrait. The portrait, while obviously a copy of the photograph, had taken on a life and force of its own.

Phil returned to the canvas with his coffee and went back to work, putting finishing touches on his portrait, glancing at my body but not my face. When finally he realized that I was staring at him, he jumped as if kicked. Then he smiled and stepped over to the bedside. Scooping up a blanket, he covered me adroitly and sat down beside me on the cot in one smooth move. Then realizing his own state of undress, he pulled on a pair of dry pants.

"You almost drowned," he said, his voice quavering. "Lucky to be alive. How're you feeling?"

I groaned. My throat and bronchial tubes ached, and I heaved and coughed, spitting up some water. He held up the steaming coffee pot.

"Coffee?"

I nodded. The last thing I needed was something to drink, yet my insides still felt chilled through.

"Better black, unless you like curdled evaporated milk. I'll mix it with a little something to take the chill out."

The alcohol replenished the strength that had sapped out of me in my terrifying struggle for life. And yet at the same time I felt I could sleep forever.

I awoke to find myself alone in the studio cabin, but I could hear children's voices far, far away, playing hide-and-seek: *Come out, come out wherever you are!* Lightheaded, I sat for several minutes trying to dispel the spasms that raked through my overfull stomach as I heaved up yet more sulfurous water. I coughed through a rasping throat.

I still had nothing on under the blanket. I cast about the room looking for my clothes, then focused on the easel propped in front of me. Suspicious, I pulled it around so that I could see Phil's latest painting.

To me, at that time, a painting should approximate the subject, a recognizable depiction of the object that was being reproduced. Although he had captured my basic features, Phil had made me look—different. I looked older than I felt, my face leaner.

In a doorless cupboard to one side of the stove I saw a biscuit box. I stood up shakily, shrugging off giddiness, then holding my blanket in front of me walked stiffly to the cupboard, took out one of the cookies, and nibbled it. Wrapping the blanket around me tightly, I reassumed my position on the bed, searching the room all the while with my eyes. I tried to remember what I had been wearing. And then the night before came more clearly into focus, more by supposition than by memory.

Phil had saved me from drowning, had removed my wet clothes, had toweled me dry. His own wet clothes were in a pile just inside the door. And yes, there was my night dress, just a glimpse of it peeking out from beneath his jeans and shirt. So it had not been a dream; I had not remembered wrongly! He had undressed me completely and had thrown my nightdress down on the floor, and then had undressed himself, tossing his clothes on top of mine.

So what was the big deal? Wasn't he my husband? Or husband-to-be? Was I at that point merely his girlfriend, or his fiancé, or was I already his reclaimed, rediscovered, humbled-if-not-mortified wife, bent on reconciliation? I had no sense of my status.

Gripping my blanket, I stepped over to the clothes to touch them with my toe. All soaking wet. I laughed at myself. As if Phil—I trembled through my whole body, feeling at once thrilled and chilled by the thought, the evidence, that somehow, after all these years of coasting in neutral—Phil *desired* me.

There was a rack of paintings at the foot of the bed, and I slid out the first one, examining it through a haze of wooziness. A round squiggle with trees. Could be anywhere. The second painting was of a stylized iris, rather well done but unfinished. I went through them all, examining them critically in an amateurish way, until I came to the last half dozen or so. They were rough sketches of a nude, hardly paintings at all. Just a few lines on each canvas—but lines defining a face and form recognizably my own.

I carefully extracted each canvas from the rack. The paint was still wet.

I stared for a long time at the sensuous outlines of the last, most detailed nude in the rack, knowing that they were the features of my own body. I unwrapped the blanket and looked down at myself, then back at the painting. There was no doubt. Phil had painted me while I was asleep. Had taken off my wet night clothes and rather than covering me up had painted me. I could almost feel his eyes flitting over my body again. The breasts were definitely mine, with too-small nipples just a shade high. The hint of pubic hair was my maiden hair, the face my face. Careful not to smudge the wet paint, I slid the canvas back into place in the rack and lay back down on the bed munching my biscuit.

I was still lying there daydreaming about the appearance of my portrait in all the famous galleries of the world when I felt rather than heard approaching footsteps. Phil entered and immediately saw that I was awake.

"Hi," he said. "How do you feel?"

"Thirsty."

He laughed. "After all that water you drank last night?"

"I took a pee in that chemical toilet. I don't know how to flush it."

He took care of it in short order.

Why was he being so nice? Why didn't he hate me anymore? Or was it I who had changed? Had the crack on the head straightened me out, made me more bearable? Surely I should feel some sort of animosity for the way he had ignored me, year after year?

Or was that yet to come? At one level, we seemed too intimate, and at another nowhere near intimate enough.

"I'll have some of that coffee you gave me before," I said.

He fixed me the drink and poured himself a generous measure of liquor, tossing it back with a slight coughing sound. "Good stuff!" he said. "Now, what do you want to eat? I have granola, porridge, baked beans—soup." He laughed bitterly. "All kinds of soup."

"Campbell's?" I teased.

"Old joke!" He sipped his drink, glowering sullenly. Obviously what I had said did not sit well with him. "Half a dozen flats a flight, he brought me. They added up. And I'm sure the son-of-a-bitch—forgive me, I know how you must feel about him—deducted it from the profits!" He reached up into the cupboard, picked up a silver can and examined it, trying to adjust his temperament. "Gets a little damp in the cellar, so the labels peel off and you take your chances. Pretty sure this one's Fiesta Tomato. But mixed with a can of Cream of Mushroom, it makes a passable puréed English breakfast."

I shuddered at the thought. "Anything else?"

"Can of beans with wieners. Sorry, there's no toast—we're fresh out of bread." He poured the coffee. I sipped it, yawned, stretched, and then winced. My head hurt.

"I don't feel nearly as sick as I did," I said. "Just—weirded out."

"You were taking a midnight dip and nearly drowned. Lucky I heard you scream. And lucky there was a full moon!"

"I don't even remember how I got to the pool!" I said, wincing against the headache.

"Perhaps you sleep-walked. You were still dressed in your nightie when I fished you out." He examined the swollen cut on my forehead, then my eyes. "Your eyes are wonky. You probably still have a concussion. Should get that looked at next time we're in town."

When I had finished eating my beans and single piece of soft wiener I sat on a chair to watch him as he layered in some details on the painting on his easel. As if organic, the canvas metamorphosed from the smiling innocence of a slumbering child to agonizing panic verging on despair, the face staring fearfully straight out of the canvas, the hair floating out, curling at the tips under the surface of rippling water. One cheek and the chin were beneath the surface and water slopped into the open mouth. The right arm was raised and clutching as if in supplication. The eyes, set in a face pale with grief and struggle, hid a hint of the happy child beneath, seeming to tell a story of their own, of utter fatigue and helplessness, so that she appeared to be pleading at once for salvation and forgiveness.

Perhaps I am reading too much into a memory. The painting was just *there* for me, and it was an experience that stayed with me, although blocked by the years. Perhaps the painting was not as good as I then thought it was. I remember the details because I saw the artist put them there, saw the painting grow, first one stroke and then another, deftly filling in the agony and tension, every mark on the painting a surprise to the watcher. Oh, he had a talent! And it was a rare experience to be able to see him at work. Yet at the time I did not really appreciate what I was seeing.

"Is that what I looked like when you saw me in the pool?" I asked.

"When? Last night? No. It's more—much more—what I *felt*!"

17

As I soon discovered while at his studio, Phil was obsessed with his belief that he had been thoroughly cuckolded by his agent and (according to all accounts) my erstwhile lover, Richard Thompson. He believed that Richard had not only cuckolded him but had been so integrally "involved" with me over the years that he had fathered two of our four children! Even in my retrospective dream it seemed odd that he should have aired his suspicions of my far-ranging infidelity, putting all the blame on Richard rather than on me. But by then, he was already well down the path to insanity, as future events would show. And so, apparently, was I.

"Halloween!" he concluded. "That's when it must've happened, right?" He daubed paint on the canvas. "That was the only time he was around." He painted furiously. "That's what I get for doing the right thing. Fuckin' shotgun wedding." He sighed. "Then fuckin' *Tom!*

"Know what? A husband knows when he's not the father. Maybe it's chemistry, but for years after that little bastard was born I couldn't stand the sight of him! At some level I always realized that he wasn't mine. Jus' like I knew Colleen wasn't mine! Neither one of 'em is right in the head, you know? Bad genes! Fuckin' nympho bitch!" Even though his misogynistic curse was directed at my image on the canvas rather at me, it frightened me. He took a long swig from his bottle. "But now it all makes sense!"

It does? How? It didn't make sense to me!

He took the painting off the easel and propped it against the corner of the stove. He looked at it distastefully, then set yet another blank canvas in place on the easel, one of perhaps twenty waiting for his brush.

Despite his anger, I did not feel the least bit afraid of him. Rather, I felt admiration. I was blown away by the painting of me he had been working on. It was not dissimilar from some of his earlier work—including some images that Roy had included in his book. The fetal faces were full of expression, ageless beyond caricature, but there was no doubt about their gender as they hovered on the rock in the center of the pond, standing steadfast against spiraling ripples of water and rays of light. The forest behind the immediate line of trees was obscurely black and mysterious, each tree resembling a fine tornado, stringing rope cords connecting the earth and heavens and reflecting obliquely toward the rock. Between the trees, the blackness was pierced by filtering shafts of sunlight, which caught the early morning mist and flashed around the rings of the pond in fine arcs. The figures on the rock were surrounded by the halo of pond, and the light streaming down and reflecting upward from the surface created a luminosity on their naked skin that allowed them to live in an eternal now; for the woman pushed her companion playfully, and he was suspended precariously over the water. She held a flower in one hand, bright white, a water lily, and he in his descent reached out for it but never would succeed in grasping it, for he was falling, falling away from it. His face reflected panic and determination; hers impish innocence modified by concern. While she pushed with one hand, the other holding the flower seemed to beckon the boy back. Suspended as he was, the boy seemed intent on clutching the petals and the supporting hand, while the other strained toward the water, his arm emblazoned by the sun. Tiny greenish flowers, unrecognizable, were scattered about the rock, muted for effect so that they did not interfere with the integrity of the larger blossom that was the focus of the piece.

As the marketplace had determined over the years, Phil's unique west-country landscapes were among the best in their genre. He was the Tony Onley of Alberta, as successful an artist as any in Canada. But as a man, I came to realize, there was no longer any integration. To me, his paintings betrayed his fragmentation. His anguish was conveyed in his tormented human figures, each superimposed or inserted uncomfortably into the scene. This, I believe, was a reflection of his own psyche. He suffered such a surfeit of anguish that it overflowed all around him, into his life, into his relationship with me, with his children, with all of us.

Unfortunately, rather than directing all of this anguish into his canvases, he attempted to flee his acute awareness of the tragicomedy of his life by resorting to the bottle. The drunker he got, the more maudlin and moody he became. I remember him holding aloft a cup of moonshine, toasting the portrait of the woman in the framed photograph.

"Mother," he said. He kissed the tips of his fingers and pressed them to the mouth of the figure in the portrait, which he peered at with such adoration that I felt a pang of jealousy.

"You miss her?" I said.

"Nope. Bitch came and went." He snorted. "Mos'ly went. Saw her twice in my life, that I recall—tha's it."

"How'd you get the portrait?"

"Painted it from a pho'graph. When I was a kid." He pointed to a dusty framed photo on the windowsill. "That one. Sketched it in charcoal, drew it in pencil, painted it in water-colors, poster paint, acrylic. Finally oils." He looked at the painting again. "Ev'ry fuckin' medium. Yeah. That's oil on canvas. My first one, just about!" He spoke to me with easy familiarity. "Rick's mother ran an arts and craft shop in Rocky back then, when she wasn't teachin', so I got all my paints wholesale. Tha's where I made my first sale, in her store—when I was ten." He picked up the framed photograph of his mother. "She also gave me this portrait of my mother. I drew it a few times before I painted it—over and over. So I musta been—thirteen?" He dismissed the oil portrait of his mother as craft rather than art because it was painted from a photograph and driven by curiosity, which didn't amount to a pine cone compared to the passion portrayed in his greatest works. "Paintin' with a live model, explorin' all she means at the moment and all she could ever mean—tha's art!" he said as, drunk, he sat beside me on my bed. Once again he kissed my swollen forehead. "That's quite a goose-egg," he said. I pecked him back on the cheek and gave him a hug. He stretched out on a throw rug spread out on the floorboards. "Tha's art. I'm *through* with copyin'!"

"Are you going to sleep there?" I asked, as if it wasn't obvious. In answer, he punched his windbreaker into a pillow.

For several minutes, we both remained silently contemplative. Then, leaning on my elbow, I watched the dark hump that bulged on the floor beside me.

"Phil?" I felt comfortable with the easy familiarity of his name.

"Hmmmm?"

"When are you going to finish that painting of me?"

"It's already finished."

"No, I mean the other one. The last one over there with the rest. The nude."

The silence roared.

"Will you finish it tomorrow?" I persisted.

"We'll see."

"Because I'd very much like to pose for it!"

18

The next morning, I got Phil up earlier than he was used to, and he was hung over and grumpy, incommunicative at first, answering most of my questions with gestures and grunts as he opened new tubes of oil paint and smeared blobs of color onto his palette. He returned to his painting in earnest, using angry strokes rather than dabs to express a deeper emotion. I allowed my bent leg to fan back and forth as I lay nude on my side on the bed.

"Sit still," he snapped.

"Sorry." I froze. "Are you pissed off at me?"

He closed his eyes as if counting to three, then started painting again.

"Sorry. Is it because I woke you up so early?" I sighed. "I just couldn't wait!"

He ignored me. I shifted my weight to get comfortable.

"This okay?"

"Look, if you want to do this, just lie still and shut up!"

I lay there for ten excruciating minutes.

"You said passion is the driving force of your art," I said at last, "but what about love?"

"What about it?"

"Isn't love a form of passion?"

"Passion is not an emotion. It is the quality or *intensity* of an emotion. It has no verb form. You can love or hate or adore passionately, but you cannot 'passion' anything." He dabbed paint, rocking the whole easel with strong, short strokes. "Word to the wise—just stay away from Tom from now on, okay? Save yourself and me and him a pile of grief, and stay away from him!"

So he knew! He knew!

"He's bad news. Always has been, always will be. How do you think I lost Alice to Richard?" Noting my puzzlement, he continued: "At first I thought it was an April Fool's joke. Which of course it was, in a sense. But LaPierre bought right into it. Or seemed to. It was a matter of *availability*, you see. Who else could the father have been? I'd forgotten all about that fucking *Richard*!" He smeared a huge gob of white paint on the canvas. "I don't mind that he exploited me, my art, don't even mind that he made ten times more money from my paintings than I ever did. But I could never forget that I had lost her to that soul-sucker! He was a vampire, a sociopath, a fuckin' social leech!" He was into the reds now. The painting looked furious. "And his stupid flats of Campbell's soup," raged Phil. "Andy fucking Warhol copyrighted *that* joke half a century ago!

"I know you loved him—probably still do and always will—but try to see things from my point of view. I've got to tell you straight up that the first thought that entered my head when it became clear that he had been killed in that crash was not, *Oh shit, what am I going to do now, without an agent?*" He snorted in disdain. "No, that wasn't it at all! No, my first thought was, *I'm glad the fucker's dead!*"

I jerked fully awake with a startling realization.

I had been with my husband Phil after the plane crash!

19

Each time I returned to the Big Bang that marked the origin of memory, it produced a different universe. This time, instead of an erupting bomb of gasoline blasting me from a plane, the explosion in my mind was illuminated instantaneously by forks of lightning, a storm of unbelievable intensity with thunder and lightning and hail and rain and tremendous winds. It was slashing about across the trees as well as down them, flashing like the blades of a giant automated scythe. As I watched, a blinding lightning bolt smashed into a jackpine near the creek upstream from the cabin directly across from where I stood. The log cabin seemed little protection. Flinching from flash to flash, I cowered into the corner of the studio, huddling under a blanket, shaking and shivering, eyes wide and frightened in the pitch-black darkness between the flashes, the lightning ironically my only illumination. More lightning bolts flashed farther off. The wind roared through the trees, snatching at the logs, shaking the cabin and its plank floor. Water splashed through the loose windows, rain beat against pane, the patter of hail.

The door burst open just as lightning struck again, backlighting a male intruder. He stood there silhouetted for an instant in the doorway, holding the door ajar against the wind. To me, he was a far greater threat than the storm itself.

I guess it was just the timing—the door flying open and the crashing flash of lightning and the electric smoke, all at once, that drove me into hysteria so that every particle of my being writhed, yearning to get out through the walls! Putting my hands over my ears, I screamed at the top of my lungs, then ran for the door. I couldn't let any man do that to me again.

Couldn't! Wouldn't!

Clutching my blanket, I fled headlong into the thickest part of the woods through pitch blackness. Sleet beat the aspen leaves in an endless drum-roll punctuated by thunder. Rain sheeted down. Wind tore at my hair. Deciduous twigs and spruce needles ripped at my face like cats' claws.

The intermittent lightning was still my only illumination. I ran blindly through the whipping wind and woods until I fell exhausted, to be tended by—

Tuanahaki. She had come to my side. Was that then or was that later? Two separate incidents, then many, came to mind.

I had killed a porcupine to eat, clubbed it with a stick, and one of the quills had lodged in my hand, penetrating the flesh at the base of my thumb. I closed my eyes in pain as Tuanahaki pulled it out, twisting just enough so that the barb could not grab the tender flesh. Hardly a miracle, but a memorable medical feat nonetheless to somebody as in pain as I.

Then there was the sow bear whose cubs I had surprised while I was gathering saskatoon berries along the creek. She ran after me, grunting with each stride, but instead of playing dead as Tuanahaki said I should in such an encounter, I ran along the creek through the shallow water screaming for help, the bear in pursuit. How incredibly fast she ran! I stumbled and fell into the water and cowered away from the bear, expecting her to tear into me and rip me to shreds. But Tuanahaki was there, my fount of protection. The venerable shaman did not run. She just stood there behind me, quivering with fear, perhaps, but no coward she, confronting the bear so that it stopped as if shot in its tracks in the creek, and stared at us. Then, far off from where I had come, the squealing of the deserted cubs wrestling with each other beside the water caused the mother bear to leave off the chase and run back up the creek to protect and reassure them. Patiently, Tuanahaki took me back through the rules of engagement with black bears. If it had been a grizzly, she said, we'd both be dead.

When I got sick from eating a poison mushroom I'd mixed up with the others, Tuanahaki stayed by my side, urging me to drink lots of water and the root of wild sunflower and the pith of bulrushes. Tuanahaki had done countless many things to help me, to protect me, to provide. I worshipped her, I suppose, or at least worshipped what she stood for. We accepted the hardship that was our lot—especially in the winters when we sipped hot soup, huddled against the bitter cold and week-long blizzard winds. We accepted each other, found fulfillment in each other's company as if we were each a part of a larger entity bent on survival in the bush.

Tuanahaki was always there in later trouble. Am I just assuming that she was there during the trauma of that first storm? What mania drove me out into that sleet, running headlong through the woods away from the archetypal man?

And then it was there, the memory of the terror, almost palpable. No matter how fast I ran, the man devil followed, hair ablaze with electric flashes, hurling substantial lightning bolts, laughing deeply with rumbling thunder, *hohohohoho*, throwing spears that were instantly transmuted into branches, twigs, and needles. The blanket became a burden, slowing my race against the man devil who trod with giant strides beneath the clouds. And in an instant of wretched vision, a horrific flash from bulbous cloud, the flash of ax blade descending to the mortally injured pine swaying in wind, the clean vertical sweep to split the tree, ax wielded by Phil Bunyan of the sky, and I felt the blue flash enveloping the tree the grass the leaves the forest the water the world and my own prone and exhausted shell.

You can't tell me that lightning doesn't strike twice!

Later, a disarray of branches and trees smashed by the storm emerged from the still mist, a mishmash of trunks twisted, torn, and contorted. The memory itself limped into my mind in lame, indiscriminate disorder, but gradually it cleared—as had the woods. It was dawn, but the sun took its time, for the sky was heavily overcast to the east, black with passing rain. The creek had swollen to a river, but flowed so fast it promised quickly to subside. Tuanahaki stood there motionless beside me beneath the screen of trees, and we watched dispassionately as Tom, wielding an ax, chopped a negotiable path through the destruction, hacking down flattened saplings until he could survey the creek. Trees stood deep in what was now a river, the edge of which licked around limestone outcroppings on the other side. Already the high water level had dropped slightly, leaving brown slime in an ugly line, below which the newly eroded bank was washed bare of leaves and needles.

We stood silent beneath the dripping spruce trees at the edge of the bluff, watching as Tom waded waist high out into the flooded area toward the huge pine that had been struck and struck again by lightning the night before. The current snatched at him with such ferocity that he would have been swept downstream had he not hooked the ax around a birch sapling and pulled himself back into shallower water. He bent over to pick something from a puddle a meter from the creek and held up a flashing trout that now, too late, was game for a fight. Then he looked wistfully about for more. Seeing none, he returned to the studio and opened the cabin door. He held the fish aloft as he entered.

"Breakfast!" he shouted and disappeared inside.

We resumed our vigil, although I, having been awake all night, could not keep alert for long. At about noon, the sound of chopping resumed. I looked back down to the creek. Tom had waded out to the split pine again and was chopping deep, glancing blows first downward and then upward from beneath. He hacked and hacked until he was worn out. That's when

Phil emerged from the rocks on the far bank overlooking the creek. Seeing them together, I began to tremble uncontrollably. Tuanahaki noticed and shifted closer. She put her arm around me, and we huddled together beneath the silent trees.

"The barn's down," Phil shouted. "Damn cow got pinned under one of the beams."

"Dead?"

"Is now. Broken back. I had to slit her throat. Can't get her out to skin her. Salvaged what I could of the meat."

"What about Angel?"

"She's okay, except for them cuts to her legs. Weathered out the storm in the paddock."

Fully clothed, Phil dove far out into the swollen creek. Gripped by the current, he swam with it to the willows on our side where the creek meandered around the hill toward the jetty. Then he pulled himself through the fronds of willow, resisting the current, relying on the strength of the twigs.

Tom followed him along the shore, watching him work from willow to willow until he had cleared the current and could stand. I could not hear them once they were together, but Phil laughed at something Tom said and tousled his hair. They walked together back to the pine, and Phil swung the ax so that the chips flew, landing in the water and whipping out of sight one by one down the creek. He kept going until the tree was three-quarters severed, and then, obviously exhausted, handed the ax back to Tom, who started chopping higher up on the other side. Soon, every swipe seemed to shake the whole tree, and then, as he chopped, it began to lean slightly and creak, the vertical wound from the crown down the trunk appearing to widen. Five more swings and the tree tottered with a horrible creaking groan, showering drops of water and needles into the creek.

"Hit her again, Tom!" Phil shouted.

One, two more blows, and over she went, wood splintering as Tom retreated from the water to watch it fall. The crown of the tree landed well up the far bank, and held, the trunk suspended from its own stump a foot or two above the water. Tom and Phil let out a simultaneous triumphant whoop that echoed through the woods.

Tom slung the ax over his shoulder like Paul Bunyan. Phil draped his arm over Tom's shoulder and they marched up the hill together to the cabin, proud and smiling, looking for all the world like father and son.

Later still, we watched them crawl like caterpillars back across that felled tree. Once on the other side, they skirted the overflowing creek down to the trailhead, then made their way in single file up over the limestone and shale toward the pasture. Peering from our natural shelter of felled trees, we waited until they had disappeared, then climbed through the trees down the escarpment toward the studio.

I kept my head low behind the undergrowth, terrified of being seen.

Tuanahaki stood at the edge of the woods as I made my way to the cabin door and peeked inside. There was a moment of disorientation as I saw myself asleep on the cot, heard myself snoring gently. I filled a pillow case with a bag of rice, a bag of barley, several cans of soup. Shivering, I snagged a couple of blankets from off a pile on a footlocker. Then I saw better fare: a scarlet-and-white floral cotton dress and a chestnut-colored sweater, hanging on a peg near the stove. I put them on, panting in my nervousness and haste, and almost tripped over a pair of mud-clogged women's shoes. I put them on too. I stepped back outside and threaded my way back through the trees to Tuanahaki.

She looked distastefully at my dress. "Tiptoe," she whispered, "so that you do not leave marks with your heels."

I followed her up the wooded bluff and through the trees to our hiding place in a cave deep in the forest. There, we shared kinnikinnick tea sweetened with the honey of wild bees.

Perhaps an hour later, Tuanahaki suddenly placed a pot upside down on the hot but tiny fire that she had built at the back of the cave beneath a natural chimney that passed the smoke into a hollow snag even higher up the bluff. I had heard nothing, but her hearing, indeed all her senses, was finely tuned to the wild from decades of life at the very edge of death.

We returned by a different route to our lookout, from where we could see the black branches of the freshly felled tree. Its needles, accentuated by the horizontal posture of the tree, shone bronze in the dusk and danced eerily as Phil crawled across, lopping off the branches even with the trunk. That is what Tuanahaki had heard, the ringing of the ax.

Phil picked his way back through strewn debris toward the cabin. He entered cautiously as if trying not to disturb me, but two seconds later he threw himself back outside. He ran a short distance, looking at the ground. My new shoes had no doubt left telltale tracks in the mud, but if so, he quickly obliterated them in his zeal to follow me. In any case, the tracks would have petered out among the leaves and underbrush where I had started to tiptoe.

A woman, looking gaunt, appeared in the doorway, clutching a blanket around her. She leaned on a blonde teenaged girl for support. "Philip?" she called weakly.

Tuanahaki signaled silence. "Your sister," she whispered.

Find your sister. Perhaps she will help you find yourself.

Phil returned to the cabin, took one last look around outside, ushered the women inside, and shut the door firmly behind him.

That was me, wasn't it? She was showing me me*!*

We retreated to the cave to sip more kinnikinnick tea and eat a meal of berries and roots, then an hour or two later returned to the crest of the bluff, each wrapped in a blanket. We stood sentry—or rather, lay there, keeping watch—much of that evening, listening to muttering chatter punctuated by the occasional burst of laughter.

Tuanahaki had been there all along, watching our sorry lives unfold, hearing Phil regale me with tales, plying me with his coffee amply laced with booze of his own concoction.

How could I be there and here at once?

When all at last fell silent, we returned to the cave by yet another route, picking up newly fallen branches for the fire. Tuanahaki had tales of her own to tell, many tales—all of which steeled my resolve.

That was my second all-night vigil in a row, and I discovered a part of me only accessed by fatigue. They were transformative—the longest followed by the shortest night of my life.

At dawn, at Tuanahaki's urging, I climbed back down the bluff, then crawled on my hands and knees across the felled jack pine's trunk. The water had subsided substantially and the tree bridge seemed higher above the water than I had imagined it. The bark was rough enough, but slippery. Conscious of the noise Phil had made on his return the evening before, I crept down its length to the other side. Soon I reached the crown and stepped down through twigs and branches, trying to find the ground. I walked briskly the short way down the creek to the trailhead, then up over the limestone and shale on the other side—where in some other life I had helped Tom carry the canoe from the pasture to the creek.

I gazed back the way I had come. Tuanahaki stood in plain sight on the bluff above the cabin, her white mud mask fairly glowing in the predawn light as it filtered through the trees. Accented by her wimple, her face seemed to float in midair like Lewis Carroll's Cheshire Cat, her black-gowned body all but invisible among the trees.

But she was not smiling.

20

"It would be really helpful if I could have prints made of all these negatives," I said, squinting at the rolls of eerie images Roy had handed me in a file box.

"I'll have Derek make you up a set of contact prints tomorrow."

I had developed a tension headache in my neck and behind my eyes from concentrating so earnestly. I felt feverish and told Roy I'd have to turn in soon if I wasn't to be desperately ill. "D'you mind if I take over the sofa?" I asked.

He immediately vacated and returned moments later with a glass of water and two aspirin. "It could be from lying scrunched up on the sofa," he said. "Why don't you sleep in my bed tonight?" Then he added, pointedly, "I'll sleep out here."

It was the first time in memory that I had slept in a king-size bed. I sank luxuriously into the mattress and pulled the covers up under my chin. Then my brain slowed and a kind of fragmentation of ideas past and present swept through my mind as the aspirin took effect. Ghostly images drawn from the series of negatives presented themselves as a backdrop in my imagination. A flurry of activity took place before them as on a public stage. That window—had someone not fallen from it and dangled there? Those bright bars across the window, were they not wooden slats, charred by fire? Had I not seen a face there, pale and terrified? A tear-streaked, wretched face, drawn by fear?

Yes, Colleen, my little Colleen peeping through the bars!

I had been a mere observer, powerless to help as smoke billowed around the screaming little girl. Margo was outside, armed with a stick of shiplap, prying at the boards.

"Hang on, Colleen!" she cried. "We'll get you out, Sweetie!" She pushed sideways with all her might until the thin lever snapped.

The screaming turned into a fit of uncontrolled coughing. Colleen disappeared.

Margo turned to me in a panic. "We've got to get her out! Can't you help?"

But I could not help. I was powerless because, caught in the dream, I was not really there.

Waking, I found myself alone in the strange, huge bed as if I had been ripped out of the earth, a clematis stuck in a pot. I reflected that once again I was without identity, rootless, torn from the earth where once I had grown into a fertile flower in the woods alongside Tuanahaki. In the hospital, I had wilted, and now I cried out for rain, knowing that it could come not on my terms—never on mine, but only on *theirs*—on *his*. Was I destined to become a domestic variety of a wildflower that never would be able to adapt to the greenhouse?

I called Roy to me, called him to his own bed and mine, hoping that the warmth of his body would be comforting. He seemed to understand at first that my need was for companionship, and he kissed my wrinkled face and gently stroked my hair, and I kissed him, clinging to him as if he were a lifeline. I trembled as his hand soothed my smooth skin, and soon his fingers were resting lightly on my breast, the ball of his thumb gently caressing the nipple. I couldn't tell him that even that was too much.

"My God, you have a beautiful body!" he breathed. "I had no idea!"

There was no magic, really. Just a yearning to be held, to communicate with a source of human warmth and caring.

Naively, I tried to exchange my needs for his, to fill his in exchange for his fulfilling mine. Roy warmly gave, proud in his giving, and suppressing my natural alacrity, I accepted his gift, involving myself with the soft comforts of his warm flesh as if it were a balm. But once aroused, he fumbled, then probed with thick, insensitive fingers that made me flinch away from him. I steeled myself for the inevitable entry.

Although painfully anticipated, his penetration was a relatively painless inoculation. He grunted in surprise and satisfaction, then moaned, then groaned, gasping in my ear. He did not move much, just lay there as if in suspended animation, and soon I realized he had lost his erection.

"It's okay," I said. "It happens sometimes, when the guy's too anxious." Where had *this* arcane knowledge come from?

"I came already," Roy admitted. "I'll try again in a minute."

I must have dozed off, because next thing I knew, he was hard again, and thrusting. It was an annoyance, frankly, being awakened that way, but I tolerated the intrusion. If I felt anything at all, it was wetness rather than warmth.

Roy knew my mind was off in the distance, knew I was not with him, though he could not know that through some feat of mental projection I was looking down on us, detached and at the same time integrally involved in his ludicrous tattoo. Feeling my passivity and yet out of pride denying to himself the possibility that anyone so close could be so removed from the experience, he became lustful, thrusting and panting. The more physical he became, the more I grew afraid. He was hurting me, and I tensed, pushing him back, trying to push him away. This resistance excited him. There was a marked savagery about his persistence, and although our arms engaged in battle his hips drove his rigid cock into me again, again, again. He kissed me roughly, then gasped as he ejaculated a second time. In a panic of revelation of horrors past, I twisted, yelped, and bit, and he yelped too, as I wrenched his invading cock out of my vagina.

It was only then that I gave any thought to protection.

Disgusted, I fled from the bed, from the room. I stumbled to the washroom and locked myself in, not bothering to turn on the light. And there, leaning against the locked door, I wailed and wailed while Roy rattled the handle and called through the door again and again out of alarm and incomprehension.

I screamed.

It had been too much, that final vision, that final neonic pulse of memory realized. Everything seemed to come together in a single numinous flash, the luminosity of lightning raping pine. Elbow gently grasped and squeezed, and a whisper: *Shh! Don't wake your sister!*

"Hmm-mm?" Eyes opening sleepily. Smile. "Hi."

"Do you want to finish that portrait? Because I'm in the mood to paint." Phil, breath heavy with liquor, artificially brave. Yawn, stretch, groggy glance around me. Nod.

"What time is it?"

Whisper, whisper: "Not very late. Eleven or so." He picked up the blanket and I followed, humble. Distant rumble. Thunder? Yes, lightning in the clouds to the northwest, but to the south the sky was clear, stars muted by the moon's full light.

Phil breathing fast, nervous, just another drink. He strode across the hilltop, and I fell in slightly behind, feeling my way with bare feet, watching his silhouette against the moonlight. He had already placed the easel on the hillside and now spread out the blanket on the leaves and grass, in a clearing behind low bushes. Moonshine of a different order had already been poured. A romantic night out.

The evening was not too chilly, yet both of us shivered. A slight breeze blew around us, yet the first candle, when he lit it, hardly flickered.

I knelt on the blanket and struggled with my soiled nightie, trying to take it off.

"Here, let me help you," he whispered as if we were in church and it was sacrilege to raise one's voice in normal speech. He pulled it gently over my head, and I lay back in the position I had assumed earlier in the day, rotating hips, letting down my weight gently to find a comfortable spot.

Phil set another candle on the brush bar of the easel, then another—votive candles in little glass cups. Not enough light, so he lit more candles around me at the periphery of the blanket, had me hold one, even, below my face, above my breasts. Finally he took a paintbrush and began to work, pausing only for an occasional drink. He worked feverishly for several minutes, breathing hard as if his exertion were more physical than aesthetic. Then he looked at the painting, looked at me, full of concentration, and, catching my eye, looked back at the painting again.

I squirmed my hips to get comfortable, then broke pose to extract a twig from directly beneath my blanket. Regaining the pose, leaning on my elbow, I gave him a sleepy smile. The moon was high in the trees by now, and Phil paused to reposition a couple of the candles closer to me so that their flickering light illuminated the front of my body.

Phil painting by moonlight! Phil in a distant world, eyes glazed, as if dreaming a wistful dream, absorbed for half an hour in a private reverie. Then suddenly he set down his palette and brush, took off his shirt, unbuckled his belt, and stepped out of his trousers. Huge flash of flesh—the shank of his penis shone by the light of the moon! Then he was there upon me, lying full length, pinning me beneath his weight, my tiny body beneath his own. I tried to cry out but he muffled my cries with his mouth. He forced my legs apart with his knees, ignoring my kicks, my nasal squeals, my squirms. He pressed his pubic bone against mine and thrust, thrust, thrust at my maidenhair, bruising my labia as I writhed and kicked and tried to scream, to bite, to fight for air and freedom. He cleared his sinuses, spat into his cupped palm, reached down with his hand, and smeared his snot onto my vulva. He crushed my labia apart with his fingers, stuck one wet, stubby finger inside my vagina, then steered his penis into me, jerking his hips in a final long push that found the mucous.

I screamed in agony, shock, horror.

"Alice," he groaned again and again, "Alice!" Then he cupped his wide-open, reeking, whiskered mouth over mine, biting my cheeks to hold my face in place. As I cried out in terror, I felt the terrible pressure of his penis forcing into me like a wedge into a timber, felt myself splitting before the wedge as he ripped me apart. He turned me inside-out. His hardness filled me painfully, painfully deep again and again in his mad animal activity, and he gasped as he ejaculated, forgetting for a moment to cover my mouth. And as I felt his final jerking spurts, I screamed in anguish and mortified terror as I had never screamed before or since, the wild shriek of a dying anything—a cat, a hawk, a horse.

He clapped his hand back over my nose and mouth, his face shining wicked and drunken in the distant lightning, and it was over, the preliminary storm, as quickly as it had begun. Yet, filling me still, he lay panting, sprawled on top of me, covering me entirely with his sweating bulk, whispering *Alice, Alice* over and over and *I love you, Alice!*

The memory was a truth. Or was it a lie? Was I his Maggie? Or his Alice? Which?

Find your sister. Maybe she will help you find yourself!

In his drunkenness he relaxed his grip over my mouth to let me breathe, then flung himself off me, exposing my sweat-drenched body to the cold wind. I wept bitterly, moaning and writhing under the growl of thunder, while Phil, suddenly sober, quickly dressed. I clutched the blanket about me, abject, out of breath, injured, bleeding—

Raped.

I reached down between my legs. My fingers came away wet with blood and semen. I tried to crawl through last year's leaves back toward the cabin, but he followed me, berating me, calling me down.

"Slut!" he yelled. "Whore! Fucking cunt! Now look what you've made me do!"

Kneeling, I vomited in the leaves, the blanket my only protection. He had hurt me, hurt me more than any man could ever have hurt me, for I had trusted in him, had loved him. For he was—he was—he was—

Warm blood trickled down the insides of my thighs, dripping onto the leaves and blades of grass as I crawled away from him.

"Fuck, you're bleeding. Why didn't you tell me you were on the rag?" He laughed. "Well, at least we know I haven't knocked you up!"

I began to keen. Then the enormity of what he had just done seemed to sink in through his thick skull.

"I'm sorry, Honey!" he whispered hoarsely. He touched my shoulder. He too was crying now. "Oh, God—what have I done?"

I shrugged him away.

"Try to understand. God knows, I didn't mean to do that! I didn't mean to! God, God!" He put his arm around me, held me. "Please, can you ever forgive me?" He stroked my hair with trembling fingers. He knelt before me in the leaves so I could not crawl on, could not struggle away, could just kneel there helplessly in the humus, shivering, head between my hands, fingers probing beneath the dead leaves to clutch the earth. I trembled and moaned and heaved with growing nausea, the bloody blanket a shroud against the gathering wind. And all the while he said over and over, "Oh my God, oh my God," piteously, "oh my God, what have I done?" He stroked my hair, tenderly now, as he might the plumage of a frightened bird shot and injured by mistake. And then, in spite of a deep, inner pain, a pang never to be lifted from my heart, I started laughing, laughing, laughing at myself and the world and men and the universe at large, laughing as one demented, laughing from shock, laughing from pain, laughing, laughing!

I turned to him, tears standing in my eyes, lips trembling in shadow face, and stared at him as his semen and my blood trickled in cold rivulets down the insides of my thighs. He wept as he held me to him, clutching my limp body against his own. He patted me gently on the shoulder.

"There, there," he said. "There, there."

"There, there," I echoed, my voice trembling not in mockery. "There, there."

The moon was obscured by cloud, but the lightning from the gathering storm illuminated his panic-stricken face. Then another bolt flashed off to the west and the thunder, a rolling kettle drum of sound, crashed closer. The rain spat cold. Phil grabbed his easel and paints and returned to the hut as the rain became a cataract spreading wider through the woods. He came back to take me and my blanket in his arms, a shuddering bundle. He carried me through the rain to the hut and set me back down on the bed beside my sleeping sister.

Then he hastily scribbled a note:

I am so, so sorry!
I'll make it up to you, I promise -
Please, please forgive me!
P©l

When he ran back out into the darkness, the door slammed shut behind him. Rain sleeted against the window.

"Maggie! Are you all right in there?" Roy banged on the bathroom door, then scratched the knob with something metal, trying to release the lock spring.

"I'm not Maggie," I sobbed. "I'm *Alice*, *Alice*!" I tried to hang on to the revelation. Grasping a towel from the rack, I wrapped it tightly around my torso, holding it together with a tuck under one arm. I opened the door. "Not Maggie," I declared again. "Alice!"

"Jesus, Maggie! I'm sorry, Maggie, honey," he whispered.

"Alice."

"I didn't realize you weren't ready. I'm sorry."

I wept bitterly, leaning against his shoulder. He hugged me, stroking my hair. "I'm *Alice*! Those are even my shoes!"

"Alice, then," he said. It was more of a statement than a challenge, but I knew what was going through his mind. *You're not making sense.*

Alice, like all the others, was dead!

21

"Have to get to work," Roy said as he drank his coffee standing up, gulping huge mouthfuls. He leaned over me and gave me a kiss on the scar at my hairline, exactly the way I remembered Phil doing at the studio. "Fix yourself some breakfast," he suggested. "There's eggs in the fridge." He gave me a more intimate kiss, and I caught a whiff of expensive cologne, fresh and stirring. My heart raced as our lips touched and softly yielded. Slight prickle of shaved beard, touch of tongue tip, flash of tooth—

"Wow," he said. "That was—unexpected." He ducked out of range of my lips. "Got to run. But read the file. The Alice thing—you'll see—it just won't stand up." He pointed to a file on the buffet. "There's absolutely no doubt that Alice Thompson was shot to death by Phil before he turned the gun on himself."

"And a week later, their bodies were burned in the fire that killed Colleen," I said. "I know that's what you think. I read the articles. Hey, I'm in your scrapbook. That's me! I'm Alice!"

"Well, what can I say to that?"

"Nothing. Except—people make mistakes. Including you."

He shrugged dismissively.

I watched him from the window as he crossed the four empty lanes of 55th Street, looking out of habit first one way and then the other. Then he jogged across the park, already ten minutes late for work.

By the time he got home that evening, Roy was even more adamant that I could not be Alice Thompson, having encountered major resistance to the theory from the medical examiner's office in Calgary. He brought a file box of materials with him.

"Dr. Sutcliffe says it's not possible a mistake was made," he said.

"Who's Dr. Sutcliffe?"

"The medical examiner. The pathologist who pronounced you and your family dead?"

"How could he have pronounced me dead when he hasn't even seen me!"

"But he has seen *Alice Thompson*, that's the point—he signed her death certificate. *Eight* death certificates, and he's equally adamant about all of them. And he's not to be trifled with, I found *that* out! I asked him if he had ordered DNA testing on all the deceased. He said that is done only when the identity of the deceased is unknown. In any case, it would have been very difficult, since after a fire, sometimes there are only fragments of bones left, especially if it was fueled by an accelerant as volatile as gasoline. He said DNA testing is not necessary where it is possible to deduce the identity of the victims from witness statements. I asked him point-blank if it is possible the witnesses made a mistake about the identity of Alice Thompson. His report with respect to her is unambiguous: Her burned body was found alongside those of Phil Campbell and Colleen Campbell in the ashes of the upper cabin. All three were positively identified by their next of kin."

"Let me guess, by Tom and Margo."

"Sutcliffe isn't backing down. Seems to think his professional reputation is at stake."

"Let me get this straight. You regard Alice as dead only because her supposed murderers identified a body as hers?"

"Tom and Margo didn't murder her. The arson charges against them were all related to the deaths at the lower cabin."

"Then, just because Sutcliffe's signature is on my death certificate?"

"In this province, that's a pretty big 'just because'! He's threatened to sue the newspaper if we publish a story saying he made a mistake. He even phoned my boss, who of course didn't know anything about it, because I haven't been working on this as a news story. So I'm in shit." He sighed. "And so, by the way, are you. The police are still looking for you—or at least for Sister Jane. Ponoka wants you back."

"Why? You saw the consent order. I've already done my time!"

"It's not a matter of doing time—you haven't been convicted of anything. But there's a warrant out for your arrest because you were supposedly in lawful custody when you disappeared. I challenged that, and it boils down to Dr. Romano not liking his psych patients taking French leave."

"You talked to Dr. Romano?" It felt like such a betrayal!

"I phoned him to see if they'd kept samples of your blood. I was hoping he could arrange for a blood type and DNA comparison between you and Tom—or Margo, as the case may be. He said they hadn't kept any samples as exhibits, and in any case they would be subject to doctor-client confidentiality. He suggested I contact Inspector Roberts.

"*Inspector*?"

He nodded. "He's been promoted. Based in Edmonton now. Roberts said even though Tom and Margo's DNA is on file, it's doubtful we could access it under the Freedom of Information Act. Said you'd have to do private DNA testing to determine whether you are related to Tom or Margo. They have do-it-yourself DNA kits now that would do that, but even those are a couple of hundred bucks, by the time you factor in the lab costs. And you need all parties to cooperate. I know Tom won't, for sure."

"Surely Margo would—assuming I'm her mother?"

"She is absolutely adamant that she saw her mother dead. When I persisted, she hung up on me. As for Tom, he has refused to see or speak to me ever since I mentioned that his mother might be alive. You'd have thought he would've been elated!"

"After what she did to him! Did you tell him that that wasn't me—that I'm not Maggie, after all, that I'm Alice?"

"That's what I'm saying—you'd think he would want to help us clear up the question of your identity. Maggie's the only missing person who fits your profile. Don't you see? If you are not Maggie—and you are certainly not her sister—then we're back to square one: You're just another missing woman."

"I'm *Alice*! I remember Phil calling me that, over and over!"

Roy could not conceal his frustration. "I tell you, the police, the medical examiner, the coroner's office, and the attorney general's office are all on the same page: convinced that Alice Thompson is dead, along with the rest of her family—all except Margo." He flipped to one of the images in his book of Phil Campbell's paintings. He tapped it with his finger. "That's you," he said.

"No it's not!" I pointed to the scrapbook Alice. "That's me!"

"How would *you* know? You're suffering from amnesia, remember?" The apparent oxymoron gave him pause. "Look, let's not fight about this, okay? I concede that you *resemble* Alice—and why wouldn't you? You're her sister, after all."

"It doesn't make sense that Phil would have shot Alice, his sister-in-law. It makes more sense that he would have shot his wife!"

"Unless he wanted to cover up the rape. Remember, you'd been estranged for a couple of years. Perhaps you threatened to rat him out for that. But put things in perspective. He was after all still your *husband*—and you were his *wife*!"

"He called out my name! Not once, but over and over!"

"So at a moment of rejuvenated passion, he calls out your sister's name. Where's the crime in that?"

That's when I started throwing things.

All the more convinced that I was Alice Thompson, I once more slammed the door on my memory bank, padlocked the vault, forgot the combination, swallowed the key. I could no longer bring myself to focus on the past, even though so many questions still needed to be answered.

Convinced more than ever that I was Maggie Campbell, Roy gave off asking questions of me and turned to other sources instead. He found more than answers. Much more. Sometimes it seemed he did not need me any more at all.

22

The winter had come late to Red Deer and the weather was mild compared to that in the mountains. Oh, it got down to twenty below zero sometimes, but only for two or three days at a time. Nothing like the intense, unremitting pain of foothills weather.

I'd had no access to thermometers in the bush, but from what I remember of the cold it was far more savage than that on the prairies, an almost unrelenting iciness that only heavy blankets could protect us from. During some of those freezing spells, we remained in our shelter for weeks without venturing forth more than a few feet, to set rabbit snares outside our lair or to gather snow to eat when we became thirsty. We virtually hibernated during those long winter months, eating ever so little to make our supply of dried berries, fish, canned soup, and frozen meat last as long as possible. Often, I stayed in my makeshift bed all the time it was dark, from five in the evening to nine o'clock in the morning, when wandering outside would be suicide. Now, thanks to Roy, I was sheltered from the cold that had become for me my one insurmountable fear in the woods.

Although Roy and I lived together and shared the same bed, we were quite independent. Often he would be away for days on assignment in Edmonton, covering "provincial affairs"—or so he told me.

Having rediscovered books at the hospital library in Ponoka, I now wanted to find out all I could about my personality—even if it was as split as the swaying pine. I was less sure than ever as to my identity, though Roy persisted in calling me Maggie. I accessed Roy's computer and spent hours on the Internet. Although I had no desire to go to university, I could at least read what thinkers of my age had to say; and so I devoured books, mostly modern and contemporary, starting with those on Roy's bookshelf, hardly ever moving, hardly ever eating, just reading, reading, reading, skimming or skipping the boring parts to find the juicy bits, finishing one book and going on to the next with hardly a break. Roy pointed directions, suggesting titles and authors, sometimes bringing home books from the office, review copies that he had not had time to look at. And because he did not have the time to read or review books himself, I reviewed them for him and wrote up lengthy and (I think) insightful comments of new books recently off the press. Starting in March, I published them once a week under the pen name Thomasina Allison, an approximate inversion of Alice Thompson. To that degree, he indulged my fantasy of being Alice.

I would have preferred "Sister Jane."

My first reviews were so popular that the editor wanted a "thumbnail" picture of me to illustrate them. Had my real picture appeared in the paper, it would immediately have attracted the attention of the staff at Alberta Hospital, not to mention Inspector Roberts. So Roy supplied his editor with a black-and-white print of his mother (as a young woman, of course). I instantly bonded with her photo, until I came to believe that that was my picture, that I at one time had enjoyed those features, her wistful smile, her intelligent eyes, her freckled but blemishless skin.

On one occasion, Roy introduced me to the local Member of the Legislative Assembly as Thomasina Allison, the book reviewer. "No doubt you've seen her picture in the paper?" he suggested. The politician stared aghast at my marred face, but then said politely, "Oh yes! Of course! Thomasina!" Roy and I laughed ourselves silly just recalling how sincere he seemed to be. Through his intervention, Roy managed to get me a Social Insurance Card in that name, as well as an Alberta Health Insurance number, although I was afraid to use it lest I be recognized.

My adherence to a schedule revolved around the open hours at the Red Deer Public Library. I could never wait to get in; often they would have to throw me out. I would sit there and daydream by the hour. The library was a sufficiently anonymous place to allow me comfort and freedom—freedom to travel vicariously around the world, or back in time, or to the most profound recesses of the most brilliant minds.

On the first of April, the chief librarian posted a notice for a part-time job, working mornings reshelving books that had been left in disarray the evening before. I took the notice down off the bulletin board and followed him into his office.

"It says here you are an equal opportunity employer," I said. "It isn't just a distasteful joke, I hope." He gaped at my face, aghast at the implications of hiring me, although he'd seen me around the place often enough. "Well? Do you hire the handicapped? Even when they're scarred and wrinkled and burnt?"

"Of course! Miss—uh?"

"Thomasina Allison, the book reviewer for the *Record*? It happens I need an extra job."

"Uh—it's minimum wage."

"I don't mind."

"Well, then. That's that."

Spending each morning shelving books in the stacks meant I could avoid the public as much as possible. And I had lots of opportunity to read and daydream—or more precisely to remember and relive the past as the devout and religious Alice, allowing my mind to catch up at last, not only by gaining access to knowledge I had bypassed while in the bush, but also with knowledge of myself, of every aspect of myself, including those parts of my past that I had experienced and often lucidly remembered but had never understood.

Yet always with Roy I maintained the illusion, now that I had found myself, that I was the enigmatic "Maggie," my sister and hated nemesis.

Occasionally Roy dropped by the library at noon and we walked to a nearby cafe for soup and a sandwich. It was during one of these lunch breaks that he came up with the idea of interviewing me more or less formally to glean what information he could from my past and write it down so we'd have some kind of record. I had followed Dr. Lenski's initial suggestion of keeping a journal, but usually I ended up writing such mundane things in it about the here and now that it wasn't of much use to anyone, least of all myself. Roy seemed determined to leap into the breach.

We seemed, frankly, to have experienced a subtle inversion of obsessions. Where I had been concerned with uncovering my own past, with disclosing the hidden truths that had lain dormant during my years as a recluse, now I wanted earnestly to forget or at least to leave alone those fearful glimpses into my private soul. Roy, on the other hand, became more and more intrigued by them, especially where they concerned his hero, Philip Campbell, for they were an inexplicable mystery full of incomprehension and contradiction. No newspaper reporter could live with the anomalies my distant remembrances seemed to evoke. He was fascinated by the irrational, by the urges that motivated human beings to fearsome actions like those that everywhere seemed to be implied in my terrifying memories—or terrified imagination. On the other hand, I now sought solace in his world, in the measured galaxy of literature, the universe of books. And so we each had a shifting of emphases, of perspectives, or to be more precise, a trading of attitudes, each of us adopting the other's but moving beyond.

Naturally enough, the bond between us became strained. His persistence in trying to fathom the depths of my personal mystery was an irritation, an intrusion. I soon came to resent his endless inquisitiveness and even to question his motives in keeping me in his apartment, grilling me every night for weeks on end, gleaning, gleaning, pouncing on every inconsistency, elaborating, refining, probing into areas of my mind that, by this time, I so desperately desired to keep confined. I wanted my glimpsed can of personal horrors contained, enclosed, boxed away, kept in the dark. He wanted it opened so that all its ugly contents could squirm out and be scrutinized by the clear light of logical analysis.

As Alice, I realized that I was not a very pleasant person. Yet I could live with that. I had been a person of faith. Who was he to challenge that? I began to take up once again with Jehovah's Witnesses, and that more than anything he regarded as a slap in the face.

Much in my mind and memory defied his probing logic, and this was yet another thorn that stabbed deep. The more he tried to fit the irrational and inexplicable into systematic patterns, the more frustrated he became. His obsession with rationality was itself irrational. He could accept nothing, or rather *would* accept nothing, that did not live up to his own narrow standards of what could or should *be*. Anything other than the scientific method was deemed to be *less* rigorous, as if a spiritual life of asceticism such as I remembered leading with Tuanahaki—and now began to live as a reconstituted Jehovah's Witness—meant nothing at all to him.

At the same time that we seemed to be drifting apart in fundamental ideology and approach to my personal problems—or at least, to the facts of my past that seemed so obviously unfocusable—Roy and I became closer and closer friends. Perhaps that is the crux of the whole paradox: As our friendship grew and stabilized, we wanted more and more to understand each other, to come to grips with facets of each other's personality, to reach out and grasp or comprehend why and how the other was moved to act in this way or that. Each of us wanted to know the basic truth about the other that could be a touchstone for a deeper understanding. The trouble was, the more Roy pressed me for information about the personal visions that illuminated my past, the more I forestalled him. The more I remembered, the more I willed myself to forget.

There came a point where I could no longer distinguish between the horrors of the real and those of the fantastic. It seemed to me that I was constantly remembering wrongly, that what I remembered simply could not be. Constantly I came to deny the truth of my memory, until I could trust nothing and the whole fabric of my mind became once more a confusion, a gyre, even a galaxy, with nothing at the center as a point of reference. Nobody *really* believes in the still point at the center of a spinning wheel, even though logically it is an absolute truth, just as surely as the theory of the Big Bang is, logically, an absolute fallacy.

In Roy's view, I no longer *wanted* to remember. Why else would I so adamantly refuse to read the file that he had concocted about the case? He had been careful not to sow seeds that might germinate into full-fledged "false" memories. Yet the images were there, distorted and in disarray, the images that I myself feared could possibly be the truth. I preferred to close my mind to them, to occupy myself with more worthwhile if mundane projects and with my reading and reviewing of books. My reading became an escape away from the haunting ogres of a past that, after all, was unchangeable in terms of event, yet malleable in terms of memory—malleable because of the very capacity to remember selectively.

By any conventional standard, Roy had been very patient with me. We touched often. I liked to feel his strength as he hugged me, to feel the slight scratch of whisker and breathe the hint of cologne with each kiss. I yearned for contact with him in the same way that I had needed to feel close to Tuanahaki, who in the beginning had been all I had, all the companionship, my sole comfort. Now that Roy filled her place as confidante and friend, I longed to reach out to him, too, in love. I told him about my memory of the fire, told him out of a shackled horror that I had witnessed from afar the death of Colleen (but how could you have, he pointed out, if you were Alice?), told him that this time I could not tolerate his probing questions, that I had to leave it be, leave it be, accept what was there and run away from it to other things. I suppose my remorseful tone triggered in him a feeling of compassion but also a curiosity that he could not abide unassuaged.

All the time I was on my own personal voyage of discovery, Roy was off on his. At the same time I was reading the sensuous prose of Anaïs Nin, Isabel Allende, and Doris Lessing, he was reading and re-reading his old files and his notes of what in those first weeks I had said in our "sessions." He was organizing, reshuffling, probing, researching on his own. In May, he returned from one of his many trips to Edmonton with more material on Philip Campbell than he'd ever gotten from me.

His work at the *Record* suffered. He was asked time and time again to pull up his socks, to get to work on time, to stay later, to do his fair share—and when it became clear that he no longer gave a shit, he was fired, once and for all. I was sick with worry as to how we were we going to make ends meet. I tried to be encouraging, urging him to apply to other newspapers in other cities, but either his reputation for tardiness preceded him, or he blew his interviews. He had several interviews in Edmonton, but it soon became clear that, despite his assurances to the contrary, they were not for jobs. Nor had he ever been "on assignment" there in any formal sense.

After he lost his job, Roy sold his Volvo for a good price and bought an old crate—a Toyota Corolla hatchback, which he insisted on registering in the name of Thomasina Allison. Other than that, my meager paycheck from the library and a tiny stipend from the newspaper for my column were all we had to live on.

Roy seemed constantly preoccupied and yet happier than I had ever remembered him. Naturally I suspected that he had met another woman. When I put that to him point-blank, he laughed heartily and kissed me on the forehead and said, "No." I didn't want to push it. Nonetheless, it caused me constant anxiety, his posited philandering. No woman in the world was less attractive than I, I reasoned, examining my marred face in the medicine cabinet mirror. The wrinkles had stretched a bit, allowing my features to reassert themselves. But they were not features of which I had any memory, nor were they features in which I could take pride.

23

One day in late June, Roy told me that some old friends of his were getting married in Edmonton on Saturday, and would I care to come along? Frankly, anything that might nudge him in that direction was most welcome. I had not had a period for six months by then, though I still hadn't told Roy, afraid he might bolt or at least balk at the prospect of parenthood. I certainly didn't want an abortion.

"Who's getting married?" I asked. I assumed it was Roy's best friend, Derek Saunders, the photographer at the *Record.* He and his partner, Joanie, had been talking about getting married before moving to the States, where he had been short-listed for a job as an aerial photographer for a real estate company in Los Angeles.

"We have to be at the church for two o'clock," Roy said.

I bought a new-for-me three-quarter-length dress at the Salvation Army Thrift Shop—white with green bands diagonally across it that I thought would hide my swelling belly, and matching brocade shoes. Roy already had a decent suit, dark blue, and he wore it with a white shirt and red tie. We clashed.

Just before noon on Saturday we started out for Edmonton, taking Highway 2A instead of the four-lane because our car could not do much over fifty and burned almost as much oil as gas, it seemed, we had to check it so often.

We arrived at Edmonton just before two, and he drove like a maniac through the unfamiliar streets, chuffing a cloud of smoke and laying down a slick of oil like a snail trail. Roy pointed out the university, over behind us as we crossed the 105th Street Bridge. Between us and the High Level Bridge to the west, the provincial legislative buildings overlooked the river; ahead and to the right, the downtown core mushroomed upward like an infection.

We got to the heart of the city in ten minutes flat. Roy parked the car illegally against a yellow curb, helped me out of the car (the door on the passenger's side wouldn't open from the inside), and walked briskly with me on his arm toward an imposing Unitarian church. We mounted the concrete steps. The huge, arched oak door stood ajar, emitting organ music. The bridal party had already arrived, and a bridesmaid fussed with her gown in an alcove of the church as an usher came hesitantly forward.

"We're press," said Roy, flashing his card. "Reporters for *Canadian Press*. Might have to slip out in a hurry to meet a deadline. Could you seat us at the very back?"

"Very well, sir."

The groom was already at the altar along with the best man and an usher. They all wore tuxedos. The groom's dark hair was neatly styled, long enough to cover the ears.

It was not Derek.

Just then, the organ music struck a more strident note and the wedding march began. A flower girl and two bridesmaids entered, a respectful distance apart. Then the bride entered, and we stood up to watch the procession. It was a simple dress, floor length with a lace hood and trace of train draped over her head, obscuring her face. Even across the church I could see from her profile that the bride was well along in her pregnancy—much further along than I!

At least her kid will be born legitimate, I thought.

We were so far back in the church that I could not hear much of what was said. The minister spoke for the fifty-odd people clustered in the first three or four aisles. I don't think he even saw us sitting there. I didn't feel very – Jehovah's Witnessy.

"I can't hear," I whispered. "Can't we move up?"

"Shhh! He's only reading a scripture."

I waited patiently as the minister droned on. "Are you sure he isn't reading the whole damn Bible?"

"Shhh!" He stood up. "He's saying a prayer."

"How do you know?" I said, standing up beside him.

Roy bowed his head, although he was an avowed atheist, and closed his eyes. I followed suit, but then peeking up at the others suddenly became aware that we were the only people in the church with our heads in prayerful attitude. "They're not praying," I said aloud. "They're not even standing!"

"For God's sake, Maggie!" he whispered. "Do you want to get us kicked out?"

"We're the only ones standing in the whole damn church!"

"That's not true."

"It is true. We're the only ones standing besides the minister and the wedding party."

At the front the couple was exchanging vows. Whereas before I could hear an echoing murmur, now I could hear nothing but gnats. There was the exchanging of the rings, the "I now declare you," the invitation to the groom to kiss the bride.

The bridesmaid pulled back the hood around the bride's neck so that it draped down her back, revealing blonde hair. Then everyone stood again and the bride and bridegroom, now husband and wife, turned and paced jubilantly arm-in-arm to the aisle by which we sat. They turned into the aisle, the man dark-haired with a noticeable limp, and suddenly, seeing their radiant faces, I realized who they were.

"Margo!" I cried. "Tom!"

Roy tried to hush me, holding my arm like a vise. The couple hesitated an instant as I cried out. They glanced at Roy in recognition. Tom glanced at me, then looked back at Roy and shook his head in mingled consternation, distaste, and confusion. Margo stared at me as if trying to focus on the blurred details of my face. Her eyes widened, then her jaw dropped in astonishment.

"Emmy?" she squealed. "Oh my God! *Emmy*!"

"Holy fuck," Tom groaned.

Breaking all decorum and every rule of etiquette anywhere, Margo sprinted the remaining three yards toward me. Roy, astonished, let me go, and I flung myself into the aisle and into my sister's arms. Her full tummy pressed against mine. "Oh, Emmy," she cried. "You're alive! But—my God! How did you survive?"

I gripped her shoulders fiercely—and burst into tears.

"Roy," said Tom, "what the hell is this? I thought you said—"

"I thought she might be your mom," Roy said lamely.

"Fuck, man!"

His hostility struck me like a blow to the stomach. As did the full implications of the wedding I had just witnessed. I recalled Phil's allegations from eons ago that Richard Thompson had fathered his eldest son.

"You're marrying *Tom*?" I said to Margo.

"Past tense. She just *did*!" Tom snarled, one eye fixing each of us.

"Couldn't wait any longer," said Margo, hefting her belly. She glanced at Roy, then laughed nervously. "That's off the record," she said.

"You'll have to have it annulled," I said. "Thank God it isn't consummated!"

"*What*?" asked Tom.

"You can't marry your own sister!"

"What the fuck's she talking about?"

"Daddy—Richard Thompson—is his natural father," I explained to Margo, "so he's your half-brother!"

"No fucking way," said Tom.

"Yes way!"

It was a conclusion drawn solely from my fractured memory of Phil's expressed concerns about Tom's parentage.

The whole congregation was bottled up in the aisle behind them. Roy extended his hand to the groom. "Congratulations, Tom!"

Tom ignored the hand. "We were separated for years by the parole board. We finally got the no-contact condition lifted—and look who shows to fuck things up! *You* engineered this? Thanks a lot!" Then, to me: "You aren't anyone I know!"

"Tom!" scolded Margo. "It's *Emily*!"

"One thing for sure," Tom said pointedly to Roy, "she's not my fucking *mother*!"

"You're coming to the reception?" Margo asked me.

"No!" said Tom, his eyes dancing frenetically. "She isn't. Read my fucking lips!"

"I'll make sure you have a special seat beside me so we can talk," said Margo, ignoring her new husband. She kissed and hugged me, seemingly oblivious to my wrinkles, and I kissed and hugged her back. "It's been *years*! How did you—?" She scrutinized my face. "Oh my God, Emily! Oh—my—God, how you've *aged*! And I thought *I* went through hell!"

PART TWO: EMILY

24

I couldn't help feeling annoyed with Roy for not having told me exactly which of his "friends" were getting married, and was equally puzzled that Tom and Margo seemed to know him so well. By the time of the wedding, I had lived with Roy for six months and had come to assume that we did not have any major secrets from each other—that I was at least acquainted with his circle of friends. But, of course, they were not "friends" to him so much as subjects to write about. Or more precisely, *objects*.

I forced myself to remember that his intention in bringing me here had been to resolve once and for all the question of whether I was Maggie or Alice by taking me to my son's—daughter's—wedding. Now the question of my identity seemed to have resolved itself in quite another direction. The fragments of memory that I had salvaged from my broken brain had to be reconfigured, but I was not about to forsake the underlying truths that they contained.

Immediately after the ceremony, I felt alienated as never before. Unfortunately, the primary catalyst for my alienation, it seemed to me, was the very person on whom I had come to depend so totally: Roy Farquhar. Yet the sad truth was that without Roy's manipulation, I would not even have been there to witness the wedding.

He'd had good reason to keep it a secret. Had I known that he intended to take me to Tom and Margo's wedding, I probably would have refused to go, working myself up into a lather in the "knowledge" that they had been convicted of killing my children.

When the small crowd filed out of the church to spewing confetti and rice, and the newlyweds climbed (after pausing for pictures) into the rear of a rented limousine, I found myself viewing the whole scene with a cynical detachment. Where, exactly, did I fit in? And how? As they drove off and the cluster of well-wishers dispersed toward their own vehicles, Roy offered me his arm to escort me back to Bolts. I declined and strode briskly down the sidewalk slightly ahead of him on my wobbly shoes so that he had to run a couple of steps to catch up.

"Hey, what's wrong with you?"

"I do not like practical jokes!" I snapped.

He laughed. "You think marriage is a joke?"

I stopped short so that he walked a pace beyond me and had to turn to face me.

"That," I said, "was a particularly bad one. Now take me home."

"Hey, I'm sorry. We were both thrown a curve." He scrutinized my face. "Are you really Emily, do you think?"

"Take me home!"

Since other wedding guests were climbing into cars immediately in front of ours, he did not reply right there. Instead, he opened the passenger door for me like a gentleman, although he slammed it a little harder than necessary before walking around to the driver's side.

"If we're going to have an argument," he said, "let's have it out right here and now!"

"Drive me home."

"But what about the reception?"

"Home!"

"We've accepted the invitation. They're expecting us now. Besides, Margo was elated to see you! And you heard what she said about giving you a place of honor. You're her sister, for God's sake, her only living relative."

"And *his* sister too, if I am Emily. That's why I can't condone this bullshit wedding!"

"I don't get that."

"You wouldn't." My frustrated anger resolved itself into tears. I was so confused! Roy leaned over to try to comfort me, but for several minutes I was inconsolable.

By the time I stopped crying, my indignation had worn off. After all, how could Roy, myself, or anyone else have guessed that I was Emily Thompson? I had to remember that Tom and Margo had been convicted of Emily's death by arson. She had been declared every bit as dead as all the others. So once again I had to ask, *How is it that she—I—am still alive?*

For the fourth time in the nine months since I had first been rescued as "Sister Jane," I had a new identity to adjust to—not counting the assumed personality of my nom de plume, Thomasina Allison. Was this yet more evidence of a dreaded multiple personality disorder, compounded by progeria? When would this craziness end?

I thought about the encounter in the aisle. I had recognized Tom and Margo instantly, but it seemed to be a struggle for Margo to recognize me as Emily—while Tom had been reticent about giving my identity as Emily any traction whatsoever. What was *that* about?

Were they "playing" me? Had they recognized me at first glance? Tom had initially denied that he even knew me. Was I in fact a total stranger? If they knew me, had they recognized me as Emily, or as Alice?

Tom had seemed adamant that I was not his mother. Was that because he knew I was *Margo*'s mother? Alerted by Roy, had Margo been preparing to "dis" me as soon as she saw that I was alive? After all, as next of kin she had already identified Alice as dead. If Alice now surfaced, would it not beg the question as to why she had misled or lied to the authorities about the circumstances of her mother's death?

Her initial hesitancy in recognizing me, was that due to the shock of recognition that I—Alice—was still alive after all? Had she been taking a moment to think on her feet? Tom had lagged behind—was that because Margo had left him for the moment in the dark? Had he so pointedly dismissed the notion that I was *his* mother as a signal to Margo that he was on the same page—that while he recognized me as Alice, he was prepared to go along with Margo's calculated suggestion that I was Emily?

Surely I was too old to be Emily! Emily was in her twenties. I was in my forties. If I was Emily, I was younger than anyone (including myself) had imagined.

Ever since my stay in the hospital I was aware that chronic malnutrition had taken its toll, giving me permanent wrinkles, aging me prematurely—I had thought by a year or two. Had everyone assumed that I was much older than my actual age? Dr. Lenski had initially toyed with the notion of adult onset progeroid syndrome but had not followed through with it. Was that why he and the rest of the hospital staff were reticent about reinforcing any notion I may have had of adopting an identity other than Sister Jane?

Officially, I knew, I still remained Sister Jane. Identifying me as Maggie had been Roy's pet project. My own inclination, still, was to regard myself as Margo's mother Alice rather than her sister Emily, a woman I didn't know and could not even visualize.

Yet I began to feel curious about how things might go at the reception. How would Margo play this out? What would Tom do to keep abreast of Margo, if this was all a scam? And if it wasn't, could Margo, Tom, and I somehow effect a reconciliation?

I could not easily forgive them for what they had done—either way, they had killed three of my children.

But no, I was no longer Alice. I must get used to my new identity. This pair of murderers had killed my brother and sister and at least two cousins—God knows who else. As for their incest, they seemed genuinely in the dark as to their (*our?*) shared father, Richard Thompson.

"I had no idea at all that you were sisters," said Roy when I made it clear that I wanted to go to the reception after all.

"Nor did I."

"Now we're facing the same conundrum as we were with 'Alice,'" he said. "Emily Thompson is supposed to be *dead*! Sutcliffe signed off on her death certificate, just as he did on Alice Thompson's. As I recall, they found Emily's ashes in the ruins of the lower cabin. They figured she'd tried to ward off the heat of the fire with a rubber mat. Emily, I mean. Sutcliffe identified her from the shape of her charred hip bone. Besides, you are way too old to be Emily. She was only a year older than Margo—and just look at her! She's twenty, twenty-one. That would make Emily twenty-two at most."

"I'm still inclined to believe I'm Alice," I said.

"And I'm still inclined to believe that you are Maggie. I brought you here because I wanted to give you a surprise reunion with your *son*!"

"Not my daughter?" It was distressing to know that he gave my opinions as to who I was no consideration whatsoever.

"Just look at you. It's far-fetched to even think of you as Margo's sister!"

"I know. She was flustered—until she figured out how to play her upper hand."

"At least she recognized you!"

"Yeah, isn't *that* a miracle? Fact is, despite what she said, I don't think she recognized me as *Emily*. Suppose she recognized me as Alice but didn't want to admit it, for some reason."

"Oh, come *on*, Maggie! You sound like you're in denial that Phil shot your sister and then turned the gun on himself."

"What steps did they take to confirm *Alice*'s identification? Perhaps *Margo* has a reason for lying—for wanting her mother to remain 'dead.' She set fire to one of the houses—how do we know she didn't have a hand in killing Alice, too?"

"You can't hurl accusations like that around so lightly!"

The remaining guests straggled by our car. Both of us stared straight ahead as they walked past. Clearly rumors as to my supposed identity had spread thick and fast, because I was conscious that every person in that final cluster peered in at me through the windshield with unconscionable curiosity. Perhaps they had seen me weeping.

"Just look at those gawkers going by!" I said. "I bet they were lingering just to talk about how that deformed monster disrupted the wedding by publicly accusing the bride and groom of indulging in incest! 'She looks so *old*!'"

"Oh, Maggie!"

"*Alice*!" I shouted. But it occurred to me that Margo would be using a different name for the next two or three hours. "Or—Emily. *What-ever*!"

25

But it was not "whatever." I revisited in my mind the time that I had posed for Phil at his studio. I was not his wife, nor yet his lover. As I imagined it, I was much younger than either of them. I doted on Phil mostly because he was a famous artist, but also because he was—

My uncle.

It seemed so clear now. I was fifteen when he "mistook" me in his drunken stupor for my mother. Fifteen, and a virgin. *And he had raped me!*

Revisiting the memory, I watched Phil as his clever hands defined lines that lent some kind of meaning to the painting for him, I suppose, but simply obscured it for me. I'd asked him all sorts of inane questions about his taste in art. What was his favorite painting? How much would he be able to sell that one for? Did he prefer landscapes or portraits? But he was too absorbed in his work to give detailed answers. Only when my mother's cry from the creek shattered our peace did I stop my questioning.

"*Philip*!"

My heart leapt into my throat. *My alter ego!*

His hand stopped in midair. He set down his brush and strode to the door.

"Whatever you do," I whispered urgently as he wrestled with the doorknob, "don't tell her I'm here!"

Shutting the door behind him, he walked down the steps toward the jetty. Already she – *I?* – was climbing toward him. I could at first overhear only a little of the mumbled conversation. I crossed the main room of the cabin, testing every footfall, since the pine floor creaked. The window and door were open but screened. There was no breeze outside, and sound carried almost preternaturally in the woods. Only the white noise of the creek muffled their words.

"They're both gone," I heard "Alice" say.

"The canoe's gone, too," said Phil. "They probably went fishing. Imagine that, paddling off into the sunrise without so much as a 'Howdy, how are ya'? Anyways, I wouldn't worry."

"Of course we should worry! What if they're tempted to— you know!"

"Fornicate? Oh fuck, no! God help us! Not fornication!"

"It's against God's Law!"

"*Love* is against God's Law? I thought He invented it! Isn't He the God of Love?"

"Not love. *Sex*!"

"Yes, He invented that, too! I'm sure I read it somewhere—"

"We're not just talking fornication or even adultery here. We're talking *incest*!"

"Why are you so damn' judgmental, Alice?" His tone softened. "You didn't used to be."

"Do you have another canoe?"

"Nope."

"Can you ride after them on Angel?"

"The way her legs are cut up, Angel won't be walking with any weight for at least a month."

"We've got to stop them! Warn them! Their everlasting life may be at stake!"

"Jesus Christ, Alice! Listen to yourself! How can you believe that shit?"

I – my other Self – began crying. "I'd been meaning to talk to her, to counsel her—but I'm not much good at that sort of thing." Then, bitterly: "It's the man's job!"

"Fine, I'll talk to 'em as soon as they get back."

"It'll be too late! Don't you understand? They don't *know*!"

There was a moment of silence, and then she took on her reproving tone. "May I please borrow your Jeep?"

"Sure. The keys are in it."

"I don't know how to drive it. Will you drive me?"

"No," he said.

"Why not?"

"It's a wild goose chase! First, we don't know for sure where they went. Second, we have to follow the fire trails in the Jeep, and most of them are blocked off by deadfall. Can't follow the creek, that's for sure. Third, live and let live. Let them figure things out for themselves, for once, what's right and what's wrong."

"She talked about going back to the site of Richard's plane crash. You know how obsessed she is about that. I'll drive as close as I can to see if they've gone there. But if I don't find them, Phil, I'm driving straight on to Nordegg and calling the police!"

"Okay by me. I'll look in on the kids from time to time."

"That's not good enough! Look, I don't know what can be so pressing down here—"

"I'm working on a new series of paintings—a 'retrospective' of a different order."

"Where are your priorities? You can't neglect your children like this!"

"Nor do I have to phone the police every time one of them takes a walk in the park."

"Even if you know what he's doing is evil, immoral, a mortal sin?"

"Well, at least it's not a crime."

"Yes it is. It's considered immoral and made illegal for a reason. It pollutes the gene pool! It's a crime against humanity!"

"*Sex*?"

"*Incest*!" This time, she fairly screamed it. "What if she gets pregnant?"

A jolt went through me like an electric shock—both then and now:

Colleen!

26

Roy drove the streets of Edmonton with less passion than previously as we crossed the High Level Bridge toward the University of Alberta. But he did not turn off there. Rather, he drove west along the river, then turned down a narrow paved lane into a cemetery. We cruised past endless rows of tombstones and grave markers until he arrived at a family plot surrounded by a concrete replica of a rail fence. He pulled over partly onto the grass. Inside the rail fence was an oval pool of smooth concrete on which "swam" a V of concrete Canada geese, eight goslings following two larger adults.

"Heading south the hard way," Roy remarked dryly as we approached the memorial.

The first goose in the cluster was marked by a plaque set into the concrete pool: Richard Thompson. Second from left was Alice LaPierre Thompson. Was that me, or was I the next name—Emily Thompson—which graced the first of the goslings? Margo's plaque had a blank date; then came plaques for Willis Richard and Sandra Carmen. According to the plaques, Emily, Willis, and Sandra had all died on the same day.

"So, one way or another, this is where my mortal remains are buried!" I said. My skin crawled at the thought.

"No bodies are buried here," said Roy, missing the irony of my remark. "They were all cremated."

"For a second time?"

"This is just a memorial. Margo designed it."

"Really? Who paid for it?"

"Your grandmother."

Mother-in-law? I thought. It was amazing to me that Roy had so quickly bought into the notion of my being Emily, given his steadfast resistance to my being Alice.

"She's buried over in the corner of the plot alongside her husband, see?" He added, "George and Elizabeth Thompson."

"Must've cost a mint!"

"Actually, not that much. Margo said she bought preformed concrete statues of Canada geese and had them set in a concrete slab. The most expensive things were the plaques."

"But you've got to admit, it does look impressive!"

We walked around to the other side of the memorial, where beside the first large Canada goose, ironically sharing it with his arch-rival in love, was a plaque for Philip Campbell. Margaret LaPierre Campbell similarly shared the second goose with her sister Alice. The four Campbell kids, like us Thompsons, each had a personal gosling. The death dates for Margaret and Tom were blank, while the last three shared as a death date that singular day of hell.

"Where are all the ashes?" I asked.

Roy nodded toward the nearby North Saskatchewan, which meandered east past the cemetery. "Margo told me she sprinkled them into the river."

How fitting, I thought. Hundreds of miles upstream, Camas Lake, the hot spring, the tiny unnamed brook, and the larger creek were all part of this mighty river's headwaters. I felt a new respect for Margo—and an appreciation for her efforts at inclusiveness.

27

Bolts shook her way back to the University of Alberta, where the reception was scheduled at The Ship, a student-run café in Lister Hall. The heavy wooden furniture, built solid to withstand the onslaught of generation after generation of penknife-wielding graffiti artists striving for immortality, seemed a trifle ludicrous for the event, set as the tables were with all the finery of a catered wedding reception. Even the paper doilies seemed somehow out of place, let alone the wineglasses and silver cutlery. But then, I approached the whole party with a cynical attitude. Whereas at the actual wedding I had been ebullient when I first recognized Margo and morose after I suspected that she had somehow disinherited me as her mother while at the same time "adopting" me as her sister, here I sought to prove that I did have a modicum of control, that I was not totally impulsive and irrational, that in "normal" situations I was quite capable of a refined if snooty dignity. After all, wasn't it my sister (*daughter?*) who had just got married? To my—brother? I wilted under the thought of my own possible relationship to Tom, recalling once again Uncle Phil's anger toward my father (*husband! husband!*) for having cuckolded him. Uncle Phil obviously believed that my father had not only stolen the love of his life – Alice – but had twice impregnated Margaret, leaving Phil to bear the burden of parenthood for both Tom and Colleen. All the lucrative art sales in the world didn't seem to compensate for those atrocities!

Had Uncle Phil raped me just to get even?

Most of the wedding guests, including the bridal party, were university students, friends of Margo. A few sitting at a table to the far right may have been former fellow inmates of the Youth Development Center, sporting brightly dyed hair and prominent piercings. They formed a klatch of their own that seemed to me impenetrable. No matter how I tried to convince myself that I could handle the situation, I began to grow more and more uneasy. Everyone everywhere I looked seemed to be looking back at me, their eyes wearing away at my social armor, leaving me feeling horribly vulnerable.

"Let's go over and talk to the other guests," said Roy.

"Let's not and say we did." A stale old rejoinder from the misty past.

Despite his appearance of suavity, Roy too, I realized, was nervous. He was sweating a little and had loosened his tie just enough to undo the top button of his shirt. The arm to which I clung like a barnacle was steady, but his right hand was constantly working, jingling keys and coins in his pocket, picking imaginary lint off his jacket, smoothing stubborn wisps of hair that stuck out over his right ear (that tuft always did), checking and rechecking his chin to ascertain if he needed another shave, as if that might be a good excuse to duck into the can if things got hot.

"We can't just stand here looking silly," he said at last. "Margo and Tom will be coming soon. Let's stroll up to the head table and find out where we're sitting. And maybe introduce ourselves to some of their friends."

"They're obviously strangers," I said, eying the punks off to the right.

"Let me guess. You recall your mother telling you never to talk to strangers but don't recall her telling you to make an exception of guests at your sister's wedding reception?"

His words were a knife, stabbing and twisting. I couldn't explain, if he didn't want to understand. I let go of his arm and ran across the room toward the double doors, barely able to contain tears of humiliation. I crashed through the double doors, only to run into Margo and Tom, who chatted with the minister who had performed the ceremony. I almost bowled the poor man over in my haste.

"Emily!" said Margo. "We have to talk—"

I was biting my lower lip, quivering all over. "I—I have to go to the, to the—" I searched for a euphemism polite enough for the minister's ears. "To wash up." Even this was not what I had intended to say, and again stricken with a pang of humiliation, I ran off down the hall. "I'm sorry, Margo!" I cried. "I'm sorry!"

In the washroom, I locked myself in a cubicle and wept. I was conscious of the squeak of the door opening, and Margo was there outside my cubicle, recognizable by the floor-length bridal gown visible under the door.

"Emily? Are you all right?"

"Yes," I sniffed.

"Hey, what's the matter?"

"I'm sorry, Margo," I said again. "I don't want you to see me like this."

"I've arranged it so that you can sit beside me at the reception. I've explained to Ann, my bridesmaid, that I want to catch up on things since I haven't seen you for—what, six years?"

"'Bout that."

I stood up and automatically flushed. And suddenly I had a tremendous rush, a feeling of *déjà vu* more powerful than I'd ever experienced before, of the mental hospital in Ponoka, sitting in the men's john just as I had been sitting there in the Lister Hall women's washroom, hiding. In an instantaneous flash of total recall I relived one of our mother's sermons, resurrected from my mind on that previous occasion too, about Tom, and sex, and marriage.

Alice was my mother! I could finally see it. *Our* mother, Margo's and mine.

Nobody had told *Margo* not to fool around with Tom—she had been too young for sex education, in our mother's book. And now, six years later, she was obviously pregnant with his child!

I blew my nose on some toilet tissue and emerged from the cubicle.

"Sorry. This all—just took me by surprise," I said. "Roy didn't tell me it was going to be you and Tom. I know I sound like a blubbering idiot, but well, I'm so happy for you, and do so want everything to go off well, and yet, well, I've wrecked everything, haven't I? I mean, I'm wrecking everything by being so cut up and uptight and nervous and weepy."

"Don't be silly, Emmy! It's made my day, your dropping in out of the blue. It was a wonderful surprise!"

"The crazy thing is, even after you told me who I was, I couldn't accept it. Until this minute, in fact. I've been thinking that I was Alice—Mom—all this time."

"Mom is dead."

"I know. I saw your memorial. But then, so am I, right? So what was I to think?" I washed my hands, avoiding as usual the shriveled horror of my face reflected back from the bank of mirrors. "What are you going to call the baby?" I wondered. "Alice?"

"Philip," she said. "We know it's a boy."

"Not—Richard?"

"I don't think Tom would approve of that!"

"Why not? He was his father."

Margo frowned. "Emily—you're a little mixed up. Richard Thompson was *our* father."

"Yes, but his too. That's what I was trying to tell you! Have you had a blood test?"

Her eyes flared. "Yes. Everything's fine. So drop it, okay?"

"Did they check for that?"

"Of course they would have!"

At last I steeled myself to look at the image of myself in the bank of mirrors above the row of basins across from the toilets.

The puffiness of my eyes from weeping muted the wrinkles on my face, although this was more than offset by my bloodshot eyes and bedraggled hair. "I can't go back in there like this," I said, truly mortified. "Not and sit at the head table!"

"Of course you can," said Margo, struggling to remain civil. "Here, dab your eyes with cold water." She took a paper towel from the dispenser and ran it under the tap. Then she reached up and ever so gently stroked my face, focusing on the multiple wrinkles, her eyes softening until they were full of compassion and concern, trying to compare it, no doubt, with the Emily-face she had known so long ago. And it occurred to me once again: This is the girl who had been convicted of killing me? Of massacring my family? She had freely admitted it!

The door opened and the bridesmaid, Ann, came in.

"Everything okay, Margo?"

"Sure," she said.

"What's wrong with her?" There was a coldness about the question that betrayed an insider's knowledge of my situation: I had been cast as the enemy, where she was concerned, not fully human, disanthropomorphized into an animal or thing.

"Oh, nothing. She's just a little upset. All right now, Emmy?"

"The caterers are waiting. And I think Tom's getting a bit impatient."

"I won't be long, tell him." And Margo stayed with me, smoothing my hair, soothing with small talk. "Where've you been living?" she asked.

"Red Deer. I'm staying with Roy."

"With Roy," she said, a statement, not a question.

"Yes. Didn't he tell you?"

"Roy raises all kinds of questions but doesn't give many answers."

"Yes, I know. I find that aggravating, too. But that's what journalists do."

The baby kicked and I held my belly for an instant. I was not quite used to the sensation.

"Cramps?" she asked.

I shook my head and nodded at her tight little belly.

"No way!" She brushed my hair away from my wrinkled face, examining it with a worried frown. "Roy's?"

I nodded, grinning through my tears. "He doesn't know yet."

"Fuck! How far along?"

"Six months. You?"

"Eight. How long have you lived with Roy?"

I blushed. "Six months."

"Prick! He *used* you!" She gave me a tentative hug and glanced toward the door. "Now, let's go in there and kick ass! Knock 'em dead! The Thompson sisters rise again!"

28

We emerged from the washroom and walked in a measured pace down the hall. We did not have to rush as we had thought, because Tom was at the pay phone. The best man, a puny little guy, stood beside him and tapped him on the shoulder when he saw us coming. Tom quickly wrapped up his business on the telephone, stuck on a smile to cover his obvious annoyance, and walked over to greet Margo as if he hadn't seen her all day. Me, he totally ignored.

Roy stood like a praetorian guard just inside the door. He looked in concern at my red eyes. "You okay?"

I nodded. "Yes, everything's fine."

"Hey, they've given us prime seats!"

"I know. Margo told me."

Ignoring the usher, we followed Tom and Margo to the head table. Margo's smile seemed radiant, but Tom's was pasted on. As we reached our places, most of the guests cast a critical eye in my direction. That made me all the more self-conscious, and inadvertently I sat down before the bride, again a humiliation covered by the patient Margo. Tom stood on the other side of my sister, his eyes ablaze as he realized that I had somehow usurped the divine order of things once again. He glanced at the best man, on the other side of me, and ever so slightly rolled one of his eyes. Then he and all the rest sat down.

If I was not going to make a total ass of myself, I'd have to follow the lead of the others at the head table, and so I fixed *my* eyes on Margo's hands beside me as a touchstone of etiquette. She unfurled her serviette. I followed suit. Then she reached out and took her water and sipped. I automatically reached out, too, but wasn't watching what I was doing and knocked the glass over. My face flamed as the water streamed under my paper doily and dribbled onto my lap. Feeling the ice-cold water on my lap, I stood up suddenly, jarring the table with my thighs. This action not only sloshed water all the way along the table but caused me to yelp and flop back down in my chair in considerable pain. Tom grabbed for the wedding cake intending to stabilize it and ended up sticking his thumb into the icing. He licked it off with a grimace.

Margo smiled, taking everything in stride. "So tell me all about yourself," she said when I had regained a modicum of composure.

"First of all," I replied, "*I* need an honest answer. Are you positive I'm me? Emily, I mean."

She gave a nervous little laugh. "Of course! Aren't *you*?"

"You're not just yanking my chain?"

"Yanking your—no! Why would I do that?"

"Do you have photographs of me?"

"Of course." She glanced at Tom, who with Ann was trying to do a repair job on the icing, then lowered her voice. "Actually, no, not anymore. But we used to."

"What do you mean?"

"I inherited all the photo albums, both from Mummy and Grandma Thompson, but—I don't know how to say this, except—Tom has this thing about you. This—thing."

"Why?"

"Because of his leg—because of—*everything*! Everything went *so* sideways! You remember."

"No, I don't."

"Roy has interviewed us for his book several times. Last fall he asked to see some photos of the way things were. I showed him our photo albums, only to find that Tom had altered the pictures." She looked at her new husband with a scowl.

"Altered them how?"

"He burned the faces off with a cigarette. Just your face, actually. As I went through the albums, it was the same story: Every photo in which you ever appeared had been—mutilated."

My heart raced out of control.

"You mean Tom—"

"—systematically eradicated all images of you from the album."

"With a lit cigarette?" I said, more loudly than I had intended. I was in shock. Tom glanced back and caught my dismayed stare. He leaned toward us.

"Margo," he said, "for Christ's sake be careful what you say to her!"

She smiled and blew him a kiss. What a consummate actor! The assembled company took this as a cue to tinkle their wineglasses, and she and Tom stood up in front of the cake and kissed. Then she sat back down, her veil awry.

"He's worried about our inheritance," she said. He overheard.

"No, I'm worried that you're talkin' about that shit with *her* at our wedding reception!"

But she was defiant. "According to Gran Thompson's will, all her surviving grandchildren were to get an equal share of the estate."

"Margo!" hissed Tom in a mixture of anger and alarm. "Will you shut the fuck up?"

"I won't take a minute, Sweetheart. We've just got some catching up to do."

He grimaced but resumed his conversation with Ann.

"Grandma Thompson had a stroke not long after the fires," said Margo. "She couldn't get her mind around the fact that all her remaining family except me had died in the fire. And she couldn't believe that I had deliberately set it. Not her favorite blue-eyed blonde-haired little chickadee! But I had already admitted to lighting the fire. I was so distraught I told everyone—the foresters, the firemen, the cops. There was no doubt I set fire to the *bushes*. That was the plan, remember? Create a distraction at the front of the house so you could run in the back and rescue Sandy. But the flames spread so quickly to the house it was impossible to stop them."

"Gasoline does that," I said, recalling in my mind's eye the image of bucket after bucket of purple gas splashing on the weathered shiplap siding.

"As I told the cops, I didn't mean for anybody to die!" Margo continued. "I just stood there staring at the blazing house, burning torch still raised high."

"Statue of Liberty," I said drolly.

"Hardly! I couldn't believe I was responsible for that! But there was no doubt that I was the one who torched the bushes—and therefore the house. They said that in trying to implicate you, I was blaming the victim. But really, I didn't want anyone else to take the blame. Especially not Tom. And before I knew it I'd given confessions to anyone who would listen.

"I heard the shotgun go off from within the house, but I couldn't move. I just stood there fully exposed in the front yard, feeling the heat of the hell I'd created. Another shot ripped out the grass right beside me. Then Tom grabbed me from behind, hauled me to the ground. I screamed and fought him, but he yelled, 'She's shooting at us! The crazy bitch is shooting at us!' He wrestled the torch out of my hand and tossed it as far away as he could into the grass. He rolled on top of me, and we rolled together over and over toward the longer grass nearer the lake, out of range of the shotgun, then lay there hiding in the hay, panting and shuddering, while the sky lit up with sparks from the flames.

"I lay there in his arms for perhaps half an hour, afraid to move. I could feel the heat of the flames in front of me, the heat of his body behind. He had passed out, clutching me in the grass, determined not to let me go. I couldn't loosen his fingers. It was like rigor mortis had set in!

"The flames lit the sky and flickered off the mountain peaks for miles around. At last I heard planes. A water-bomber dropped its load on our house up on top of the embankment, which Willis had set afire, then landed on the lake to refill its tanks. It dropped another load on Uncle Phil's house, the one I had lit. The house seemed to explode like a steam bomb, billowing thick, acrid smoke. By the time the flames took hold again, firemen on the ground were pumping water from the lake, dousing what was left of the house.

"Tom still didn't move. Didn't wake up. Just clung to me. I thought for a minute he'd been shot, that he was dead. But he wasn't cold to the touch. Quite the opposite! And I could feel his chest rise and fall against me. I learned later that he had gone into toxic shock from the gangrene in his broken leg. But he'd saved my life!" She glanced at me nervously, reading my face.

"And all along, Tom thought *I* was shooting at you?"

She nodded. "He thought you still had the shotgun. He'd been down at the dock, you see. He didn't know that Willis had managed to wrest the shotgun away from you, had set fire to our house, had taken Sandy hostage, had locked her up. He didn't know anything about our plan to rescue her. Tom was completely in the dark!

"It was so unfair, what they did to him. Just because he was older. They wouldn't let me take responsibility—said there had to be a criminal mind behind it, that Tom had me under his power, his spell. And it didn't help that he admitted to putting the boys up to staging a raid on our cabin to free Colleen. 'Similar fact evidence,' they said."

I was fixated on the notion that Tom had thought that I had been shooting at her. "But couldn't you *see* that it was Willis shooting at you from the attic?"

"I wasn't looking. And neither was Tom, of course. But later, Tom told the police that *you* were shooting at us from the attic.

That's what he told his lawyer, and that's what his lawyer told the court at his bail hearing. His story didn't jibe with mine. And he couldn't corroborate it, especially when the police found your body, what was left of it—I'm sorry, what they *thought* was your body—at the other end of the house near the bottom of the stairs, not far from Sandy's. So it's come as a *real* shock to him that you survived the fire!"

"So why is he so angry at me now?"

"His leg, I suspect. He lost it. That's why he limps. Cheap prosthesis. He blames you for that. Remember, it's difficult for us to adjust to the knowledge that you survived. We haven't had a chance to talk about it. *I* certainly didn't expect *you*. In fact, from what Roy said, I half expected you to be Aunt Margaret."

I glanced at Roy, who was deep in conversation with the minister. Then I picked away at my salad.

"But if you didn't intend to set the fire, and were prevented by Willis from putting out the blaze, why did you plead guilty?"

She smiled sadly, then shrugged. "Because I *felt* guilty. I had killed my own brother and sisters! I think Tom felt the same way about his two brothers—felt guilty about failing to protect them. Feeling guilty allowed us to *plead* guilty. Besides, if we hadn't pled guilty, we would have gone to trial—and been *found* guilty of much worse charges than those for which we were convicted. Like first-degree murder.

"They had the smoking weapon, so to speak—both our fingerprints were on that torch. It was a piece of wood like the one I'd tried to use as a splint on Tom's leg. That was another, more direct connection the police made between Tom and the fire. I told them he had grabbed the torch from me to put out the flame so that Willis couldn't see me so easily."

"I handed that torch to you!" I suddenly realized with a shock. "Did they find *my* fingerprints on it?"

"I don't know." She took a forkful of salad into her mouth, chewed, then flushed it down with water. "My lawyer advised me to plead out. She was pretty good. But she refused to listen to me when it came to exonerating Tom. She explained that her job was to get me off or negotiate a low sentence. Tom's lawyer was nowhere near as effective.

"I have another lawyer now, who is helping me with Mum's estate. The whole matter is going back to court. And that's what I need to talk to you about—how we can get a hundred percent of the money, despite my conviction for killing three of my siblings. She has argued that the Proceeds of Crime Act which the Crown says prevents me from profiting from my crime does not apply to youths, since a youth record is expunged two years after the sentence is complete. Therefore I am deemed not to have been convicted. Also, the intent of the provision is to protect victims from being exploited directly, or through insurance claims. If I had killed Gran Thompson, for example, I would not have a leg to stand on." She glanced at Tom. "Sorry. Unintentional." Then she resumed: "My lawyer argued that killing my siblings without premeditation of any kind, before she died, is too remote an act to be deemed a breach of the provision.

"But there is a way to beat the government at its own game. Part of it will hinge on your being able to prove who you are—Emily Thompson. But I don't know how we can do that without inviting the Crown to reopen the case. Believe me, you don't want that!"

The tinkling of wineglasses by the wedding guests once again ascended toward crescendo. Rolling her eyes, Margo rose for yet another insincere kiss from the disgruntled groom.

As soon as she had regained her seat, she outlined for me how, together, we could beat the criminal justice system and become instantly and incredibly rich.

29

"As you know, Daddy's painting collection went automatically to Mum when he died—a warehouse full of them," Margo said. "Her will was a mirror-image of his—the spouse was the beneficiary unless predeceased, in which case the kids inherited everything. But there's a law that says a convicted criminal cannot profit from her crimes. Because I was convicted of killing all three of my siblings, I can't claim more than twenty-five percent of her estate, and a lot of that will go to legal fees. The other seventy-five percent goes to the public trustee, unless we can throw up some sort of block. My lawyer is still working on that. In the meantime, it's held in trust by the government."

"So what happened to the collection?"

"It's still in the warehouse. It's fabulous! Dad represented a lot of artists, and we had to return many of the paintings to their artists when we couldn't prove he had actually bought them. I agreed to let Tom claim most of Uncle Phil's paintings because there's no evidence Daddy ever paid him for them. But there's still a huge collection. A whole lot of big prairie artists. He bought wisely in New York and London, Moscow, all over the place. I'm talking hundreds of paintings by famous landscape and portrait artists like Wyeth, as well as inferior abstracts by Warhol, Picasso, Miro, and Dali. Eventually, they may fetch even more than Gran's estate. My lawyer's talking about selling off some of the paintings at auction through Sotheby's, whatever we don't want to keep."

Tom leaned over in front of her and fixed me with one of his eyes. "But after all the shit we've gone through? There's no fuckin' way you're gonna get a red cent!" His eye was full of hatred. I flinched back into my seat away from him, but he leaned back behind Margo to continue his harangue. "Not one cent from either estate! You can be damn sure of that!"

Margo seemed genuinely appalled by his demeanor. "What is *with* you, Tom?" she said.

"Don't you get it? It's a con!"

"You're being ridiculous. How is it a con? It's *Emily*, Tom, remember? What are you *on*?"

Tom beckoned over his best man, who left his chair beside me. The brief storm seemed to be over.

"*Either* estate?" I prodded Margo.

"Yeah. Similar thing. I stayed with Gran Thompson after the fires, but she had a stroke and I ended up taking care of her rather than the other way around. After I was arrested and charged she managed to visit me at the Youth Development Center once in a while, and toward the end I was given UTAs—unescorted temporary absences—from the YDC to visit her on compassionate grounds. After she died, her lawyer came out to YDC to read her will. I was the only beneficiary, you see."

"So she'd changed her will?"

"No, that's the trouble, not since just after Dad died in the plane crash. That's when she bequeathed her estate to all of her surviving grandchildren. My lawyer said that's not unusual, that she probably wrote it that way to make it clear that she did not want *Mum* to be the beneficiary. The lawyer told me that her estate would be liquidated and all the proceeds from the sale would be put in a trust account, held by the public trustee until I reached the age of majority—eighteen—from which I could draw as long as I remained in school or university. But again, there's that law that says I cannot profit from my crimes. Since I was convicted of killing three other potential beneficiaries—including you—I could only access twenty-five percent of Gran's estate, the share that I would have inherited had my siblings not died in the fire."

"But if you didn't intend to kill them—"

"My lawyer fought it, but lost, so now it's black and white. On my eighteenth birthday, only twenty-five percent of the estate transferred to me, less legal fees and any amount that I've drawn down while in university."

"And the rest?"

"Until you surfaced today, I had two options: allow the seventy-five percent to be held in escrow for the province, or convert it into a scholarship fund in Gran's name. But it occurs to me that now that's all changed. All you have to do is prove to the public trustee that you are Emily Thompson, the grandchild of Elizabeth Thompson, and you stand to inherit—"

"—seventy-five percent of the estate!"

"For fuck's sake, Margo!" snapped Tom.

"*We* can't benefit from it," Margo retorted. "Better she gets it than the Province. I don't want those bastards to get a penny!"

"How much are we talking here?" I asked.

"All told? Coupla million bucks. Whereas with my share alone? I couldn't even afford to buy a condo!"

The guests started tapping their glasses, and Tom and Margo bobbed up like automatons to kiss each other yet again. What a charade!

A waiter served me my Cornish hen, about the size of a spruce grouse, with peas and potatoes.

"Are you telling me I stand to inherit more than a million?" I asked agog when she regained her seat.

"Plus interest!" she said as she dug into her main course.

I followed suit. Roy and I had grabbed toast and coffee for breakfast earlier that morning but had skipped lunch to get to the wedding on time, so I was famished.

I tasted a bit of the bird. Mmm! It brought back memories of that spruce grouse Tuanahaki had killed with a stone, sneaking up on it, dumb bird, until she was within ten feet. We had roasted it over the campfire and devoured it—we hadn't eaten for two days, other than a few edible greens and berries and some unripe hazel nuts. Tuanahaki did not even bother to strip off the feathers; rather she soaked the whole bird in clay from the bank of the creek and we roasted it until the clay was hard and the bird steaming, the same scent as I experienced now. We cracked open the clay and the feathers came away from the bird, leaving the tender flesh. We each took a leg first, and we snorted and giggled and dribbled as we ate. There was no one to laugh at us or point or jeer or mock, just each other, feasting, happy, knowing precisely how good the other felt just then immersed in grease. We each took a half, sharing, gnawing the bones to get their marrow, munching, chewing, slurping the salt, swallowing the smooth and filling meat in easy, sliding gulps.

Suddenly I realized that, as so often happened to me, I had transported myself in more than mere memory, was there in fact, sitting at that fire, eating that way. Except that, physically, I was still there in The Ship, dripping and dribbling grease, half of a bird in my hand, gnawing.

Even Margo was embarrassed as I slowly set the naked ribs of my chicken beside the leg bone. I reached automatically for my serviette but grabbed the tablecloth instead, besmearing it with grease.

My serviette had fallen on the floor. Margo came to the rescue by giving me hers. Again I was on the verge of tears, aware of sneers of disgust from the pit.

"It's all right," Margo whispered. "I'll explain everything." Just one more thing to add to the burning of my ears: my younger sister, the bride, having to explain away her inappropriate older sister in public at her wedding!

We toasted the bride and groom, and again they stood up and kissed each other in response to the ringing of tapped wine glasses. But Margo didn't take the opportunity to explain me, thank God.

Having cleaned the grease from my face, hands, and arms, I could not face the prospect of putting on another demonstration for my ogling audience, and so I ate nothing. I just sat there looking up at the ceiling, wondering when my usual presence of mind would return to me. Certainly I had never been put on a stage and made to perform like today. I could hardly wait to find out how Margo would explain away my actions.

Roy pressed his hand onto my shoulder. "I'm just going to the men's room. Everything okay?" He addressed the question more to Margo than to me. Margo smiled at him, nodded, then turned her smile into a glare as he walked away.

"You and Tom should at least have a proper DNA test," I said, prompted by a premonition I did not then comprehend.

Tom dropped his napkin on the table. "Are you on about that again?"

"It might have been interesting to compare your DNA with Colleen's," I shot right back.

His reaction was over the top. "Get rid of her!" he hissed to the best man, who had resumed his seat to my left.

"Colleen's DNA would be closer to ours than his," said Margo, glancing at Tom. Then she added: "We don't have any secrets."

"I know. I heard the tape of him describing his affair with Aunt Margaret."

"That wasn't an affair," said Tom. "That was sexual abuse—sexual assault, actually!"

"From what you said, it was consensual—it went on for months!"

"He was a minor. Minors can't consent!" Margo followed Roy's retreating form as he left the hall. "Roy wasn't supposed to share that! I didn't even know he'd kept it!"

"Consent or not, it doesn't alter the net result," I said, working it out. "Tom admitted they had sex over and over, practically every night. Until Aunt Margaret dumped him for her new stud: Richard – your – *our* dad!" She looked at me, still puzzled. "Tom hasn't told you that he got Aunt Margaret pregnant?"

"What? No! He told me *Daddy* got Aunt Margaret pregnant."

"Oh, really?" I leaned over in front of her. "Tom? Who is Colleen's father?" It was a stab in the dark, but given his reaction to my suggestion of a comparison of his DNA with Colleen's it suddenly made so much sense! Were Tom and Colleen full brother and sister, as I had intended to imply—or even *more* closely related?

He glared at me with unmitigated hatred. That just triggered me to attack.

"Lucky, wasn't it, that Dad and Aunt Margaret didn't take Colleen along on their final ride. But for the grace of God and Thomas Campbell, your little daughter would have died as well!"

His eyes bulged and danced and his nostrils flared as he stood up, pointing his finger directly in my face. "You are one fucked up bitch!" he hissed. "You can't throw around accusations like that! Not on my wedding day!" Then: "*You* killed Colley, you fuckin' who-er, lockin' her up like that!" His voice sounded choked. His face red with rage, he walked around to the back of my chair, fists clenched. I flinched away, fearing he would strike me.

In the absence of the best man, the minister stood up, ready to intervene. Tom leaned on the table, arms straight down with white knuckles, looking for all the world like a wild-eyed gorilla. "I agree I should've taken care of Colley myself. That's my biggest regret, leavin' her in your care. A real father would have protected his little girl from the likes of you!"

"You mean—it's true?" said Margo, aghast. "Colleen *was* your daughter?"

He was trapped. He bit his lower lip, took a deep breath, and nodded. "Yes, she was my daughter. Do the fuckin' math!"

30

In all of Lister Hall, not a glass tinkled, not a fork scraped a plate as Margo suppressed an anguished cry. Defeated, Tom sat down sideways in the chair vacated by his best man. Every wedding guest gaped at us—especially at me, because now I sat between the bride and groom, the obvious cause of yet more grief for the newlyweds.

Once conversation in the hall resumed, Tom tried to explain with a lowered voice.

"When she found out she was pregnant, Mom panicked. She ended things with me and started an affair with your father. I don't think she ever loved him; she just took him on as a lover to protect me. She wanted Dad to believe that Colleen was Uncle Richard's kid." He looked at Margo with eyes full of regret. "Dad sure as hell knew she wasn't *his*."

"So Colleen was the product of your incest!" said Margo aghast. "That's why—"

"She was wall-eyed, damn near retarded? Yeah!"

"And now the incest is happening all over again," I added. "Phil—Uncle Phil—told me that you are our father's son!"

"You're so full of shit!" Tom polished off the best man's wine in a single gulp. Someone took this as a cue for a toast, and the tinkles continued for a full minute before Tom and Margo stood up on either side of me, leaned over me, and kissed.

"*Ménage à trois!*" somebody yelled.

Hoots and catcalls.

"Piece o' cake!"

Scattered laughter. Several guests started chanting *Piece, Piece, Piece, Piece, Piece*, until the majority of the crowd drowned them out with chants of *Cake! Cake! Cake! Cake! Cake!*

"Come, on Tom. We'd better cut it," said Margo, handing him the knife. As they sliced into it together, she said with a quavering voice, loud enough for all to hear: "*Let them eat cake!*"

The best man regained his seat beside me. He was meticulously polite.

"There's a gentleman to see you," he told me casually as he resumed eating.

"Yeah, right!" I said skeptically.

"No, seriously. He's waiting over there, just inside the main door."

I glanced across at the stranger. He was tall, heavyset, ruggedly handsome, neat, and businesslike, dressed in a dark suit fit for a funeral. He smiled at me and nodded.

"Why would anyone want to see *me*?" I glanced at Roy, who had also returned to his seat, but he was engaged once again in earnest conversation with the minister. I set down Margo's borrowed serviette, grabbed my purse, and headed for the door as if going to the washroom. The stranger followed me out into the hallway.

"Sister Jane Doe?" A quiet, polite voice.

Busted!

Measured tone. Steady: "Yes."

"Also known as Margaret Campbell? Also known as Alice Thompson? Also known as Emily Thompson?"

I nodded almost imperceptibly, cocking my head suspiciously to one side.

"I'm Constable Evarts." He flipped open his RCMP identification wallet with its buffalo insignia. Can you show me some ID?" Flustered, I fished my license and social security card out of a pocket in my purse. He looked at it. "'Thomasina Allison'?" he read. "Is this *another* alias?"

"No," I mumbled. "It's my real name."

"I have to ask you to come with me."

"Go with you?"

"To the Detachment."

I was horror-struck! I did not know whether to faint, fight, scream, or run. As if anticipating my dilemma, the officer added, "I would suggest you come quietly, so as not to cause further embarrassment to the bride and groom."

He had a point there. Meekly, I walked beside him down the hall and outside along the sidewalk in front of the building to a waiting cruiser. A uniformed constable sat at the wheel.

Evarts held my head as he helped me into the rear seat, then slammed the door behind me. He opened the front door and sat in the passenger's seat in front of me. I was protected from the officers by a steel grill. There were no interior handles on the rear doors.

We drove down the alley toward the road. The driver's window was open. I was aware of a number of students on the sidewalk watching us. We paused beside them waiting for a campus truck to pull out of the way.

"Yeah, it's the narcs," I heard one of the students say as we pulled out into the stream of traffic.

"Who'd they bust?"

"I dunno. Some chick."

"Fuckin' pigs!"

31

At one level, I was not surprised to find myself in custody. For six months I had assumed that I had committed some kind of offense by hopping into Farquhar's car and leaving Ponoka. A series of clichés rang in my head, suddenly meaningful. The long arm of the law had finally caught up with me, was about to mete out just punishment. I would be locked up forever on the forensic ward of Alberta Hospital, never again to see the light of day, never again to be allowed to walk the woods or read a book, my obvious insanity corroborated by fifty-odd wedding guests, all witnesses in the long-drawn-out trial before mother-god-judge, faceless Mothergod looming behind the bench:

Do you recognize the defendant?

And mushy sounds as the mouths of my mother and Uncle Phil opened ragged in firelight: *Yeththth.*

What distinguishing marks?

Her headlethneththth.

Constable Evarts ushered me out of the cruiser into a low, concrete building painted a sickly pale yellow. We walked under a buffalo crest with a red crown on top, down a long corridor to an office with a tinted glass door, which he opened without knocking. There was a secretary inside, her neat stockinged legs wrapped around each other under the desk.

"Sister Jane Doe," the policeman said. "Inspector Roberts wanted to see her."

"Thank you, Constable Evarts," said the woman. "Will you have a seat please, Sister? I'll tell the inspector you're here."

She disappeared into a back room, leaving me with the horrible sensation that I was about to be inspected not by a policeman but by a medical doctor on a psych ward. After all, I had never met this man outside Red Deer General Hospital—and he had signed my unused committal papers.

It occurred to me, fleetingly, that nobody was there watching me, Constable Evarts having disappeared into the woodwork. I could run. Or rather walk. I could get up, open the door cool as lard, and slip down the corridor to freedom! Last chance. Opportunity going, going—

Gone. Inspector Roberts entered the outer office, carrying a file. "You may come in now, Sister Jane," he said as the secretary regained her seat at her computer. I walked past him into his office.

"Inspector," I said.

"Ah, you remember me."

"You were a just a corporal last year. Congratulations on your promotion. Let's get one thing straight. I'm not Sister Jane Doe or Maggie Campbell or Alice Thompson or even Thomasina Allison. I'm – actually, I'm – I'm Emily Thompson."

"Yet another ingenious alias. 'Alice Thompson'? No, of course not. But unfortunately Emily Thompson, like her mother, is stone-cold dead, and so is her case. The medical examiner is understandably reluctant to reopen that file."

"If there's any doubt about my being Emily Thompson, just ask my sister," I said.

"I assume you mean Margo Thompson?"

"Margo Campbell, now. She just got married—"

"—to Tom Campbell, her co-accused in Emily Thompson's murder. Yes, I know. How convenient! I confess it caught us by surprise that he would marry her! Probably believes his new wife can't be forced to testify against him. That just confirms for us that he has something to hide." He shook his head in consternation. "She's twenty now, and he's put in two-thirds of his sentence, so the parole board let him out on mandatory release without a no-contact condition. He seems to have forgotten that there was a court order as well, although he might have some success varying that now.

"More surprising still is that you should opt for their company, considering that, if you are indeed who you say you are—Emily Thompson—they've already been convicted of killing you!" He opened a file folder and shuffled through it. "Here's the judgment. Pleas of guilty to arson causing the death of Roger Campbell, William Campbell, *Emily Thompson*, Sandra Thompson, and Willis Thompson. So you see, you are dead. *If* you are Emily Thompson. Which of course you are *not*, because you're standing here in front of me, as large as life itself! And here are copies of their death certificates including—" He held it up for me to see. "Ah! Emily Thompson."

"There's been a mistake."

"Mistaken identity? No. As far as the police are concerned, you are still Sister Jane Doe, also known as Margaret—not Margo, mind! She's your niece—Campbell. *Period*."

"Margo recognized me instantly as her sister!"

"Of course, she would, wouldn't she? She's been convicted of killing you, and now conveniently, on her wedding day, someone purporting to be her sister reappears—someone who has already been diagnosed as delusional and suffering from amnesia." His eyes narrowed. "Don't you see? You're being played here! She and Tom Campbell are convicted killers." He sighed in frustration and became less strident, more intense. "We are very aware of Miss Thompson's attempts to obtain what she regards as her 'inheritance.' If she succeeds in this scam, she'll be facing serious criminal charges—this time as an adult. And if you help her, so will you!

"They've killed before and, given the pot of money under consideration here, might just kill again. I'm surprised that Roy

Farquhar would expose you to such jeopardy!" He swiveled in his chair, picked up an even slimmer file folder from a small stack, and completed the revolution, setting it on his desk. He laid it out before me. "Here is a school photo of Emily Thompson from junior high. Do you honestly believe that you are the same person?" The bright, attractive-looking girl had bronze-colored hair, scads of freckles, and reddish eyes, reflecting back the flash of the camera. It looked vaguely familiar.

"Yes," I said. "That's me."

He glanced at the photo, then at me, then at the photo again. "Then you've changed," he said, frowning. "Radically. But that's not the point. I am not concerned with who you are or claim to be, but who you were while at Ponoka Hospital." He produced another document and set it before me. He was suddenly very formal. "I would request you to swear out this prepared affidavit saying that you are Sister Jane Doe. Then we can officially stop looking for you."

"But you weren't 'officially' looking for me in the first place. I'm *dead*, remember?"

"Emily Thompson is. But Sister Jane isn't. There's no compunction to return you to Ponoka, if that's what you're worried about." He glanced at a form attached to the affidavit. "True, you discharged yourself from a secure psychiatric hospital facility without a doctor's approval, but there's no breached order of committal or anything like that. I can vouch for you on that score—you voluntarily consented to a thirty-day examination. You're still on the missing persons list, that's all. We can at least stop looking for you. Remove you from the system. One more file resolved." He sighed. "What's that name again? Thomasina?" As if by sleight of hand he produced my license and social insurance card. "Allison. Good enough for me."

"Why didn't you just send the papers down with Constable Evarts? I could have signed them there just as easily."

"For one thing, he's not a commissioner for taking oaths in the Province of Alberta. For another, I wanted to be sure that you were the same person I saw in Red Deer."

"Well, now you know, why don't you just remove the name from the list? They'll take your word for it. After all, you are an inspector now."

He smiled grimly. "Third thing, someone phoned in a complaint to the city police about someone interrupting a private wedding reception. He agreed to file a formal complaint that you were an uninvited interloper falsely claiming to be Emily Thompson. Given the criminal profile of the complainant, the matter was referred to us. We had to take it seriously."

"Who?" I challenged. "Who would have done a thing like that?"

"Tom Campbell!"

32

I felt myself spiraling down, down, down, Alice, Alice – definitely Alice – falling down the rabbit hole, sinking in a giddy faint into my chair. My own cousin, brother, brother-in-law, son, nephew—*whatever!*—himself a criminal convicted of my death, had been so injured by my conduct that he'd called in the law, in the process disclaiming my inheritance and my identity! Despite his criminal record, he'd had the guts and gumption to telephone the police to lay a formal complaint against me: *What's sauce for the gander is sauce for the goose.*

What opportunity did he have to do that? He had never left the head table for a minute. So it had to have been before, while Margo and I were in the washroom. Yes, he was on the pay phone. Was that when he made the call? Or had the best man called on his behalf?

And then he was there, my "cousin," by the brook, coming up behind me so that I had the strange feeling that time had been wound back several days. He stood in the shade of the trees, hidden from the house, just looking at me as I worked with the clothes, hands blistered, clothes clean now, but I still scrubbing them, washing like Lady Macbeth out of some compulsion that I could not understand, rinsing out the blood-and-semen stains of a rape and rage more deeply rooted than both of us, a miscarriage of justice, of integrity, of trust, of love.

I was aware of someone being there even before he spoke. I reached for a rock.

"Hello, Emily," he said. I started back, snarling, holding the rock threateningly in my hand. Tom advanced no farther but sat down at the side of the brook, trying to ignore my bluster. "Remember that time we wrung out Willis's gaunchies here, and you said you wished his balls were in 'em?" I stood glaring at him, eyes alert and blazing, rock poised. "You might as well sit back down," he said. "I'm not goin' nowhere, no matter how much you carry on. Not gonna hurt you, neither. Like you too much for that." He smiled, but his disordered eyes betrayed a deeper forlorn expression that seemed to override his superficial nonchalance. "I just want to say that I'm sorry about what happened. About the horse, I mean, runnin' away with you like that and tripping on the wire. It was my fault. And I guess that was the start of it, wasn't it? You were right. I shouldn't have come on to you so strong, bein' cousins an' all. It was wrong."

I shook my head slightly but did not put down my stone. He kept absolutely still, sitting there across the brook. Ages passed, and we were frozen in time and space, I with rock raised, he contemplating the water without a murmur. What a ridiculous picture we must have created—Diana the Huntress, armed and dangerous, confronting Rodin's passive Thinker!

Gradually I lowered the rock to my side, then dropped it utterly so it fell to the ground beside my foot. Only then did he look up. "When Willis strung that balin' wire across the trail he meant it for me," he said, "to get even for that time I busted his bow and arrows, that time he shot you with 'em."

It all came back in a rush, the encounter between Tom and me at the fence when we had flirted back and forth and he had adjusted my saddle. Later, after our swim, we had walked back through the pasture from the creek, hand in hand, leading the horse by the reins. When we reached the rail fence that marked the edge of the pasture, we kissed, and he slid his hand up under the fabric of my tank top to caress my breast.

In the middle of the kiss, a rubber-cupped arrow swished by our heads and hit Angel's saddle. I shrieked in alarm, spooking the already jittery horse, which cantered off into the pasture the way we had come. Three little savages daubed with chicken-shit war paint stood before us, bows drawn. Willis's was a rubber-cupped city set, while Billy and Roger held crude hand-made bows made out of twigs and butcher string.

"Okay, you caught us," said Tom with an embarrassed grin. "Now, put 'em down before you hurt somebody!"

Roger and Billy immediately obeyed, but Willis continued pointing a second rubber-cupped arrow at my face. He grinned behind his ludicrous makeup.

"Point that somewhere else, you little jerk-off!" I yelled.

The arrow struck me full on the breastbone. I hurtled backward toward the rail fence with a whimper of shock.

"Fat squaw stay with Injun chief!" shouted Willis, drawing another arrow from his quiver.

Fat squaw? Fat *squaw*! That was it. I charged at him, flailing nails. The third arrow swept zinging by my head. Then I was upon him, punching and clawing, kicking and screaming, searching for some flesh that I could bite. "You fucking little bastard!" I screamed.

"Cunt!"

Tom pulled Willis away from me toward the railing, lifted him, and dropped him on the other side. Then he vaulted over the fence into the pasture and confronted him. Willis cowered down into the grass.

"Tell her you're sorry," said Tom.

"For what?" replied Willis. "It's just a play arrow. It was only a game!"

"You hurt her. You don't hurt women. Not on my turf!"

"It was a toy fucking arrow!"

"Tell her you're sorry," Tom repeated.

"I'm *not* sorry!" Willis crawled away through the grass as Tom advanced. "Okay, okay. I'm sorry!"

Tom turned back toward me as if for direction. But Willis misread his hesitation. "Anyways, we saw you feeling her up, and I'm *telling*!" said Willis, dusting off his clothes.

This time, Tom hoisted him off the ground by his shirt. "You won't tell no one *nothin'*!" he said.

"Okay, okay!" Willis squawked.

"You do, and I'm personally gonna kick the shit right outta ya!" Tom dropped him and vaulted back over the fence with one smooth leap, leaving Willis lying in the grass. In quiet rage, Tom broke Willis's new store-bought bow under his foot, and each of the arrows.

"You didn't have to do that," Willis blubbered, "ya fuckin' wall-eye!"

Tom did the same with his brothers' home-made weapons, then worked a book of matches from his jeans pocket. He grabbed a handful of dried grass, struck a match, and lit first the grass and then the string and feathers. We watched the fire flare, waiting for the larger pieces to catch fully alight.

"We'd better go back separately, the way we came," I murmured to Tom out of earshot of the boys, who kept their distance. "I'll round up the horse."

He nodded and continued tending the fire.

The sun was low in the sky before I finally cornered Angel. She had returned to the creek and stood beside the canoe munching dogwood leaves. I suppose she'd often been tethered there and considered it her second home.

By the time I mounted her, I had lost all patience. I slapped the tip of the reins against Angel's flank and we charged up the hill at something akin to a gallop. Limestone rocks flashed by on either side. Completely unprepared, I straddled the saddle, my sandaled feet out of the stirrups. I simply could not keep my balance. Low branches swept by my head, and I pulled on the reins as hard as I could and yelled *Whoa!* over and over. But Angel seemed deliberately to misinterpret my signals. She veered sharply to the right so that I was forced to cling to the saddle horn with both hands as she galloped into the pasture. I was aware of grass sweeping past and grasshoppers flashing out ahead of us. And it wasn't until that moment that I remembered the height of that fence! I screamed at the horse to stop, but that only egged her on. I pondered jumping off, but large stones were strewn at random across the meadow, half hidden in the grass.

Clinging to the saddle, I closed my eyes as the horrible barrier loomed closer. I felt the horse give an extra lurch and realized we were airborne. I opened my eyes just a second to see the twisting fence below me. I was suspended for an instant directly above the ashes of the fire. No horse was beneath me, no pommel was in my hand, no reins. I heard my own shriek as the ashes and dirt punched up at my face, heard it echoed by an even louder agonized whinny from the horse, felt in an instant of timeless apprehension Angel brush past me, heard her snorting and limping, descending a hidden trail behind a huge spruce.

My whole head rang, clanging from the jarring blow. I tried to open my eyes but saw nothing but red with purple streaks and the image of fire. The fire seemed to be alight, burning my face, consuming flesh. Each flame was a molten arrowhead, and Willis was there, malicious bastard, seeming to take delight in poking each burning arrow deeper into my flesh, branding me forever. I tried to pull back, moaning, but my hands were powerless. I clutched at the hot ashes as the red grew darker, duller, and finally the flames of pain flickered out.

"I'm sorry you were the one got hurt," Tom was saying. We were back at the brook, weeks later. I snorted in disdain. He didn't know what hurt was. "My Dad told me everything."

I cocked my head at that. "*Everything*?"

"Told me it was best I heard it from him. He's gonna marry Aunt Alice. Proposed last night, and she agreed. So we'll be stepbrother and stepsister, I guess."

Step? Step?

I felt a shivering wave shudder through me, chill and absolute. "They can't get married."

Tom frowned. "Well, I don't see why not. See, Dad's marriage to my mom was never registered nor nothin'. The wedding was a pagan handfasting, was all. Common law, plus a contract with Grandpa LaPierre." This was news to me. "Dad told me he'd been engaged to Aunt Alice once before."

"But they called it off!"

"Sure," said Tom. He was blushing. "And d'you know why? 'Cause Grandpa LaPierre objected. And why did he object? 'Cause Mom was pregnant with me!"

"That's not all." I suddenly felt very tired. "That's not all." And I turned away from him, away from my washing, and walked slowly back up to the house.

That's not all. That's not all. What other terrible knowledge did I possess? What was that other elusive memory, more horrific, perhaps, than all the others? I remembered then, but could not remember now, however hard I might try.

33

Inspector Roberts waited while I pulled myself together, gasping air to my soul.

My effort to collect myself was assisted by the welcome sound of Roy's voice shouting in the next office. "*Where the hell's Roberts*?"

"In his office, sir, but he has someone in there right—" The inner door crashed open.

"You son of a bitch, Roberts!" Roy yelled as he entered. "I should've known better than to trust you!"

"Hey! Calm down, Roy!" barked the inspector. "And that's a warning!"

"What the hell are you doing to her, putting her through the third degree?"

"We received a formal complaint—"

"You'd better have it in writing!"

"—forwarded from the city police. We agreed to handle it." What a contrast to their first confrontation in the hospital!

There was a sharp rap on the door, which opened again, and Constable Evarts stood there, filling it. "Everything all right, Sir?" the constable asked Roberts.

"No, everything is *not* all right!" snapped Roy. "Why the hell don't you go out and entrap somebody else! I'm not kidding!

Any more shit like this, Roberts, and *I'm* going to register a formal complaint!"

Evarts remained standing in the doorway. His secretary poked her head in around him. "You have another visitor, Inspector," she said.

"Give me a minute. Roy, as I explained to Sister Jane here, we have to respond to formal complaints—"

"Especially when it's from the groom at a wedding," I added. "Tom says I'm an imposter!"

"I know. When Margo found out what he'd done, she had a fit. She insisted on coming here with me."

"Thank you, Constable Evarts," said Roberts. "That will be all."

As Evarts turned to leave, Margo swept by him, an albino luna moth looking stunning in her bridal gown. She closed the door behind her. Her eyes were red and face puffy from crying.

"Tom didn't give you guys the straight goods," she said. "Emily isn't impersonating anybody! I'm sorry, Emmy!" she added to me. "I don't know what's come over him!"

"You left your own wedding reception?" I replied, astounded. "For *me*?"

"He had no right to complain to the police. You were my guest, my only relative, you're my sister!"

I watched the two men communicate straight across, a facial ballet without words.

"Emmy?" said Roberts at last. "Who's Emmy? Surely not Emily *Thompson*, your sister, one of the kids you were convicted of killing!" The silence was palpable. "Think about it," he continued. "If it ever became obvious that the *original* Emily Thompson was alive, we would have to open up the investigation all over again." He glanced at Roy. "And after challenging Dr. Sutcliffe the way you did a few months ago, he would have both our balls even for *suggesting* that he can't count heads!"

"It's my duty to expose the truth," said Roy. "Yours, too! So if that's what it takes!"

"What 'truth'? Your theories? They've got us nowhere. My duty is to expose the *facts*."

"Then *do* it," I said.

"All right." He swiveled once more in his chair, returning to face us with yet another file in his hands. He opened it. "Remember, at the time, we merely wanted to determine whether you were Tom Campbell's mother. We didn't get these results until after you'd flown the coop, so to speak. 'Mitochondrial DNA comparison between Thomas Campbell and Sister Jane Doe, also known as Margaret Campbell.' Do you want me to continue?"

I nodded eagerly.

"And you don't mind my disclosing the results to present company?"

I glanced at Margo. "No. I have nothing to hide."

"There's a greater than ninety percent chance that you are *not* his mother."

"Only ninety-nine percent?" said Roy. "What happened to the usual 99.99999?"

"While you and Tom share a lot of DNA," Roberts told me, ignoring Roy, "you are not likely his mother."

"So what's our relationship?"

"It doesn't say. We didn't ask."

"He's our cousin," said Margo. "Half-cousin, actually. Any closer and we wouldn't have gotten married."

"There you go."

Alice bubbled to the surface. "So I could be his aunt?"

"You are not my mother!" Margo expostulated.

"Thank you," said Roy.

"Remember, they're only looking at the mitochondrial DNA," said Roberts. "In fact there's a note here that says a more detailed analysis of RecQ is essential. That's a gene associated with premature aging."

"Not surprising after all she's been through—but she's definitely my *sister*!" exclaimed Margo.

Inspector Roberts regarded her with barely veiled contempt. "Emily Thompson is dead. Read my lips!"

I began to remonstrate, but Roy took me by the arm. "*Jane*," he warned me, "don't say another word!"

What had I missed? Why did I feel that a door had slammed shut, even as another—several others—had creaked open?

Roy escorted me out the door and around the rigid Constable Evarts, who stood on guard outside it. Another policeman was waiting in the outer office with the secretary. All three stared at us as Roy pushed past them for all the world like a professional bodyguard. We stepped in pace through the door into the hallway. Margo trotted behind, trying to keep up.

"Oh, Sister Jane," called the inspector, "you forgot to swear your affidavit!"

"Shove it up your ass!" yelled Farquhar as we marched briskly down the hall.

34

“We’d better get you back to the reception,” said Roy to Margo as he held open the main door of the police station. “The guests will be waiting to see you off.”

“Where are you going for your honeymoon?” I asked her.

“Sylvan Lake for a couple of days, then Camas.”

“Camas Lake? But there’s nothing there,” said Roy. “Both houses have burned to the ground.”

“Tom wants to rebuild eventually, if we’re allowed. He wants to take in a prefab package, then live in the studio or in a tent next summer while we start to build the house. That’s what’s in store for me!”

“What about the baby?”

“Oh, we’ll come back to Edmonton long before then!”

“It’s June—still a little chilly for camping in the mountains,” said Roy.

“I know. So this’ll be a short trip. We’ll take stock, look around, measure the foundations, see if there’s anything salvageable—that sort of thing.”

“Some honeymoon!”

A blue sedan bedecked with white plastic pom-poms pulled into the parking lot beside us. The best man was driving with

Tom riding shotgun. Tom climbed out and limped across the tarmac toward us, still dressed in his tux.

"Margie?" he yelled. "Jesus Christ, Roy—I can't believe you brought her here in the middle of her wedding!" He limped past him to Margo's side. "I'm sorry, Honey!"

"It's not me you should apologize to!"

Tom glanced at me, then closed his eyes in frustration. "You're right, I wasn't thinking. I shouldn't have phoned the police. I should've let you handle it. Okay? I didn't realize you'd be so upset. But we have guests waitin' for us to lead off the dance. So let's get back to The Ship to enjoy whatever the fuck's left of our wedding day!"

"Apologize to Emily right now, or I'm getting the marriage annulled before it's even filed!"

"Christ!" He glanced at me. "Look, I'm sorry, okay?" Then he turned back to Margo. "But this is the whole of the rest of our lives we're talkin'! I mean, you're carryin' my child for Christ's sake!"

"'I'm sorry, Emily,'" Margo coaxed him.

"I've already fuckin' apologized to her!"

"Say it again, and this time, *mean* it!"

He glanced at me with one eye, struggled with himself, then turned and limped back to the car. "Fuck you!" he said as he climbed back into the sedan.

"Not likely!" But she followed him to the car. The best man jumped out and opened the back door for her. Careful of her dress, she got in and quickly rolled down the window.

"Listen, we're not going back to the reception," said Roy, craning to look into the darkness of the car beyond the best man. "We're heading home to Red Deer. I just want to thank you both for inviting us to the wedding—and for all your help in researching my book. And to say that I'm sorry for the balls-up. I honestly thought Maggie was your mother."

"Maggie *was* my mother," said Tom. "*She* is not!"

"Anyway, in case we don't see you again, congratulations!" He reached in through the rear window to squeeze Margo's arm. "Best wishes," he said.

That made Margo cry. With her smudged makeup and bedraggled hair all awry, she looked as thoroughly defeated as I had in the women's washroom.

It was my turn to comfort her. Standing beside Roy, I leaned over to look at her through her open window.

"Thanks," I said, "for standing up for me like that."

She grasped both my hands. "Believe me, you *are* Emily. And Tom has every reason to be mad at you."

Tom shook his head in apparent consternation.

"Stay in touch," Margo whispered. "Roy has my address." Then: "I'll look you up in Red Deer on the way back. We'll get together again soon, and *really* talk!" She caressed the scarred skin of my face with the balls of her thumbs. Then holding my face in her slender fingers, she closed her eyes and kissed me full on the lips. I felt my lips yield, and I couldn't help but kiss her back. "Love ya!" she whispered, breaking off the kiss. She glanced over my shoulder at Roy, who had retreated several paces to stand beside Bolts. "Be careful," she murmured in my ear. "He's a slippery one!"

Puzzled, I waved her out of sight, then got into Bolts beside Roy, my white knight. He looked me up and down, focusing on my belly. "Margo said you told her you're pregnant," he said tersely, now that we were alone. "Why the hell didn't you say something?"

I shrugged. "I thought you would figure it out."

"As if! How far are you along?"

"Six months. It must've been that first time. Remember? When I was so upset? I haven't had a period since."

"Fuck, fuck, *fuck*! We'll have to have it aborted."

"Too late for that. Besides, I don't want 'it' aborted!"

"How are you going to take care of it?"

"Well, I was hoping that *we* could make a family, the three of us."

"Look at yourself, Emily. Do you really think you're ready for motherhood?"

"I'll make a great mother!" I said confidently.

"Great mother! You don't even know who you are, for Christ's sake! And nor do I!"

35

My brush with the police, Roy and Margo's rather bold "rescue" of me, the confrontation with Tom, Margo's too-familiar kiss, and Roy's seeming rejection of my essential Self including the fetus within—all these events conspired to trigger in my mind a flurry of remembrances, reconstructions of similar confrontations midway through that horrible summer at Camas Lake. In my mind's eye, the house echoed and reechoed as I strode to the front door. Tom ran toward me across the lawn.

"Emily!" he yelled. He stood pale and quaking as I confronted him, his eyes all over the place. He backed away from me, arms out in a hyper-extended plea. "No! Oh, no!"

The other boys approached from the barn. I leered at them with a determined frown and raised my voice so that all could hear. "You listen, all of you," I cried, suddenly brave. "From now on you boys are not to come anywhere near our cabin, or else! You're to stay in your own cabin, and we girls will stay in ours. Don't even think about coming up here!"

The boys stopped, waiting for Tom's answer to this edict. As the oldest, he was their spokesman. But he had nothing to say. Instead, he led a calm retreat down the path toward the other house, Roger, Billy, and Willis falling into stride beside him, plying him with questions.

I stepped back into the house and slammed the door, then stood watching out the window, trembling like an aspen leaf. *The bluff had worked!*

There was so much to do before the other girls got home. Sandra and Colleen were not that far away down the trail. Was Margo with them? What did it matter? I had already committed them by my declaration to be a part of a new political *mise en scene*.

I searched through the kitchen drawers until I found a padlock to secure the old slide bolt on the master bedroom door. The bolt had been painted open and had not been used for years. I hammered it over into the hole with the heel of my shoe. Then I slammed the kitchen drawers shut, and the back door, bolting it too from the inside. Hearing familiar female voices, I glanced out the kitchen window. All three girls were yapping away, oblivious to their newfound independence. I stuck my head out the front door and looked around. Coast clear.

"You girls'd better get in here before they come back!" I yelled.

"Why? What happened?" asked Margo. She carried an armload of irises and other flowers.

"The boys tried to raid the place."

Margo glanced around the living room as she sauntered through it into the kitchen. "Where's Mum?" she asked.

"Gone back to the studio with Uncle Phil," I mumbled.

"I can't believe she's still letting you wear her dress." She poured some water from a bucket into a vase and began to arrange the irises.

"Where did you get those?" I demanded, knowing damn well where.

"D-daddy say pick 'em," said Colleen defensively.

"Yeah, we met Uncle Phil on the trail," said Margo.

"When?"

"Couple hours ago. He told us about this cool place to pick a bouquet of flowers for Mum—wild irises and water lilies—no death camas, right Colley?"

Colleen laughed knowingly.

"Took longer than we thought. They were hard to get at. But they're just gorgeous, aren't they?"

"Had to walk right round to the far end of the pond," said Sandy. "I got a soaker. Hey, how come this door is locked?"

"Mummy locked it. The boys tried to steal the supplies."

Margo glanced at the bolted door to the master bedroom, puzzled. "There's a latch on the trap door. Why not just lock *it*?"

"It broke off."

"No way!"

"This is the first line of defense against the boys. This way they can't break into the cellar and steal our food again."

"We're not at war, for God's sake!" said Margo.

"Yes we are." I put the key to the padlock in my pocket. Later I made a necklace for it out of braided cotton thread.

At supper, I gloomily picked over my scalloped potatoes and ignored the meat. When Margo persisted in asking the exact nature of our quarrel with the boys, I slammed out of the kitchen into the living room and lay down on the sofa, nursing a chronic migraine. The other girls whispered in the kitchen.

I could not sleep. I hallucinated my father's eyes, staring at destiny for that last God-awful second as his plane careened into the verge of the slough, smashing into a tree, lopping off a wing. Did he have any inkling as to who or what had killed him? I imagined a bloodied Aunt Margaret, too, refusing to give up the ghost. And a thousand times a vision of fused flesh flared into my mind. Tensed against the nightmare of retribution, I felt a rat inside my head gnawing its way out through the cracked skull, starting at the temples and working around inside the sutures, a terrible pressure on each side and the top behind my eyes, a sick headache that seemed to clasp my throat low down as well. My whole brain throbbed red, the vision of merging flesh pulsing behind my eyes, red on black, larger, larger, the little eyes inspecting me, dilated yet beady, close together, until the whole redness of the flesh was nothing but eyes, eyes,

eyes, bloodshot and horrible, an eye among a thousand eyes, all staring, leering, yet dreadful in the genuineness of their remorse, until they streamed past me becoming one huge Horus eye, the eye of Polyphemus in the center, spreading and spreading until it engulfed my being.

36

The next morning, Margo freaked out when she realized that the bedroom door was still padlocked from the outside: obviously, Mum had not come home the night before.

"Where did Mum and Uncle Phil say they were going?" she demanded, shaking me awake. Sandra and Colleen stood in the living room archway.

"Back to the studio," I replied. "Where do you think?"

"Why would she lock her door like that?"

"I told you – she doesn't trust the boys."

"More like, she doesn't trust *any* of us!" said Sandra.

I dangled the key in front of them. "She trusted me. I'm the gatekeeper."

"*Wha-at?*" exclaimed Margo.

"I promised to protect you from the boys."

"Why, what did they do? What *exactly* did they do?"

"What d'ya mean? They *shot* you," I said. "You've got the pellet in your leg to prove it."

"It was a BB. It stuck in my skin, just below the surface. I squeezed it out."

She meant it as a denial, but I took it as an affirmation. "See?"

"B-Billy p-push me," said Colleen.

"Me too!" said Sandra.

Colleen's good eye made a complete circle of the room. "I hate b-boys!"

"You guys're putting wrong ideas in Colley's head," said Margo.

"Anyway, we shouldn't have any more problems. I've told the boys to stay down at the other house. They're not to come up here at all. The laneway's the border."

Sandy cheered. Margo groaned.

Later, Margo conducted a brief search of the kitchen cupboards. "What're we eating tonight?" she asked.

"There's more of that porky casserole on the counter."

"Yuck. It tastes like spruce needles," said Sandy.

"What I mean is, we're almost out of supplies up here," said Margo. "Just soup and baked beans, a little rice, and spaghetti, but no sauce. And the boys will need some supplies."

"Fuck the boys!" I snapped. "We're not giving 'em *anything*! There's not enough to go 'round."

"What d'you mean? There's tons of tinned food down in the cellar—flat upon flat of soup! Gimme the key, I'll go get some."

"I'll stock up when we need to, when it's safe!"

Margo glanced out the window. "It's safe *now*."

"We have to train them to stay down at their own house. Including Billy and Roger."

"Billy p-push me," said Colleen. "So did Rog!"

"Yeah," said Sandra, "and Willis punched me again and again, and we had to hide in the outhouse, Colley an' me, didn't we, Colley?"

Colleen nodded emphatically. "We almos' coulda d-died!"

"That's nothing," I said. "Roger actually *shot* Margo. Show her the bullet hole, Margo."

"It was a BB pellet!"

"*And* Willis pulled you off that top bunk," said Sandra.

"Well at least you weren't *raped*," I said. "I was *raped*!"

That was a conversation-stopper.

"When?" said Margo.

"What's 'rape'?" asked Colleen.

"Just about the worst thing that can happen to a woman," said Margo, fixing me with a skeptical eye. "It's when a boy forces a girl to have sex against her will."

That was Margo for you. Clarity. Simplicity so slick it made me sick. No wonder my mother wept!

"It wasn't a boy. It was a *man*." I looked up at Colleen, loathing her for being Philip Campbell's daughter, wanting her to share my pain. "I kicked and screamed, trying to get him off me. He covered my lips with his own filthy germy stinky mouth. I couldn't breathe. With one hand he lifted up my nightdress and yanked down my panties. His cock was already big and hard. He cleared his sinuses, spat his snot into his hand, reached down, and lathered me with it. He forced a filthy finger inside me, lined himself up—and wedged his cock right into me, splitting and tearing me open 'til I bled!" I covered my face with my hands. "It hurt so much! So, so much! So much I threw up! And all the time he was tearing me apart, he said he was doing it because he loved my fucking *mother*! '*Alice! Alice! Oh, Alice!*'" I burst into tears. "That's what rape is!"

Margo put her arm around my shuddering shoulders. "Oh, Jesus, Emmy. Not Uncle Phil!"

"*Yes, Uncle Phil!*"

My scream commanded silence. Then Sandra joined Margo in hugging me. But Colleen would have none of it.

"*D-daddy*?" she whimpered in disbelief.

I nodded and blew my nose. Put on a brave face. "And Tom tried it too," I added.

"Tom?" said Margo. "No!"

"Yes! I fought him off, but—" I could see I was losing credibility. "So you have a choice," I said quietly. "You can still go and join the boys if you want to. But of course, they wouldn't trust you because you're a girl. Certainly Willis wouldn't. I mean, would you trust him? And of course if you went over to them, we couldn't guarantee your safety, because we couldn't trust you, either. You'd be a traitor, you see."

"What's 'traitor'?" asked Colleen.

"A scab. A scumbag."

"I'm staying with Emmy!" said Sandy.

"Me too, me too!" said Colleen.

"Okay, you can stay. But only if you do exactly as I say."

Another pause. Then Sandra's words ripped the silence like paper: "I don't know how women could ever marry men!"

"Nor do I," I admitted.

"Jeez, guys," said Margo. "I mean—they're not *all* like that!"

"Around here they are!"

Suddenly, there was a loud knock on the front door. Reflexively we screamed and scattered in all directions—even Margo. "It's *them*!" squealed Sandy.

I approached the door, trembling.

"Who is it?"

"Tom."

"What d'you want?" I barked.

"Willis's clothing and some food."

I looked out of the window to make sure that Tom was alone on the verandah. The three other boys stood well back on the far side of the laneway near the trail which led down to their house. "Go stand with the others," I yelled through the glass. "We'll gather up his clothes."

Tom retreated halfway across the front lawn. I gestured to Margo to get the clothes, and she dumped the top drawer of the dresser into a green plastic garbage bag.

"Get back farther!" I shouted from the shadow of the house.

"Can we talk?" asked Tom.

"What about?"

"About us livin' all together, sharin' chores."

"There's nothing to talk about!"

"Yes there is! Look, we don't have no food down at our house."

"Hunt some. That's what 'men' are good at, isn't it? Hunting?"

"We don't have guns. Just useless shells."

"You've got Roger's gun, you liar!" shouted Sandra accusingly from the door.

"It's a BB gun! Can't even kill sparrows with that!"

"Then go fish," I suggested bluntly.

"Yeah," said Sandy. "Go 'Fish'!"

"Where's the shotgun?" Tom asked.

"It's right here," I yelled from the shadows, holding a broomstick against my waist. Margo glanced back and saw the bluff. She grinned. "You stay back," I yelled, "or I'll pull the triggers!"

"Look, you give us the gun and we'll hunt for you, and you can cook for us. That's the way it should be."

"Male chauvinist pig!" I screamed, advancing to the door.

Tom retreated halfway to the laneway, then turned. "Can't we all be friends?"

"Brothers and sisters?" I said ironically.

"Yes! It ain't natural, dividing ourselves up like this!"

"This is our country!" cried Sandra from just inside the door. "Go home!"

"That's crazy," said Tom. "This whole area belongs to all of us."

"This a g-girl house!" piped in Colleen. "Right, Emmy?"

"Right!"

"Colley, Sweetie—"

"We hate b-boys!"

Tom's shoulders drooped in despair. Resigned to our decision, he returned to his main refrain: "Can you spare us just a little food?"

"Why don't you eat the dead cow?" I asked, lowering the broom.

"She's all flies. She stinks!"

"For God's sake, Emily!" sighed Margo. "There's plenty of food in the cellar for everyone."

"Yeah, there's food in the cellar in your house," chimed Sandra.

"We don't have a cellar—just a crawl space full of junk. There's no food in it, trust me!"

"We want food!" Willis chanted. "We want food! We want food!" But nobody joined him in the chant.

"Dad shot that porky for all of us!" added Roger.

"That's a thought," said Margo. "Let's give 'em the rest of the casserole!"

I nodded. We all hated porcupine meat—it was stringy and strong. Besides, I was not much good at negotiations, especially this kind of brinksmanship.

"Go back and wait with the others," I said to Tom hoarsely. He returned to the edge of the lane, standing silent and dejected, in contrast to the other boys, who stood in eager expectation. Then Margo stepped out of the house with the garbage bag full of Willis's clothes. "Go back farther!" I shouted to the boys. "The trail's the boundary."

They obeyed. Margo walked toward them, placed the bag among the trodden-down grass and camas in the center of the trail, and trotted back to the house. Willis streaked forward, grabbed the bag, and ran back to the others. He rummaged. "Hey, there's no food in here!" he yelled.

"It's coming, greedy-guts!" shouted Sandra, holding the casserole dish before her.

"Willis, this time you just keep back and stay there till I tell you, or I'll shoot!" I yelled.

Sandra carried the dish to the center of the laneway. Smelling food, Ragtime and the pregnant Baloney joined her. Sandy tried to shoo them away.

"Don't let them get it!" cried Willis.

"Tom, call off Baloney!" I shouted. "Here, Ragtime! Here, boy!"

Baloney obeyed Tom, but although Ragtime glanced confused at the open door, he pranced around Sandra excitedly, leaping up at the bowl.

"Call him off!" she squealed.

"Set it down and run back here!" I replied.

Sandra did as she was told. But the instant she turned her back to run, Ragtime threw off the lid and had his muzzle deep into the food, guzzling it. Willis gave him a kick in the ribs that lifted him a foot in the air. Yelping and winded, the dog limped out of harm's way, tail between his legs.

Tom doled out the food to the other boys and then helped himself.

"Remember," I yelled. "The far side of the laneway is the border!"

Chewing greedily, the boys descended the footpath to their residence.

"Hey, good bluff!" laughed Margo, holding the broom to her shoulder. "Pow! Pow!"

"But how long will it last?"

We needed to get serious. We needed to purge the boys from the valley. That is what motivated me, eventually, to burn down their house.

37

Later that night, after the younger girls had gone to bed, Margo demanded more information about the rape. I could tell from the skeptical tone of her voice that despite her earlier show of compassion, she did not believe me. Yet I needed her as an ally. I started to cry again. She looked at my dress, my bedraggled appearance, then reached over to hug me.

"It must've been awful! Did you tell Mummy?"

"I wanted to. I tried to. But there's no point. She wouldn't have believed me!"

"Sure she will. She'll put him in his place, if anyone can! Tell her about it, promise? If you don't, I will!"

"It's not that simple!"

"What he did was wrong!"

"It's too late!"

"But Mummy'll know what to do."

"No she won't. She can't do a damn thing! Because she's *dead*."

"Don't be silly!"

"Uncle Phil shot her, don't you see?" I said, working it out. "Murdered her, just like he murdered Dad and Aunt Margaret!"

"Murdered?" She looked at me aghast, then laughed, incredulous. "*Mummy*? No way! Why would he do that to her? Come on, Emily! Can't you see they're in love?"

"You're not listening."

"Well, it's nuts! I just saw Mummy this morning. And, and Uncle Phil—we saw him down at the end of the lane. He told us where to pick those flowers."

"Let me guess. He had his gun with him?"

"The shotgun. Yes."

"I don't know what they had been arguing about, but he came here, out of control, held that shotgun to Mum's head, forced her to undress, and then shot her dead."

"Wha-at?"

"Then he shot himself."

Margo reflected on this, then shuddered as she looked at the locked door, trying to put two and two together.

"How do you know?"

"Because I saw. Saw it all through the crack in the door. Remember how it wouldn't shut?"

"In there?" she said in a hushed voice.

I nodded.

"Can I see?"

Again I nodded, glad to be able to share the awful secret. I stooped low enough for the key hanging from a thread around my neck to fit into the padlock. I opened the door, then lifted the oil lamp higher as we entered the forbidden chamber. It reeked of dead blood.

I could hardly bear to look at the two naked bodies locked together on the bed. They seemed to be in an interminable struggle against gravity, leaning as they were against a corner of the windowsill. The double barrel of the gun pointed toward their bloody temples. Mum's right arm was draped over the barrel of the gun in a leisurely way, as if cradling her favorite possession. Uncle Phil's left arm dangled lower, all business, his forefinger resting on the dual triggers, supporting the weight of the gun.

A blowfly buzzed in the windowpane. Margo shrieked, then started weeping soulfully. I joined her in her contagious wail.

"That's what I've been trying to protect you from!" I cried, nearly as distraught as she. "See his finger? Isn't it clear to you? He raped her, then shot her, then shot himself!"

Trembling, Margo moved closer to the bodies with the lamp. "We have to get the police," she whispered in horror.

"The nearest phone is a hundred kilometers away."

"If we get to the forestry trunk road, there should be trucks with radios. Hey, didn't he have a short wave radio?"

"It's down at the other house."

"We can ask the boys if we can use it. And Mummy has a cell phone. Where's that?"

"In the kitchen. But the battery's dead. There's no way of charging it."

"It plugs into the car's lighter!"

"She left the adapter at home. And in any case, it's out of range. No service."

We stared transfixed at the bodies for several long seconds. Margo knelt on the floor, shoulders drooped in despair, and seemed to pray silently, then leaned against the bed, her hand resting on Mum's arm even as it caressed the barrel of the gun. It was as if Mum recognized in it the agency of peace. Feeling the coldness of their flesh, Margo sobbed for several minutes while I stood there, feeling awkward. What was done was done.

"We should at least cover them," Margo said at last, fanning away another fly. "Lay them out." She tugged on a blood-soaked sheet, but it was under the two bodies, bearing their weight. She waved away the odor of dead blood.

"We can't move them," I said. "We have to let the police see them pretty well the way they are."

Margo looked around the room to drink in other details of the scene. Mum's clothes were neatly stacked in a pile on the armchair, her brassiere on top. Uncle Phil's pants, shirt, and socks, by contrast, lay in an untidy pile beside the bed. She leaned over to examine the gun more closely. "His finger's in backward," she said, poking it.

"Huh?"

She shuddered. "It's cold, just like a glove! But see? The back of his finger is toward the triggers."

"So?"

"So the gun must've discharged accidentally."

"I don't think so. If he shot Mum first and then himself, it must've been deliberate. His hand probably turned that way in a death spasm."

"Unless he flicked the triggers with the top of his finger."

"Two shots, two shells, two triggers," I said. "He killed her with the first shot, killed himself with the second."

Margo held Mum's arm in one hand and nudged Uncle Phil's finger back against one of the triggers with the other. His hand shifted, and the gun slipped off his finger. The shoulder rest bounced off the floor. We both shrieked as Mum's arm lifted, caressing the whole length of the barrel of the gun as it slid toward us. The dead were coming to life!

Margo caught the gun and pulled it free.

"You shouldn't have touched it," I said. "You've seen *CSI*. This is a crime scene, and that's evidence!"

Still holding the gun, Margo looked at me in alarm. Then we both gazed at the bodies on the bed as Mum's arm moved in a subtle arc against Uncle Phil's wrist exactly as if she were feeling for his pulse.

"Well, now you *have* touched it, we'd better hang onto it," I said. "It could come in handy." I laughed grimly. "Beats a broomstick!"

38

That night, neither Margo nor I could sleep, so we visited the cellar to bring up enough canned food to stock our kitchen cupboards. Margo filled a large cardboard box for the boys with a flat of soup and baked beans, a bag of rice, cornflakes, evaporated milk, powdered milk, cocoa, sugar, flour, salt—you name it. We carried it together to the crest of the bluff and left it on the laneway near the path to the lower house. By noon the box had disappeared.

For the rest of that week, peace seemed to come to the valley and the lake. The boys did not challenge our sovereignty in the house up on the hill, and we were not in the least bit interested in challenging them to any more acreage. Although we weren't particularly interested in intruding on their privacy, one evening we did sneak through the long grass at the brow of the hill to see how they spent their time. We heard the noise of glass breaking and the pop of stones hitting wood: the boys at target practice with their slingshots and the air rifle.

In the second week, Tom came up the trail to beg for more food. Colleen, digging in the compost pile, was the first to see him.

"I find w-worm for you go fish!" she cried.

"Thanks, Honey!"

Sandra screamed and ran over to Colleen, dragging our little cousin back to the house. Margo followed slowly. As soon as they were inside, Sandra slammed and locked the door behind them. I glanced out the window to make sure he was alone, then swung open the door.

"All right, Campbell!" I shouted. "Stop right there. You've just crossed the border!" Tom, seeing my determined eyes and the long double-nostriled snout of the shotgun, stopped and sat down in the grass in front of the house. "Back up, you bastard!" I yelled. "Back to the other side of the trail!"

"Come on, Emily. Cut the horseshit!"

"You know the rules! Back up or I'll shoot!"

"Then shoot. I wanna talk."

But I couldn't shoot. He probably had figured that out by then. The only shells I had were the two spent ones in the dual chambers of the gun.

"What d'you want to talk about?"

"What do you think? More food."

"There isn't any more."

"Sure there is," he said. "All them hams and canned meats and vegetables and soup your dad brought in. The cold cellar was near full at the beginning of the summer!"

"We're rationing it."

"Why can't you share?"

"Why should we?"

"Because they're ours as much as they're yours," he said. "They belong to all of us. We'd share anything we caught with you, you know that!"

I sneered at him. "Why don't you hike into Rocky Mountain House, pick up some food of your own?"

"We don't have no money. And it's more'n sixty miles through the bush!"

"You could all go together. And good riddance!"

His voice suddenly had a hard edge: "Would you really want us to do that, Emily?" he asked. "Because the first place we'd go would be to the police!"

"Then fetch the police! We have nothing to hide!"

His eyes widened. "Nor do we," he said quickly. "Margo told me what happened. Dad shot Aunt Alice and then turned the gun on himself. They're gonna want to investigate that."

"You get back to the other house!" I yelled, loathing him. "You'll never, ever get any more food from us!"

I re-entered the house and slammed the door behind me just as the car door slammed, waking me from my reverie. Roy had filled Bolts up with gas at a self-serve station. Soon we were on Highway 2 again, heading south, spewing blue smoke.

39

Bolts came sighing to a halt in the parking lot of our Red Deer apartment building. As I reached back to get my coat and purse from off the back seat, I noticed Margo's bridal bouquet.

"What's this doing here?" I asked.

"She said she forgot to toss it at the church," Roy said as he locked up his side of the car. "Said she wanted you to have it."

"Now *there's* a hint!"

"May as well bring it in."

"Sure. Anything to brighten up the place," I muttered.

But as it turned out, there was no place to brighten up. Almost everything that Roy owned had been stacked on the second floor landing. The landlord had pinned a note prominently to one of the boxes.

> *MR. FUCKWAR. You no pay rent for 3 month, spite our letter. Other tennants complaint you kipping women again rule of hose. I unerstand you no have job and not able pay rent no more. Because aparment scarse alot people wants yours and wiling pay. So this fomal "evicsion notice." Lock change so no try get in. I kip small apliance + dammage deposit cover rent. Rest funiture belong me.*

It was signed with an unreadable scrawl.

"Shit!" said Roy, trying his useless key in the lock. He shouldered the door, but it was bolted solidly against any effort of intrusion. He examined his precious Campbell paintings, stacked unevenly against the foyer wall.

"What are we gonna do?" I asked.

"I don't know."

"Didn't you really pay your rent for three months? Surely we haven't been that short!"

"I'm not 'short' at all! I just forgot."

Before I came along, while he was at the newspaper, he had lived a reasonably comfortable life, content with his bachelor lifestyle, including his apartment and fancy car. Now he had neither. Too proud to approach his parents, he had sold his car to clear up other debts, though I couldn't imagine any more pressing obligation than the rent.

Dejectedly, he opened a couple of the file boxes to check their contents. "Shit, they've thrown all my papers and books into boxes any which way. And look! All our clothes in garbage bags! The food as well." He opened another box. "They've got my tapes and discs all out of order," he sighed. "It'll take some doing to sort everything."

"Never mind the tapes," I said. "What are we going to do with all this junk? And where are we going to sleep tonight?"

"I don't know. Do you have any money on you?"

"About fifty bucks."

"Not enough for a motel. And we might need that money, anyway." He flipped on his phone. "I'll make a couple of phone calls to friends of mine."

"There's an ATM machine at the corner store," I reminded him.

"I'm overdrawn at the bank and my Visa's maxed out."

"Shit, Roy. Really?"

He waved me silent as he spoke into his cell phone, walking away as he talked.

"Do you want me to start loading some of this junk into the car?" I called.

He nodded okay. "Careful with the paintings!"

When he got off the phone, he fished out a set of adjustable racks for the car propped up against the wall in the corner. "We'll just take the essential stuff, leave everything else for Sally Ann," he said. "Let's put the paintings on the back seat."

It was a strange feeling to know that nearly everything practical that two people possess could be loaded into, or more precisely onto, a tiny Toyota Corolla sedan. By the time we had finished packing the first load, the trunk wouldn't shut. Roy secured the three-foot-high pile on the roof with a clothesline purchased at the corner store and a dozen bungee cords.

As we pulled out of the parking lot the car lurched from side to side as if to advertise our plight. We drove to 49th Avenue in silence and turned right to cross the bridge over the Red Deer River. Then we headed north up Highway 2A as if retracing our path to Edmonton. We pulled off into a storage facility and took another half hour to unload the art. We returned to the apartment for a second load, and a third. Finally, we retrieved the camping gear from the storage unit, including tent, sleeping bags, inflatable mattresses, and propane bottles. Our clothes and food were still piled high on the racks.

"Where are we going?" I wondered as we headed even farther north.

"Derek's cottage at Sylvan Lake. Hey, we may be in luck! He landed a job in L.A., doing aerial photography for a real estate firm. They're moving down there in a couple of weeks. I'll hit him up for a loan. Joanie's family's coming in tomorrow from Ontario, but Derek says we can crash there tonight. After that, we're on our own." He shrugged. "Beggars can't be choosers!"

We turned left onto Highway 11A. As we bumped roughly over the Canadian Pacific Railway tracks, the load shifted ominously on top of the car.

"It'll ride," Roy muttered as if he were trying to convince himself. "I'll just take it easy, that's all." We passed over the four-lane Highway 2 and kept heading west, the car straining and struggling up each successive hill; it seemed along this highway that we were riding the top of the world. Lights twinkled to the horizon in every direction.

"What town is that over there?" I asked, pointing to a cluster of lights to the northwest.

"Bentley," he said. "And over beyond that, right on the horizon, Rimbey." He turned to look over his shoulder in the other direction. "And believe it or not, that bunch of lights over there to the south is Innisfail. That's about twenty-five miles away."

"And up ahead," I said, "is a cop, flagging us down."

Roy groaned. "RCMP," he said. "As if we hadn't had our fill of them today!"

It was an Alberta Checkstop, designed to catch impaired and drunk drivers. Roy rolled down his window as he pulled to the shoulder.

"Hello, sir. May I see your driver's license and registration, please?" said the officer.

"Oh, God. I wouldn't know where to look!"

"May I suggest your wallet?"

Roy turned off the ignition to minimize the fumes, then fumbled about in his wallet. Several of his cards fell out onto his lap. "Damn!"

"Have you had anything to drink, sir?"

"No, not since this afternoon. Wedding reception in Edmonton. But I sure could use a stiff one!"

"Would you please step out of the car, sir?"

"Sure."

"You know there's a minimum fifty-dollar fine for hauling uncovered garbage?"

"Garbage! Oh, yeah." He patted a garbage bag tied to the roof. "Would you believe these are my household possessions?"

"And a minimum one-hundred-dollar fine for excessive fumes."

"You're kidding!"

"I'll let you off with a warning—but you'll have to have your muffler fixed and report back a week from today. You can bring in your license and registration along with your car for a follow-up check." He began to fill out a warning ticket as a second policeman sauntered up. He immediately recognized Roy as a newspaper reporter.

"What's the problem?" he asked.

"Hi, Paul!" said Roy. "Can't find my damn license."

"He's press," Paul explained to the cop who had stopped us.

"I know. He flashed me his press card." Then he added in an undertone, "That's what peed me off, arrogant son of a bitch!"

"I'll handle it."

The first officer grunted and moved on to the next car. I shuffled through the cards on the driver's seat. "Here it is!" I called out the window.

"Ah, thanks, uh, Thomasina," said Roy. "We're moving today. Out to Sylvan Lake. Came back from Edmonton to an eviction notice, if you can imagine that!"

Paul laughed. "Just not your day! You have the pink insurance slip?"

"Yeah. Em—uh, Thom, could you reach into the glove compartment there?"

I retrieved the temporary ownership slip. "It's registered in my name," I said. "I've just owned this car for a couple of months. I know it needs work. Roy's just driving it for me because of the heavy load. Guess I didn't tie it on very securely."

Paul did a double-take, staring at my wrinkled face. He shuddered. "Fine, Miss Allison," he said, handing back my documents. He eyeballed the pile above us. "Just one thing. Garbage—"

"—has to be covered or it's a fifty-dollar fine," I parroted brightly. "Yeah, your partner told us. Thanks for the break!"

40

It was after midnight when we arrived at Derek Saunders's cottage not far from the lake. He and Joanie were still up listening to CDs, an open bottle of Mateus on the table between their flaccid beanbag chairs. "C'mon in!" Derek called. "We're already blasted, so youse guys've got some catchin' up t'do!"

As far as I can remember, I had never toked up on marijuana before. Before we even had a chance to sit down in the smoke-filled inner sanctum Derek passed a joint to Roy, who took it and inhaled the smoke deeply several times, and then held his breath. He passed the smoldering joint to me. I took a puff or two. The smoke grated in my throat. I coughed.

"Take another toke, Thomasina!" Derek whined off the top of his breath. I did, and then passed it to him. He took a deep draw so that the end of the paper flared in the gloaming, and then passed it to Joanie. She in turn inhaled deeply and passed it back to Roy, who followed suit, and it came back to me. This time it went out, and Derek had to light it again, holding the browning paper between the prongs of a hairpin. "Joanie, it's your turn to rescue some hash from the stash!"

Joan pulled aside a Persian area rug and lifted a trap door, then descended steel rungs inside the concrete well. "*Ding dong bell! Pussy's in the well!*" Derek sang as she disappeared down the hole. "Bring up a bottle o' wine, too, Honey. That ol' well's our wine cellar, cold cellar an' stash all rolled up into one," he explained. "Talkin' of which, here, you may's well get started on this li'l fatty!" He handed Roy another lit joint and Roy inhaled, then passed it to me. I took a tentative puff and coughed again.

I already felt light-headed. I gazed down into the bowels of the dry well as Joanie emerged with a bottle of wine and a vial of hash oil. Derek handed her the fat joint and she inhaled deeply as if savoring a steak. She handed the joint to me, and absently I took it.

I was mesmerized by that trapdoor. I recalled the trapdoor in my mother's bedroom at Camas Lake, which had witnessed such horrors with its Horus eye. Indeed, the well holds a certain fascination for me to this day, even though since moving in here I have nailed down the trapdoor securely, for safety's sake. Little Philip and Alicia are precocious kindergarteners now, and mothers can't be too careful. The floor is now covered with battleship linoleum, quality underlay, and a dense wall-to-wall shag.

The others broke up at my seeming preoccupation as I watched Joan close the trapdoor and unroll the rug over it.

"Sure you don't want another toke, Thom?" Derek asked me. "There's plenty!"

"No thanks," I said absently. "I've had enough." Derek and Joanie thought that was the most hilarious thing they'd heard in years.

There was an awkward silence.

"Then, d'you mind sharin', Honey?" asked Derek.

It hadn't registered that I was still holding the joint. Joanie whooped with laugher and Derek snorted. Roy, too, chuckled and the candles flickered and the music crashed into the room. Too quickly, I handed the cold joint to Derek, then, thoroughly humiliated, stood up—and immediately fell flat on my ass.

"Oooh, you okay, Honey?" said Joanie.

"She jus' lost her balance," said Roy.

"No, I di'n't lose my balance," I slurred as I carefully regained my feet using the wall for support. "I jus' never found it."

They laughed all the harder. I couldn't do or say anything right, it seemed.

"Goo'night," I said. "I'm real bushed! Where do I crash out?" And then: "Comin', Roy?"

"I'll be along, Thom," he said.

Joanie hooted. "Well I'll be a Long Tom!" she cried.

Roy cracked up. "And a Long Tom I shall be-oh!" he sang. "You better believe it!"

I stood self-consciously in the doorway. "Don' call me Tom, 'kay?" I slurred. "I'm *Thomasina*!" All three of them screeched with laughter.

"Yeah, that's the long and short of it," said Roy with sudden sobriety. He joined the other two in what seemed an interminable chant: "Tom! Tom! Tom! Tom! Tom! Tom! Tom! Tom! Tom! Tom! Tom! Tom! Tom! Tom! Tom!" Then, in a mocking falsetto: "Thom-a-*seeeeee*-na!"

Fuck them! Fuck them all!

41

The next morning I awoke to the mingled aroma of fresh coffee, well-cooked bacon, and buttered toast. Joanie's kitchen sounds were as welcome as the rich scents that filled the air, and I had a strange sense of having returned home at last. For a fleeting second I imagined my mother in the kitchen, and then, recalling where we were, reached a different level of *déjà vu* as I relived an earlier visit to Sylvan Lake, long a favorite Alberta holiday destination. Margo and I had paddled in a rented canoe out past the swimmers. We were horsing around, splashing each other with our paddles, and both of us twisted in the same direction at the same time so the canoe tipped. Margo, never a strong swimmer, was terrified, sure that we would never make it back to the shore. She had clung to the canoe and I had gone out ahead, swimming, the rope tied around my waist. We hadn't gone more than twenty meters when, still a hundred meters out from shore, I could touch bottom and I waded all the way back to the beach. Meanwhile, my mother, who had been watching us, ran frantically down the beach for a lifeguard, in the process assembling a small army to rescue us. She stood there in shame and confusion at the bluster and fluster she had created as we waded to shore.

I remembered too that other time when we girls had made a huge sandcastle on the beach and Willis had jumped on it because it was the biggest and best, and his own castle kept crumbling as the sand dried.

Back in the present, Roy leaned over and kissed me. I gave him an exuberant hug, pressing his naked chest against my breasts, and kissed him back. I held his penis, felt it stir.

"I think breakfast is almost ready," I whispered, feeling him grow larger in my hand. "Otherwise . . ."

He ran his hand from my breasts to my round belly. "Boy or girl?" he asked.

"How should I know?"

"What's your best guess?"

"She's too well-behaved to be a boy."

"Just wait a month or two!"

I flopped over on the bed, clutching a pillow between my legs.

"Yesterday seems like such a dream," I said.

He yawned. "Grass does that."

"No, no. I mean the whole day. The wedding, the police station, the eviction, the trip here."

". . . The trip after we got here . . ."

"Where are we going to live? Where are you going to work without an apartment or any place to go?"

"I talked to Derek and Joanie last night after you turned in. There's a very good chance we can take over this place at the end of the month, once they head out to L.A. All we'd have to pay is utilities and taxes. They'll be gone at least a year."

"End of the month? Sounds great, but what're we going to do until then?"

"We'll join Tom and Margo—camp at Camas Lake." It came as a pronouncement. "It's the logical place for me to finish my research. And I've got to finish this book. It'll be my only source of income. I've got a contract with the publisher in Edmonton and he wants to see the manuscript by August, otherwise I don't get advance royalties against expenses. I have to go back to Camas Lake anyway, to get a feel for the country again. It's been nearly six years."

"I lived there for most of those years," I said. "Suppose I don't want to go back?"

"You said you loved the woods!"

"Do you have any idea how lonely it was?"

"Even with Tuanahaki?"

I was about to counter when Derek called the reveille: "Hey, lovebirds! Breakfast's ready when you are!"

We sat around the drop-leaf table in the kitchen, first savoring and then devouring the grilled bacon, fried eggs, and buttered toast, and drank orange juice and coffee.

"What time do your guests arrive?" I asked Joanie.

"This afternoon some time," she said. "It's my sister and her family from Ontario. She's straight as a nasal hair. They're on their way out to the coast. Lots of kids. Hey, stay, if you think you can hack the racket."

"We'll be heading out about noon," said Roy firmly.

"Where're you going?"

"Camas Lake, southwest of Rocky. Remember those pictures you took, Derek? There's one I want to use for the cover of my book, the one with the fish-eye lens. I'll give you full credits and everything."

"Sure. Full credits and everything—but *cash*!" joked Derek.

"Hey, you won't be short of that in Hollywood!"

"What's your book about again?" asked Joanie.

"It's a biography of Philip Campbell."

"My uncle."

Derek and Joanie looked at me in surprise.

"The artist," said Derek. "But you already did one on him. I took some of the photographs of his paintings."

"That was a coffee-table book of his art. This is a biography—although there will be some overlap. I'll re-use some of your images, give you credit. And royalties, of course. In fact, the way things are going, it'll be illustrated with dozens of his paintings. I'm trying to make it popular enough for the general reader to pick up."

"Well, as I said last night, when you're finished out in the West Country, c'mon back and set up house," said Derek. He slapped a house key on the table. "We'll be long gone! You pay the taxes and utilities and maintain the place, and we'll be happier'n pigs in shit!" He laughed. "We'll even leave you our stash!"

"Don't want to be caught with *that* at the border!" said Joanie.

Roy grinned. "*Ve'll be back*!" he said in his best Arnold Schwarzenegger imitation. He pocketed the key.

After breakfast, I took Roy on a guided tour of what I recalled of my old holiday haunts along the lakefront. We crossed the main road to the beach and sauntered across the grass, breathing in the fresh breeze that purified the shoreline. The lake side of the highway—a public park with lush lawns and trees—contrasted with the strip of false-fronted shack-like vending outlets on the other side. But closer to the center of the village, the shacks had been supplanted with a row of modern motels.

We had just drawn parallel with one of them when we heard a sharp shriek of tires. A blue sedan with white dots of plastic pom-poms burned rubber as it pulled out of the gravel parking lot, turned left onto the pavement, and took off up the road away from us. It sported a tattered cardboard sign on the trunk and bumper: *Just married.*

"That was Tom and Margo!" cried Roy. "I'm sure it was. That's their car!"

"Margo said they were coming here for their honeymoon."

The car disappeared around the curve behind the trees, so that we caught only glimpses of it as it skirted the lake, clearly exceeding the speed limit as it headed west past the government wharf.

"Wherever they're going, they're in a hurry," said Roy as he strode across the road toward the motel. "C'mon! Let's check it out!"

"Roy, you're not a reporter anymore!"

"No, but I'm still his father's biographer!"

42

A tired-looking middle-aged lady answered the ring of the counter bell. “Excuse me, could you tell me what room Mr. and Mrs. Tom Campbell are in?” Roy asked.

“That’s easy. Room 201. The bridal suite. Right upstairs, above *our* apartment.”

Roy laughed. “They were busy last night, huh? Any idea how long they’ll be here?”

“They booked it for the week to get the cheap rate. Paid in advance, too, more’s the pity. Are you, uh, friends of the newlyweds?”

“Relatives,” I said with a grim smile. “I’m their sister.”

She looked at my wrinkled face. I still looked twenty years older than either of them.

“His sister or hers?”

“Both.”

“But they told us they were married!”

“They are. I’m half-sister to both of them.”

“Different parents,” Roy explained. “It’s complicated.”

“Well, they’re off to a rocky start. I don’t mind a little lovemaking, banging of beds, that sort of thing. That’s expected. But they’ve been at it all night!”

"This is a *good* thing on your wedding night," said Roy.

"When she's eight months pregnant?" I said, alarmed.

"No, no! They weren't making love. They were *fighting* all night long. Arguing back and forth, calling each other down, throwing things—I hate to think what. Kept us awake all night. My husband didn't get to sleep until four a.m. Sorry, nor did I. That's why I feel a little cranky this morning. And we have to put up with this for a week?"

"You didn't complain?"

"Who to? We own the damn place!"

"We saw them take off a few minutes ago," said Roy.

"*He* took off, cussing and swearing all the way to his car, spewed gravel getting out of here—just look at that rut! See the black tire marks where the gravel becomes pavement? That's him! Left rubber twenty feet down the highway!"

"So *she's* here still?"

"Must be." She cocked an ear to the ceiling. "I don't know. It's awful quiet up there compared to what it was!"

"Can we go up?"

"Be my guest. Want me to phone first?"

"Might be an idea," said Roy.

We could hear the phone ringing distantly upstairs, but no one answered it.

"You have a master key?" asked Roy. "We'd better go up, take a look. Do you mind?"

"Should I phone the police?"

"No, no, that won't be necessary. But we should check to see if everything's all right, don't you think?"

"She's my sister," I reminded her.

A *Do Not Disturb* sign hung from the doorknob. The manager tapped on the doorframe, then rapped more loudly on the door. "Housekeeping. Ms. Campbell?" She waited a couple of seconds, then unlocked the door with the master key. Opening the door, she knocked again on the wall. “Ms. Campbell?” She paused for a moment. “She must've gone out. Funny, I didn't see her leave. Unless she took off last night. I wouldn't blame her, poor soul.”

“What were they arguing about?” I asked as I pushed the door fully open. Roy followed me into the suite.

“Most of it was too muffled to hear the words. I gather she didn't want to go somewhere with him to the lake.”

“Camas Lake?”

“Well I assumed Sylvan. And at one point she let the whole neighborhood know she didn't want his blankety-blank baby. Which it's kind of late to worry about that sort of thing, I should think. You say she's eight months?”

“At least,” I said.

I scanned the room. Except for one dented lampshade, the table lamps were intact. One of the chairs had tipped over on its side against the king-size bed. Scattered shoes included a man's running shoe, a lady's pump, and a pair of hiking boots. Two matching Samsonite suitcases lay on the floor, the open one spewing its contents, including an open pink floral toiletry case, Secret deodorant, and a bag of pink disposable razors.

The main bed, while turned down and rumpled, had not been used. By contrast, an open hide-a-bed at the far end of the room had been slept in.

“Do you mind if we go through it, while you're here?” I asked.

The manager shook her head.

“Margo?” I called into the kitchenette. Then I tried a door. It was locked.

“Where's the bathroom?”

“That's it.”

“Margo?” I knocked on the door. “She must be in there. How do we open this door?”

The manager promptly produced a hairpin. It took her no time at all to release the lock.

I entered the bathroom, glanced around, and pulled back the shower curtain. Margo lay there naked in half a tub of water, her upper torso and distended belly covered with a white bath mat. Her left eye was swollen shut, and below it her cheek was puffy and red. A bump just above her forehead oozed blood. A rolled towel supporting her neck was stained red.

"Land sakes!" said the manager. "I'm phoning the police!"

"There's no need to do that," said Roy. "Let's find out what happened first."

"It's my duty!"

"Then it's my duty as a newspaper reporter to report this incident fully in the press. What's the name of this motel again?"

Margo's breasts rose slightly in the water, then sank again.

"She's breathing," I said with relief. "She's alive! My God, you had me convinced she was dead!" I stroked her hair, avoiding the pronounced bump. "Margo, Sweetie? What happened?"

She twitched and stirred, lifting one knee. I dropped a towel over her lower belly and bruised thighs.

Roy picked up an empty wine bottle from the floor beside the tub. "Liter and a half of Gato Negro," he said. "See? It's not as bad as it looks. She probably drank too much and slipped in the tub." He pocketed a much smaller but equally empty bottle from the lip of the tub: Nytol.

"Unless she swallowed this!" said the manager, picking up an empty box of Epsom salts from off the floor beside the tub.

"No, she's bathing in it," I said, pointing to a residue of white crystals lining the inside of the tub at the water line. "Margo?" I cried, shaking her shoulder. "Margo, Sweetie! Wake up!"

She groaned. "Huh?"

"Should I phone for an ambulance?" asked the manager.

"Not unless you intend to pay for it; they're way too expensive," said Roy. "I have a car. I'll take her to the hospital."

"Wha's goin' on?" slurred Margo. She focused one eye on Roy. Blinked. "Oh, hi, Honey!"

"Looks like you ODed on red wine and sleeping pills," I said. "Are you okay?"

She looked at me. Refocused. "Oh, you!" she groaned. She closed her eyes again, did a double-take, then sat up a little too fast. The bathmat flopped down across her thighs, exposing her full breasts. "Oh God, things are going 'round and 'round! I'm gonna—"

She spewed deep red vomit over herself the full length of the tub, staining the towels and bathmat. She groaned. I supported her shoulders, her head.

"Uh, uh, uh—do I feel sick!"

"Oh my God!" said the manager, eying her pink-splotched towels. "It's much better for *everyone* if you would just throw up in the toilet!"

And another blast of red.

The manager held out the empty carton of Epsom salts, waving it in Margo's face. "You didn't swallow this, did you?"

Margo glanced at the box and shook her head. "Miscarriage," she whispered, heaving. "He was—trying—to—"

She barfed again.

"Induce a miscarriage? At eight months?" said the manager. "Are you crazy?"

"I think we can handle it from here, ma'am," said Roy. "Thank you very much. Feel free to add any extra cleaning costs to the bill."

"They paid in advance."

"Then you have lots of security! With any luck, they'll be leaving early."

"Don't worry, we'll rinse out these towels right away," I added as I supported the heaving Margo.

"No, I'll take 'em with me right now, before the stain fixes." She gathered them up. "I'll bring fresh."

"Thanks."

"All that alcohol can't be good for the baby! Nor can them Epsom salts!"

"At least she's getting rid of the Nytol and the wine," said Roy. "Thanks for being discreet about this!"

"She should have the bump on her head looked at. And that black eye!"

"What can I say? Sometimes things go wrong even on your wedding night!"

"Your brother—brother-in-law should be charged! Nothing justifies beating a pregnant woman like that!"

"We don't know what happened yet," said Roy, escorting her to the door.

Once we got Margo talking, nothing could slow her down.

"I jus' tol' him the truth," she said, "tol' him what you tol' me—that he's my half-brother." She began to cry. "He said if that was the case, the baby was the product of incest, like Colleen. 'Incest's is a criminal thing,' he says, 'we'll both end up back inside.' Says my baby's gonna be deformed: 'We gotta get rid of it!' he says. And he punched me in the belly."

"No!" I gasped.

"Again and again," Margo sobbed. "He's changed, Emmy. Tom's changed!"

I seethed. "That *bastard*!"

"I tried to protect myself," Margo sobbed. "I yelled, 'You have no right! It isn't your baby!' That's when he really lost it!"

She coughed and gagged over the side of the tub, then dribbled and spat yellow bile onto the floor.

"Whose baby did you tell him it was?" asked Roy.

She glared at him with loathing. "Is," she said. "*Is*! I told him the fucking *truth*, Roy!" She glared at Roy with unmitigated hatred. "The baby is *yours*, you fuck!"

43

Roy did not look at me as he ran the water in the tub to get the right temperature. He stood my younger sister up under the shower, and neither one of them seemed fazed by her nakedness. He soaped her all over and rinsed her off until she was purged of vomit. She held her battered face to the stream of water and started crying, a low, soulful moan. While Roy supported her, I turned her around and washed her back with a facecloth. Between us, we helped her out of the tub, draping a second bath sheet over her shoulders.

"Are you okay now?" I asked. "Do you want to lie down? Come on, we'll get you to the bed."

She sat down on the toilet. "I hafta pee."

"Will you excuse us, Roy?" I said.

He left, and I supported Margo on the toilet. "You said it's Roy's baby," I said quietly. I needed to know she wasn't simply naming the first man that came into her mind.

She nodded, then read the alarm on my face and shook her head. "Oh, God!" she whined. "I forgot. I'm sorry."

"*Is* he the father?"

She closed her eyes and nodded. My heart turned upside-down.

I helped her stagger to the bedroom, where she flopped onto the bed on her bruised belly. I winced, feeling sorry for the unwanted fetus within. *Give it a chance, Margo! Give it half a chance!*

"I'll pack her duds," Roy said. I had never seen him so humble. "She can't stay here." Both suitcases, though open, were already full of Margo's clothes. "Where's Tom's?" he asked.

"He took 'em with him."

"Do you know where he went?"

"I don't give a shit!" Then: "Prob'ly Camas Lake. I told him I wasn't going."

I touched her cheek gingerly with my fingertips. "I can't believe that son of a bitch did this to you!"

"Nor c'n I!" She felt her face, then sat slowly up as she took stock of her aches and pains. "Fuck. As if I would want *his* damn baby!"

"Don't blame the baby."

"Tell that to Tom! He was the one who tried to kill it!" She began to weep. "He's a fucking low-life scum murderer, after all."

"Yeah?" said Roy a little too sternly. "Who put the Epsom salts in the water?"

"*He* did! Said he'd heard it was a remedy for unwanted pregnancies."

"Well, if it isn't his—"

"You're *defending* him? You *fucking* men! You're all alike!" She held her head in her hands. "Tha's what he wanted, okay? The baby gone, his baby, your baby whatever."

"Did you tell him who the father was?" Roy asked anxiously.

"He knows. Figured it out in no time. I told him he was a dumb fuck for not doin' the math sooner. Threw *that* back in his face. He was in Bowden Institution when you knocked me up. Remember?"

"He was out on parole for a while," Roy remonstrated, "living with you!"

"Yeah, and that put him in breach of his no-contact order with me—his co-accused. So they took 'im back in and he had to stay 'in' until his warrant expiry. Then they had no control over him. I told him I was pregnant, and we arranged to get married as soon as he got out. Which was a coupla months later than either of us expected."

"So it could be his baby—"

"That's not the point!" I snapped. "While we were living together, you had an affair? With my *sister*?"

"It was before you moved in. Besides, I didn't know she was your sister. I thought she was your *niece*!"

"Oh, brilliant. That makes it right!"

"Roy interviewed me about Uncle Phil and what happened at Camas Lake," Margo explained. "It was Halloween."

"The interview went longer than expected," added Roy.

"He offered to take me to supper, but I said I could fix dinner in no time. So I shoved a frozen pizza in the oven, and we kept right on talkin'. One thing led to another, I was lonely, I guess, and frustrated that when warrant expiry came they tacked on another coupla months for the breach. That's how it started.

"But the baby's only part of it—" She hiccupped. "Tom's pissed because he thinks you're after our money. The money we can't get because it's proceeds of crime. Not that money's a big issue." She shook out her purse onto the bed. "Here, Sis! Wan' some money?" A roll of bills fell out along with a makeup pack, lipstick, and a small mirror. She peeled off several one-hundred-dollar bills and tossed them into the air. "How much d'ya want? One thousand, two thousand? Ten? It's jus' an advance. You stick with me, an' we got more money comin' our way than we'll ever know what to do with!"

"You shouldn't be throwing that around!" I said, gathering up the bills and shoving them all back into her purse. "Look, this has nothing to do with money—it just has to do with my finding out who the fuck I am. And that's the truth!"

"I know that. I know that! I'm sorry, Emmy—" She groaned again. "And to think I thought you were Aunt Maggie! From what Roy said. Not that *Tom* did, though. Oh, no, not for a minute. He had that one figured out right quick!"

"What do you mean?"

"See, it di'n't add up, did it? Here's Roy tellin' me Aunt Maggie's alive, and I thought, *Great! I'll go see her, compare notes*, y'know? But Tom tol' me not to go. Says he di'n't want nothin' to do with it, nothin' to do with you, nothin' to do with *her*. I mean, I'm obviously a damn fool, Roy, and a sucker, and a patsy, and for a while was your cheap trick—think how many free fucks you got out of me!—but I believed you when you said Tom's mum was alive. I figured him refusin' to see her was jus' plain ignorant. I mean, even if you have issues with your mum, you should at least check it out, don't you think?"

"Struck me as odd, as well," Roy mumbled.

"I jus' couldn' figure it out. And then him gettin' so upset when he first saw you at the church. Sure, you've aged more'n most of us, but it wasn't as if he didn't know who you were! So why the hell would he phone the police, risk mischief charges tellin' em you're not who you say you are?—'specially when you hadn't even *said*; *I* was the one who first recognized you as Emily—and he knows damn well that you're my sister! He had the hots for you long before he ever even looked at me! *Concept!* I mean, what an asshole!

"So drivin' down here, I put it to him, asking why he'd tried to give us all the gears like that. He tol' me he was afraid you would open up the investigation all over again. I said, 'So what?' And he said, 'There's too many bodies!' See, here's the thing: S'long as you were dead and Aunt Maggie was missin' there wouldn't have been any further questions—an' this was a good thing. But once you arrive on the scene, alive, claimin' to be Aunt Maggie—"

"That was Roy's theory, not mine."

"No matter. For Tom, his mum bein' missing was a convenient 'truth.' Let sleepin' bitches lie, he said. That's who he was referring to when he said that. But on the way here, he tol' me that what he shoulda done was gone down to the hospital in Ponoka when they first asked him to, and said, 'Yep, this is mah mom!'—even though it wasn't true."

"Why would he have done that?"

"'Cause your remains could only have been Aunt Margaret!" She tried to think this through, but gave up. "I 'member readin' statements Tom an' Rog an' Billy, and I think Uncle Phil, gave the police sayin' Aunt Margaret was on the plane with Daddy. Later, Tom and Roger both told me when she wasn't found at the crash site that she must've survived. So when Roy told us someone he thought was Maggie Campbell had been found, it struck me as odd that Tom did *not* want to meet her."

"Yeah, that bugged me, too," Roy repeated.

"Well it isn't too surprising to me," I said, "considering the abuse she put him through!"

"But that was—shit, eleven years ago now! I thought it was crazy for Tom not to invite his own mother to his wedding. I mean, what're weddings *for*? He would've had no family there whatsoever. That's why I agreed when Roy asked if he could bring you along—as a surprise for Tom."

"I was still absolutely convinced that you were Maggie," said Roy. "I knew you couldn't have been Alice. Sorry, Honey."

Margo's voice cracked. "I thought I'd killed you, Sis!" She held out her arms, offering a hug. "Drivin' down here, Tom said that if they believed you were Emily, they'd soon put two and two together. I asked him what he meant and he said, 'Supposin' that hip bone they found belonged to Ma?'

"'You mean, I killed her too?' I said, trying to track. I thought he meant that Aunt Maggie had somehow been hiding out in the cabin all that time and had burned to death with the others.

"'No, no—I mean, suppose she was long dead,' he said. 'S'pose someone had buried her there, under the cabin.'

"'Who would have done that?'

"'Who knows? My dad, your dad—'

"'Not *my* Dad!' I said. 'He was killed in a plane crash, remember?'

"'That's the day I'm talkin' about,' he said, 'Uncle Richard filed a flight plan to fly from Edmonton to Camas Lake and back on the same day. He spent the afternoon with my Ma. They were talkin' about flying out of Camas Lake together with Colleen to get her checked out—he thought she had Fragile-X or some such thing. When he come back to his plane there was a great big oil slick on the lake—fuel from his airplane. Both drain plugs had been pulled and were hangin' by a wire, the drains still drippin'. He got into the plane to check how much gas was left—

"'Zip!'"

44

"Tom said that at first Daddy thought Maggie was trying to stop him from leaving," Margo continued. "They had a terrible fight over that. Then he thought it might be Phil. Then he thought it was him—that is, Tom—or Roger or all three boys. That about covered the waterfront. Tom said Daddy spent that evening carrying pails of purple gas down to his plane from the barn, filling one of the gas tanks. Next day, when he took off, Tom thought he'd taken Aunt Margaret with him, because her bed was made and she was nowhere around."

"The boys all told the Transport investigators they saw their mother in the plane," said Roy. "They and Phil all signed statements to that effect."

"Yeah—I've seen 'em," said Margo. "Tom said the investigators drew up identical statements for him and his brothers and asked each of them to read it over. 'But none of us was big on readin',' he said. He signed it anyway, and so did his brothers and father. Rog swore up and down he'd seen his mother on that plane! Tom wasn't so sure."

"Are you saying your dad *didn't* give Maggie Campbell a ride?" asked Roy.

"Point is, what if Roger was mistaken? If she wasn't on that plane, whatever happened to her must've happened that night—

before Daddy took off. Tom said she wasn't around after that. He told the police that if his mother wasn't on that plane, she must've run off."

"Run off," said Roy. "Makes sense."

"And leave Colleen? No way!"

"So who tampered with the gas tanks? Someone who knows about planes, I would guess."

"Tom denies it."

"So—Uncle Phil?" I wondered.

"Tom said Uncle Phil knew Daddy and Aunt Margaret were having an affair. Of course, Daddy may not have *known* that he knew. But once someone had tampered with his plane, Daddy must've thought Uncle Phil was suddenly gettin' protective of his wife. That would explain why he was in such an all-fired hurry to get away that he would risk using stale gas—his life may have depended on it! But Tom says, if that was the case, why di'n't he fly out that night—land at Abraham Lake or somewhere else close by so he could fix his plane and get the proper fuel?"

"Why didn't he radio for help?" asked Roy.

"The radio was fucked. Aerial probably disconnected or something. I don't know. Tom said earlier on Daddy asked him to help unload the last of the art supplies he'd brought in for Uncle Phil—the boys had already unloaded the groceries when he'd arrived earlier that day. They lifted down a plastic bin containing fresh art supplies—Tom said it was about five feet long—the kind with three hinges on one side. He said they carried it up to the house, leaving it with a bunch just like it in the dry storage area in the crawl space under the house. That's where Uncle Phil kept his paint supplies, so it wouldn't freeze in winter—paint both for his art and for around the house, like latex house paint and varsol and oil-based fence paint and enamel—you name it. Once it freezes it's good for nothing, and Tom said most years it froze. So there were dozens of plastic bins under the house, filled with old paint, with no place else to stash it. He said that's why it didn't surprise him when the house went up like a bomb. He said the crawl space had a dug dirt floor and everything got covered with dust unless it was sealed up tight. Most of the storage bins were sealed with duct tape to keep out the dust.

"Tom said when he and Daddy got back to the dock, Daddy gave the pontoons and the surrounding water a blast of the fire extinguisher, spraying fire retardant all around and under the plane and the dock until the canister was spent. He said all the time Daddy was spraying he was lookin' around him, like into the trees and into the hayfield, and up at the path, and all around, scared shitless!

"Tom said Daddy stank of gasoline. When they finally went back up to the house, Aunt Margaret was all apologetic and said she'd heated up the water for a bath. She'd added a cup of dish detergent to cut the grot and make a bubble bath. He said—I can hardly believe it, but he said Daddy let Aunt Margaret scrub his back, and then she took off all her clothes and climbed into the tub behind him. Tom said, 'Uncle Dick kept eyein' the door, expectin' my old man to walk through into the kitchen any second.'"

"Tom was watching them?" I said in disgust.

"Well, you remember the layout of their kitchen. Kind of hard not to look! He said while they were bathing, he and Roger cooked up some spaghetti and meatballs. Roger was really pissed. After dinner, Daddy took Tom aside and told him he'd need help carrying gas from the tank beside the barn down to the plane. He told Tom he was going to fly out with Aunt Margaret and Colleen in the morning—'Take 'em away from this madness!'

"Aunt Margaret had already told the boys she wanted to take Colleen to see a specialist in the city, and that she hoped to go with Richard," Margo continued. "She asked Tom if he would mind taking care of the two younger boys for a few days. Tom said Roger got real upset, sayin' she couldn't leave. Tom said she glared at Roger as if to tell him to shut the fuck up. After that,

Rog refused to help, and Tom actually hid Colleen. Abducted her. Locked her in the cellar up at the other house."

"Poor kid," I said.

But Roy kept her on focus: "So Richard and Maggie had patched things up—sharing a bath, sitting down together at dinner," he said, coaxing her to continue.

"Tom figured things fell apart later that night, after Colleen went missing. Aunt Margaret thought she might have wandered away, got lost. She had one of the boys—Billy, I think—go down to the studio to see if Phil had kidnapped her. By evening, Aunt Maggie had gone completely squirrelly."

"So would any mother," I said.

"Meanwhile, Tom helped Daddy refuel the plane with purple gas. He says he didn't think any more about it: Gas is gas. Next morning Daddy tried to fly out of there at first light. And as we all know, he crashed. Killed himself. Question is, why was he so anxious to fly out of Camas Lake so early, even though the plane was backfiring and stuttering from the bad gasoline?"

"If the body they thought was mine was in fact Aunt Margaret's, it must've been under the house all along," I said. "Nobody checked those bins from one year to the next."

"If there was a decomposing body among them, you'd have thought they would have smelled it!" said Roy.

"'Not if she was floatin' in purple gas and the bin was sealed with duct tape.'"

"What?"

"I'm telling you, Tom had an answer for everything. He said if 'her' storage bin was sealed up with duct tape like that, it would match all the others—and nobody would ever guess. More to the point, nobody would ever check. And it makes oddball sense.

"Two years later, the house burned to the ground. The fire burned through the floor and the heat melted through the plastic lids of the storage bins in the crawl space beneath it, working from the top layer of bins to the lower layers. When the flames ignited the gas in Aunt Margaret's bin, the explosion would've blasted away any debris from the floor that may have fallen on top of the bin, exposing her burning corpse.

"Remember the pathologist's report? He said it looked like Emily had tried to shield herself from the heat usin' a plastic door mat, which had melted over her. That same effect would be achieved if Aunt Maggie's remains were partially covered by the melted lid of her plastic coffin."

I could see it all now: What was left of the storage bin would have melted inward, along with the plastic residue of the upper layers of bins, and the lid and bottom of her bin would have adhered to her charred bones.

Roy nodded his understanding. "Gruesome," he said, "but plausible."

Perhaps *too* plausible. As Margo had wondered, how could Tom have surmised all this detail without himself having some inside knowledge of his mother's demise? How could Tom have come up with such a comprehensive explanation so quickly? Had he been complicit in the murder? Had he tried to cover for his own father, who finally like an outraged Odysseus had sought vengeance against Aunt Margaret's suitor for the many times he had flown out to Camas Lake to be with her? Had Tom killed his own mother and attempted to preserve her remains in gasoline? Or had that been a group project? Was that why Tom had been so reluctant to meet me, once I had surfaced—because he knew that I *couldn't* be his mother, since he himself had stashed her dead body in gasoline to cut the stench of death?

Was he concerned that he might be accused once again of murder—this time of matricide?

"I told Tom I didn't want to move back to Camas Lake, even for the summer," Margo was saying, more sober now but petulant. "Can you imagine my saying that? What a nerve! Both our families died there, so we might just as well go back there for our honeymoon, right? That's where Daddy died, and Mummy died, and Sandy died, and Willis died, and Emmy—" She looked at me and her eyes bugged slightly. "That's where you died. Or were supposed to have. He hates it that you *didn't* die!" She tried to rein herself in. "His family died there too—all of 'em, parents, brothers, sister—and yet he says that's a good reason to go *back*? I say that's one fuck of a good reason to stay away!" She coughed. "Oh God, I talk a lot! Roy, Honey, can you get me a glass of water?"

Roy let the bathroom tap run and poured her a glass.

I picked up her hairbrush from off the bed and started tidying her hair, pulling it back off her face. I brushed her hair for a full minute as she sipped her water. "You're beautiful," I said, reaching over to show her to herself in the mirror. She held my hand, adjusting the mirror so that it reflected both of us, displaying my smaller wrinkled face in the background, her swollen eye and cheek in the foreground. "Beauty and the beast," I said.

We locked eyes in the mirror, then she leaned back and kissed me on the cheek. "You're one lovable beast," she whispered.

Roy was on the phone. "Derek's on his way," he said as he hung up, then he added, for Margo's benefit: "Derek and Joanie are close friends of mine, you'll like them—"

"They're loads of fun," I confirmed somewhat cynically.

"They know all about Camas Lake. He was the photographer who took pictures of the crime scene. They have relatives coming in from Ontario for the next few days, but if you're going to be here, they'll look in on you."

"I'm not gonna stay here! What if Tom comes back?"

"Well, I was hoping he *would*!"

"Jesus, Roy!" I said. "After what he did to her?"

"Derek said that after their relatives leave, you can crash there until we get back."

"Get back from where?" I asked. "Where are we going?"

"Yeah, where ya goin'?"

"Camas Lake."

"You're kidding me!" I said. "With Tom on the loose?"

"What'd I tell ya?" said Margo. "Men! The fuckers always stick together!"

"I told you that was my plan," Roy protested.

"Suppose Tom's out there waiting for us?"

"Oh, God, how romantic!" Margo glared at me. "'Snot you he's mad at. It's me!" She blinked at Roy—or was that an attempted wink? "I wouldn't mind going out there with ya, just to face up to that bastard—long as I don't have to stay!"

"Not gonna happen," I said.

45

We piled Margo's cases and shoes into the back of Derek's Explorer and Margo into the passenger seat. There was room for extra passengers, but Roy and I had much to talk about, so we retraced our steps along the lakeshore. Still stung by Margo's claim that Roy was the father of her baby, I walked beside him with arms folded. Black-capped Bonaparte seagulls hung in the air above the lake, gliding on the breezes and air currents, almost motionless against the trees.

"So, is it true?" I asked, my voice quavering.

"Your father offing your aunt? Seems a stretch. But Tom's explanation of how Maggie's body could have been confused for yours—brilliant!"

"You know what I'm talking about! You seemed right at home with each other." I blinked away hot tears. "You slept with her, I have no doubt! Was that her reward for sharing all that information?"

"That's ridiculous!"

"You were visiting her whenever Tom was away, weren't you?"

"I interviewed them both."

"But mostly Margo, alone!"

"It's not that simple. Look, Tom wasn't straight with me. He didn't tell me that one of the conditions of his parole was that he have no contact with Margo. When I interviewed them together at her place, it was clear he was living there, and I put that in the story. As a result of my article, Tom was busted for breach of parole. He was some pissed!

"I felt so bad that I arranged for both Margo and me to attend the hearing of the Parole Board to be witnesses on his behalf, but they tacked on two months to his sentence for breach. Later that afternoon, Margo and I went back to her place to commiserate and—well, one thing led to another. We did it. Okay?"

I flopped down on a park bench facing the lake. When he sat down beside me, I shrugged away from him.

"Emily, listen to me. She needed comfort right then, and I was there. And then later, well, it was kind of—follow-up."

"'Follow-up.' Great! How long did *that* last?"

"Until Tom got back out last Christmas, this time with no conditions. They've lived together ever since. Since then, I haven't had much to do with them. So it's—not like you think. She never loved me and I never loved her. It was a relationship of—convenience, okay? I first met her months before you came along. And all along, she made it clear to me that she would always be loyal to Tom—"

"You call that 'loyal'?"

"—even though while he was locked up she was not being strictly *faithful*. The point is, I don't love her. It's you I love. *You.* I love *you*, Emily!"

I blinked away my tears. "Say that again," I said.

"I love you, Emily."

I melted. We kissed softly, our lips just barely touching, little kisses and then longing glances, gazing deep into each other's eyes. For long minutes the magic lasted, and when we rose Roy gave me a huge bear hug, lifting me off my feet and swinging me back and forth. "I love you too!" I cried, and we kissed once more.

Why was I so forgiving? Was it desperation? The fear of being left alone once again?

Arms linked, we paced slowly back along the beach and across the road toward Derek and Joanie's place. When we got there, Margo was fast asleep in our bed.

"She had half a cup of coffee, a piece of dry toast, and an Alka-Seltzer," said Joanie, "in that order. That should keep everything down."

"Who can blame her for tying one on?" added Derek. "He must've really belted her, to give her a shiner like that!"

"Her legs are bruised, too," I said. "And her ribs and belly. I hope the baby's okay."

"Joanie's a nurse. She'll take care of her."

"Babies are quite resilient," said Joanie, "and they're well protected by amniotic fluid. I could hear the baby's heartbeat—it sounds fine. If that changes, we'll take her in to Red Deer General."

"What about your relatives?"

"Margo agreed that my family can stay in the bridal suite, and she'll crash with us. That way, her husband won't find her, and if he shows up at the motel he'll have me and my big sister to contend with. Been itching to show her some real action in the wild, wild west!"

"Talkin' of which, I was tellin' Joanie how great the mountains look from the air at this time of year," said Derek. "All the alpine blossoms. Told her I'd fly her out to see the Rockies before we forsake our country for good. So if you don't mind visitors droppin' in—"

"Sure, come on out and visit us after your guests go," said Roy.

"'Kay, it's a plan. Camas Lake, next Saturday. I'll book a plane. We should get there 'round about noon."

"Cool."

"I hope that old claptrap of yours can make it!"

46

The road west to Rocky Mountain House seemed vaguely familiar from years and years ago. The distant mountains were at once a magnet and a barrier, the end of the world, the point where the horizon ceased to unfold. We reached Rocky at two-thirty, and sought a store that might be open on a Sunday. We had lots of food and other incidentals in boxes on top of the car, but Roy felt that we had to pick up some canned vegetables and soups, just to be on the safe side. We spent my remaining fifty dollars on the food, and he filled the car and a spare gas can using his sole remaining credit card.

By three o'clock we were heading out of Rocky, still driving west beside the North Saskatchewan River, then southeast on the Forestry Trunk Road, an interminable gravel ribbon that snakes its way around hill after hill after hill. There was still snow deep in the ditches along the road and on the shadow sides of the mountains. In some places, especially in the deep woods, the drifts seemed hardly to have melted, although the road itself was bare.

Seeing the familiar stands of lodgepole pine edged only occasionally with trembling aspens, I thought of Tuanahaki, lying in her death lodge beneath her rock grave, guarding an anonymous creek. Only nine months had passed, yet what a transformation in my life!

Roy knew the best route from the Forestry Trunk Road to Camas Lake, but there was quite a contrast between the way he drove down the rutted trails and the way Uncle Phil had driven the Jeep on our first trip from Rocky Mountain House. I saw again the faces of my sisters, grimacing but laughing in the back, and Willis's pale fear as he clutched the backs of the seats in front of him, his face glued to the tortuous trail every inch of the way. We lurched too, Roy and I, but it was a slow, cart-horse lumbering under the load of his possessions.

In spite of the familiar feeling about the trees and trails and creeks, there was no sense of homecoming for me. Rather there was a fear, with every passing mile intensifying, that I was somehow going back to a hell I had already chosen to forsake.

"This is where I got bogged down before," said Roy, "where that ford crosses the road." He braked and stopped the car. We were perched on top of a rise, and before us for perhaps a quarter of a mile there was a sea of mush. "I'll walk down, check it out," he said. "At least it isn't totally flooded like the last time. I had to hike miles!"

He soon came back, his face full of optimism. "Some logging trucks must have gone through," he said. "And at least one car—probably Tom. It's pretty solid underneath—ice with about four inches of slushy mud on top. We'll take a run at it and try to keep going."

Bolts had never displayed such fine pickup. We roared down the hill, careless of the swaying load on the roof, and struck the mud at close to sixty miles an hour. It spattered over the front bumper and hood, blanking out our windshield. Roy drove blind for five or ten breathless seconds before the laboring wipers cleared the glass enough for us to see. The tires spun and mud sprayed and we swayed and lurched and danced through the muskeg, fishtailing all the way. Roy grunted and sweated as if he had a fever, swinging the steering wheel first one way and then the other like a seasoned rally-driver. And only barely did we make it through.

Once up on the dry road on the other side, the car lurched to a stop.

"We lost half our load," he said.

"Great. Just great!"

"Look!"

Battered, besmattered boxes of our food and clothing were indiscriminately scattered in the mud over a hundred yards like colored sprinkles on a chocolate cake.

"We'll gather up as much as we can," Roy said, taking off his shoes. We hoisted our jeans above our knees and waded into the muck.

The sun was already low above the mountains by the time we had gathered most of his belongings, fighting off flocks of mosquitoes and blackflies that descended like clouds in spite of the cold. The mud oozed between our toes and nearly froze our feet. The clay beneath the mud was still frozen. By tomorrow, once the sun had shone another day, the road would be totally impassable.

Since the food was already out and down, we ate before we continued on our journey to Camas Lake—bread rolls with no butter, stuffed with salami, lettuce, and sliced tomato, enough to make any stomach explode. After the snack, we retied all our dirty belongings back on top of the car once again, stringing the clothesline back and forth over the nondescript bundle of boxes, loose clothing, the tent, two suitcases, and the spare can of gas.

"Not far to go from here," Roy said. "Just a mile or two before we see the lake! And look, fresh tracks!"

"Tom," I said.

When we started off once more, we'd completely lost our muffler and Roy complained that the steering was stiff from the mud caked up in it. The woods roared with the echo of our exhaust and blue smoke trailed behind us worse than ever.

The trail was high with thistles and grass and a variety of alpine flowers: Indian paintbrushes, wild onion, lupines. We took it on faith that some solidity existed midway between that line of trees and this. The general aspect of the entire area was unfamiliar and I did not recognize the site of the house where so long before I had stayed with my mother, sisters, and brother, until Roy drove right up through the foot-high grass of previous years to the very foundations of the ruins. The back corner of the house still stood, complete with its murderous window frame. That window had backlit the silhouettes of my mother and father having noisy, energetic sex in a benighted final union. I had later slammed that same window down on Tom's leg, snapping his shin and tibia as he fell backward over the fulcrum of the window frame. And later still, that window and its ugly charred slats had framed Colleen's pale, panic-stricken face amid billowing black smoke and the ominous orange flicker of flame.

"We'll pitch the tent over there," Roy declared, indicating the very spot that had riveted my attention. He had pulled right into what had been the back yard of the upper cabin. "This is where I camped last time. That piece of wall makes a good windbreak against the breezes off the lake."

"Can't we go lower, closer to the lake?" I asked with a shiver.

"Too exposed. Look! The outhouse is still intact. And as I recall, there's a rill over by the trees there for fresh water. Everything we need!"

At least a ready supply of firewood awaited us in the ruins of the upper cabin, and it did not take long to set up camp. But I did not blame Margo one bit for her reluctance to return. After all, she had spent one hellish summer here, less than two months total time, in which she had lost both her family and her freedom.

"I'll wash the mud out of our clothes in the morning," I said, my mind casting back to the times I had been stuck with that chore. I recalled Tom helping me wring out Willis's underpants ("Wish his balls were in them," I had said). Later, I had threatened Tom with a rock at that very same spot.

The trails were overgrown with brome grass, which competed with lupines, larkspur, alpine forget-me-nots, and clumps of pussytoes. The charred ruins were themselves overgrown with fresh fireweed and Indian paintbrush.

As I trod a path through the ubiquitous death-camas, the very ground felt strangely too familiar, as if there hadn't been a lag of years between the then and the now. Something seemed to infect the very atmosphere, a strange unnerving tension from the knowledge of the tragedies that had occurred there. *Where was Tom?*

There is no doubt in my mind that the place is haunted.

47

That night, sleep did not come easily. For one thing, we were camped practically on top of the spot where Tom had ended up after falling from the window after it slammed down on his ankle, breaking his leg. I remember seeing Margo kneeling beside him beneath the busted window, hugging him as he moaned in pain. His leg was stretched out straight before him. Margo was crying, but if I felt sorrow for whatever had happened to him I did not allow myself to express it.

"That's what comes of snooping about, spying," I said. "Leave him there."

"We can't just leave him," Margo retorted tearfully. "His leg's broken."

"Serves him right. He was trying to break in!"

"He's in shock. We have to make him warm and comfortable!" She began kissing his face, his lips. That infuriated me.

"He could have raped us, even killed us for all we know!" I proclaimed for the benefit of Sandra and Colleen.

"Don't be ridiculous! He wouldn't hurt a fly!"

"He could've killed us all!" parroted Sandra.

Colleen looked at Tom doubtfully. "Didja see my d-daddy?" she asked him.

Tom reached out for her. "Sweetie!"

I pushed Colleen back against Sandy, who held her with a not unwelcome hug.

"You climbed in there, didn't you?" I accused him, striding over to him. He vomited on the grass, and I suppose this had something to do with the disgust I felt for him right then. That, and the knowledge that he had actually succeeded in peering into the forbidden room. Margo cradled his head in her arms. "What did you see?" I demanded.

"Nothing!" he gasped.

"Liar!"

"Emmy—please! Leave him alone!" cried Margo as I descended upon him.

I jumped with all my weight on his broken leg.

The horror of what I had done gripped me now so that I had to struggle to focus. Why had I shown him no mercy? In my mind, I jumped on his broken leg not just once but again and again, until I heard it crack and splinter. Margo grappled with me, grabbed my hair, and finally dragged me off him. We fought, two sisters, shrieking and clawing with nails and fists and feet and teeth. Finally she broke free and ran to the house and slammed the door on me. I knelt beside Tom, just looking at him. Colleen and Sandra stood just outside the screen door, and I heard little Colleen say to Sandra in a hushed voice, "Emmy hurted Tom w-weal bad!"

I felt a wave of horror as I stared at Tom's leg. It was horribly bent halfway between the ankle and the knee where no leg should have a joint, and it seeped blood. I felt physically ill just looking at it.

Margo unbolted the door and carefully opened it to peek outside. Realizing that my temper had cooled, she walked toward me cautiously. When she saw the angle of Tom's broken leg, I thought for a minute she would pass right out, but she knelt down beside him, across from me. Tears streamed down her face, and her chin trembled. She tried to tear the denim of Tom's pant leg, but however hard she tried, it would not give.

"There's a pair of scissors in the string drawer," she said, sniffing away tears. Sandra went into the kitchen and a few seconds later returned with them. Margo carefully cut along the seam of Tom's jeans. She was a born nurse.

It was horrible! Jagged broken bone protruded through the skin at least an inch, oozing blood. I was completely disoriented, never having been much good in emergencies.

"There's no way to get a doctor," Margo said. "We'll have to try to fix it ourselves."

"We can't fix that!"

Margo frowned. "Last time, I just pulled it straight." She looked around and saw Sandra and Colleen, silent now, gawking at Tom's exposed leg. "Sandy, we need two boards about the length of his legs. And Colleen, you go get a bed sheet from off my bed, any one will do." She checked the open wound. Blood seeped from the gash, but no artery was broken. "He'll never be able to walk properly again!" she lamented.

Once the girls had gone, Margo gently grasped Tom's ankle and pulled as hard as she could, her foot jammed right into his crotch for leverage.

"Thank God he isn't conscious!" I said and laughed. Margo gave me an angry scowl and full of grim determination pulled Tom's leg straight, cringing as if she herself felt the pain that the unconscious Tom could not. She worked the fracture back into place with her fingers, picking slivers of bone out of the clotting gore.

Sandra returned without any boards. Leaving Tom's side, Margo pulled one loose from the side of the house, lay it over the porch steps, and jumped on it to break it in two. She hammered the rusty nails out with a large rock. Then she ripped the sheet into long bandages. She even poured some rubbing alcohol over the tear in the flesh.

Tom's leg was already purple and beginning to swell, but Margo bound it with strips of the sheet and placed the splints on either side. Sandra and I held the boards in place while Margo slowly wound the torn sheet around and around the leg, splints and all, pulling tightly until it was completely bound. We spread a blanket on the grass beside Tom and used it as a stretcher, dragging his limp body across the patch of lawn.

Sandy and I took his head and Margo his feet, while Colleen shuffled along behind. He was much heavier than I expected. We hauled the blanket around the side of the house to the front, right to the center of the grassy trail that marked the boundary, the border—the no man's land, between the boys' leaderless kingdom and our own.

48

In the days that followed our arrival, I became peculiarly perceptive to what might be called the psychic flow—if not of beings outside myself, then of the ghosts within. Every five minutes I felt my hair trying to stand on end, and the down on my arms tingled as if it had life of its own. I kept recollecting, reliving, trying to visualize it as it had been, and yet even that was unnecessary, because the "had been" very succinctly was right there and then being revitalized by my terrified imagination.

A rational explanation? No. My feelings while I was there defied the rational. It was more than mere uneasiness. It was a feeling that everywhere I turned I was being not watched but *touched,* caressed as if by fingers of breath or wind. My skin crawled.

As Roy and I walked through knee-high camas down the hill toward the charred and shattered barn for the first time, I felt drawn not toward the ruins on the right but toward the trees down through which flowed the brook. Turning my back on the ugliness of the overgrown ruins of the Campbell cabin, which sprawled like a dark scar across the meadow, pocked with fireweed, I absorbed the beauty of the woods and the pure brook, captured in a waterfall that in a single sweep cleared almost twice my height and then raced on down the hill in a series of secondary cataracts that bounded right to the lake. Why had I not remembered this?

The lake too lived, and it spoke to me as never before. The evening breeze pushed choppy little waves across its surface, and the water flamed in the dying sun as it sank behind the nearest ridge of mountains. *Flap, flap, flap, flap*, the waves slapped the pebbles along the beach with monotonous regularity and lapped at the shrubbery along the shore. A loon quavered querulously in the twilight then loomed into view suspended between air and water, its sparkling necklace bobbing with the wavelets. Even as we watched in hushed awe it dipped out of sight, reappearing briefly with its mate twenty meters farther out until I could no longer see them but only heard their mournful scales. I wished for a moment that I was a loon, that Roy was a loon, that together we could swim and fly wherever we wanted without impediment.

As the evening grew dark, I knew I would have to leave the world of the waterfall and the loon behind, dismissing them as a fool's paradise even as Roy was beginning to see and hear and understand for the first time, perhaps, the attraction of the woods. For me, the waterfall, the brook, the lake, the loon were a touchstone. For Roy they seemed to be a signal beckoning.

Despite the proximity of the window frame that had witnessed so much horror, we both slept soundly that first night. We zipped our sleeping bags together so that we could be close and consummated our arrival in an ecstatic burst of lovemaking that lasted past midnight, and left us at once plenished and exhausted. If anything, my pregnancy seemed to excite him. I had never before had such wonderful sex.

I did not wake until the sun beaming almost directly down on our tent told me it was nearly noon. I looked at my watch seeking confirmation. Roy still snored gently, his face a picture of contentment, and I managed to sneak out of the tent without awakening him. I decided to go once again down to the lake and waterfall, just to marvel and adore.

The waterfall was white with its rushing, tinted with the turquoise hue familiar to mountain tarns. I felt an overriding urge to cleanse myself, felt that I needed purging as perhaps never before. I stripped off all my clothes and steeled myself against the frigid water. I stepped into the clear, cold brook, wading through it ankle deep, arms out, hands cupped, until my palms were filled to the brim with sparkling water, which I drank and savored. Then I stepped right beneath the arc of the falls, holding my breath after the first rushing intake, the involuntary squeal as the icy water splashed over my head and shoulders and breasts, spraying purging needles of white pain from fingertip to fingertip. I willed myself to believe that it was boiling hot instead of freezing cold. The water rolled down my pale, nude body, flowed over my full breasts and jutting belly and pubis and down my thighs. I felt my baby kick as if in protest. Despite the chill I felt at one with the waterfall, at one with the entire brook.

I did not stay there long. After fifteen seconds my skin was numb from the cold, blotched white and red as my blood retreated to a warmer zone. I emerged from the water into the noon sun, but a brisk breeze worked through the trees so that in spite of my wetness I put my blouse and jeans back on over my goose bumps to ward off the chill. The baby kicked again.

I heard Roy chopping wood. The sound of the ax reverberated from the hills and echoed across the lake. I hurried back up the trail to the camp.

"Morning!" I called, exhilarated.

He leaned on the ax. "Hi." He looked at my hair. "Been for a dip in the lake? You must be crazy." He shivered. "Look!" He pointed across the lake. "There's still ice floating in it!"

We set up an awning between the tent and the car so that Roy could work in the shade. Soon he was keyboarding away full tilt on his laptop, plugged into the cigarette lighter of the Toyota. He had dozens of notebooks to get through and perhaps thirty cassette tapes of interviews held with everyone from Inspector Roberts and Dr. Sutcliffe to Tom and Margo. Most of the tapes were about Uncle Phil as he had been in life—Tom's memories of anecdotes that his father had told him in the woods. Most were drab, tiresome accounts, some of which Roy admitted were surreptitiously recorded during prison visits; others were transcripts of telephone conversations. A few were taped during Tom's period of freedom before he was locked up again for breach of parole for having "contacted" his co-accused (in fact he had been living with her for months). Some of these were taped at Margo's apartment, but several contained background bar talk and music, testifying to the circumstances under which they had been recorded. I listened to some of them with half an ear as Roy transcribed them. They ranged from the romantic to the graphic.

One tape was particularly revealing of the close relationship between my sister and Tom:

Margo: *I felt real uneasy about the zeal with which Emmy and Sandy swatted those flies! I stayed in my bedroom with Colleen until the operation was over, then changed into some slacks and went off to meet Tom. We had this special place where we met, at the rail fence down by the clearing. It was so peaceful there. I climbed and straddled the fence, sitting on the top rail. The morning sun warmed the slight breeze, and I remember my ponytail sweeping gently over my face. A gorgeous red-tailed hawk marked time high above the clearing, searching the grass for field mice—taking a good look at me, too. And then close-by, over near the creek, I heard the hollow howl of a timber wolf.*

That wasn't a big deal in itself—we heard them at a distance nearly every night—but I had never heard one so close, and never when I was alone at the edge of the woods. I shuddered, thinking of all the stories of big bad wolves that I'd heard since I was a little girl—"Little Red Riding Hood," "The Three Little Pigs"—you know. I knew a bit about wolves from school, like "Never Cry Wolf," but my teacher said a lot of it was fanciful—so I didn't know whether to stay put or run. It howled again and far off, the howl was answered. Then I heard one of the dogs clamoring down at the Campbell house—must've been Ragtime. But in spite of all that, in spite of the adrenaline rush I got from that wolf howling maybe a kilometer away through the trees, the woods seemed more peaceful than home.

I guess that's the point I'm trying to make. The horror of that house was indescribable. But there in the clearing there were speckled butterflies of all varieties—lots of brilliant blue ones, and fritillaries, and tiger swallowtails, and those white ones, what do you call them?

Tom: *Mountain butterflies. Pernicious.*

Margo: *Parnassians! There were more howls, and I heard the chattering of a squirrel, a chipmunk, really, come down to scold me. Then a shadow swooped in front of the sun, and the hawk—I had completely forgotten about it—shot down like an arrow, soundlessly. The squirrel leaped up in the air in a frantic attempt to fool fate, but the hawk was much too quick. Its talons gripped the squirrel around the belly and the hawk struck her tiny head with his beak twice, three times, while the little animal squealed horrifically. The hawk pecked until the squirrel was motionless, and then, leaping out over the clearing with the squirrel in his talons, he spread his great wings and soared over the bushes and trees, out of sight, his dinner dangling beneath him.*

Roy: *Wow!*

Margo: *I wanted to cry out, to run toward the hawk, to scare it off, to save the squirrel. And yet I was so filled with dread that I could not move. It seemed so incredible that God would let a hawk do that to a defenseless little squirrel. So incredibly right for the hawk. So incredibly wrong for the squirrel. I wondered what would happen to the squirrel's babies—she had obviously been protecting her nest. I felt like that squirrel must have felt in her last futile attempt to escape. I could see the talons of a giant hawk looming down in that last awful second, the final frantic leap. And I realized, suddenly, that I was in fact a squirrel with no true home to hide in, out in the open with no functional parent to protect me.*

It may seem ironic to you, but I find violence abhorrent—I always have, especially then, so soon after having been one of the hunted, one of the hurt. Up to that moment, God had existed for me as a sort of vague Santa face that streamed through the universe in my dreams, His beard the Milky Way. Despite this image of Him stretching trillions of light years across the firmament, I did not doubt that He could see me personally, right there and then was watching my actions, reading my thoughts. But God seemed to have forgotten Camas Lake.

Perhaps the Indians were right—the place is cursed. Was that why He had turned a blind eye on what was going on there? First Dad and Aunt Margaret, and now Mum and Uncle Phil—both sets of parents dead. It seemed so unfair! So I told Tom about what had happened, from my point of view—that his dad had killed my mum, then killed himself. That's the way Emily explained it, and that's what I believed. And I knew that neither we girls in our house nor the boys in theirs could hope to cope alone, that divided we would fall, that the only real hope we had was some form of reconciliation. And Tom seemed to be our best hope for survival.

Tom: *Yeah, right.*

Margo: *You were! You were the only one old enough or sensible enough to be able to get help, to get word out about what had happened, to call the police.*

Tom: *Are you blamin' me?*

Margo: *No. Far from it! I adored you, you Bozo. I regarded you as our potential savior. I worshipped you. Of course, I was all of thirteen. No, I'm just telling you what was going through my mind while I was waiting for you down there at the rail fence.*

The wolves were coming closer and closer; one was near the creek and the other was farther south. Then there was the sound of a third wolf from across the lake. And suddenly I felt something in the woods, moving through it. I felt eyes looking at me, although nothing was visible. The sound of a wolf, panting, padding within yards of me, rustling behind the spruce just meters away! I was trying to scream, to shout, to run, but instead my body remained frozen as the beast approached, growling. I swung down off the fence, keeping the railings between me and It. My scream seemed to rebound between the hills, and then Baloney lunged into the trail—followed by you!

Tom: *That scream sure scared the shit out of me, I can tell you! I didn't see you till I was practically at the fence. I thought* she *was a wolf, the way she howled!*

Roy: *So you'd heard the wolves as well.*

Tom: *Sure, of course. I'd heard the wolves howlin' down around the lake and then I seen the paddock had been left open, probably by Willis. The horse wasn't there. So I went off down the lake lookin' for her. It bothered me that there seemed to be so many wolves around. Bothered the dogs, too. But I had this hot date I didn't want to miss, so I cut through the woods to the clearing to meet Margo.*

Roy: *And?*

Tom: *As I say, she scared the shit out of me! And the wolves kinda wrecked it for us. Margo told me she'd seen a wolf down toward the crick, so to impress her I decided to check it out.*

Margo: *Was I scared! I told him I wasn't, of course, that I wasn't afraid as long as I was with him. But I felt my heart pounding in my chest every pace of the way, saying* liar, liar, liar, liar, liar, *over and over. Tom handed me some stones, remember? You told me wolves always run when human beings get close. So we moved together across the pasture along the trail to the woods. Tom whistled, and we heard some snorts –*

Tom: *More like a half-assed whinny.*

Margo: – *way off through the trees. Baloney came to Tom's whistle, but she whined and barked. And then we stopped in our tracks. A silver form flashed across the rocks ahead of us, giving us a wicked sidelong glance. He must have paused there for a full second, eh, Tom? Confronting us, just about fifty meters away down the trail. Completely fearless. Completely in control. Then he disappeared.*

Tom: *And so did we—in the other direction. What a rush! He was huge!*

Margo: *And then we heard the loudest howl of all, coming from the rocks, a mocking laugh that went on and on and on. And we ran back across the pasture, Baloney running way out in front, tail between her legs! And that was about the last time we saw each other, right? Alone, I mean. The day we saw the wolves was the same day Emily booby-trapped the window and broke your leg.*

Tom: *It wasn't a booby trap. She said it was. But she was inside the room, waiting for me, I swear. I remember seeing her through the glass as I fell. She slammed the window down on my leg as I tried to crawl through, crazy bitch. Then later she jumped on the break, stomped on it with Aunt Alice's shoes. Broke it good.*

Margo: *We didn't get together again very much after that. Hardly saw each other!*

Tom: *Emily fancied herself Aunt Alice, and wore her clothes.*

Margo: *Yeah, for a while there, she believed she was Mum. And wore Mum's clothes to the very end.*

Roy: *What do you mean, "to the very end"?*

Margo: *Right up to the time of the fire. Emily died wearing Mum's red floral dress—and those awful shoes!*

49

After I first listened to that taped interview, soundless tears welled hotly from within my heart, tears that told of a longing for forgiveness where none could ever, ever be found. Yes, I remembered waiting there in the dark, serving as sentry, knowing that Tom would eventually sneak around to the back of our cabin to take a peek. I remember the adrenaline rush when, after days of standing guard, I saw his fingers grip the sill as he jumped up to the window, then saw his booted foot appear and slide over the sill like a snake. I leaned with all my weight on the window, and down it came with a crash on his exposed ankle. I remember the pained expression on his face in the instant before he fell as he stared in at me through the windowpane for a split instant before he fell, his leg snapping sideways at a ridiculous angle, twisting the window from its sash. I remembered his searing scream.

I remembered too a time before that, when I shivered at the shadows, not daring to undress out of my mother's clothes because of the Things behind the lamp and under the bed and behind the walls and beyond the ceiling and beneath the floor. And I myself hid, shuddering beneath my covers, clutching my blankets around my neck, high, high under the chin, just my face protruding, or ducking my head beneath the pillow in an effort to ward off the hands grasping from all sides in the darkness, skeletal hands, as I moaned a pitiful prayer for understanding and forgiveness to the faceless mothergod. And long into the night I cried into my pillow to myself, believing in my despair that my prayers would never, ever be answered.

On the night I heard Roy's interviews with Tom and Margo, the answers came, one by one, each itself a separate nightmare. I slept only fitfully, listening for mosquitoes. Other sounds shook me to the marrow. Owls. Wolves distantly howling, competing with coyotes. And I had a whole series of dreams, intertwining images, most of them oh so lucid of a past (oh let me be just let me be) campfire and a flaming pit. But it was the dawning sun that more than anything else triggered a memory so vivid that for several minutes I relived a past event as if I were actually going through the motions once again. Burned, bruised, shell-shocked, I was wandering almost aimlessly down the trail toward the creek. I puzzled over the changed scenery, the fallen pine, then limped down the tiny trail to the pond where eons before I'd raced Tom to the water. But all that was left was a muddy quicksand puddle with a dead horse, half eaten and half buried in muck, filling the muddy bottom. Wolf tracks were thick here, and the odor of death was overpowering. Angel's eye sockets were empty, her ribcage exposed to the flies.

It was then that my *own* savior appeared to me with soft tread of her moccasined feet and gently placed her hands on either shoulder, lifting the weight from my heart. I hardly dared open my eyes, but rose to be with her, holding her wrinkled hand. She smiled slightly, harbinger of peace, and turned away, not following the path but flowing through the undergrowth, seeming to move freely through it to another destiny. And I followed. Followed. Followed her forever. Followed and adored.

And then in a blinding flash of vision, she was there, Tuanahaki, *there* where the sun shone through the fabric of the tent. And she spoke as she had spoken, her black habit as alight with rainbows as a raven's plumage.

"*Emily!*" she called. "*Emily*!" And I was transported into a worldspace not my own, reliving the horror of it all, and the joy. Transported by joy I saw, not heard, the holy accented words, and they in turn lit up other vistas flashing with white lightning. There was a tiny fire and a face white with ash and mud. Tuanahaki lived again in that instant, her mouth working, her words dropping on my ears like music of the spheres, in hypnotic chromatones.

"I am Tuanahaki," she'd said on the night of the storm, her voice hardly rising above the wind. "I have lived many years in this valley. I know its secrets. For many years I have watched and waited, waited and watched. I have seen my own father destroyed, my own daughter taken from me. I have seen the sickness brought to this valley by your grandmother long years ago, a woman not from the woods but from your world.

"My father, Thundermaker, was a Cree trapper. He sent me to a mission school where I could learn English. I did well there and learned to love the Virgin and the Savior. Eventually I became a Sister of the Blessed Virgin. Because my own people were not yet truly Christian, I sought to help them, and I returned to my people, to my father, and I taught the children of his camp—my nieces and nephews—about the Christchild and the Virgin. And I taught them English.

"While I was away, my father had taken to drink quite heavily. At the bar at Rocky Mountain House he met a white girl, perhaps your age at the time, who said she'd had a falling out with her family. When she discovered my father had a camp in the foothills, she begged him to take her home with him. And so he did.

"By the time I returned there, she had settled in, was running the place, young though she was. She knew no Cree, although she tried hard to learn, and my family knew little English. She knew I spoke English and, trusting my nun's habit, talked to me for hours about what she should do next. She was afraid of her abusive father, she said, and could not return home to Calgary because she was pregnant with his child. I urged her to return to her own people, to the whites in Rocky Mountain House, but she stayed for several months at the camp on the Kootenay Plains until her baby was born. She left the baby with my brother's wife, a jolly Cree woman who fed and cared for him for several years. She called him Woodbird because of his red hair. I taught him English and brought him little children's books and coloring books and colored pencils, but he preferred plain paper and watercolor paint. He disliked me because I was not colorful like my brothers at the powwows but wore my habit—and because I used to discipline him when he painted the summer tepees red. He helped paint drums—that's what he loved to do."

"Then he wasn't raised by the Thompsons, like he said?"

She looked at me inscrutably, and I apologized for being so presumptuous as to interrupt.

"Woodbird was maybe four winters old when your grandpa LaPierre first came to the valley. Francois LaPierre, a French Canadian trapper and fur trader, came from nowhere to build a frame house on Camas Lake, where he had his trap lines. He used to paddle down the North Saskatchewan to Rocky Mountain House with his pelts. He loved to gamble. I didn't know much about him except that he was always coming around. He was interested in little Woodbird; I guess because he was white. He gave him stuff. Told my father he wanted to buy him, take him home. But of course my brother and his wife said no.

"That same year, the boy's birth mother returned to the camp—just visiting. She had sunset hair like her son. She was older now, but everything looked perfect on her face. My father fell in love with her all over again, and so did my brothers. That's the way she was.

"My sister-in-law wanted to keep Woodbird away from his natural mother, wanted to claim him for herself. His birth mother did not seem to mind. She thanked me for trying to teach him English and asked us to send him to the separate school in Rocky Mountain House—spare no expense. She gave me some money, because I was a nun. So when he turned five, I took him to Father Peste to arrange for him to stay with white folks in Rocky Mountain House. He lived with George and Elizabeth Thompson for a while—your father's parents. George was a realtor whose son Richard was the same age as Woodbird—a little older, perhaps—and I was allowed to visit him there sometimes. Woodbird still returned to see my brother, though, and sometimes he and Richard would paddle there in the Thompsons' canoe, just to visit.

"One spring, LaPierre said he planned with his new boat to transport my father's pelts to Rocky Mountain House for a cut of their worth. My father agreed, and they shook on the deal, then drank until my father was too drunk to be wise. And all the time he kept me there to translate, that the deal might be fair and clearly understood. I wore this same habit, took pride in wearing the rosary and the cross. My habit is all I own to remind me of those days.

"My father lost his wisdom and began to gamble with sticks, the Indian stick game. He thought no white man could play that game as well as he—surely no white man would have skill in a game so Indian! He lost first little things and then his pelts, a bundle at a time. Every time he lost he drank some more and laughed, pathetic to see! I begged the trapper to leave us, but LaPierre eyed me viciously and asked my father if he would play just one more game: all or nothing. And the stake, he said, would be I myself, my father's daughter.

"My father seemed to think that very funny. So did my brothers, rolling drunk on the floor. So did LaPierre. And so they played, despite my pleading protest, and again my father lost. But when the trapper rose from the hides on which he had been sitting and began to load my father's pelts into his canoe, a whole season's catch, my brothers realized that all their hard work was about to disappear the way of the liquor. Furious, they roused my father and told him what LaPierre was doing. It was the livelihood of the whole band, that catch, for a year to come, and I could not let LaPierre take it all. "'Take me with you,' I said, 'and leave my drunken brothers to their pelts. I shall be your servant until the debt is paid. Better a willing servant than a reluctant slave!'

"LaPierre and me, we paddled across the lake and up the river to the creek, from where we portaged to his cabin on Camas Lake. He assured me that he did not need me for sex; he had a wife, but he needed a housekeeper because his wife was having difficulty with the baby. And when we got there, I met again the young woman with the sunset hair. How she came to be there I do not know.

"He bullied her constantly, and I was glad I was only his servant, not his slave. He told her he'd hired me as her cabin maid, with the blessing of Holy Mother Church. She was skeptical, of course, but we lived for months like that, and I served them well, working off the debt for my brothers.

"Then one evening LaPierre got drunk and had an argument with Alicia, which turned into a violent fight. She ran off for a while until his temper cooled. While she was away LaPierre came into my room where I was sleeping. He said my days of freeloading were over—his wife was gone—I must make love. When I refused, he grew violent, trying to tear off my nightgown. I struggled and screamed—until he held his hunting knife across my throat. And then he raped me. Again and again he raped me.

"I will not say he raped me every time, because after a while I came to revel in his abuse, to love his power when drunk and his gentleness when sober. But yes, that first time, the first few times were rape. After that, once I became his, I could not stop myself.

"Once, and only once, Alicia came home at a time when we were making love. She stood silent in the doorway, watching us. I was more frightened of her than I was of him, the way her eyes burned. She just turned away and went outside. I never saw her again. She took LaPierre's canoe and left the valley. She visited her son in Rocky Mountain House, then disappeared. That is all I know. She left behind her little daughter, Alice—your mother. It was because of her that I stayed on at the cabin with LaPierre.

"I prayed a lot during that time because I knew I had given my soul to God even as I had given my body to LaPierre. It did not feel good to be torn that way. But I thought myself blessed, not cursed, when I became pregnant, and doubly blessed when I gave birth to a little girl. I hoped she would grow up to become a nun like me.

"Father Peste heard that I had broken a holy vow. He came to explain the nature of my sin. He told me I was no longer a Sister of the Church. He would not listen to my pleas, my explanations. I even followed him back to Rocky Mountain House, and in confession I told him there had not been any choice. But I knew in my heart that that was not true.

"I was able to visit Philip—for that is what they called Alicia Campbell's son by then—but even that, they said, was an affront, for I was an adulteress, a fallen woman, a harlot. The priest railed against me, turned Philip against me even though he was still a little boy, and I returned in shame to Calgary, where the Mother Superior of the Convent of the Blessed Virgin said that I was no Bride of Christ. I had made a mockery of my Sisterhood, had shamed the Savior and the Blessed Virgin and the Holy Mother Church. In the eyes of the Church, in the eyes of Christ, in the eyes of God Himself, I was excommunicate. And so in shame I journeyed on, as far north as the Grande Cache highlands, as far south as the Land of the Long-Knives, and as far east as Hobbema, where at length I met a medicine woman who was prepared to teach her craft. I lived with her for many years before returning to my valley.

"When I returned, I lived in the old cabin that your Uncle Philip now uses for his studio. My daughter had become a beautiful teenager of whom I could be proud. From there I watched LaPierre's daughters growing taller, blooming into womanhood. Sometimes they would go with their father on his rounds to visit the Stoney and the Cree and what was left of my father's camp. But my father and brothers knew that he had shamed me, and my father cursed him for taking me away. I think he blamed himself for my misfortune.

"My father told Philip many stories, but his favorite was about the time the Frenchman tried to buy him. Camas Lake, my father told him, was accursed. He warned Philip to stay away but did not tell him why. And of course, with a curious boy it had the opposite effect.

"When the boys were teenagers, George Thompson sold his realty company in Rocky and moved to Edmonton. Elizabeth invited Philip to join them for a while to attend school, but every summer the boys would return to the Kootenay Plains and Camas Lake, farther to the south.

"When my father died, everyone was invited to the funeral, whether white or Cree. We traveled many miles to mourn his passing and celebrate his arrival in the holy place. A whole busload drove in from Rocky Mountain House, including Philip, who thought it right to be with my brother and his wife at their time of loss. He brought Richard with him to the ghost dance.

"LaPierre traveled with his daughters from Camas Lake to pay respects, thumbing his nose at my father's curse. The girls did not understand what was going on, or why, and nor did Philip, really. How could he? But that was Philip's first contact with my Margaret—as a teenager. Anyone could tell just from looking at him that he had fallen in love.

"He was a handsome young man, skillful with his hands, and he carved and painted and took delight in sketching the girls and showing off his work. LaPierre invited him to visit with them, and he and his foster brother, Richard—your father—borrowed a canoe from my brother and paddled to Camas Lake, following LaPierre and his daughters. Quite a difference from the way your father would later travel, flying his own plane!

"I watched the couples courting from afar, never interfering, though they noticed me often enough. They must have thought me crazy. After all, the Sisters of the Blessed Virgin had long since forsaken their cumbersome habits for shorter skirts." She stroked the black fabric. "But I could never discard it." Tuanahaki shook her head sadly and looked up into my face before continuing with an anguished cry: "LaPierre knew that Philip was Alicia's son. But only I knew that Philip himself was the product of incest. Surely that sin invites the wrath of God!"

Her words echoed through the woods, themselves for all the world like a curse. But when she spoke again, dignity had supplanted indignation.

"Philip went away to study at the university for awhile, but his heart was not in it. He returned to the mountains each spring, spending more and more time developing his talents as a painter. He would come back from a trip to the mountains with a hundred canvases strapped to a travois pulled by his horse. But most summers, he spent in the valley.

"Usually he drove in alone, but sometimes he brought Richard. Margaret, my daughter—the younger of the two—seemed to be left out at first but soon became accepted. I was happy when Alice left the valley to marry Richard, and Philip took my Margaret as his bride. Unlike LaPierre!

"After that, peace came to the valley. Margaret helped Philip build the larger house at the south end of Camas Lake. Alice never visited, although your father did often enough. And Philip became quite accomplished in his art. Your father took many of his canvases to market.

"Although their business flourished, Philip was not happy. Despite the fact that he had two houses at the lake, he evicted me from my cabin in the woods so he could use it as his studio, as if space alone were to blame for his lack of inspiration. He struggled with every canvas in frustration, driving himself to drink. More and more he depended on your father for supplies. But he no longer kept a bed at home. Philip and Margaret had grown apart, you see. Richard's plane would come more often, when he was away. Then came the plane crash that killed your father.

"I should have seen it coming. I knew how cruel and ruthless Philip could be. I knew his craziness whenever he drank. I know what he did to you last night; I know what happened. I heard what he said to you; I heard your screams. I know he has hurt you as only a man can hurt a woman, as I myself was hurt by LaPierre! Perhaps he has forgotten, perhaps he has never known, that he is your uncle not just by marriage but by blood!"

Tuanahaki looked me directly in the face, the flames of the fire flickering on the caking white mud of her mask.

"There is one thing worse than rape: the curse of incest. Nothing is more disgusting in the eyes of God, because it not only pollutes the sacraments and soils the souls of those who indulge themselves—deprived of sanctifying grace, they are lost forever—but it taints the souls of all the misbegotten children who follow, generation after generation. Such mortal sin must be severed at the root!

"Ever since the plane crash, Philip has yearned to court your mother. He invited her here this summer for that reason only. I believe he intends to marry her. Neither of them knows that they share the same mother—Alicia!

"But you can stop them. Tell your mother everything that I have told you. Tell Alice what your Uncle Philip has done to you. If she believes you—and she surely must!—she will take her children from this valley and leave it to its curse!"

O Tuanahaki! You who knew so much about the valley! Why did your omniscience not reach into the womb of woman? How was it that you could give me such a burden, even as I fixed my eye on heaven! I only did your bidding—as best I could!

And in the twilight of sleep I cried out to her, my savior and protectress, even as she faded from my sight. Yet she was there again, running toward me as I relived that day of smoke and pain and terror when the flames seared my flesh. It was Tuanahaki who braved the fire to smother the flames that engulfed me. She ran with me to safety, yelled at me to keep on running as the inferno erupted around us, my face still afire even in the darkness of the fabric of her habit. I heard once again Sandy's final frail lament, and joined it in a piteous wail that awoke Roy with a jolt so that the tent shook and assumed its proper physical form.

"My God, Emily! Are you all right?'"

I wept on his shoulder and told him of Tuanahaki's visitation, and he soothed me with soft hushes and smoothed my hair.

50

And then I knew all, knew everything, everything was there as a gift, gift of a dying sun. Colleen had tried to sneak the boys food. I caught her leaving it beside the compost heap, pretending it was garbage. We could no longer trust her. I told the other girls we couldn't afford to feed ourselves *and* the enemy, so I made a prison for her with wooden slats for bars. I only intended to leave her there that night—not forever. Her punishment for treason and insubordination had seemed just at the time—yet what a punishment! Incarceration among the bodies of the dead and damned, an incarceration ending in immolation. Even the innocent had experienced Hell at my hands!

Yet how innocent had she been, being herself the product of incest, generation after generation? Daughter of her own brother, granddaughter of her own mother?

Let she who has not sinned cast the first stone!

Besides, I had not killed her. Not really. How could I have known that the boys would raid the place that very day and raze it to the ground?

When Tom told him that the food supply line had again been cut, Willis decided to sacrifice my dog to the cause of the boys' survival. I heard him calling Ragtime—"Here, Ragtime! Here, boy! That's a good dog!"—and I strode to the top of the hill to investigate. The trusting spaniel was already fastened to a leash, and I realized that I was the one Willis was really calling—to witness the event. As soon as he saw me appear at the crest of the hill, he stabbed Ragtime in the hip with a butcher knife.

"No!" I screamed, a yell echoed by my dog who yelped and howled, wrenching around to snap at the source of pain. Willis, in high excitement, plunged the knife again and again on the other side so that the dog screeched in agony at this new injury.

"Slit his throat!" I heard Roger yell. "Slit his throat!"

"No, no. You stick a dog," I heard my brother say.

As long as I was watching, horrorstruck, he kept stabbing. Finally, I wrenched myself away and fled back to the house, confirmed in my belief that the boys were evil, evil, evil! Evil incarnate!

The boys roasted him that night and, no doubt feeling emboldened by his spirit, one of the boys stapled Ragtime's bloody head to our door. The next day, they paid us another visit to leave a severed paw.

Predictably enough, Willis decided to steal more staple food. I heard a cast-iron stove lid being replaced and smelled the distinct smell of smoke. Someone was sneaking about, going through the cupboards in the kitchen. Heart hammering in my chest, I scooped up the shotgun.

"Who's there?" I demanded, striding into the kitchen. Willis had hidden behind the hall door. As I came through the doorway, he slammed it into me and seized the barrel of the gun. He swung a lit firebrand in my face, setting my hair ablaze. We wrestled for possession of the gun and, screaming in pain, I fell into the kitchen closet. Willis dropped the burning piece of wood among the clothes, and then by main force he wrenched Phil's shotgun away from me and ran out the door.

As my hair flared with its sickening odor, I panicked. Sandy grabbed a basin of dirty dishwater and threw it over me. Reflexively, I attacked and wrestled her to the floor.

"The closet!" Sandy screamed. "Look at the closet!"

The fire consumed our coats, lapping at the walls and ceiling.

"Water! Get more water!" Sandy yelled, making toward the door.

I grabbed her arm and swung her around. "Willis is out there!" I warned her. "He's got the shotgun! They've got the shells!"

Margo rushed in. "Where's Colley?" she demanded.

I shrugged in confusion.

"The key! You've got the key!"

I reached for it, but in my struggle with Willis the thread necklace that had held it had broken. I gestured toward the flaming clothing. "It must be in the closet!" I choked and heaved, gasping against the acrid smoke for air that wasn't there.

"Keep your head down!" cried Margo as she guided me toward the door.

Willis was outside, his newly acquired gun trained on the door. As I stepped through it, he pulled both triggers. It still hadn't dawned on him that the shells in the chambers were spent.

Down at the other house, Willis had all the ammunition he needed. I therefore had to regain possession of the shotgun before he got there. Yet the upper cabin was on fire, with Colleen still trapped inside.

Margo came out through the smoke, a damp dishtowel around her face. She was gagging, choking herself hoarse.

"Colley's locked inside!" she screamed. "Roger, we need buckets! Help me!"

"It's a trick!" cried Willis, still trying to figure out how the shotgun worked.

"No! No! It's on fire! It's spreading! Where's Tom?"

"He's down at the lake, tryin' t'fish," said Roger.

Alone, Margo re-entered the burning house, but try as she might she couldn't get to Colleen. A minute later she came charging out, choking and crying, and fell on her hands and knees, gagging away the smoke. "Get Tom!" she gasped. "Get Tom!"

51

But even worse than the torment of condemning an innocent little girl to hell, was the knowledge that out of a responsibility for retribution that I still could not quite comprehend, I had executed my parents with the coolness of white rage. At the time it had seemed inevitable, the only solution to a very complex problem. Perhaps it had seemed the solution only because it was so obviously simple as an answer to the dilemma that had been posed by a combination of little bits of knowledge, terrible in their very formlessness, that had filtered into my terrified imagination and which suddenly came together in an explosion impossible to contain. It had started before the conversation with Tom at the brook, before he told me of his father's intention to marry my mother. Yet still I could not quite remember when. I just knew I had to stop them, knew I was the only one who could, knew why I had to, knew why I should.

"*I did it for their sake!*"

But that was an utter lie.

After the rape, I had bled. I had finished a period a week before we left Edmonton. I had brought no napkins of my own, not fully appreciating the inconvenience of being so isolated from drugstores, and so when my period came, somehow brought on by the rape, I had no choice but to use what was available—toilet paper and Kleenex, a very unsatisfactory arrangement. Sandra, who had not yet reached puberty, was particularly unsympathetic.

"Look, you're bleeding over everything!" she said shortly after I arrived back at the upper house dressed in my mother's clothes, and later I heard her say to Margo, "She's gone corky!" Margo nudged her hard with her elbow. "Ow! She has!" Later, after my mother returned to the house, I was washing out my soiled underclothes down at the brook when she suddenly appeared and sat down beside me on the bank. It was just before I had threatened Tom with a rock, that same afternoon.

"You're wearing my dress," my mother said in a hoarse voice. Her nose was stuffed, and she coughed. I reacted defensively, clutching the red dress to me.

"It's okay. I don't mind. You can keep it. It suits you, actually." She patted her hips. "And I've outgrown it." Then she added quickly, "Sandra told me you're bleeding. Everything all right?"

I shrugged.

"There's probably nothing to worry about," my mother said reassuringly. "In fact, I'm rather relieved. It means you're not pregnant."

She searched my face for a reaction, but I felt nothing but puzzlement.

"When you and Tom ran away together, did he—do anything to you?"

Of course I wanted to deny that we had run away, but then I would be caught in another, even more serious lie. If I hadn't run away with Tom, what had I been doing? Should I tell her about Uncle Phil? Describe how he had smothered me with his alcoholic halitosis as he pinioned me to my blanket and ripped me apart?

Why couldn't I have just done Tuanahaki's bidding?

I shook my head slowly, then wrung out my panties until I felt the fabric tear.

"Nothing?"

Shake.

"Well, that's *really* a relief!" she said. "I just wanted to explain to you exactly why you and Tom must be so careful. I suppose it's a confession that I have to make to you, but I know that you're mature enough to understand. It may surprise you to learn that your Uncle Phil and I were once engaged to be married."

If she expected a reaction to this, she was disappointed.

"We loved each other, you understand," she continued, "or at least I loved him and believed that he loved me, but—well, as you know, he married your Aunt Margaret instead."

Old news, old news.

The only sound was the water of the brook, bubbling over stones.

"Men are different from women," she continued at length. "Very different. Often, they are quite thoughtless. I've told you that before. And sometimes they don't mean to be that way. Sometimes they're forced into situations by—well, by us, by women. And they feel compelled to act in the way that—animals act."

I felt myself flinch and blink. "They fuck," I said.

"Yes, to put it crudely. We must accept that," she continued quickly. "That's just the way men are." She coughed. "Oh, I don't want you to get the wrong idea. Men are essential, and I suppose it's right that Jehovah has given them their needs so that they would compete to be breadwinners and love and protect their wives and families after they're married. Anyway, before your Uncle Phil and I fell in love, unknown to me, of course, he was already treating Margaret—like a wife."

"They fucked."

"Well, yes. Even though they weren't married, of course. I knew they fancied each other. But I allowed myself, foolishly, to fall in love with him regardless—especially after he proposed! And after we were engaged, I too treated him as if he were—well, already my husband."

"You fucked."

Her eyes filled with tears. "We *loved*," she said. "You see, we were going to get married the following May, so there didn't seem to be any risk." She blew her nose. "But even before we could tell my father that we intended to get married, Margaret had told him that *she* was pregnant. My father went berserk. Not only would he not let Philip marry me, but he took Phil aside and forced him to sign a contractual agreement to marry Margaret instead."

She took a stick and poked nervously at the soil of the brook bank.

"The day after Margaret's pagan wedding, Daddy took his own life—or so it seemed. He blew his brains out with his shotgun—the one Philip uses now. He left a will bequeathing everything to Philip. Nothing to me. That was the arrangement they had come to, you see, the two men. In exchange for entering into a contract of marriage with Margaret, Philip would inherit everything."

Her eyes filled with tears. She blew her nose again.

"I'd met Richard out here at Camas Lake several times, and he'd invited us all to stay at his place whenever we were in town, just being polite, I'm sure. He'd been deep in his graduate program and hadn't had a chance to visit much—just one trip the previous Hallowe'en. But of course he remembered me fondly, as I did him, and he let me crash there at Gran Thompson's place, and I never really left. Moved in with them. Became a fixture. That's how I came to move to Edmonton. I'd already skipped a period or two by then. And believe me, I prayed and prayed for one to come. But it never did—because I was already pregnant with you. It never once dawned on Richard that you might have been Philip's child instead of his own!"

I was on my knees, wailing, writhing, sucking air to my soul in great sobs that merged into a scream. My mother held me around the shoulders, clutched me to her, trying to steady me.

"There, there!" she cooed. "I'm sorry, Baby. I knew it might shock you, but I had to tell you. Now you understand why I was so worried about you and Tom going off together. You're not just cousins, you see. You are actually brother and sister!"

"No we're not," I shrieked. "No we're not, you stupid woman! No we're *not*!"

"Shhh, shhhh! It's no good denying it anymore! I know you feel attachment for him, but I'm telling you the truth! Not that that would make much difference, of course, but one thing could lead to another if you didn't know—"

She stood slowly up, shaken by the depth of my anguish.

"You didn't—do anything, did you? With Tom?"

For her, my pain must have spoken for itself.

"Oh my God, Emily! You did, didn't you! May Jehovah forgive you! You *did*!"

"Yes! I did." Then I screamed at the top of my lungs: "*We fucked! We fucked! We fucked! We fucked! We fucked!* All right?" My words echoed across the lake.

"Oh my God, Emily! That's *incest*!"

Still kneeling, I worked my body into shuddering, agonized circles, eyes slammed shut, and felt the tears roll down my cheeks. I wailed inside and out.

"I want you to keep this our secret," my mother was saying. "God knows, I tried to tell him—but not even your Uncle Phil knows you're his misbegotten daughter!"

And later that afternoon, Tom had stood there on that same spot as I wrung out for the hundredth time, perhaps, any molecule of blood and semen from my soiled panties, semen left there by my own natural father, semen left there when he raped me, raped me mere hours before turning his attention to my mother and asking her once again to marry him.

"They can't get married!" I had told Tom as I turned to run to the house. *They can't! They can't!*

Yet another memory clutched at my being and I threw it back, tried to suppress it, knowing that it was too late, because unlike a fading dream, once a memory has been glimpsed it is seen in the full light of day. So I braced myself, fearing the worst. I could not believe, could not *conceive* that our simple lives could have become such a mess, so utterly ugly, incestuous violation after incestuous violation, shattering of taboos. It was up to me, that I knew, that I had been told, it was up to me, me, Emily, who had been wronged, to right the wrong and to prevent its furtherance. I wanted a purging then, a cleansing more profound than washing my soiled underwear in the brook. I had to confront my mother with the facts, to tell her everything that Uncle Phil had done to me in the woods so that she would reject him utterly. Was that not the plan? Even if she would not accept the fact that Uncle Phil was her own half-brother, surely she would reject him, even prosecute him on my behalf if necessary, as the father of her daughter, whose own daughter he had husbanded in rape! They cannot, cannot marry!

Rejecting my mother's shoes at the front stoop, I entered quietly and crept in bare feet down the hall toward the kitchen, heart thumping. From the adjoining bedroom, I heard my mother's scream of triumph and ecstasy as she achieved orgasm, followed by my father's low groan.

"Oh God!" my mother cried exultantly. "Again! Again—oh, *God*!"

They cannot! It cannot be! Only you can stop them!

And the door slightly ajar.

And Uncle Phil, my father lover, sprawled atop my mother pumping, pumping like Ragtime on Baloney. And I remembered how I had been burst and bitched, so deeply, deeply hurt by this evil man, screwing sister, daughter, lover, aunt, mother, dribbling spit, lunging, lunging, genitalia of Earth, plunging in, ripping open pinned flesh lying Philalice producing another lost Emily and another and another and where would it all end? Alice Alice yes Alice panting, moaning on the bed not suffering but smiling, kissing back while writhing under him, blushing-nippled breasts under hairy sweaty chest oh Alice Alice Philip Philip panting panting it cannot be! It cannot be! *You are the only one who can stop them, Emily!*

I grasped my grandfather's shotgun propped against the doorjamb and listened, hating, loathing yet loving, found myself sighting down the twin barrels of the gun, found myself demanding justice in spite of love, found myself more calm in anguish than I'd ever been, coolly aiming broadside at the preoccupied faces through the crack in the door. *Our Father*—coolly squeezing on both triggers—*which art in Heaven*—watching Satan writhing on his demon love as he held his head aloft in ecstasy—*hallowed by Thy name*—squeezing, simultaneously squeezing—until at their moment of mutual climax the unanticipated kick from the dual explosion thrust me backward down the hall—and them to Kingdom Come.

The bedroom door swung open from the force of the dual blast. Father Phil, eyes alone intact, stared back at me in pain and supplication, faceless father Phil, eyes set like reived rivets in a steak of dripping fresh flesh, mirrored in the side of my mother's mutilated head. They moaned, still suspended, aware, oh so aware of my disapprobation and of God's as, still coupled, they moaned in chorus and settled softly onto the bed, inclining by dint of gravity toward the windowsill, flesh glued to flesh, both spurting blood, heads merging in a single sea of crimson, facelessness to facelessness fused together forever in an incestuous embrace!

52

Incest. That was the knowledge the memory of which I could not bear for so long. That final taboo was the disease, the curse, with which my family appeared to be afflicted—a family curse extending from generation to generation. The revelation that I was both a product and a victim of incest struck me with such horror and disgust that anything, anything at all, seemed justifiable to assuage and expiate the guilt, to remove the stain of the ultimate unforgivable sin, the taboo that even animals seem to honor. I was at once stricken by remorse and by a sense of relief that at least my complicity was accidental, that I did not knowingly seek to sleep with my father, as had Lot's daughters with God's blessing. Yet neither did Oedipus—who died blind and in grief—knowingly sleep with *his* mother. Unlike Hamlet, I had "murdered" my parents in bed, while they were playing. They had no time at all to pray.

At some level, Tom must have known what it was all about. He had been there. He did not accuse me of the murder of Mum and Uncle Phil because he knew I would have retaliated immediately with allegations of my own. He knew that there was no doubt in my mind that he had tampered with my father's plane, not to kill his mother, whom he loved and sought to protect, but to kill a rival lover, my father, of whom he was so jealous. He had every reason to try to have me recommitted as the delusional "Sister Jane."

But not wholesome reasons. Selfish ones. He wanted to keep me from sharing Margo's inheritance, for one. Why had he really beaten up Margo? Surely not because she balked at the idea of coming to this hellhole that she had the best of motives to avoid? Was it because she had surmised too much about his mother's death? Was it because she carried Roy Farquhar's child instead of his own?

I could forgive Roy, but could Tom? Until he surfaced, I feared for Roy's safety.

Roy was as anxious to see Phil's studio cabin as I was curious to see my pond, so on one particularly dreary day we hiked down the trail to the rail fence—our first venture from the immediate vicinity of the lake. A section of the fence had been scattered, the jackpine rails strewn left and right into the grass. Fending off the drizzle, we crossed the boulder-strewn meadow and slithered and skidded down the overgrown shale trail toward the creek, each of us in the remnant of a rut.

"Tracks," said Roy. "Car tires. Relatively fresh."

"Down here? But how?"

At the creek, the ruts turned left into the willows, which had been crushed to the ground in parallel lines. We followed the tracks to the rocks overlooking the hot spring pond—the very spot where I had skinny-dipped with Tom six years before.

Only then did I recall the dream memory of the devastation. In confusion, I cast my eyes about, searching for some point of reference, something recognizable in the heart of the woods where my own heart had resided for so long. And I realized that my dream was a truth: The landscape had irrevocably changed. Death had visited with a swift wave and new life grew in its wake. And I knew that in my pool of paradise, my fool's pool, I'd find nothing but quagmire, and perhaps a bone or two of a dead Angel.

"Polluted," said Roy, pointing as a cluster of bubbles broke the surface. He knelt to feel the water. "Funny, it's still cold."

"I remember the hot spring being further over," I said.

He tossed a rock among the bubbles. Seconds later we heard a hollow metallic thump.

"What was that?" I asked.

"I don't know. Let's try a larger one."

He picked up a second rock, four times the size of the first. He balanced it on his palm like a shotput, then hurled it off his shoulder into the pool.

"Thousand and one, thousand and two—"

Clunk! A hollow, echoing boom like *Inside the Great Pyramid*. This time, something floated to the surface up the watery path left by the missile.

A plastic pom-pom.

Roy and I exchanged horrified glances but said nothing. But on the way back through the crushed willow bushes, I found another pom-pom, and another. For Tom, it seemed, this journey to Camas Lake had been from the outset a one-way trip. And it wasn't the memory of the lake that had drawn him—it was the memory of innocence signified by this pond.

I knelt in the pathway and closed my eyes, trying to visualize him as he had been. Had I ever loved him? Perhaps, those first few days—up to the time his father had raped me. Had he loved me? Yes, definitely, until he transferred his affections to Margo.

And I. I loved Margo too, even though I should have hated her.

Roy seemed even more cut up about Tom's apparent suicide than I as he whispered silently to the primordial bubbling mud. I picked an iris from a clump beside the muddy pond and in a final tribute to lost love, tossed it as far as I could out over the pond—overhand.

53

It was midsummer, a time of new life, yet all around us there were endings as much as there were beginnings. Even the few remaining needles of the pine tree bridge were red with death—a shadow of the living tree felled years ago by Tom.

I gazed up to the top of the cliff overlooking the woods, where I'd climbed with Tuanahaki on the night of the storm. I had stayed with her up there for the most meaningful night of my life, listening to what she had to say about my family, about our history, about the outrage of the double curse brought down upon our heads by the actions of my grandparents—my not-so-great great-grandfather, to be precise. Alicia had brought the curse to the valley and had tried to leave it here, spurning her own children, the products of incest and rape. And Francois Lucien LaPierre had been no better, abducting my grandmother, trying to buy her son, settling for Tuanahaki, Margaret's mother.

On the far side of the creek, the woods were overgrown, so we had to force our way through to the log cabin, getting drenched in the process from the rain-soaked foliage. I found a trail that skirted the embankment above the creek, leading to the front door, which overlooked the long-demolished jetty. The door was partly ajar but frozen in place by snow that had piled inside, swelling the wood. The tree-shaded rear door of the cabin stood ajar but was blocked by a melting snow drift, which we waded through to get inside.

"Too bad some asshole left the door open," Roy said. "Looks like the snow drifted right though!"

He gestured with a flourish for me to enter first. And there on the floor was the hideous thing of my own creation built mindlessly on instructions from my mentor: more rocks, *huge* rocks, most of them—hardly liftable alone—neatly piled in long, tidy rows exactly where I had left them covering—Tuanahaki's body.

As Roy had noticed, the snow had drifted over the rocks. The smell of death seemed pervasive.

I cried out as if my entrance into the hut were an intrusion into a holy place, the tomb of a god. And so it was! For Uncle Phil's studio cabin and Tuanahaki's long-forgotten death lodge were one. Around the lodge, weathered now, were strewn the knickknacks of my magic, feathered and beaded and buckskinned. Several books had been scattered about—books on herbal medicine and wildflowers and survival in the woods, as well as books on Indian lore that I had used month after month not only to make my isolation in the woods more bearable but to feed my dreams. And there were paintings, too—canvases not only by Uncle Phil but by myself, sketches of Tuanahaki, mostly, painted year after year during the frigid winters when survival itself seemed a gift.

Roy, insensitive oaf, had lumbered in behind me.

"So this is it, huh? Hey! Quite the dump!" He glanced around with a huge, wide-eyed smile, then sniffed. "Stinks!" he said. He picked up a sodden book off a cot and kicked a pile of blankets into disarray. "He was quite the survivalist!" He examined some of the paintings stacked in a rack behind the metal cot; others lay beneath it. Only a couple of paintings hung straight on the wall. One of them was the portrait that Uncle Phil had painted from a photograph, which, dusty and water-damaged now, still stood in its place of honor on the bookshelf.

"What the hell?" Roy said, picking up the picture frame and wiping off the dust with his sleeve. "Where'd this come from?"

"It's a portrait of Uncle Phil's mother," I said. "It was his most treasured possession. See? He tried to paint it. But the portrait came out looking more like *my* mother."

Roy shook his head and peered at the photo again.

"My God, so that's why she collected his art!"

"What do you mean?

"I didn't even know they knew each other. I thought she just liked his art. She collected enough of it—of course!"

Roy bent aside the pins on the back and removed the weathered frame to examine the photo in its more pristine form. Then he flipped it. "See?" he said, tapping it. "Right here. Alicia—" He faltered. "Campbell! My God! You see, this explains it. *That's* why Mom was so interested in Phil Campbell's work! She was his mother!"

And then I recognized where I had seen that face before. The sepia photograph was not identical but certainly was from the same photo shoot as the thumbnail portrait of Thomasina Allison.

"Alicia Campbell is *your* mother?" I said. "But how could that possibly be? Wasn't she an Allison?"

"As in Thomasina Allison? No! That was just an approximate inversion of the name you had adopted at the time. She was Alicia Peters when she hooked up with my dad, John Farquhar. They married just before I was born, so I have his name. But d'you see what that means? D'you see how this enriches the biography?"

I nodded slowly.

Grandma!

"Philip Campbell was my half-brother! That's why she collected his art!"

Our baby once again kicked, as if protesting this further outrage. Once again my heart seemed to flip upside down. I sat down on a corner of the cot, feeling sick, knowing exactly how Margo must have felt: *I don't want this baby!*

"You're my uncle!" I whispered in horror.

Roy frowned. "Huh?" Then he laughed. "Not really. No. Not at all. Phil was your uncle by marriage, that's all. And only the husband of a half-aunt at that!"

But I shook my head in horror. "You're my uncle twice over! Don't you see?"

"Whoa, whoa! How do you figure *that*?"

I gasped for air in the black horror of the obvious. *Where could I begin?*

"Tuanahaki told me—"

He laughed again and glanced around him at my paintings, putting it together. "What, just now?" he said. "Or last year? Or was it six years ago? Great! Face it, Emily. Dr. Lenski was right: Tuanahaki was a figment of your sick, injured imagination. Your imaginary friend may have helped you survive for years in the bush. But don't truck her out now to rain on my parade!"

"Philip Campbell was my natural father, you see!"

"Oh? I thought he was your *lover*!"

"My own father raped me."

"So you say."

I spoke calmly, the voice of reason. "You are the younger brother of both my mother and my father. I am the misbegotten product of their incest—"

He laughed. "'Misbegotten', huh?"

"You are my uncle, and I am carrying your child. A child conceived of incest."

"'A child conceived of incest!'" he mimicked. "You're delusional." He set the photograph face down on the table. "Getting pregnant was a very clever ploy, Sister Jane! You and your whore sister!" He knelt down beside the mound of rocks, visually checking its height. "You say you put these here, right?"

I nodded.

"Why?"

"Tuanahaki told me to bury her body."

"*She* told you? Before or after she was dead? Now there's a test! Well, I'll bet you ten bucks—no, a hundred!—that there's no body buried under here!"

He picked up a large jagged rock. I followed suit. He tossed the rock out through the door and reached for another, and another, and another.

"Well, I'll be damned!" he said.

And as he struggled with rock after rock, revealing first my mother's charred red and white floral dress, then the sorry rotting body of the saint who wore it—her white hair and white painted skin a mockery of my own distorted flesh—I knew, knew as never before, that I had to make a choice.

54

My hell had become Roy's heaven, his heaven my hell. Once, briefly, the Rocky Mountain forests had been paradise, a haven and a home. But now I knew myself as never before, knew too that my relentless beau would never have desisted from his quest for a nebulous truth. Forever he would have searched and never found, and even had he found would he ever have understood?

I went back to the car, a familiar trek, to fetch his best suit for the ritual. It still had a carnation boutonnière on the lapel—not even wilted. I picked a bouquet of death camas blossoms from the hillside and plucked the creamy yellow petals to use as confetti. I changed into my best dress for the return trip and carried my hand-me-down wedding bouquet in my left hand. Retracing my path to the creek, I paused to gaze once more at the hot spring pond where my first love lay. Then I gathered up all the plastic pom-poms I could find.

Roy looked somber, agonized in death. His staved-in head had bled all over his camping duds. A part of me wished I had not hit him quite so hard, but at least he had died with a single blow.

By the time I had finished laying him out in his wedding garb, Roy looked as if he had come fully to life again, at least a shadow of his former handsome self. The residual blood, confined to his chestnut hair, had darkened it a bit, if anything. But he was still my Roy. I wept for him.

I imagined Tuanahaki standing in the gloaming of the darkening cabin with unblinking cynicism, somehow knowing that this ritual—complete with sacrifice—was for her.

Roy's lips were cold when I kissed them, and his body was heavy as I lay him down in readiness for his passage into the holy place. I lay down full length on top of him—and I wept to heaven.

How could this be happening?

I kissed his cold lips all the harder, trying to make them warm, to bring them to life so they could laugh again and tell me that they loved me. And I felt our baby stir.

I sang the Blackfoot ghost dance song, which Tuanahaki had taught me, over and over, until, exhausted, I fell asleep.

When I awoke at dawn, Roy's face was pale as a ghost's, and one eye was slightly open as if he were taking a final peek at the world. I placed the plastic pom-poms on his chest and the wedding bouquet in the crook of his left arm. I kissed his cold lips a final time, then buried him beneath the rocks from which he had released Tuanahaki's tempestuous spirit.

I had long since used up Uncle Phil's paints, but a couple of rusty tins of scentless turpentine occupied the bottom shelf of the kitchen cupboard. I sprinkled the clear fluid all over the inside of the log cabin, all the time uttering the songs Tuanahaki had taught me so many years before. I made a fuse out of Roy's camping clothes, salvaging his wallet and ID. Outside, it was pouring rain, so the turpentine kept beading on the wet surface of the logs. But I did my best. I lit the fuse and retreated through the woods. By the time I had reached the pine tree bridge, Phil's studio—Tuanahaki's death lodge—was guttering flame.

55

On Saturday, Derek and Joanie landed on the lake after a spectacular demonstration of barely curbed insanity that left me for a moment wondering if hell might not just be a safer place than heaven, and I realized that Derek and his ilk could never be grounded for they were like my ghosts, creatures of air. My uneasiness dissipated as the rented Cessna set down, sending up a plume of water as it taxied swiftly to the shore. I waited alone on the wooden wharf to greet them.

"Where's Roy?" asked Derek as he moored the plane.

"Off with Tom," I said, "researching his book."

"So Tom's here?" said Margo excitedly from the back seat. She leaned forward into the doorway, looking pale. "God, am I seasick!" Favoring her swollen belly, Margo somehow squeezed past the co-pilot's seat and teetered on the edge of the doorframe above the right pontoon. Derek and Joanie helped her swing down to the dock. She gave me a hug and kissed me full on the mouth. "Tom surfaced?"

Such a blunt question, so on point!

"No," I said. Then, "Yes. That is, he was here. He and Roy took off a couple of days ago. Haven't come back."

"Oh shit! They went off *together*?"

"Where'd they go?" asked Derek.

"They were going to check out Uncle Phil's old studio cabin, down through the woods. They took Tom's car."

I could practically see Margo's memory rolling back like an odometer. "Couldn't get very far in that," she said. "There's no road to the studio, and the banks of the creek are too steep to ford. Unless they got stuck somewhere. But then they would've walked back. I mean, it's not that far."

We passed the huge black and pinkish-purple patch that I had tried studiously to ignore—the ruins of the lower cabin overgrown with fireweed. The charred staircase still stood in the center of the livid scar, a sentinel to sun and stars. Derek photographed it as Margo gaped at the ruins in awe, then ran to a spot in the overgrown hay field that eons ago had been the semblance of a lawn. "This is where I stood when Tom rescued me after the shooting began," she said. "He hauled me down into the grass right here!"

We climbed the path up the embankment to the other ruins, and once we reached the camp sat down beside Bolts on the trampled death camas and brome grass. I had already packed everything of Roy's in the tent and had rolled up my sleeping bag in anticipation of the plane's arrival.

Derek and Joanie seemed more distant and withdrawn than they had been at their home. Thoughtful. Sober.

"When'd they leave, again?" asked Derek, feeding a stick of pink chewing gum into his mouth. He offered me one, but I declined.

"Two days ago."

He glanced around him, clearly spooked. "Son of a bitch! I mean, he knew we were coming. We rented a plane, flew all the way out here as we said we would. When I go to that kind of trouble, I expect him to be here, goddammit!"

"Hey, Derek, don't shoot the messenger!" said Joanie. She gave me a maternal hug. "He probably just forgot, or lost track of time."

"Quite likely," I said.

"He should be here, that's all I'm saying!" said Derek. "Which way's the cabin?"

I pointed in the general direction. "You flew right over it coming in."

"Perhaps they heard the plane," said Joanie. "How long would it take them to hike over here?"

"Half an hour."

She glanced at her watch. "So, they'll be here any minute. Hey, sadsack! I thought we flew out here so you could show me the West Country. I'm impressed, okay?"

"I for one have had enough of it," I replied. "If you are flying back to Sylvan right away, I'd like a ride."

"No problem! There's always room for one more—both in the plane and at the house."

"Tom and Roy can drive out on their own when they're good and ready," said Margo. "In the meantime, you and I can crash at Derek and Joanie's place, if that's okay. We have to get cracking on the inheritance business. I phoned my lawyer yesterday, told her how you're in the picture now, and she sees the wisdom of making a joint claim. You might have to retain a lawyer of your own, but in the meantime, she's prepared to stake us for all the necessary DNA tests to prove kinship. Should be simple enough."

"I'm not sure I trust DNA tests," I said. "Supposing we don't have the same father? How would that help my case?"

"My lawyer says that even if our tests are negative or inconclusive—even if one of us was adopted, say—the central question is not consanguinity but whether you were raised as part of the family. I'll swear an affidavit that you are my older sister, that my parents always treated you as their daughter, that we grew up together assuming that we were sisters by the same parents. I'll testify to all that in court!"

"The judge will just say that it's self-serving. Especially if the end result is that you double your money."

"I wouldn't be doubling my money. I would still receive my twenty-five percent. You would get the balance. Don't you see? You'd be crazy not to push for it!"

Derek poked the ashes of the campfire with a stick, trying to get it going. "What're all these sheets of paper in the fire?" he asked.

"Roy's first draft," I said, glad of the distraction. "He couldn't get it off the ground."

"And the cassettes?"

"Extraneous research."

"But you can use this kind over and over!"

"Not any more."

Derek shot several exposures of the fire pit, then turned his attention to the ruins of the upper cabin. A distinct path led through the ash and rubble up to the charred trapdoor leading to the empty cold cellar. I had inadvertently left the trapdoor open. He photographed this, too, then walked to the remaining chunk of charred wall and hit his fist against it as if checking its strength. It gave a little, and the windowsill where last I'd seen little Colleen's panic-stricken face seemed to come mockingly to life. Derek photographed it, then pushed the wall harder until with a creak and a groan the remaining chunk of house collapsed inward, rotted from beneath. The wall landed on the trapdoor, slamming it shut with an echoey finality that sealed the cellarage forever.

Joanie clapped and cheered, the lone applauder. Derek shuddered and looked around nervously as if he'd seen an apparition.

"I don't know what to do. Roy told us he'd be here, and I hate to leave without saying hi, but that plane's costing us five hundred an hour!"

I shrugged. "Inspiration," I explained. "It rarely seems to come for him, and when it does, he likes to take full advantage."

"But you say he's been gone two days? It doesn't make sense!"

"You don't know Roy. He's obsessed with this story. It's a sacrifice he hasn't been able to make before, giving himself up totally to something beyond himself."

I had piled most of Roy's stuff in the tent except his laptop and accessories, which I commandeered as mine. Derek and Joanie helped me carry my few other possessions back to the plane, where we stacked my bags on the wharf. Margo lagged behind, crying out Tom's name into the wilderness.

"How's the fishing in this lake?" Derek asked.

"The lake's polluted," I said. "It's been dead for years, ever since Roger drained out the gas from my father's plane." *I had worked it out.*

"But it looks so pristine!" He peered into the water, then took a tiny strip of pink chewing gum from his mouth, flattened it, fashioned wings, and flipped the missile high above the surface toward a clump of reeds. A huge trout lunged out of the lake, snapping the gum out of the air.

"Not polluted anymore," he said.

A scant hour after they arrived, we took off from Camas Lake and flew over the charred ruins of the cabins, the lush camas meadows, and the trail. Derek stayed low, and I could see the double tracks of Tom's car leading toward the muddy hot springs, and what was left of Tuanahaki's smoldering death lodge, its smoke blending almost imperceptibly with the mist-shrouded trees. Derek circled lower, his camera at the ready.

"Take the controls!" he shouted to Joanie above the roar of the engine.

"Again?"

"Just for a minute. I need this other lens!"

He bayoneted a telephoto lens in place, then took over the controls again to bank the plane sharply over the creek. We descended to within ten meters of the trees. As Joanie held the controls in place, Derek snapped a series of photographs of what was left of the pond. He took the controls again and we flew higher, then came in low and banked again as he snapped away.

"Oh, no," groaned Margo, looking down past the screen of treetops. "Not again!"

"What?" I asked, feigning ignorance.

"The studio—it's gone, burned to the ground!"

"You're kidding!"

"It's a wonder it didn't start a forest fire," said Joanie.

"No sign of Tom or Roy," said Derek. "They'd be trying to get our attention if they were there."

"Do you think they would've gotten out okay?"

We ascended, and Derek took yet another series of photographs with a smaller lens as we spiraled up higher and higher until we could see the pond and the ruins of the log cabin in perspective. And deep in the pond, I could see clearly what had drawn his attention—the outline of Tom's car, where the mud had settled.

Margo suddenly threw up into a motion sickness bag. She heaved and heaved, then leaned against me, weeping silently. I felt nauseated too.

As we left Tuanahaki's death lodge for the final time, I wondered if she would be able to sleep in peace with Roy and Tom so close, or if she might visit me again someday in a golden flash that the rational mind cannot quite comprehend.

O Tu-an-a-hak-i, take care of them in the woods!
Help them in whatever they do, wherever they go.
That they may be happy.
O pity them! Pity their bodies!
Help them find the heaven they search for.
Make them skillful in what they do.
Ageless among our children!

56

A month after Derek and Joanie left Sylvan Lake for California, I sat with Margo through the delivery of her son at Red Deer General Hospital. She had decided not to call him Philip after all.

"What should I call him?" she asked me as she checked him for the hundredth time for defects that might have arisen from inbreeding. After all, Roy was her half-uncle, too.

"Why don't you name him after his father?"

Margo glanced at my distended belly. "And steal your thunder? No way! How about the next generation? What was grandpa's name? Not George but the other one."

"Francois Lucien LaPierre."

"Oo-oo!" she said with mock trepidation. Then: "Hey, I like it! He looks the part, don't you think?" She gently kissed the soft spot on the top of the baby's head. "My little French-Canadian!" she crooned. "I'll have to buy you a toque!"

"Francois?" I said.

"*Mon dieu, non*! Pierre, Mum's maiden name. How can Tom or Roy complain about *that*?"

"They can't."

We both laughed heartily, a measure of our moving on together.

Eleven weeks later, Margo held my hand as I gave birth to Alicia in a difficult breech delivery. I screeched with every new contraction that I hated Tom, Philip, Roy, Adam, Jesus Christ, and every other son-of-a-bitching man who had ever had the temerity to exist. Tears streamed down Margo's cheeks as she relived her own recent torment.

"Push, Baby, push!" she cried, looking in the mirror to see the progress of the delivery. She gripped my hand with all her might.

"Whose side are you on, Bitch?" I screamed as I bore down on the stirrups.

"Ease up now, Emily. Easy!" said the pinch-hitting obstetrician as if I were a horse. "We don't want her ending up on the floor!"

"How do you know it's a she?" I gasped.

"She's all out except her head. Here she comes! Now one more gentle push!"

"God damn you, Roy!" I screeched as I bore down. "God damn you to fucking *hell*!"

And it was done.

57

Margo and I arranged to buy the cottage in Sylvan Lake from Derek and Joanie after it became clear his new job in California would be permanent and they would not return. We liquidated enough of our father's art collection to get by until I could challenge the public trustee for the right to inherit Granny Thompson's estate. All it took was a declaration from the court that I was who I claimed to be: Emily Thompson. Margo was the star witness, attesting that she had known me as her sister both before and after the fires. The court likes nothing more than continuity. "I recognize her," Margo said, gazing at me with adoration, "by her eyes."

But the clincher was the mitochondrial DNA evidence, which showed that Margo and I shared the same mother. Definitely not our father, but a mother! But that was okay, because as far as the court was concerned, it didn't matter. Even if I was not the natural daughter of Richard Thompson, my grandmother would not have known that, and she clearly intended all four grandchildren to inherit equally. The results lent credence to my claim that we had been raised together as siblings. On the balance of probabilities, I was more likely than not Emily Thompson. Despite my wrinkled face—the dark badge of my progeroid syndrome—my birth certificate showed that I was born two months after Richard and Alice got married. I was therefore a child of the marriage and could claim all of Granny Thompson's estate that had been held in escrow: almost a million bucks!

Margo and I have invested it all in blue chip stocks for the children.

I myself will not enjoy it for very long. I have been diagnosed with adult onset progeria, a double recessive affliction resulting in premature aging and death by fifty. That explains my short stature, my doctor tells me. And the fact that I look two or three times my age.

Despite my growing deformity, Margo and I have become partners in every sense of the word. We are adept at creative love-making. We present ourselves to each other squeaky clean, breaths fresh as peppermints. She loves the taste of my lotus blossom, she says as she gently opens my petals, and I've gotten used to the taste of hers. Even so, I miss the feel and shape of Roy—that whimsical touch of whisker. As I lie here, naked beneath the sheets, half awake in a twilight world of daydream, my slender lover rolls over on top of me, hugs me, and gives me a soft kiss on the lips. I taste a trace of my own vagina from last night. She straddles me and busses the perimeter of my burns.

"Y'know these wrinkles and scars kinda grow on you," she says.

"Thank God for that! Can you imagine what I'd look like if they *didn't*?"

She laughs, then sighs with satisfaction. "I love you," she says.

"Good, because I *adore* you!" Gently I caress her breasts, feeling her little nipples stiffen beneath the soft balls of my thumbs. "That was good last night."

"Mmm," she murmurs. She absently rocks her hips forward and back against my pudendum, arousing me all over again.

"But we have to be careful, nonetheless—it's still against the law."

"*This*? Get real! Even same-sex marriages are legal now." She tickles me, and we wrestle squealing in glee, rolling over and over on the king-size bed. "Think about it!" she says. "How can anything that feels this good, this safe, this wonderful—this *right!*—possibly be against the law?"

She is in much better shape than I. Panting from exertion from our impromptu wrestling match, I lie on top of her, pretending to pin her down by the wrists, brushing her naked belly with my wrinkled breasts, kissing her perky ones, her slender neck, her cheek, her lips. I am like a scrawny elf on top of her. In any case, she knows I wouldn't hurt her for the world.

"Making love to your sister is still *incest*, that's my point," I say.

"Oh, *that*!" she says.

"Yes, *that*. And incest is a still a crime. Fourteen years max! I looked it up."

"But we're consenting adults! And we couldn't produce children if we wanted!"

"It's a *victimless* crime, but a major crime nonetheless."

She sighs. Scowls. "Then I wish you weren't my sister after all!"

Her petulant words are icy water across my spine. "We'd all be the poorer for it."

She catches her *faux pas* and claws it back. "What I mean is, if we weren't sisters we wouldn't have the *law* hanging over our heads every time we make love. Hell, we could even get married!" She leans upward from the pillow to give the tip of my nose a tiny peck. "You win, okay?" She jumps her hips against me impatiently several times, maidenhead to maidenhead. "Now will you get off me? I've gotta get the kids up and off to school!"

She walks the children to kindergarten every day. Has no choice: Besides progeria I suffer from chronic agoraphobia and can't go out. Simply *cannot*! Sometimes I think I am destined to remain in this cottage for the rest of my not-very-natural days, a prisoner for my foreshortened life in a jail of my own design. Self-condemned. How's that for natural justice!

Sometimes I weep for hours, deeply depressed. *Roy didn't deserve that*, I think still. Or *None of them deserved to die!* But then I begin to qualify: *Except Willis!* Or *Except Uncle Phil!* Or *Except Aunt Margaret.* Generally, I have turned it around to give the whole scenario biblical proportions. They were mythic victims of circumstance . . .

Yeah, right. What innocence! What naiveté! And at times like this I think of myself as very much on my own. Not that I feel guilty, particularly. No, I don't feel guilty in the least! Because I was put here for a purpose greater than myself. I am an avenging angel with wings of flame, ruled by righteous indignation, sent to the vicinity of Camas Lake by God or Destiny—a gyre of pure, spinning energy, more mindless than intelligent: a blazing tornado raging upward from a burning bush, a burning cabin in the woods—three burning cabins, if you want to know—leveling, consuming, purifying, cauterizing, purging the land of its incestuous scourge with more intensity than Oedipus purging Thebes.

The other deaths were accidents. All accidents. Collateral damage.

Except Sandy—

Except Colleen—

Except—

Tom. Now, *that* was suicide, any way you look at it!

Yet, "Murder-suicide," the police had familiarly pegged it.

Derek Saunders had penned his first and last news assignment for the *Record* before heading off to his new job in California. He had helped the police piece it all together in the same way that Roy had helped them piece together that I could be none other than Margaret Campbell. That was the only way Derek could get the *Record* to pay the rental cost of the Cessna.

Suspected murder-suicide

FOUL PLAY SUSPECTED IN REPORTER'S DEATH

By Derek Saunders
Record staff reporter

NORDEGG—Former *Record* staff reporter Roy Farquhar was killed by a severe blow to the head, provincial medical examiner Dr. James Sutcliffe has determined. Police say they extracted Farquhar's body Saturday from beneath a pile of rocks in a log cabin previously used as an art studio. His body, soaked in turpentine, had been set on fire.

Police said a second man, possibly his assailant, drowned after driving his car into a nearby slough at breakneck speed in an apparent attempt to flee the scene.

Farquhar had been interviewing convicted killer Thomas Campbell about the death six years ago of Campbell's father, well-known artist Philip Campbell, who along with his sister-in-law Alice Thompson was shot at close range in what police then believed was also a murder-suicide. The house in which they were found had been torched presumably to destroy evidence, police said.

Farquhar was the artist's biographer. Roy Farquhar is survived by his father, Rocky Member of Parliament Colin Farquhar, the former Minister of Foreign Affairs, and by his mother Alicia.

Although Tom Campbell was not charged in connection with the deaths of his father and aunt, he later pled guilty to manslaughter by arson of five children, including his two younger brothers and three cousins. He was released on parole last Christmas, and married his co-accused Saturday. Farquhar attended his wedding.

RCMP Inspector Dale Roberts of the Criminal Investigation Branch in Edmonton said the Farquhar murder fits Tom Campbell's MO. "Although no fingerprints were found at the crime scene, this homicide has his signature," he said, adding that by his estimation up to a dozen homicides could be attributed to him in four separate sprees of arson and murder.

Dr. Sutcliffe said skeletal remains found at the scene of Farquhar's murder were likely those of Tom Campbell's mother, Margaret Campbell, who went missing seven years ago and is thought to have survived a plane crash.

Mitochondrial DNA comparison of the woman's remains with Campbell's were "inconclusive," the pathologist said, but some of the main genetic markers were identical, indicating a close familial relationship.

Police said it is possible Farquhar uncovered Margaret Campbell's remains and confronted Campbell as to his role in his mother's disappearance.

"What a crock," said Margo to Derek when she first read the account in the newspaper. He had driven back to our place specifically to deliver his article. She picked up the urn containing Tom's ashes, one of three matching urns still gracing the mantelpiece, and kissed it thoughtfully. "Hey, Em, think I should sue on Tom's behalf, or on Roy's?"

She was kidding, of course, but given her propensity for litigation, Derek wasn't so sure. "Why, what's wrong with it?" he asked.

"Tom didn't plead out to manslaughter. He pled out to two counts of arson causing death."

"So? What difference does that make?"

"This makes it sound like he pled guilty to *five* counts of manslaughter! And 'the Farquhar murder'? How do they know it was murder? Maybe it was self defense—"

"You don't bash in a guy's head with a rock in self-defense," said Derek.

"Yeah, and hey, you've got to admit, he had a motive," I said, nodding at her belly.

"This? A motive? For Tom bashing in Roy's skull?" Margo slumped into a chair, legs spread, hefting her belly. "I don't get it. Why are men so fucking irrational?

"Now, I'm left with nobody!"

"Join the club," I said.

She picked up the paper and scanned Derek's story again. "Look at this. That Roberts character said Tom killed a dozen people and implies that each time he burned the bodies. That's garbage!"

"That was a quote," said Derek. "That's what he meant by his 'signature' and 'MO.'"

"But again, it's bullshit! I'm sorry, Derek, I know you're just the messenger, but fuck, man, you've made my late husband out to be a monster! He had nothing to do with the deaths of Mum and Uncle Phil. He had nothing to do with starting the fire at our cabin—or at the Campbells' cabin, either. As for Roy, maybe he deserved what he got. I'm kinda flattered that Tom stepped up to the plate like that, the outraged husband. Kinda like that Greek guy offing all the suitors that had gathered hoping to bang his wife while he was away."

"Now, there's a puzzle!" I said.

Annoyed that Margo was so critical of his news story, Derek kept glancing across at me, aware that I was a source of at least half of the information he had used. I was glad that Margo was circumspect about the identity of the remains found in Uncle Phil's studio cabin. It helped that Tuanahaki was Margaret's mother and therefore Tom's *grand*mother. No doubt that was why Sutcliffe had found the DNA comparison "inconclusive."

What was conclusive was the comparison between Margo's DNA and that of her late husband. The genetic imprint of our mutual maternal grandfather was duplicated in Tom's DNA three times over, proving beyond a doubt that Francois LaPierre, not Philip Campbell or Richard Thompson, was Tom's unnatural father. This genetic overload had been compounded in Colleen, the one child among us who exhibited serious signs of Fragile X. Like me, she'd had the defective WRN gene symptomatic of Werner's Syndrome—adult onset progeria.

EPILOGUE

I hear Margo in the shower. Pensive, I crawl into my housecoat and head to the kitchen to make the coffee and set the breakfast table: knives, spoons, and napkins, mugs for coffee, glasses for milk, bowls for cereal, plates for toast, sugar, cream, a jug of milk, a jar of strawberry jam. Toweling her hair, Margo grabs a triangle of toast as she passes through the kitchen on her way to wake Pierre and Alicia. I remain pensive as they come to the table, half awake or half asleep, but dressed at least.

"Hi, Mums!" Pierre mumbles as he eases his favorite cereal from a variety pack.

"Pipi," I say, and I bend over to take his usual morning smooch on my cheek. He is undeterred by my wrinkled face and faded scars. Gently, I wash his face with a damp facecloth. As usual his blond hair lies neat and flat, at worst the target for a comb. He is his mother's son.

By contrast, Alicia's shock of copper curls would be matted into dreads in a week without attention. To whines of complaint, I attack her with a brush.

"No, no!" she cries. "Mumsy, help! Mums is murdering me!"

I rap her head with a knuckle. "Cut it out!" I say. She begins to whimper.

Margo is off in the bedroom, trying on summery dresses. Every morning she takes her moment on the catwalk before the closet mirrors. It wouldn't matter in the least which one she picked—clothes hang on her like on a professional model. She never flaunts her beauty, just accepts it, shares it with me, moves on. It is simply *there* for her, a fact of life like a vagina or a pair of breasts. I am secretly terrified that her relaxed, natural beauty will draw the attention of some man. Or worse yet, a more attractive woman. How could I compete? I don't know *what* I'd do!

That's why I am so distracted this morning. I can't get her words out of my mind. Were they uttered in earnest or just in jest? A passing remark of no significance? No! She'd said it twice!

When she comes to the table at last, dressed in a pleated white skirt and black blouse, a white silk scarf tied loosely around her neck, I pour her a cup of coffee, fill my own red-and-white mug, and pose the question.

"What you said in bed this morning before we got up—was that a proposal?"

"Refresh my memory."

"Quote, 'Will you marry me?' unquote."

She frowns, reflects, grins as she remembers. "That's not what I said. But it's as close as you're gonna get!"

"Well then let's turn it around," I say, pressing my advantage. "Will *you*?"

"Will I what?"

"Marry *me*?"

"You guys're gonna get *married*?" says Alicia with a gasp. She claps her hand over her mouth to suppress a giggle and gapes at Pierre with round, green, mischievous eyes still bright with a trace of tear. "Mums and Mumsy are gonna get *married*?"

"Nah, they can't. They're both *ladies*!" says Pierre.

"That's okay," I say breathlessly, gazing at Margo. *God, what beauty!* "Ladies can do that now."

Pipi glances up at the dimpled Ali and shakes his head in obvious disgust. I know where I have seen these kids before. On the Campbell's soup mug that I nurse in my hands, the one with the kids diving into the lake on one side and sitting on the fence on the other. It's the one possession I've kept with me since my hospital days. Except for the reversal of hair color, our Campbell Kids are the spitting image.

Which is it, Margo? Do we take the plunge, or continue sitting on the fence?

"Well, when I grow up," says Ali, "I'm gonna marry Pipi. Aren't I, Pipi?"

Blushing, Pierre starts counting out his Wheaties.

"But *we* can't marry," says Margo, more to the kids than to me, "because we're *sisters*, remember? We discussed this!" She casts a worried glance from one child to the other to see if *they* understand, then says to me: "I believe that was my point!"

"Only half-sisters," I say. I shudder. *Déjà vu.*

"That's what I mean. Point is, we could never get a marriage license in the first place!"

"Perhaps we can," I say with deliberation. "I'm still Thomasina Allison, remember?"

"Also Sister Jane. Are you *sure* you didn't take a vow of celibacy?"

"My SIN, my driver's license, all my IDs, even Alicia's birth certificate, bear that name!"

"Yes."

"And despite the court's declaration for the purposes of the inheritance, nobody's ever reversed or invalidated Emily Thompson's *death* certificate. In fact the judge gave judicial notice that a death certificate is valid on its face! So officially speaking, Emily Thompson is still dead—"

"Yes."

"So there's really no impediment to our getting married—"

"Yes."

"—if we want to. We've been together five years now, going on six. We've got two delightful kids—"

"Yes."

"So what do you say? Will you marry me?"

"Yes! Yes! Yes! Yes! *Yes*!" she says with a grin. "Why do you never *listen*, woman?"

I stand there for a second, stunned. Then abandoning our mugs, we lock in an embrace and kiss each other in the middle of the kitchen floor. We dance like we used to as children, jumping in a manic circle round and round. My breasts and buttocks and flabby belly jiggle up and down beneath my floppy terry housecoat.

Pierre looks at Alicia and rolls his eyes. *Mums and Mumsy—when will they grow up?* he seems to say. Alicia shakes her head in mock despair, then with an impish grin showers Pierre with a cluster-bomb of Sugar Pops. He responds with a well-aimed Wheatie fired from a teaspoon catapult. Their food-fight escalates to toast before we can intervene.

"So, who gets to wear the engagement ring?" I ask when peace has been restored. I wince, awaiting Margo's answer, feeling vulnerable, frumpy, misshapen, deformed.

"Both of us, Silly," she replies. "That is, if you want to. We'll buy a matching set. Now fix your housecoat. You'll catch your death of cold!"

She herds the kids to the door ahead of her. Alicia is first out of the chute, as usual, yanking on Margo's pinky.

"Come on, Mumsy! We'll be late!" she cries as Margo pauses for my kiss.

"No we won't!" says Pierre, looking up at the hallway clock behind me. He clutches a real Chinese abacus—one Margo bought at a garage sale for a buck not knowing what it was. He hasn't figured out how to work it yet so far as I know, but it's just a matter of time. "We got five minutes," he calculates. He lingers on the bottom step, looking back, his blue eyes assessing me from toes to nose. He gives me a charming smile. "Bye, Mums!"

"Bye, Pipi!"

"I love you."

"I love you too!"

I feel a pang of angst as my new fiancée sways gracefully away from me down the sidewalk with a *flick, flick, flick* of white-pleated hem, accompanying our perfect children to the school. A picture of innocence, they walk hand-in-hand beside her, Alicia carrying her latest drawings for Show-and-Tell and Pierre his abacus. They are good kids, I think. *Great* kids. Not just creative. Smart. All that worrying for nothing about the effects of inbreeding. How lucky we are! Hard to believe Pipi can play computer games already and can count to a thousand. Ali prefers to spell out words, and she draws and paints. But they have a lot in common, too, these kids of ours: They watch TV, play video games unsupervised for hours at a time while we make love, and hardly ever quarrel.

Like Mums and Mumsy, they simply adore each other.

OTHER TITLES BY THE SAME AUTHOR

Non-fiction

The Theatre of Protest in America
Computer-Assisted Instruction of English As a Second Language
Thinking As a Hobby: The Novels of William Golding
The Orwellian World of Jehovah's Witnesses (with Heather Botting)
Fundamental Freedoms and Jehovah's Witnesses
Leadership: An Anthology (with M.E. Symons)
Chief Smallboy: In Pursuit of Freedom
Extradition between Canada and the United States
Wrongful Conviction in Canadian Law
Halsbury's Laws of Canada: Extradition and Mutual Legal Assistance
Extradition: Individual Rights vs. International Obligations
Canadian Extradition Law Practice

Plays

Prometheus Rebound: A Dramatic Poem
Perambulance and Pipe Dream: Two Plays
The Box Beyond
Crux
Winston Agonistes
Prime Target

Poetry

BumweltS
Streaking!
Monomonster in Hell
Lady Godiva on a Plaster Horse
Freckled Blue and Other Poems
Lady of My House and Other Poems
Isabeau: Poems of Lust and Love
Streaking: The Collected Poems of Gary Botting

REVIEW REQUESTED:

If you loved this book, would you please provide
a review at Amazon.com?

CPSIA information can be obtained at www.ICGtesting.com
Printed in the USA
LVOW10*0138160415

434613LV00001B/2/P

9 781628 573121